WHISKEY 601

//MARK NELSON//

Published 2015 by Mark Nelson

First Edition

Library and Archives Canada Cataloguing in Publication

Nelson, Mark (Mark Robert), 1963-, author

Whiskey 601 / Mark Nelson.

ISBN 978-0-9732825-4-2 (pbk.)

I. Title. II. Title: Whiskey six oh one. III. Title: Whiskey six zero one.

PS8627.E573W45 2015   C813'.6   C2015-902211-8

Dedicated to Mom and Dad

"The Earth is blue... how wonderful. It is amazing."

Yuri Gagarin, April 12, 1961

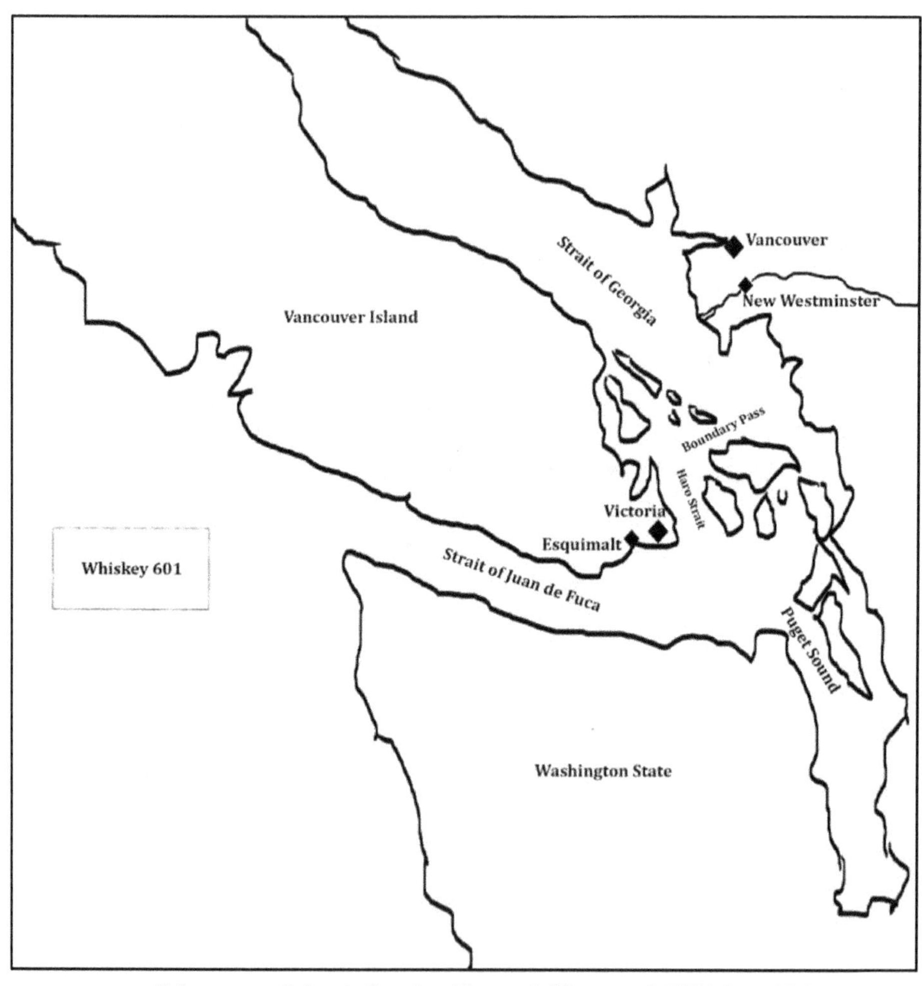

Vancouver Island, Strait of Juan de Fuca and Whiskey 601

PROLOGUE / WHISKEY 601

In 1983, "Whiskey 601" existed as an imaginary rectangle of ocean located approximately forty miles off the west coast of Vancouver Island. It was relatively insignificant in size, a mere 20 miles wide and 10 miles high. It was its location, near the entrance to the strategically important Strait of Juan de Fuca, which gave it significance.

Its official name on a nautical chart was Exercise Area W-601. However, it was more often referred to as "Whiskey Six Oh One", or as Canadian Navy sailors had shortened it, "Whiskey". Of course, the name gives the notion that there is a connection with libation. However, the curious title is simply due to the military's desire to use the phonetic alphabet to spell out letters. This is why the "W" in W-601 is vocalized as "Whiskey." As one might surmise, there is not an actual drop of whiskey to be found in the entire area. The only exceptions may be a few stray bottles that were held in the liquor cabinets, lockers, or bars belonging to the crews of ships that might transit the area.

Ironically, a bottle of whiskey was a certain luxury that one should probably bring along if they were headed anywhere near Whiskey 601. There was nothing romantic or luxurious about the location. The area is neither scenic nor remarkable in any way. No stoic landmasses rise up from the ocean depths to form islands. Essentially, to the naked eye there is nothing to see. Actually, it's rather boring.

The only landmarks available to the eye are dozens of miles of ocean waves, occasionally broken up by an ocean going freighter or container ship that might sometimes plod past the area, on their way inbound or outbound from the west coast.

If a piece of ocean had a personality, Whiskey 601 would surely be known as a boring crank. Her waves were consistently lackluster in colour, a dark greyish green. Yet they were unfailingly punishing. On a good day, she was grumpy. On any other day, she was angry.

To a Canadian Navy sailor, there was no exotic allure to this place. In sailor circles, Whiskey is only noteworthy for its high rolling waves. The giant swells are omnipresent and everlasting, and when you're trapped on a navy ship, the situation is inescapable. Whiskey was a seasick sailor's nightmare. In navy circles, even the strongest-stomached seaman would groan when they were told that the ship was headed for Whiskey.

The reason for Whiskey's high seas is relatively scientific. In seaman's parlance, "fetch" is the distance wind travels to arrive at a set location. It is a simple math ratio and the greater the fetch, the higher the swell. In respect to Whiskey 601, the fetch can be huge. There is nothing blocking the westerly wind for thousands of miles, as there is no land mass all the way to Asia. You can imagine that each swell started as a small ripple in the water thousands of miles away, and an unrelenting west wind had driven it to become an 18-foot swell by the time it arrived at Whiskey.

So, was Whiskey 601 ever the place to be? Certainly, especially when naval tactics were considered. Its proximity to the entrance of the Strait of Juan de Fuca, the only passageway to the important port cities of Vancouver and Seattle, not to mention several major United States Navy bases, made it very important.

In the days of the Cold War, this choke point was a location that the Soviet Navy would count upon. All maritime traffic had to flow in and out of the Strait. If the Soviets were looking to intercept certain maritime traffic, all they had to do was wait. The place to wait was in the international waters of Whiskey. Thus, Whiskey 601 was one of the common places where the Canadian Navy came face to face with the Soviets.

At the time, the Soviet Navy had no face, especially to the average Canadian sailor. To the Canadians the "Russians" were a collection of darkly painted ships that lurked just outside Canadian territorial waters. The ships were foreign in both look and identity. They featured unusually sharp lines and huge superstructures that supported massive antennas and abundant and impressive missile systems. In short, they were scary looking, representative of an awful communist system of government that was perceived as evil in every way.

In the spring of 1983, Ronald Reagan, the President of the United States, went on record as referring to the Soviet Union as the "Evil Empire". Those two words were conveniently uttered to garner support for the Reagan governments' unprecedented spending in a massive military buildup that began when he took office. Of course, now, Russia was officially branded as an evil empire, just because the President said so. Perception was always a strong force.

Even in Canada, perceptions were now strengthened. The Soviets were a communist regime, and they were a menacing empire. In turn, they were to be threatened and feared in every way. Canadian Navy sailors were to consider the men in those dark ships to be dreadfully different from themselves and conniving and evil in every way. They were spies and thieves, hostile torturers and criminals, nothing more. They needed to be feared.

It was commonly understood that the Russians were determined to steal the democratic freedom of every NATO nation. The role of the Canadian Navy was the same as all NATO countries, to oppose the USSR and hamper their operations in any way they could.

Of course, fear is what drove the Cold War, and in 1983 it was especially evident. At this time, the Soviets were acutely fearful of the recent US military buildup and, in turn, the US was fearfully denouncing the Russians as an evil empire, hell-bent on taking over the world. These fears, on both sides of the conflict, fuelled the Cold War.

In 1983, another factor that contributed to the Soviet's fear came from a brand new American missile platform. It was at this time that the Americans began to launch a series of Ohio Class nuclear ballistic-missile submarines. These vessels were state of the art, quiet and powerful, and each one carried enough nuclear missiles to level the entire Soviet Union in a matter of seconds. The Ohio Class made the Soviets especially nervous. Some were even convinced that the US was preparing for a sneak attack on Russia.

Sneak attacks were something that made the Soviets cringe. After all, it was a sneak attack in June 1941, under the codename Operation Barbarossa, that Nazi Germany invaded Russia. After WWII, certain Soviet leaders, bound and determined to defend Mother Russia, had vowed that this would never happen again.

However, the rise of fear wasn't limited to the Soviet Union. In the fall of 1983, a US national television network took advantage of the uneasy feeling of the American public and released the television movie "The Day After". It depicted the eventual extinction of humankind after a full-scale nuclear exchange between the United States and the Soviet Union. More than 100 million viewers watched the movie during its initial broadcast. Although fictional, it efficiently alarmed multitudes of US citizens. There were even reports that it startled Ronald Reagan himself.

When the Berlin Wall was torn down in 1989, the Cold War was said to have ended. Coincidentally, in 1989, Whiskey 601 was decommissioned as a Canadian Navy operation area. Was this a coincidence? Most likely, though, since Whiskey 601 was linked to the Cold War it is fitting that the end of the conflict might seem to have marked the end of Whiskey 601, as well.

CHAPTER 1 / BEAUTY AND THE GREAT GREY BEAST

There are only three things that a 24-year-old male needs: a good paying job, a nice girl and a cool place to take her where they could be alone. Matt Petersen was feeling pretty confident that he was on track. He had one of the three requirements, and he was about to score the other two.

A Leading Seaman in the Canadian Navy, Matt walked across the street with a jaunty stride. It was a beautiful summer day, in July of 1983, and he was headed to his job at the Radar School in Canadian Forces Base Esquimalt, near Victoria, BC. Matt considered everything in his life to be coming together perfectly. He had a great shore posting as an Instructor. No more going to sea for him! Additionally, since he had completed his Junior Leadership course, he was guaranteed to be promoted very soon. With the promotion, he would be making more money, and then he could finally move out of the barracks and get his own place. This was something that his girlfriend Cynthia would love. This represented the entire crux of the matter... pleasing the love of his life.

Once across the street, Matt marched smartly up to the front door of the Radar School, which was one of the great historic buildings at Canadian Forces Base Esquimalt. Situated near the top of a hill, and nestled right next to the parade square, the old brick building was built in the time before the Second World War. Since then, the only real modernization had been a large radar mast that was added to the south end of the building. It sported several impressive looking radar antennas that were used for radar training.

He quickly ducked into the main door of the school and then went directly downstairs to grab a cup of coffee. A few minutes later, he went back outside through the fire exit on the south side of the building. This was the area where the instructors usually gathered to start their day. The other guys were smoking, but Matt didn't smoke. He would just enjoy his coffee while he shot the bull with the guys.

This morning, most of the other instructors were present, though a few were missing as it was the summer, and some were on leave. Still, some of the regulars were there, Leading Seaman Sylvain Perrault the radar instructor, Leading Seaman Mel Gray, who taught "Rel Vel" and Petty Officer Ross Manson the resident Radar Technician. All three were discussing sports, as usual. Today the topic seemed to be about baseball, as the discussion was focused on the Montreal Expos and what a great season they were having.

"The Expos will take a run at the pennant this year, I guarantee it," Manson boasted as he squinted and took a long drag from his cigarette. Then he tossed his head back and exhaled as he rocked back onto the heels of his boots. He was sure of himself.

"Sure they can take a run at it. They can run all they want, they'll never get there," Perrault was quick to provide a counterpoint, demonstrating that though he originally was from Quebec, he still wasn't an Expos fan.

"At least the Expos have a better chance than the Blue Jays," added Gray. "There's a team that will never win a World Series... ever. And, I guarantee that!"

Perrault shook his head as he took a drag from his cigarette. "Face it, Canadian baseball teams suck. I don't know why we bother..."

Matt wondered if he had heard this same conversation yesterday, and maybe the day before. He just couldn't get into this kind of discussion with the guys. He didn't like baseball and he couldn't understand why the Americans loved it so much, let alone this small group of Canadians. Instead, Matt looked down the hill towards the harbour where he could see the tall masts and grey hulls of the destroyers. He loved so many things about those ships. In fact, he recalled when he, a prairie boy from Winnipeg, first laid eyes on a destroyer. It was love at first sight. Today, he was content to love at a distance. He was more thankful to be up here in Fleet School for once in his naval career, rather than down there in those great grey beasts.

Matt had done his time in the ships, and he knew that his next posting would be back in one of those hulls. But, for now, it was his turn to work ashore and maybe even have the chance to get a regular life. It is a fact, when you're posted to a ship you had no life, outside of going to sea and then coming home, just to go back to sea again.

Matt smiled. The thought of not going to sea was exceptionally agreeable to him. It gave him time to be with Cynthia...

"What are you daydreaming about, Petersen?" Gray asked abruptly, interrupting Matt's contemplation. "You're grinning about something."

"Oh, it's nothing... actually, I'm just listening to you guys talk about the Expos. I'm picturing what it would be like to see them win the World Series this year."

"You're hallucinating Petersen!" Perrault responded with a snort as he extinguished his cigarette butt by squishing it between his thumb and forefinger.

Matt wasn't going to tell the guys that he was thinking about a girl. No way! That was never done in a group like this. Besides, they didn't need to know what he was thinking.

Matt considered himself very lucky to be with Cynthia. He had never had a girlfriend like her before, and she was very special to him. Since Matt had been in high school, he was always waiting for a certain kind of girl; smart, strong yet quiet and cute of course. He was older now, he was ready to settle down, and he was now sure that he had found the right girl. Cynthia was the one. She had it all.

Matt had met Cynthia at a Victoria nightclub about eight months ago; she was a friend of a friend, and they hit it off immediately. She flirted with him, and he instantly fell for her. She was so cute with her red wavy hair and her perkiness, and she exuded confidence, which was something he just couldn't resist. They talked, flirted some more, danced and then kissed all night long. They started dating immediately. It was a crazy time for Matt because he usually didn't go wild over any girl, especially this fast, but he did with Cynthia. He often wondered how she had that special allure that worked on him, but he couldn't figure it out.

Matt tended to ignore the only real problem with his relationship with Cynthia. She thought that the navy was the wrong career for Matt. In fact, she was always trying to push Matt to quit and find a stable civilian career.

"You're a smart guy. You could do anything with your life. You don't need to waste your life in the Canadian Forces," she would say.

Matt wasn't convinced. He did love the navy, and he was being paid well. Soon, he would get an important promotion to Master Seaman, which comes with a big raise. Once he had more money, he could do more with his life, like rent an apartment downtown or maybe even buy a condo or house and move off the base.

"The navy is good to me," he would tell her.

However, he knew that his counter argument wasn't even close to be convincing for her. Anyway, she would always make a funny face and clam up when he talked about the navy, so he would end up avoiding the subject altogether. This meant that he never really knew exactly what she thought about it, though he could manage a guess. Still, he thought that Cynthia would eventually come around, especially when he got his promotion and raise. She'll see it his way eventually...

"Hey Petersen, wake the fuck up and quit your day-dreaming. The Chief wants to see you in his office."

Matt's daydreaming had been suddenly interrupted by the one person at his workplace that Matt detested. It was another one of the instructors, Master Seaman Gooch. Gooch was a higher rank and he never let Matt forget it. He seemed to love bossing Matt around.

"All right... GOOCH," Matt put an accent on the "Gooch" part, for effect. "I'll get right on that, GOOCH..."

"It's Master Seaman Gooch to you, Petersen," Gooch responded forcefully. "Now, move your ass."

Matt turned and looked at Gooch. As usual, he had cycled into work and his face was glistening with sweat. He was still wearing his cycling clothes: a yellow tank top and tight black spandex bicycle shorts. Matt hated this about "The Gooch". He would always wear his sports gear into the office and then would change into his uniform at his desk. Matt thought it was all too disgusting.

"If you put on your uniform, I'll properly respect your rank," Matt said matter-of-factly.

Matt was challenging him, and Gooch knew it. Gooch didn't fall for it though. His only response to Matt was a dirty look.

Meanwhile, Petty Officer Manson overheard Matt calling out the Gooch, and he decided to join in. "Hey, Gooch. Your bike shorts called," Manson mocked. "They're going on strike for a biker with a regular-sized ass."

This didn't bother Gooch one bit. He could be very thick-skinned, certainly more so than Matt.

"You guys are just jealous because I have such an athlete's body," Gooch said as he preened by sticking out his chest and sucking in his gut.

"Oh yeah right. An athlete? An athletic blimp maybe," Perrault added.

"Fuck you Perrault," Gooch said as he turned, and then strode back into the Radar School. He wasn't going to take any shit from a lowly Leading Seaman.

Matt wasn't sure if Perrault's retort was actually that funny, but he laughed anyway. After all, it was directed at the Gooch, and that pleased him to no end.

* * *

Just before 0800, the men looked at their watches, butted their cigarettes, and ended their break very suddenly. They quickly scurried inside the building, knowing full well that 0800 meant that it was time to work, but also that ceremonial colours were about to occur on the nearby parade square. It was not a good idea to be outdoors, and smoking, during colours.

Matt went to his office and put his coffee down at his desk. Instead of sitting down in his chair, as he would usually do, he dutifully marched down the hall and up the stairs to the Chief's office. As he went, he naturally wondered why the Chief had summoned him. Matt speculated, "Could this be my promotion?" Then he decided that it couldn't be, as promotions of this type usually occurred in the fall. Besides, he thought, a Chief never issued a promotion. Nevertheless, Matt knew that the Chief never called you to his office unless it was something important.

As he came to the top step in the staircase, he could see through the open office door that the Chief was in his office and seated behind his desk.

The Chief immediately spotted Matt coming up the stairs, and he called out to him, "Petersen, I need to see you right away."

Matt hurried across the hallway and entered the office. "Yes Chief," he said as he smartly stopped in a position front and centre of the Chief's desk. He didn't snap his heels together, but he made sure that he was standing tall, his chin was up, and his arms were lying straight by his side. You didn't want to slouch when you were called before the Chief.

"Thanks for coming upstairs, Petersen. At ease, please," the Chief ordered.

Matt relaxed a bit, moving his feet apart and placing his hands behind his back. Matt was six feet tall, and he was standing. Meanwhile, the Chief was a small man. In addition, he remained seated behind his desk. Matt had a good view at the top of the Chief's head, which sported a stringy collection of hairs that were combed over his bald scalp from right to left.

The Chief put on his glasses and peered down at the message that was sitting on his desk. He reviewed the message for a moment, and then he lifted his glasses to his forehead and looked up at Matt.

"Petersen, the *Mackenzie* is short one Radar Plotter, due to last minute course scheduling," the Chief announced in a calm tone. "They are asking Fleet School to send them one Leading Seaman for a duration of four weeks."

Matt knew what this meant. He just stood there stunned, knowing precisely what was going to happen next. He just couldn't believe it. Yet, he already knew there was nothing he could do about it. It was like this in the navy, once you were screwed. It was permanent. There was no backing up.

The Chief noticed the look on Matt's face, "Now Petersen, I know that you have just come to us recently. However, this attach posting is only for a few weeks. You'll be back with us before you know it."

Matt squirmed. He still didn't know what to say. In reality, he knew that he couldn't say anything. For example, he couldn't say "No" to the Chief. It just could not be done.

The Chief felt he had to explain, "Petersen we have no choice. As of tomorrow, you're posted to the *Mackenzie*. Finish up your work here today, tomorrow morning report to the *Mackenzie* for an in-routine. Make sure you bring your kit down there. On Monday morning, they sail for an entire month, four weeks."

Matt groaned inside... four weeks at sea? No Cynthia! No apartment hunting! No life!

Despite Matt's panic, he kept a calm demeanor. Finally, Matt nodded his head and said, "Yes Chief."

The Chief smiled, "Don't be so pitiful Petersen, it won't be so bad. You won't be at sea for the entire four weeks. Next weekend the *Mackenzie* is scheduled for a port visit in New Westminster."

The thought of a port visit didn't appease Matt. "I have one question Chief. Who is going to teach my classes while I am away? I've got a class starting in two weeks?" Matt thought that he had just brought up a valid point.

Unfortunately, the Chief had already thought of a great answer to every angle. "Since there is only one course in house this summer, I have given Perrault those tasks. Don't worry. Your trainees will be looked after while you're away... and, just in case you were wondering why I cannot post Perrault to sea, as you know Perrault has a young wife who just had a baby. We wouldn't want to send him away now. Would we?"

"No... you're right, Chief," Matt said.

Matt knew that he was stuck. He also knew that the other Leading Seaman, Mel Gray, had a period of leave scheduled starting next week. Meanwhile, Matt's leave was scheduled for the fall. Matt knew that there was no other option. Still, he appreciated that the Chief explained it to him.

"I can do it, Chief." Matt had no choice but to be agreeable.

As Matt left the Chief's office, he immediately began to fret about how he was going to tell Cynthia the news. He already knew she wasn't going to like it very much.

* * *

On his lunch break at the Base Cafeteria, Matt began to agonize about his situation. His personal life had just been getting interesting, and now it had taken one-eighty turn. Moreover, he still had to tell Cynthia the news! As he ate his lunch, he thought about how he was going to break the news to her. No matter how he thought it through, the outcome was the same... she didn't take it well.

After lunch, Matt returned to the Radar School and started to prepare for his departure. He began by tidying up his desk, sorting his belongings putting most of his things away.

"You guys don't screw with my stuff while I'm away," Matt announced to his office mates. He knew how much they loved to play pranks.

"Oh, weeeeeee woooon't," chortled Gray. "Rel Vel" Mel was the chief prank-puller in the office. In fact, Matt had actually directed his original comment mostly at him.

Matt joked back, "I'm sure you and Perrault will be too busy picking up the slack teaching my trainees to pull any pranks. But if you get enough free time to plan something, just remember that I'm the guy that's out at sea defending Canada from attack by the godless communists..."

Mel interjected, "You're just the man for the job."

Matt smiled, "Sure enough. Why don't you thank me in advance for saving your sorry asses?"

"Okay," Mel responded. "Thank you Leading Seaman Matt Petersen for saving us all from the Communists."

Matt smiled as he packed the last of his belongings into his desk drawer and closed it one last time.

"How was that?" Mel asked.

"That was pretty good," Matt said. "Just because you asked nice, I promise to defend you... but just you... Hey, do you actually think the Soviet Navy is skulking off our coast waiting for me to show up?"

"Actually, I seriously think it might happen."

"Why do you think that?" Matt asked.

"I saw a news program last night that depicted Yuri Andropov as a paranoid freak," Mel explained. "He thinks that Ronald Reagan is going to blow up Russia with a sneak missile attack."

"Reagan's not going to do any such thing," Matt said. "Are they nuts?"

"Yeah, they're nuts." Mel agreed. "Haven't you heard? The whole world is nuts."

Just then, Master Seaman Gooch sauntered into the office. He wasn't the type of person to waste any chance to poke fun at Matt Petersen.

"I hear you're heading back to sea. Ooooh, tough break Petey," Gooch bayed.

"I can see that you're all broken up about it, GOOCH" Matt replied very coolly. It was obvious that he wasn't a big fan of the Gooch.

"Hey, I know," Gooch taunted. "What is your sexy girlfriend going to do when you're gone? You know, as a buddy, I can look in on her and make sure she is doing okay without you. You know, console her..."

Matt just glared at Gooch.

Gooch noticed the glare, but it didn't stop him one bit. He continued with his teasing, "So, what do you say Petey? Can I have her number?"

Matt was plenty annoyed. "Very funny Gooch," Matt muttered sternly. "You can be sure that I'll be warning her to stay away from any hairy bagged sailors while I'm away. That's the only good advice she needs. She won't need any comforting. She'll be just fine."

"Okay, no problem," Gooch said, nonchalantly. "Let me know if you change your mind. I'm available."

"Nope, your help is not required," Matt said.

"Sure. But, what if I see her out in public and I notice that she looks lonely. I feel it would be my duty to console her." Gooch didn't know when to quit.

Matt didn't say a word. He just glared back at the Gooch.

"Okay, suit yourself," Gooch said as he walked away. "Shoot... you try to help a guy out..." he muttered, jokingly.

Matt did not laugh.

* * *

At the end of the day, Matt walked from the Fleet School back to the shacks. As he walked, he made a point to look back over into the harbour to spot the *Mackenzie* sitting alone on "B" Jetty. Things had drastically changed from the morning, when he had looked down upon the ships with fondness.

"There she is," he muttered to himself. "There's the great grey beast that's fucking me over."

With an air of disgust, Matt made his way to his room in the barracks and began to plan his method of telling Cynthia the news.

* * *

That night at about 7:30 PM, he called Cynthia.

"Hello," he said, "Did you just get home from work?"

"Oh, yes, and I'm so tired," she told him. "I had a horrible day at work. I'm actually in bed already."

"In bed? That sounds great. I can be there in fifteen minutes." Matt was half-serious.

"Oh, don't you dare go there!" she scolded him. "I'm too tired for that."

Matt knew that voice. He had learned some time back when Cynthia used that voice it was time for him to back off. Matt decided that the best thing to do was to let her vent about work. "Tell me all about your day," he said.

And, she did. She told him about a difficult customer she had, and then she told him about another customer that couldn't decide which outfit to buy. Apparently, they kept flipping back and forth, *ad nauseam*. She didn't leave out too many details, which was awfully tedious to Matt, but he still managed to pay attention to the entire affair. While she was talking, he just imagined her cute face resting on her pillow as she whispered her story into the telephone. In his mind, her red curly hair was half covering her face, but he could still imagine her soft full lips mouthing the words as she spoke. He even pictured the slight freckles on her nose. He adored those freckles...

All of this daydreaming managed to help him feel more connected to her as she told him everything about her day. Cynthia worked as a personal shopper, downtown at Eaton's. He was pretty sure Cynthia might have thought this was a dream job at one time, but that was before she realized that she had to deal with rich old ladies and spoiled trophy wives all day long. Still, Matt knew that Cynthia needed to vent about her work, and he was a good listener.

"You're such a good listener," she said. Finally, she had finished her rant. Then, she even gave him an opening, "How was your day Matty?"

First, he always melted when she called him "Matty". Second, though Matt was putty in her hands, he had serious business to discuss with her, as he needed to tell her about his posting. However, he couldn't. He was too chicken. He needed to tell her, but not just yet. He just needed to feel her out a bit. He decided to talk more generally first and then ease into the news.

"A Master Seaman at work really ticked me off today. I almost hit the deckhead," he blurted out.

"Huh, what are you talking about?" she replied. "What is a Master Seaman and why do you always say deck and heads and navy things like that when you're talking to me. I've told you before. Never use that navy language with me. You know I don't like it."

"Oh, oh," Matt thought. He had hit Cynthia's hot button. He should have known better than that.

She continued to scold him, "I'm not a sailor. I don't use that navy lingo. So don't use it with me."

Matt knew very well that this was the curse of a sailor. Even when you got off ship, you still talked like a sailor. He would have to make a real effort not to do this anymore, especially with Cynthia.

"I'm sorry," he apologized. "It's just that, from basic training, they drilled it into me that the floor was a deck, the ceiling was a deckhead and the walls were bulkheads."

She didn't respond. Matt could tell that Cynthia was getting madder.

He laughed a bit and tried to lighten the mood. "You know, to you we have ropes on a ship, but to a navy person a rope was never a rope. It's always a line... or a halyard... or a lanyard... or a hawser."

"Sorry buster," she said. "To me, a rope is always a rope."

Matt sighed. He really loved this girl, but she honestly did hate the navy so much. It was becoming a distraction.

Cynthia asked, "Please explain this to me, what's a Master Seaman? Is that a higher rank than you?"

"Yes, it is," Matt explained. "It is one rank higher than me."

"So what rank are you again?"

"I am a Leading Seaman."

"It's so silly," she said. "Using terms like master and leading. Who made this stuff up?"

Matt let out a big sigh, and he began to describe the naval rank structure, "You start off as Ordinary Seamen then you're promoted to Able Seamen, then you're promoted to Leading Seamen, and then you're promoted to a Master Seaman."

"Uh, okay. Is that it?" Cynthia asked. She may have been paying attention now, or she may have simply been asking Matt if he was done. He assumed the former.

Matt continued, "After that, your next promotion brings you up to the rank of Petty Officer Second Class, and then afterward, Petty Officer First Class."

"So you go from Master to Petty?" She was teasing him now.

"That's right," Matt continued on, ignoring her teasing. "Then you go to Chief Petty Officer Second Class, then Chief Petty Officer First Class. After that, there is nowhere else to go."

"Okay," she said. "What about Lieutenant and Commander and those naval ranks? When do you get those?"

"Those are Officer Ranks," Matt explained. "You have to be an Officer to go to those ranks, and I'm not an Officer."

"Why not?"

"Because, that's why," he said. "Just because..."

"Okay, whatever, I guess I hit a sore spot with that question," she teased. "So if I got this right you're a Leading Seaman and your next rank is Master Seaman?"

"That's correct," he confirmed.

"So, tell me this," she asked. "When will you be promoted to Master Seaman?"

"Soon," he assured her. "Likely this fall."

"Oh, that's nice," she said. "And how long before you're promoted to Petty Officer?"

"Oh, I don't know. It'll be a few years, and I have to keep my nose clean."

"Keep your nose clean?" she laughed. "What are you going to do, punch the Admiral? You're such a goody two-shoes! You've never done a bad thing in your life."

"Yeah, you're probably right about that. Still, it'll be a few years before my next promotion, after Master Seaman."

"This all takes a lot of time," she said.

"It might seem so," Matt replied.

"Do you ever think of getting out of the navy and doing something else?" Cynthia asked. "Maybe, something more meaningful?"

Matt had noticed in the past how she was good at strategically bringing up that very subject. He didn't like how she kept asking him this question.

"Yeah," he said. "I often think about doing something else with my life but I run into the same problem every time. I discover that I really love the navy."

"Well, what's so great about it?" She was challenging him now.

"I don't know," he thought for a second. "...the camaraderie, the travel, the excitement... it's not just a job it's an adventure."

"That sounds like a TV commercial," she said.

"Part of it was," he snickered.

"Yeah, I know, and that doesn't make it not lame," she retorted. "What I'm telling you is please don't answer my question with an advertisement for the navy. Tell me what YOU really think about it."

"Well, I think I like it," Matt said.

Cynthia scoffed, "That's not a good enough reason! You have to have a valid reason to like it. That's what I'm asking you. Why don't you get that?"

"What do you want me to tell you? That I like the ocean... that I like the sea air... that I like going away and visiting strange places?"

"Yeah, something like that... There has got to be a good reason you can tell me why you love the navy." She was really pushing him now.

Matt thought to himself. She's always going on about the navy, and how positive I am about the navy, and she's consistently negative about it. This is becoming an issue more often lately. He wondered where this whole episode might be headed.

"I'm just not sure what you want me to say." He sounded like he was weary of the entire subject.

Cynthia sighed, "Okay, we'll just leave it at that."

Matt sighed, as well. Then, he suddenly realized that he hadn't told her the big news yet! How could he do it now, after all that huge disagreement about the navy?

Now, Matt had a knot in his stomach. However, he decided that he had to go through with it. He couldn't delay the news, and he just couldn't beat around the bush any longer.

"I need to tell you something," then he paused. "It is interesting news... aaah... I'm attached posted to the *Mackenzie* for a month."

"What does *attached posted* mean?" she asked curtly.

"It means I am temporarily leaving my Fleet School job for four weeks, and I'll be working on a ship, the *Mackenzie*."

"Really? Are you serious? Is the ship going anywhere?"

"Well, that's just it," he said. "The *Mackenzie* is sailing on Monday morning and will be gone for four weeks straight." He cringed after saying that.

"What? Really? Really?? I don't believe it!" She exclaimed.

"Well, actually we are sailing for one week, and then we are going to be at New Westminster next weekend. Then, we are going back to sea for three more weeks," he explained.

"Okay," she said. "You mean New Westminster over by Vancouver?"

"Yes, that's the place," he replied. "I won't be that far away. You could come over on the ferry, next weekend. You know, for a visit... and maybe spend the weekend there? We could get a hotel room..."

"Not likely!" she interrupted. "You know that I work next Saturday, smarty pants."

"Oh, that's right, I forgot," he sighed, as his great idea was dead in the water.

"So basically, you'll be gone for four weeks," she conceded. "One whole month..."

"It won't be that bad," he said. "It'll go by fast."

"I doubt it," she protested. "This does suck. I will hardly see you this summer."

"I'm sorry. I'm sorry you feel this way. I had no choice," he apologized. "But, we can see each other this weekend, at least. We can talk it over this weekend."

"Yeah, I guess," she sighed.

"Tell you what, tomorrow night I'll take you out to dinner. We can work it all out then."

"I guess," she said. "Okay, pick me up at 7PM."

"I wouldn't miss it," Matt said. He was so glad she agreed to dinner.

Mostly, though, he was glad that he would get to see her the next night. He really adored Cynthia. He missed her every minute of the day that he was away from her.

The fact that he was leaving was surely bothering her, though. Matt had definitely sensed a trace of doubt in her voice.

* * *

Matt spent the rest of the evening packing some kit to bring down to the ship in the morning. He knew exactly what he would need on the *Mackenzie*: work uniforms, work boots and plenty of socks and underwear. He also packed his number one uniform, just in case he was assigned duty watch, and a dozen cassettes and extra batteries for his Sony Walkman.

While Matt packed, he did consider that there might be a positive aspect to being posted to the *Mackenzie*. He knew that his good friend Paul Legere was onboard the *Mackenzie*.

Paul and he had been friends since Matt had joined the military. He had met Paul in his Basic Training Course, and their friendship continued afterwards. As young sailors, they were both in the same OSUT (Ordinary Seaman Under Training) program in Halifax, and had both sailed in the *Margaree* together. They always had a good time when they were together, and he was a good friend.

At least he could look forward to hanging out with his old friend.

CHAPTER 2 / #4 MESS AND THE MEMORABLE MEETING WITH MELISSA JO CRABWELL

Matt had never been onboard her, but, before he had even set foot in her he felt that he already knew everything he needed to know about the *Mackenzie*. What was there to know? She was a carbon copy of her sister ships, many of which Matt had sailed in throughout his naval career.

HMCS *Mackenzie*, a Destroyer Escort, was commissioned in the 1960s, 1962 to be exact. Matt knew that he was only three years old when the *Mackenzie* had been launched. That made her 21 years old, which meant she was nearly a senior citizen in terms of the average life of a warship. However, when compared to her sister ships, she was a baby, as most of them were launched prior to the *Mackenzie*. Still, you couldn't ignore the fact that the *Mackenzie* was old and out of date, much like most of the ships in the Canadian Navy.

The navy was building new ships, but that took time and they weren't scheduled to start being operational for another decade. For now, the Canadian Navy kept finding ways to make do with old hulls like the *Mackenzie*.

To a civilian, the *Mackenzie* may have looked like a formidable war machine. She was 366 feet of light-grey sleekness. Her stylish rounded corners were designed to shed the effects of nuclear fallout. Her main mast was tall, and her radar antennas looked powerful and capable. Even her guns looked impressive. But, looks could really be deceiving.

Where the *Mackenzie* really lacked was in armament. She was outfitted with two deck guns mounted fore and aft, they were formidable looking but they were of an older design and only intended for short-range combat. As well, she had anti-submarine mortars aft and torpedo tubes amidships, both weapon systems designed to attack an underwater threat. Unlike other surface combatants of the 1980s, the *Mackenzie* lacked any modern missile systems. Therefore, she wasn't a long-range threat to anyone, and she really couldn't defend herself from a missile attack. In reality, during a bout of modern naval combat the *Mackenzie* would be a sitting duck.

Even her engines were outdated. Yes, they did put out a maximum speed of 28 knots; however, she was powered by older style boilers that fed into steam turbines. It was modern in the 1960s, but twenty years later, it was simply old school. Still, the older technology was reliable enough to take the *Mackenzie* anywhere in the world, just at a slower pace than some of the more modern warships.

None of this really mattered that much to the *Mackenzie*'s crew. They loved the ship and always did their very best to make everything work. Plus, they all knew that the *Mackenzie*'s missions were mostly low-level, as she was used primarily as a training platform for Ship's Officers. This took her in and out of most bays and waterways on the west coast. It was a low stress life for the regular crew, but taxing for the Officer trainees. Only occasionally was the *Mackenzie* ever called upon for more demanding and interesting missions.

* * *

As Matt arrived at "B" Jetty, he paused and stood in front of the *Mackenzie*. He admired the lines of the ship; he really thought all these St. Laurent Class Destroyers were beautiful. He looked upwards and appreciated the fact that the radar antennas, the SPS-12 air search radar and the SPS-10B surface search radar antennas, were both aligned in the forward position. This was always a sign that the Radar Plotters loved what they did, when they spent time to align the antennas properly when they performed shut down procedures.

His admiration was real, despite the fact that he felt that this particular ship was ruining his life right now. He realized that he was a sailor, and he still had affection for the grey beast.

* * *

Friday morning on any Destroyer, meant Friday Routine. Matt knew what that signified; the crew would be distracted by cleaning and preparing for rounds. It meant that if he was going to get any part of his in-routine done he had to start very early and finish before Friday rounds took place at 1100. Once Friday rounds began, the ship usually shut down until at least noon. He would have to work fast.

He was lucky when he arrived at the gangway at 0745, as he happened to know the Quartermaster. It was a Boatswain he knew from the shacks, Leading Seaman Blair White.

"Hey, it's Fleet School Petersen! Whatcha doing here on the Mack?" White said when he saw Matt coming up the stairs to cross the brow.

Matt smiled at White as he came up the gangway, then he saluted as he crossed the brow, as was the custom. Matt immediately extended his hand towards White, and they exchanged a handshake.

"Hey Whitey, I'm posted here for four weeks, replacing Sullivan while he is on course."

"Aaaaah, I see. Lucky you... I mean, welcome aboard!" He smiled. Matt was kind of glad that a friendly face was the first thing he saw now that he was in the *Mackenzie*.

"I trust you don't need me to give you the grand tour?" White asked.

"No thanks. I think I can find my way to the Coxswain's Office," Matt assured him. "I'm just going to head down right-away and start my in-routine early."

"Well, as I said, welcome aboard. If you need anything, let me know. I'll see you around."

"Yeah, thanks," Matt replied as he walked toward the hatch that lead to the deck below. Then, he turned to ask White a question. "I'm about to find this out, but you could tell me one thing? What's the sailing schedule for the next few weeks?"

"Yeah sure. Monday we sail for Whiskey. Next weekend we are in New Westminster. After that, we go straight back to Whiskey for three weeks."

"So, we'll be away from Esquimalt for four weeks?" Matt asked.

"That's right," White confirmed.

Matt's heart fell. It was already apparent to him that he would be gone for an entire month, but he was hoping that there had been a mistake. Now, Blair White had confirmed his worst fear. He did the math in his head... that's three weekends, two paydays, twenty-five nights, one-twelfth of a year... without Cynthia.

Matt shook his head and said thanks to White one last time. Then he slung his kit bag over his shoulder and headed through the hatch and down the ladder to the main flats. At the bottom of the ladder, he looked forward and had a view of "Burma Road", the nickname that was sometimes used for the main flats in this class of ship.

Matt headed forward up Burma Road toward the Coxswain's Office. It was busy at this time of the morning, and there were plenty of other sailors about. As he traversed up the flats, strange faces checked him out, as they always did when an outsider was onboard the ship. It was pretty much the same each time. Sailors always exchanged a glance at your face and then at your nametag.

It only took him a minute or two to get to the Regulating Office. Matt went up to the open half-door and looked inside to see if the Coxswain, or the Coxswain's right hand man, the Coxswain's Writer, were inside. He saw the back of a skinny looking Leading Seaman standing at the rear of the office. Matt surmised that this must be the Coxswain's Writer.

Matt stood there for a bit, waiting, but the Leading Seaman never turned around. Matt decided that he probably needed to get his attention, so he announced his arrival.

"Hello!" Matt said. "I'm Leading Seaman Petersen. I'm doing an in-routine."

The Leading Seaman turned around abruptly. He had a startled look as he first studied Matt's face, and then his nametag. His glasses were hanging low on his nose, so he pushed them up onto his eyes.

"Petersen, eh? Leading Seaman Petersen?"

Matt noticed that the Leading Seaman seemed very confused. Matt looked at his nametag and saw that it said, "Budge".

"Yes, Leading Seaman Budge, I am Leading Seaman Petersen, Radar Plotter," Matt smiled as he repeated his name. He always thought it was best to try to be friendly to Coxswain's Writers, as they were the ones that typed up the duty rosters.

"Petersen?" said Budge as he turned and sat down at his desk. Then, he looked down at his desk organizer and scratched his head. Finally, he said, "Petersen, I have no Petersen arriving today. Are you sure your name is Petersen?"

Matt let out a slight laugh, "Yes, I'm pretty sure. My name is Petersen."

The immediate thought that raced into Matt's mind was that this must all be a huge mistake, and he should just turn around, go back to the fleet school, and forget about this whole mess. He would consider it his lucky break! However, his good sense quickly took over, as he knew that this just was a typical navy

SNAFU. He couldn't escape this posting that easy.

Matt leaned forward towards Budge and helped to explain the situation, "I'm the guy that's here to replace Sullivan."

Budge didn't say anything. In fact, he looked even more confused. He just started rifling through papers on his desk. He was obviously just hoping to stumble upon something that had the names "Petersen" or "Sullivan" on it. Meanwhile, Budge was mumbling, "Nobody tells me anything."

Matt just stood patiently in the door of the Regulating Office and watched Budge's incessant paper shuffling. After about a minute, the Coxswain himself appeared out of nowhere. He placed his hand on Matt's shoulder as he said, "Excuse me Leading Seaman."

Matt smartly moved aside as the Coxswain stuck his head into the Regulating Office door. In a booming voice, he said, "Leading Seaman Budge, look in the morning traffic." He pointed toward an unopened envelope that was on the desk. Matt noticed that the Coxswain was a big burly man, over six feet tall with wide shoulders. His hair was dark on top, but his bushy sideburns were grey.

Budge went about opening the package and sorting through the messages. Meanwhile, the Coxswain introduced himself to Matt.

"Hello Leading Seaman Petersen, welcome to the *Mackenzie*. I'm the Coxswain, Chief Czerwinski." He thrust his rather large hand towards Matt. Matt placed his kit bag on the deck and pushed his hand forward to shake the Chief's hand. He had a solid handshake.

"Thank you Chief. Nice to meet you," Matt said.

"Don't worry Petersen, we have your information. I personally saw a draft of the posting message yesterday. Our problem is that it's still before colours, and we are a smidge behind. Leading Seaman Budge will soon locate your paperwork."

"That's okay Chief, I'm not impatient."

"Good, good. That's what we need around here... while Leading Seaman Budge is getting your in-routine ready, I can tell you some details. First of all, you'll be bunking in #4 Mess," he turned and pointed to the hatch conveniently located just across from the Regulating Office. "The 'Mess Mom' down there is Master Seaman Burke. He'll help you get acquainted."

"It shouldn't be a problem Chief," Matt replied.

"Secondly, look at the duty roster that we will be posting later today. Since you're replacing Sullivan we've slotted you into his duty rotation spot, and his name was coming up soon. That's not going to be a problem, is it?"

"No Chief, not a problem," Matt replied. What else was he going to say?

The Coxswain replied, "Great. I'm glad to hear you're okay with it."

Just then, Leading Seaman Budge interrupted loudly, "Found it!" He was smiling as he held up Matt's attached posting message. Matt noticed that Budge's glasses had slipped back down to the end of his nose.

* * *

Once Budge had finished preparing the in-routine card, Matt didn't waste any time getting started. He headed down to the Stores Office and received his war bags, gas mask, lifebelt, flash hood and gloves as well as his sheets, pillowcase, counterpane and blanket. He stacked all these items on top of his kit bag, and then he headed straight for #4 Mess to find his bunk and stow his growing pile of gear.

Matt slung his lifebelt and gas mask bag over his shoulder and picked up his green duffle bag that was also stacked with kit. Then, he gingerly stepped through the open hatch and began to descend the ladder into the mess. As he slowly came down the ladder, he took note of the mass of ventilation ducts, pipes and wire harnesses that cluttered the deck head. He also noticed that there was a bucket and some rags near the bottom of the ladder. Matt thought that it appeared that cleaning stations were just about to begin. His thoughts were confirmed by the strong smell of the spray cleaner Fantastic. As his left foot hit the tiled deck, he was extra careful to avoid the bucket. As his right foot finally touched down, he breathed a sigh of relief as he had made it down the ladder successfully with all his kit intact.

To the left of the ladder, Matt saw two Able Seamen sitting in the lounge area of the mess. On the table in front of them was a filthy ashtray, a half-eaten bag of potato chips and two Coca-Cola cans. Both sailors were craning their necks, and staring upward watching a television, which was mounted high in the corner of the mess. They paid no attention to Matt, as they were transfixed on the television program, which was the exercise show *20 Minute Workout.*

Sitting to the left of the two Able Seamen was a brawny, dark haired Master Seaman with a bushy moustache. He was reclining back on a metal chair, with his feet resting on a small side table. Matt thought that he sort of looked like *Magnum PI* with a receding hairline. He looked up at Matt and saw the kit bag. "Are you the new Radar Plotter?" he asked.

Matt looked at the Master Seaman's nametag and recognized the name, "Yes, Master Seaman Burke. I understand that there is a bunk for me here?"

Burke nodded and motioned toward the other side of the Mess. "Bunk number 19, over on the fucking port side. It's Sully's bunk, but he is gone on his TQ4 course. That's where you'll be while you're here."

Matt turned and lugged his duffle bag to the other side of the mess. There were many bunks in this mess; a total of twenty-four to be exact. The bunks were stacked three high, and they were arranged in rows. At the end of each row of bunks was a row of lockers. Each bunk had a number that corresponded to a numbered locker located nearby.

As Matt neared the far side of the mess, he noticed a pudgy shirtless sailor standing in-between the rows of lockers. He was liberally applying Mennen Speed Stick to his armpits.

Matt greeted the sailor, "Hello, I'm Matt Petersen."

The sailor looked up and smiled, "Hello Matt, I'm Ryan James." He stuck his hand out to shake hands with Matt. Of course, Matt shook his hand, even though he knew that James was offering the same hand he had been using to apply deodorant to his armpits.

"You looking for Sully's rack?" James asked. "That's it up there." He pointed up to the top rack over in the last row of bunks.

Each bunk had a set of red curtains that could be closed to give the occupant a little privacy. Matt climbed up to Bunk #19 and opened the curtains.

The bunk was about 30 inches wide, and six feet long, enough room for most grown men. On the back side of the bunk was a series of metal boxes that could be used to store his life belt, flash gear and his gas mask. At the head of the bunk was a reading lamp with a 40 watt bulb. Above the metal boxes, there was a picture taped to the pastel green bulkhead. Matt switched on the reading lamp, just to be able to see it better. It was a *Playboy* magazine centerfold.

"Oh, looky looky," Matt exclaimed.

James noticed Matt checking out the centerfold. "Isn't she a beauty? That's Miss May 1983, Melissa Jo Crabwell. Her turn-ons are diamonds and furs, vintage champagne, faster horses, traveling and going home. Her one and only turn-off is heartache."

Matt was surprised that James knew so much about her. "She certainly has nice eyes," Matt replied.

Leading Seaman James explained, "She was Sully's favorite, but I don't think he liked her for her eyes, if you know what I mean. He spent many long hours in his bunk with his curtains closed."

Matt quickly discarded the thought of Sully's private moments behind the closed curtains. It was better that he didn't think about it.

"Don't worry," Matt replied. "You can tell Sully that I won't besmirch his girlfriend."

James looked at him with a sneer, "You better NOT be smoochin' anything up there!"

* * *

As Matt was making his bunk, he could hear Master Seaman Burke begin to chastise the two Able Seamen on the other side of the mess.

"Why don't you two fuckers stop watching that fuckin' *20 Minute Workout* crap and finish off the fucking cleaning stations? It's fucking Friday rounds you fuckin' numbskulls! You know that means the Executive Officer is coming through here, and you better do a damn fucking good job in here... or it'll be your fuckin' asses in a fucking sling!"

Matt heard the response of one of the sailors, "Oh, FUCK the XO!" Matt grinned. He knew that the Executive Officer was the number two officer onboard any ship, second only to the Captain. The XO was usually either feared, or hated, or both. This sailor's remark seemed to be relatively normal.

Burke yelled back, "I'll just tell him you fucking said that! How does that sound smart guy? Now just get the fuck to work and quit your fuckin' bellyaching!"

Matt noticed that Burke's method seemed to be effective as they immediately shut off the television and furiously went to work.

Burke yelled at Matt from across the mess, "Hey Petersen, they're going to scrub the deck in here soon. You're going to have to get out of here while they work. How's your in-routine going?"

Matt replied, "It's going good. I just need to find the Operations Chief and the Operations Officer and get their signatures on my card. Where do you think I would find them?"

Master Seaman Burke replied, "I bet you ten fucking bucks that Chief Cartwright is up in the fucking Operations Room. Head up there to see him, but make your bunk first. It is fucking Friday rounds, and the Executive

Officer is a nutcase about perfection."

Matt nodded in agreement. Master Seaman Burke's ability to communicate using the "F" word seemed legendary.

Matt had no time to waste, so he quickly began to make up his bunk. First, he spread the white bottom sheet across the mattress and tucked it in on all sides. Then, he put the pillowcase on the pillow and placed it at the head of the bunk. Next, he spread the second white sheet and the blue counterpane over the bunk, covering the whole bunk and the pillow. Then, he tucked everything in tight. Lastly, he placed the folded grey wool fire blanket across the foot of the bunk and tucked it in tight, under the right and left sides of the mattress.

"There, it's all made up nice, Master Seaman," Matt called back to Master Seaman Burke. However, there was no reply.

"He's gone," said one of the Able Seamen, as he trudged across the mess carrying a bucket of soapy water. Matt looked at his nametag and noticed that it said "Morrison".

"Okay. Thanks Morrison," Matt said. "I'll be out of your way soon."

"No problem," said Morrison. "We just have to get this done. The XO is doing rounds and he is real picky."

Matt went back to his locker and pushed his kit bag inside. Then he closed the door and snapped the lock shut. He would have to unpack it later, as he needed to locate the Operations Chief to complete his in-routine as soon as he could.

Matt took one last look at his bunk, to make sure it was perfect. He noticed that Melissa Jo Crabwell seemed to be smiling at him.

"I'll be seein' you later Melissa Jo!" Matt said.

Able Seaman Morrison smiled as he began to scrub the deck in the corner of the mess. He yelled out, "You know that you're talking to a piece of paper, don't you?"

"A gorgeous piece of paper," Matt responded. "I am only here for a few weeks. I'm determined to have fun with it."

"Just not too much fun..." Morrison warned him. "Or we'll have to tell Sully."

Matt was laughing as he climbed up the #4 Mess ladder and then walked back up the flats across to the port side. Then he climbed the ladder to the Wardroom Flats. As he went by the Wardroom pantry he could hear the clinking of dishes. The Stewards were probably getting things organized for Friday rounds. He circled around the ladder and climbed the third ladder to the Captain's Flats. Then, he walked forward, through the open door of the Operations Room.

As usual, the Operations Room was dark. Matt's eyes needed to adjust before he could go further. Despite the lack of lighting, he knew this layout well. There were two large plotting tables, one on the port side and one on the starboard. In the middle was the centerline radar display, and on the port side, was the Sperry Radar display. On the left, was a cubbyhole dedicated to Meteorological business. Aft of the Ops Room were additional rooms for Electronic Warfare Operators and Sonar Operators. Forward in the Operations Room was a set of stairs and a door that lead up to the Bridge.

Once his eyes adjusted sufficiently, Matt saw Chief Cartwright sitting at a small desk in the far corner of the Operations Room. Using a reading lamp, he seemed to be going through a clipboard of printed message traffic and initialing each message. He had his dark-rimmed glasses pushed up upon his forehead, obviously, so he could read the light printing on the messages.

Matt approached the Chief, "Hello, Chief. I'm Leading Seaman Petersen from the Fleet School."

The Chief turned and looked at Matt. "Ah, Petersen. We've been expecting you." Matt watched as the Chief took the glasses off his forehead and then hastily cleaned them with a piece of white paper towel before placing them back on his eyes. Matt noticed that his eyebrows were so bushy they curled around the frames of his glasses.

"There we go," he said. "These damn old glasses don't work for reading, but I need them to get a good look at you."

Matt nodded.

"Why don't you pull up a chair and sit down here so we can have a chat."

Matt went back across the Operations Room and found a chair. He returned to the Chief's desk and sat down next to him.

"Now Petersen, the first thing I have to say, thank you for coming down to the *Mackenzie* and helping us out."

"Okay Chief, no problem," replied Matt. This was different. He had never been thanked for following an order before.

"We're lucky to get you on short notice. We thought we had a replacement for Sullivan, but that fell through at the last minute. Anyway... the Fleet School spoke highly of you. They thought you were one of the guys that could drop in here at a moment's notice without too much difficulty."

"Oh, I guess..." Matt paused as he was surprised by this statement. "...an Ops Room is an Ops Room, Chief. This should be no problem."

"I'm glad to hear it," the Chief said with a smile. "Anyway, Petersen, let me ask you, aside from Fleet School, where are you from?"

"Winnipeg, Chief," Matt said proudly.

"Ahhh, Winnipeg. We have a few sailors on here from Winnipeg. It seems like a popular place for navy recruiting."

"It seems so," Matt agreed.

"Was your father in the navy?" the Chief asked.

"Uh... no," Matt said. "Both my parents were killed in a car accident when I was pretty young. I grew up with my grandparents."

"Oh! I'm sorry to hear that," the Chief apologized.

"It's okay," Matt said. "I was pretty young when it happened. It was during a snow storm on a highway outside Winnipeg," he paused slightly. "Anyway... my grandparents were very good to me."

The Chief didn't know what to say to such a sad story.

Matt decided to change the subject, "To answer your initial question, my grandfather was in the navy. He is a World War II veteran."

"Really? That's interesting. Where did he serve?"

"He served in the *Athabaskan*. He was a Stoker," Matt said proudly.

"Really? Was he on the *Athabaskan* in 1944 when it was sunk in the English Channel?"

"Yes he was," Matt confirmed. "He regularly says that he is lucky to be alive, and he always pledged a debt to the *Haida*, the ship that rescued him and the other survivors."

"That's fascinating," the Chief smiled. "I bet he has a thousand stories about those times."

"Not really," Matt said. "He really doesn't like talking about it too much. Other than telling people he is lucky to be alive, he doesn't like to talk about the friends he lost."

"I see... I've met many veterans that are the same way..." The chief paused and looked down at his lap for a moment. Then, he continued his questions, "After the war, what did he do?"

"He worked in the CN rail yards in Transcona," Matt said matter-of-factly. "Fixing locomotives, just like so many navy veterans did after the war. Of course, he is retired now."

"Oh, and your grandparents still live in Winnipeg?" the Chief asked.

"Yes, he goes to the Legion and plays darts while my Grandma goes to the church and fundraises for the poor by making cabbage rolls and perogies. They're happy and doing well... enjoying retired life." Matt said with a smile.

"Perogies? That's a Ukrainian delicacy! Is your Grandma Ukrainian?"

"Absolutely!" Matt gushed. "And she's a fantastic cook! Both of my grandparents are Ukrainian, we even speak Ukrainian in the house, all the time."

The Chief was surprised, "Oh that's interesting. With a name like Petersen, you'd never expect 'Ukrainian'. I assume that Petersen was your father's name?"

"That's correct Chief. My grandparents are actually Melnychuks. Growing up, I was the only Ukrainian Petersen in Winnipeg," Matt said with a grin.

The Chief laughed.

"We're glad to have you in the *Mackenzie*, and I have something to ask of you. Here's the thing," he paused. "Leading Seaman Sullivan was supposed to do flash-up this Monday morning with another Leading Seaman named Legere."

Matt nodded. Flash-up was the process of switching on the radars and equipment, and testing whether it was functional. This procedure was done whenever the ship set sail, and it was something in which Matt was well versed. Matt was also well versed with his old chum, Leading Seaman Legere.

"Chief, I can do it. I can cover Sullivan's assignment. It will give me a chance to get to know the routine around here."

"That's great," the Chief said. "Legere will show you the ropes."

"It shouldn't be a problem," Matt agreed. "I know Legere."

"Okay, excellent," the Chief said. "Now, considering that you will be coming in early on Monday, and since you probably have plenty to do to get your personal affairs in order, as you're sailing with us at the last minute, I'll give you sliders this afternoon."

The Chief handed Matt a blue chit, granting him "Sliders", which meant that he had permission to take the afternoon off.

"Thanks Chief. You're right. There are a few things I need to look after this afternoon. This will come in handy." What sailor didn't love Friday afternoon sliders!

"Do you have any questions?" the Chief asked.

"Just one," Matt replied. "I wanted to confirm our sailing schedule for the next four weeks."

"Oh, okay. That's easy. Next week we are at Whiskey. Next weekend is a port visit in New Westminster, and then we are back to Whiskey for three more weeks. After that, we are going into our leave period, and you can go back to Fleet School."

Matt frowned. He had confirmed a third time that it was as bad as he was told. He would be away for four weeks straight.

"I can't believe the Fleet School didn't tell you this," said the Chief.

"No, they did," Matt said. "I just wanted to confirm it."

"I understand," said the Chief. "Well it's been nice to meet you, and thanks again for helping us out."

The Chief pushed his burly hand toward Matt. Matt obliged and shook his hand. The Chief's handshake was firm and warm.

"No problem Chief," Matt said. "It's nice to meet you."

* * *

Matt continued on to complete his in-routine. His last visit was with the Pay Office where they checked him in, and then he returned his card to Leading Seaman Budge in the Regulating Office.

Matt noticed that Budge threw his in-routine card on a pile of other paperwork. Matt thought that was funny. All Coxswain's Writers he had met in the past had been well organized. This guy just seemed to be completely confused.

Straightaway, Matt went back down to #4 Mess to finish unpacking his kit. When he arrived he was met by Able Seamen Morrison, who was standing at the bottom of the ladder.

"Leading Seaman Petersen... great. Have you seen the XO coming? We are going to have rounds here any minute, and I need to be ready," Morrison said.

Matt replied, "No. I was just up in the main flats, and I didn't see or hear them coming, so you can relax."

Morrison replied, "No time to relax, the XO is a real ball buster, especially on Friday rounds. You better get the hell out of here, at least until rounds are over."

"I just need to unpack my kit bag," Matt said. "It'll only take a minute or two."

"Sure go ahead. If I hear him coming, I'll let you know," Morrison replied. "But you'll only have seconds to close your locker door and stand by for rounds. He doesn't like to have gear sculling about, so please help me out on this Leading Seaman. I'm in enough shit already."

"Seconds you say? I think I can handle the pressure... I get it. I'll be real careful not to screw things up for you," Matt assured Morrison.

Matt went over to his locker and opened the door. He was glad to see that there were no naked posters in the locker. It was just an empty aluminum box with a hanger area on the left, shelves on the right and drawers near the bottom. At the very bottom of the locker was an open area to place footwear. He placed all his clothing in his locker, folding up his underwear and t-shirts tightly so they would fit nicely onto the shelves provided. He scooped the clean socks out of his bag and placed them in the drawer. He closed the drawer and everything just fit.

He retrieved his sea boots from his duffle bag and dusted them off. He placed them in the bottom of his locker. Then he did the same with his dress boots. He hung three uniforms in his locker; two were work uniforms and one was his dress uniform. Then, he fished out his forage cap and placed it in the top of the locker. Lastly, he removed some civvies from his kit bag, shirts and jeans, and placed them on a shelf in the locker. Now, he was ready for anything.

Matt would bring a bit more kit on Monday morning when they sailed. However, most of what he needed was already here.

Before he closed the door, he took out a picture of Cynthia and taped it to the inside of his locker door. It wasn't even a photo. It was just a caricature drawing that had been drawn by an artist down at the Victoria waterfront. It showed her on roller skates eating a huge ice cream cone. He lamented that he didn't have a regular photo, but he knew that he had some fresh photos in his camera that needed to be developed from a previous visit to Saxe Point Park. He would have to get the film developed this weekend, so he could have a real photo of Cynthia in his locker while he was away.

Just then, from across the mess, he heard Able Seaman Morrison whisper in his direction, "Leading Seaman Petersen, they're coming. Please stand by for rounds."

Suddenly, Matt heard a commotion in the main flats up above the ladder, and he heard a boatswain's call piping the still, a single long high note. Morrison was right. It was time for rounds. Matt quickly closed his locker door, making sure there was nothing laying around outside the locker and then snapped the lock shut. Then, he put on his beret and stood over off to one side of the passageway in the position of attention.

The sound of boots could be heard coming down the ladder into the mess. Then he heard the deafening sound of the boatswain's call from within the mess and a booming voice announcing, "Stand by for Rounds!"

Matt could hear Morrison reporting "Number Four Mess ready for rounds, Sir", and then the inspection began. Through the gaps between the bunks and lockers, Matt managed to get a glimpse of the Executive Officer as he was conducting rounds. Lieutenant-Commander Drapeau was a short man, about 40 years of age, with a round face, thin lips and a slight chin. He was clean shaven, but he had a permanent five-o'clock shadow. His eyes seemed to be piercing, almost hawkish. He's not very menacing looking, Matt thought, maybe except for the eyes. Matt recalled that most XOs he had met in the past usually meant business. This guy seemed to be no different.

Followed by the Coxswain and Master Seaman Burke, Drapeau continued to tour around the mess, peering into every corner. He came toward Matt's corner and went right past Matt. The XO didn't even make eye contact with Matt, but he looked directly at his uniform and his boots. Then he moved on.

Everything seemed to be going smoothly, then suddenly, Drapeau purposefully marched across the mess and pointed toward Matt's bunk.

"That bunk is not made properly," the XO stated aloud. His voice was forceful, but not accusatory. It was more of a matter-of-fact type statement.

Master Seaman Burke quickly came forward and replied, "Yes Sir. That bunk belongs to a new man. I'll let him know how the bunks are to be made in the *Mackenzie*."

Drapeau snarled. Apparently, he still wasn't happy.

"Coxswain!" Drapeau yelled abruptly.

"Yes sir," Chief Czerwinski came forward.

"Even new people should know the rules Chief," Drapeau lectured.

Matt was surprised by Drapeau's tone. He had never heard any Officer, let alone an Executive Officer, speak to a Coxswain in this way.

"Yes sir, it won't happen again," the Chief replied stone-faced.

Although he stood silently while all of this was going on, Matt was completely confused on the matter. How was his bunk not made properly? He looked at the bunk. He had made it tight, and everything was tucked in as well as any other bunk he had made in his naval career. But, he restrained himself. Obviously, it was not a good time to open his mouth.

After the inspection was over, and the Executive Officer had left the Mess, Master Seaman Burke came over to speak to Matt.

"Sorry Petersen," Burke explained. "I should have warned you, but on the *Mackenzie* the XO wants the top sheet and counterpane folded back ten inches, like in the fucking barracks."

"But that's not how it's done on every other ship," Matt protested. "On every other ship the pillow is tucked under that sheet and counterpane."

"Well, not on the *Mackenzie*," Burke sighed. "What can I tell you? That's the way the XO wants it, so we just go along with it... He can be a real fucking prick about things if you hadn't fucking noticed."

"Okay, Master Seaman. I get it," Matt agreed. "I'll fix the bunk up right."

As Matt re-made his bunk, he kept thinking about how rude the XO was to everybody. Some officers seemed to think it was their job to be rude to subordinates, but this guy really wanted to go out of his way to be a tyrant. Obviously, this Executive Officer was somebody Matt should avoid in the few weeks that he would be onboard the *Mackenzie*.

* * *

Once Matt had all his gear stowed, it was nearly lunchtime. As he went up into the flats, he heard the long-winded "hands to dinner" being piped. He queued up into the long line of sailors in the main flats waiting to be served.

The line went fast. Soon, Matt was the proud owner of a steaming hot plateful of beefaroni with a side helping of vegetables, consisting of boiled peas, carrots and lima beans.

Matt thought, "Good thing I'm hungry." As he sat down at an empty table in the middle of the Main Cafeteria, he looked around to see if there was anyone he recognized. Alas, everybody looked like a stranger to him, except maybe Leading Seaman Budge, whom he recognized from earlier. He was sitting alone in the corner eating a hot dog and reading a science fiction paperback. He looked like a serious nerd.

Matt had to agree that this "Main Cave", as the sailors often called the Main

Cafeteria, was pretty much the same as every other Main Cave he frequented. The same long tables with built in bench seats, the same sticky blue placemats and the same built-in racks at the end of the table designed to hold condiments and salt and pepper shakers. It was all too familiar.

Although he didn't know anyone at first, it only took a minute before some friendly faces showed up. Into the cafeteria came Able Seaman Morrison and right behind him was one of Matt's old friends, Leading Seaman Paul Legere.

Morrison saw Matt and came over to his table. "Do you mind if I sit with you Leading Seaman?" Morrison asked.

"Not a problem," Matt replied cheerfully. "I owe you one for that debacle in #4 Mess. I apologize for not knowing how to make my bunk. Apparently, I'm a bad Leading Seaman."

Morrison laughed as he placed a plate of beefaroni and a bowl of clam chowder on the table and sat down across from Matt. "Yes, welcome to the *Mackenzie*. Where our XO is an asshole and we all know it."

Matt smiled. He was beginning to think that Morrison seemed like an okay kid.

Morrison waved his hand towards the food line, where he saw Paul Legere was waiting for his food.

"Hey, do you mind if Leading Seaman Legere sits with us?" Morrison asked. "Don't worry, he's a good guy."

Matt realized that Morrison obviously didn't know that he and Paul Legere were previous friends. He decided to play a joke on the Able Seaman.

"Oh, I know him. He's an asshole. My whole family hates him. He seduced my grandmother," Matt said stone-faced as he ate a forkful of beefaroni.

Morrison was speechless. In fact, he looked downright confused. Finally, he replied, "What? Are you joking?"

Just as Paul arrived at the table with his meal, Matt said, "Yes I'm joking. I know this guy; he's an old buddy of mine."

Paul sat down at the table, "What's the joke Petey?"

Matt laughed aloud.

Paul laughed as well, "Don't tell me that I missed out on one of Matt Petersen's patented sly remarks?"

Morrison said, "Yes, you did. Before I knew you guys were friends,

Petersen told me that you had sex with his grandmother."

Paul laughed, "Oh, that story. He's used that one before, many a time..."

Matt laughed.

Paul continued, "I sailed in the *Margaree* with this guy, when we were brand new Ordinary Seamen. We had a trip up to Montreal together. That was a lot of fun. Remember all those French sweeties? I love those French girls, what good memories..."

Matt chuckled, "I seem to recall that you had much more success with the ladies than I ever did."

"Oh contraire, mon ami! You had a knack for attracting the talent," Paul countered. "Remember that cute French honey that latched onto you in Three Rivers?"

"Oh, don't remind me of that," Matt protested. "That's not a flattering story to tell."

"No, it's not that bad," Paul said. "Anyway, I have to tell it now that I mentioned it."

"That's true," Morrison said. "You can't just bring it up and then pack it away. It has to be told."

"Okay Paul, go ahead and tell the story," Matt said. "You tell it the best."

"Okay, we were in Trois-Rivières and Matt and I went ashore to a bar. It was Halloween, so we dressed up in costume. Matt went as a Wolfman. It was a pretty simple deal. He had a full-head mask and two furry wolf hands."

"So, he's the Wolfman, was there a full moon?" Morrison interrupted.

"No. No full moon... Anyway, here is what happened. As soon as Matt walked into the bar, like, he wasn't even three steps inside the bar, this adorable blonde came over and grabbed him by the hand and yanked him onto the dance floor. Matt just went along with it. Soon they were dancing, and Matt was showing her his moves, which are rather lame I might add."

Matt laughed. "Shut up. Quit embellishing!" he said.

"No embellishment," Paul said. "It's all true. So, as it goes, they left the dance floor and then she started buying him beer. The whole time, Matt was still wearing the Wolfman mask. He was using a straw to drink the beer through a mouth hole in the mask. It was hilarious!"

"How many beers did she buy him?" Morrison asked as he shoveled a forkful of beefaroni into his mouth.

"It doesn't matter... it was more than one," Paul replied tersely. "Just let me continue this... so now she is chatting him up in French, but he doesn't speak French. The whole time he just kept on nodding his head up and down in agreement. This continued on for what seemed like forever. They even went back on the dance floor and danced to a slow song. She was holding him tight. Things were really getting hot, but he kept the mask on the whole time."

"That part is true. She was hot stuff," Matt said.

"She was a 10. I guarantee it," Paul said. "So, like I said, they started to get real cozy and it looked like she wanted to start to kiss Matt. Then she reached over his head, grabbed the back of the mask and slowly lifted it off, revealing his face. She took one look at his face, and then she bolted."

"She bolted?" Morrison asked.

"Yes, she bolted. She ran away," Paul laughed.

Matt explained, "I think she thought I was someone else. I was just happy to go along with the whole thing. She was a real sweet girl..."

Everybody laughed.

"Hey, I think we should start calling Petey the 'Wolfman'," Paul proposed.

"Don't you mean the Lonesome Wolfman? Or maybe Lone Wolf? I'd prefer Lone Wolf," Matt said. Matt wasn't worried about the thought of a new nickname. He knew that nicknames never stuck to him, for some reason. The only nickname that really stuck to him, seemed to be "Petey".

"I like 'Wolfman'," Morrison said. "Nobody will know why it's your nickname, but we'll all know."

Of course, Matt never aspired to be a lady's man but he knew that Paul certainly did. In fact, there were plenty of good Paul stories. Matt decided it was time to throw it back at his old pal.

"Hey, Paul. Do you remember when you were asked to babysit Mr. Marbles?" Matt asked.

Paul winced.

Morrison chimed in, "Who, or what, is a Mr. Marbles?"

Paul winced again. "I don't want to tell that story. I'm still broken up about it." Actually, he seemed to be chuckling about it at the moment.

Matt piped up, "I can tell the tale." He looked over at Paul, "Just jump in here anytime good buddy."

Paul gestured with his upturned palm, in an offering, "Okay, you tell it better than I do, go ahead."

Matt had a wide grin on his face as he began, "Well as it goes... Back in 'Slackers', Paul was dating this great looking girl..."

"What's Slackers?" Morrison interrupted.

"Slackers is Halifax," Matt explained. "Anyway... she was gorgeous, dark hair, thin, face like a model. Frankly I don't know how he gets these girls, but somehow he does."

"So, she looked like a model?" Morrison's eyes were wide.

"No, she didn't just look like a model. She WAS a model," Paul corrected.

"Whatever," Matt said. "Tell me, what did she model?"

"She did a Zellers flyer," Paul bragged. "It was even an underwear ad, and it was pretty hot actually. I still have the flyer somewhere."

"Okay, I believe that," Matt said. "She was beautiful."

"Can I see that flyer?" Morrison interrupted with a smile.

Paul glowered back at him. "You're such a pig for a young kid," he said rather jokingly.

"Okay, okay. I don't need to see it. Just get to the part about Mr. Marbles," Morrison said as he began to crumble crackers into his bowl of clam chowder. He was getting fragments everywhere.

Matt looked down at the crumbs and deliberately brushed some stray cracker bits back over to Morrison's side of the table. "Okay, don't get all excited with your cracker crushing. I'll tell it. Keep your pants on!"

Paul chuckled.

Matt continued, "Well, as I said, Paul is dating this gorgeous model," he looked over at Paul. Paul nodded in agreement.

"So, this girl is going out of town and she asks our good man Paul to look after her cat, Mr. Marbles."

"He was a lovely cat, "Paul interrupted with an obviously fake sob. "I loved that beast."

Morrison immediately reacted, "Why are you referring to the cat in the past tense?"

Matt explained, "Well, that's just it. While she was out of town, the cat died. Paul, being the great humanitarian that he is, figures he can't just leave the cat where it dropped, dead and all. He needs to dispose of the corpse. But he didn't know what to do..."

Paul spoke up, "I didn't want to call her and ruin her trip by telling her that her cat was gone. I didn't want to just throw it in the dumpster, or she would be further devastated. I decided to keep it around so she could decide once she returned whether she wanted to bury or cremate the thing."

"Didn't it start to decompose?" Morrison asked.

"No," Matt explained. "Because, Paul is a genius and he knows how to deal with such things. He put it in the fridge."

"Really?" Morrison asked. "Did that work?"

"Oh, it worked just great," Matt replied. "Everything was just fine... until she came home early and decided to look inside the fridge for a snack."

Morrison laughed aloud. He even spat some chowder out onto the table.

"Apparently she saw Mr. Marbles there on the second shelf, in a clear plastic bag all cold and dead... poor girl. She broke up with Paul pretty much on the spot."

Paul smiled, "Who would think that a skinny model is going to look in the fridge?"

"Huh... Who would think?" Morrison shrugged as he laughed aloud.

* * *

After lunch, Matt decided to hit the heads before he left for the day. On the wall of the toilet stall, he saw, written in black marker, "I love the fucking navy because the navy loves fucking me".

"Well that's about right," Matt said aloud. His words echoed off the walls in the empty heads.

On Friday afternoon, Matt used the "sliders" chit that the Chief had given him to get off early. He had plenty to do before he was to meet Cynthia for dinner, so he hopped a bus into Victoria. The first place he needed to go was a one-hour photo shop. He had a roll of film that contained the photos of him and Cynthia's visit to Saxe Point Park the previous weekend. He felt it would be nice to be able to give Cynthia some of the pictures tonight, on their date.

Matt dropped the roll of Fuji 100 ASA on the counter. The clerk, a middle-aged man, rolled the cylinder over slowly and inspected it, and then he dropped it into an envelope.

"That's it?" the clerk asked.

"Yes," said Matt. "Wait... I need double prints."

The clerk looked up at Matt, "Double prints? They must be good."

"I sure hope so," Matt smiled. "I'll be back in an hour."

The clerk shoved a pen towards Matt, "Wait a minute, put your name and phone number on the envelope."

Matt picked up the pen and obliged.

"Oh, by the way, we are backed up. It'll be more like two hours," the clerk said without offering any sort of apology.

"Thanks," said Matt. "I'll be back in two hours then." Matt sighed. This was typical. They advertise "1-Hour Photo", and then they take two hours to do the job.

While he waited for his photos to be developed, Matt decided to relax and do some shopping around Eaton Place. It was nice to get off the base and away from the navy and into the real world where real people lived. He had to be careful, though, because Cynthia worked at Eaton Place, and he didn't want to bump into her. He had stopped by to see her at work once in the past, and she didn't like it. She really let him know she hated that he dropped in to see her. So, he decided to go into the mall and do his shopping and then get out fast, to lessen the chance of bumping into her.

He saw that there was a sale at one of his favorite men's clothing stores and went inside. Matt didn't like to shop at length when he bought clothes. He usually just bought the first thing that caught his eye. He managed to shop around for a bit, but then he quickly decided on a new shirt and tie that he thought looked fashionable. He could wear them tonight on his date with Cynthia.

Once he was finished clothes shopping, he went to a café on Yates Street to wait for his photos to be ready. After about an hour had been wasted, he went to the photo place to pick up his pictures. As he walked in, he looked at the clock on the wall. One hour and fifty-five minutes had passed since he had dropped them off. He sure hoped that they were ready earlier than predicted, as he really wanted to get back to his barracks and prepare for his big date.

The clerk recognized him when he walked in, "You were right. They were good pictures." The clerk reached down and pulled out an envelope containing Matt's photos.

"Thanks," said Matt. He really didn't like the thought of the photo place guy looking at his pictures.

"How much do I owe you?" Matt asked.

"Fourteen-fifty," said the clerk.

Matt paid the bill. He wasn't even out of the store before he opened the envelope to see the photos. Just as he had ordered, there were two copies of each photo. Most of the pictures featured him and Cynthia lying on a blanket together at Saxe Point Park. He had placed the camera on a bag and used the timer to snap the shots. They turned out pretty good. Cynthia's red hair was even brighter than usual as it was glowing in the sun. He really liked one particular shot where he was kissing her on the cheek, and she was smiling and beaming. Matt swooned. Her smile was spectacular.

Since the photo place had taken so long, he didn't have much time to waste, so Matt quickly hailed a taxi and made a quick trip back to the base. He needed to shower and get ready for his dinner date.

Once he got home to his barracks, Matt separated the photos into two piles. One set he would give to Cynthia, and the other set he would keep for himself. He put his own set into his duffle bag, the same bag that he would finish packing with items to take onto the *Mackenzie*, as he planned to have those photos with him when he went to sea.

Matt showered and changed into the new shirt and tie he had purchased. Of course, he noticed that the shirt had wrinkles on it where it had been folded in the store, so he quickly took off the shirt and ironed out the wrinkles. Matt knew that Cynthia would hate it if he wore a wrinkled shirt. Regardless, he held out hope that she would actually like these new threads, as he knew her well enough to know she was sometimes difficult to please.

Matt caught another taxi and sped to Cynthia's apartment, which was located near downtown Victoria, on Fairfield Road. He arrived at Cynthia's building perfectly at the pre-determined time, 7 PM sharp. He rang the buzzer, and she quickly buzzed him into the building. When he got to her apartment door, she called for him to let himself inside, as she wasn't ready yet. Matt let himself in, and waited patiently.

When she finally appeared, it was worth the wait. She was stunning.

Cynthia wore a green summer dress. The pale green of the dress matched her eyes perfectly. Her red hair was slightly curled and resting gently upon her bare shoulders. She even had a big smile for Matt. To top it off, every one of her freckles was too cute for Matt to bear.

"Oh, wow!" Matt was dumbstruck. Still he knew that he had to keep his cool. This was going to be a fabulous night.

"Do you like it?" Cynthia asked as she twirled around for Matt.

"Cynthia, you look absolutely gorgeous," Matt gushed.

She replied coolly, "I know."

Matt leaned in, hoping to be able to give her a kiss. However, she blocked him by putting her hand up to his face.

"No, you'll smudge my makeup," she protested.

Matt groaned, "Don't make me beg."

"Sorry, baby it's not going to work," Cynthia explained with a straight face. "I want to look good tonight and I don't need you pawing me up before I even set one foot out of the house."

"Okay, I guess we might as well head out then," Matt said as he picked up the phone and dialed the number for a taxi. He decided not to be too disappointed, as it likely wouldn't get him anywhere. He would have to wait until later. It would be worth the wait.

Cynthia stood and studied Matt as he was on the phone placing an order for a taxi. She waited until he was finished then she asked him, "Is that a new shirt and tie?"

"Yes it is," he replied. "Do you like them?"

"They're not too, too horrible," she giggled. "Next time you want to buy clothes why don't you let me accompany you? I'm a professional, after all."

"Okay," Matt said. "It's a date." Secretly though, he would avoid it. He didn't like it when girls tried to dress him up as if he was a Ken doll.

While they waited for the taxi to arrive, Matt decided to give her the packet of photos from their visit to Saxe Point Park.

"I have something for you," he said.

Cynthia's eyes lit up, "A surprise? I wonder what it could be." She was clearly expecting something amazing.

"These are for you," he said as he produced a packet of photos. "They're from our time at the park last weekend. I had them make double prints. These are yours."

"Oh," Cynthia said softly as she took the envelope from his hand.

She opened the envelope and immediately looked at the pictures. "These are nice," she said. "I look really good in that one," she remarked as she flipped through the photos.

Matt said, "I wrote something on the back of that one." He pointed to the one photo where he was kissing her on the cheek.

She flipped the picture over and read what Matt had written, "Dearest Big Red. I love your smile. Love Matt."

She furrowed her brow. "Since when am I 'Big Red'?"

"I don't know," Matt attempted to explain. "I just thought of it. You know that I love your red hair." He suddenly realized he was in big trouble, and he figured he could compensate by cracking as big of a smile as he could. After all, she always said she loved his smile.

She looked at him and noticed that he was sporting his trademark crooked smile. Nevertheless, it didn't change her current opinion.

"But, Big Red? Come on!" She scolded him. "...and what are you smiling about? Wipe that smile off your face."

Matt cancelled the smile. Due to the scolding, he adopted a more repentant demeanor.

"I don't like being called Big Red. I hate it! Don't ever do that again." Then, she ripped the photo in half and placed it back in the envelope.

Matt apologized. "I'm sorry. You know me. I'm kind of clumsy when it comes to romance..."

Cynthia cut him off, "Clumsy? This is almost as bad as the time you called me Madam Smiley."

Matt winced.

"It made me sound like some sort of cheerful brothel operator," she said, as she continued to berate Matt's choice of nicknames.

"You know, I really thought that it was a nice nickname," Matt tried to explain. "You know, because your smile... I love your smile! You've got a great smile."

She was still frowning a bit, but the compliments about her smile seemed to have taken some edge off her sour demeanor.

Matt decided to try the crooked smile again. To see if that could level things off.

"Keep wiping that smile off your face," she scolded him anew.

Good thing for Matt that the buzzer rang, and the taxi was downstairs and ready to go. Matt breathed a sigh of relief that they were able to get in the taxi, and there was a natural point where he could change the subject.

* * *

During the taxi ride to the restaurant, Cynthia told him all about the awful day she had. Again, Matt did his duty as a good listener. She did like that about him and Matt knew it. He felt it was his job as a boyfriend to listen, but he often found it was a challenge to maintain his focus.

Finally, she ended her discourse and gave Matt an opening.

"How was your day, Matt?"

"I had a strange day," Matt answered. "I arrived onboard the *Mackenzie*, and they didn't have my paperwork. Once they got that straightened out everything else went smoothly... until I had a run-in with the Executive Officer."

"Are you in trouble?" she asked with a slightly concerned look on her face.

"Not really. But, I had planned on 'flying below the radar' for the time I am there. But, now it seems like I am on HIS radar."

"Okay," she said. Suddenly, she seemed disinterested. Matt realized that he had used the word "radar" twice in his explanation. She probably didn't appreciate it very much.

"Sorry, I know you don't like it when I talk about all that navy stuff," Matt apologized as he slid his arm around her waist. "I'll lay off the navy talk tonight."

She didn't respond immediately. She just sighed as she leaned back a bit, pressing against his arm. Finally, after a minute she spoke up.

"Matt, you can talk about your work if you want. I can't tell you not to. I'm sorry. I just don't think that the navy is much of a career."

Matt frowned. This was never going to end. She was never going to accept his life in the navy.

"Are you ticked off that I'm leaving for four weeks?" Matt asked.

"No, not really," she responded softly. "It's your job. You have to do it. I'm not ticked off."

"Are you sure?" Matt asked. "You sure seem put off about something."

"I don't like it when you say that I'm 'ticked off', or 'put off'," she responded with a strange grin. "Listen buster, when I'm ticked, you'll know."

Matt decided that he better change the subject, fast.

"Well, I'm surely going to miss all your cuteness while I'm away," Matt said.

"Okay," Cynthia responded, rather dispassionately.

Matt was disappointed. He had actually hoped she might respond in kind, telling him that she would miss him, as well. Maybe if he cheered her up?

Matt put on a fake mope. He turned down his eyes and adopted a big lip, "It's going to be rough on me. I'm going to be surrounded by all these hairy gorillas for four weeks. I will surely miss being around a cutie-pie like you."

She just turned to him and smiled briefly, and then she turned away. That was her entire reaction. She seemed so uninterested in what he had to say. He would be gone for four weeks, and her only reaction was to be indifferent about it.

But, he thought he knew this look. She always did this when she got upset about something and she didn't want to talk about it. Still, Matt thought, maybe she was going to miss him. This just might be her way of showing it.

Matt was sure that he was never going to understand women.

* * *

The taxi pulled up in front of the restaurant. Matt got out first and held the car door open for Cynthia. She exited the taxi gracefully, and then walked up to the door of the restaurant while Matt paid the cabbie. She waited patiently, for Matt to open the door for her, which he did dutifully.

Once they were seated at their table, things began to go a little more smoothly for Matt. Cynthia decided that she did not want to talk about work. Matt was agreeable with this. Instead, they chatted about food they loved and food they grew up with. Then the conversation turned to Cynthia's future career aspirations. She wanted to go back to school and get a Business Degree. Matt listened intently. All the while, he couldn't help but think that Cynthia looked even more beautiful in the soft light of the restaurant. He couldn't help himself. He was truly smitten by her.

She ordered a bottle of wine. Matt agreed with her choice. Then, for her main course, she ordered the Pasta Primavera. Matt went ahead and ordered a steak and potato, with onions.

Cynthia frowned. "Why are you going to eat all that red meat... and onions!? You know I don't like the smell of onions."

Matt smiled, "I'm sorry sweetie. This is going to be one of my last good meals for four weeks. I think I have earned the right to eat pretty much what I want."

"Okay, I guess that makes it acceptable," she smiled back at him. "But you know that I hate the smell of onions, and now you're going to have onion breath."

"I have some gum," he said. "That'll nullify it."

"Sort of, maybe," she whispered as she took a small bite from a breadstick. "The gum just masks the odor, it doesn't take it away."

"Okay," Matt said. "I won't eat the onions."

Once their meals arrived, they ate quietly. Cynthia commented on her Pasta Primavera, as she thought it was extraordinary. Matt could tell that she really loved it. Matt ate his steak and potato, but he pushed the sautéed onions to the side of the plate. He simply stared at the juicy strips of onion. They seemed to be daring him to take just one bite. But he held back. It was easier this way.

"Mmmm, this steak is perfect," Matt said as he consumed a generous morsel of his meal. "It's juicy and rare. Just the way I like it."

Matt noticed that Cynthia didn't respond to his review of the steak. Matt could see that she appeared to be quiet and withdrawn this evening. She didn't seem to be like herself, and he wasn't sure what the problem could be.

After the main course, the waiter brought the dessert menu over. He held it up at the side of the table and began to recite the dessert specials.

"None for me," Cynthia said, rather abruptly.

The waiter turned and looked at Matt, "For you sir?"

"I'll have some dessert, "Matt announced.

Cynthia frowned. "You're not going to get dessert and eat it in front of me, are you?"

Matt thought about it for a split second, "Yes, I think that I'll get a dessert. If you don't want one then you'll have to suffer by watching me."

Matt ordered a helping of apple pie and ice cream. When it arrived, Cynthia didn't say a word. She just watched Matt, as he enjoyed his dessert.

"Well at least you didn't get cheesecake," she conceded. "I really couldn't stand it if you were eating cheesecake in front of me."

Matt smiled back at her as he swallowed the last piece of the pie.

* * *

After dinner, they returned to Cynthia's apartment. Now, Matt was hoping things might get a little more intimate. He was going to sea for a month, and he wanted to have some fun with the girl he truly loved.

Cynthia only had tea to drink; no soft drinks, or beer. Matt settled for water. They sat on the couch together; she was sipping tea, and he was drinking water. He didn't mind the lack of beverage choice as it was the girl that interested him.

Matt leaned over to kiss Cynthia. This time he was successful as she returned his advances. But, that was pretty much as far as things were about to go.

"How about we spend the night together?" Matt asked, in the sweetest voice he could muster.

Cynthia remained cool in her response. "I'm not sure I want to do that tonight," she replied.

"Well, think about it," Matt countered. "This might be the last time we see each other before I go away for four weeks."

"Yeah, I know sweetie," she said. "I'm just so tired."

"Okay," Matt said. He had a slightly sullen tone.

Cynthia sensed Matt's mood, and she felt that she needed to explain. "You know, I just don't feel like it," she said. "...and if I'm not in the mood, I'm just not in the mood."

"Maybe I'll get you in the mood," Matt said with a grin.

"I doubt it," she said dispassionately. "I'm on my period and I don't feel like fooling around tonight."

Matt's male mind automatically connected her moodiness to her monthly visitor. It could only explain so much.

"Oh," he said softly. "Okay."

Matt continued to sip his water, trying to think of some way he could lighten Cynthia's frame of mind. He still wanted her to get into a playful mood, a mood that he had seen in the past. After all, if she were playful enough, maybe she would still want to fool around a bit. Tonight, though, this seemed impossible. Cynthia just wanted to talk about work and her family, which she did. Matt listened, which is what he figured she wanted him to do. However, as the minutes turned into hours Matt got no closer to the prize he desired.

Finally, Cynthia announced that it was time for bed. Matt looked at his watch and saw that it was 1 AM.

Matt asked, "Do you want to sleep together... and just cuddle?"

"I don't think so. I already know that won't work. You toss around so much! Plus, you'll probably want to do more than cuddle."

"So you're kicking me out?"

"No, I won't do that. You can sleep on the couch if you want," she said as she walked into the kitchen and turned off the lights.

"Okay, I guess that will be fine by me." He didn't really want to go back to the barracks, and it meant that he would get to see her again in the morning.

Cynthia went into her bedroom and brought out a blanket and a pillow. "Here you go Matty," she said with a sweet voice, as she put the bedding down on the couch.

Matt sighed, "Okay, thanks. I'll see you in the morning, Cynthia."

Cynthia was headed back into her bedroom, and then at the last minute, she tiptoed back over to Matt and kissed him on the cheek.

She whispered, "Good night, Matty."

Matt put his arms around her and whispered into her ear, "Good night Cynthia, I love you."

She stopped cold. Then she placed her arms around him and embraced him, as well.

"I know," she said softly as she hugged him tightly.

They hugged for about a minute, and then she broke off the embrace. "I'm so tired. I have to go to bed."

"Okay... hey, I've got an idea," Matt whispered. "Maybe we can go out for breakfast in the morning?"

"Sure, that sounds like fun," Cynthia smiled softly. "We can go to that bistro I like."

Matt watched as Cynthia went back into her bedroom and closed the door quietly.

"Okay," Matt whispered. "Good night."

* * *

At about 8AM, Matt woke up to the sound of a ringing telephone in Cynthia's bedroom. Matt heard the telltale sounds of Cynthia answering the phone, and her muffled voice as she spoke. Matt was still on the couch, and he rolled over in an effort to get a little more comfortable.

About a minute later, Cynthia came rushing out of the bedroom and abruptly made a rather disappointing announcement.

"I've been called in to work," she said.

"Oh no," Matt sighed. "Can't you tell them no?"

"No," she said sternly. "It doesn't work that way."

"Okay," Matt said. "We can just go for breakfast now, and then you can go to work on a full stomach."

"I don't have time," she said. "I've got to be at work at 9:30. I've got to get ready and go straight to work."

Matt was clearly disappointed. It was apparent by the look on his face.

"I'm sorry I don't have time for breakfast with you," she apologized.

Matt was undoubtedly let down, but he quickly realized that there was nothing he could do.

"Okay. No problem... I will probably just take off then, and let you get ready for work." Matt began to fold the blanket that had been covering him on the couch.

She didn't respond, as she was busy scurrying around trying to get ready for work.

"So..." Matt asked. "Should I call you later?"

She was still too busy to respond.

"Maybe we could do something tonight?" Matt asked as he was putting on his socks and shoes.

Finally, she stopped and responded. "Yeah. Maybe maybe."

"Two maybes?" he joked. "Two maybes means 'yes', isn't that right?"

She just stared at him blankly. "I don't know what you're talking about Matty..."

Matt came over to her and put his arms around her. Then he moved his face toward her, in an obvious attempt to give her a kiss goodbye before he left.

"What are you doing?" she said as she pushed him away.

"I wanted to give you a kiss goodbye," he responded with a crooked smile.

"No way!" she said. "Morning breath." She waved her hand in front of her face.

Matt reached into his pocket. "Wait... I've got some gum."

"No thank you," she said. "It'll just be spearmint flavored morning breath... and that's even worse!"

"Okay," Matt said as he went to the door. Slightly disappointed, he simply left without a kiss.

* * *

Matt trudged down the street to the corner store and bought a coffee and bagel. Then he walked towards downtown to clear his head. He ate his bagel and drank his coffee as he walked.

Once downtown, he stopped at Coles Books to buy a paperback. A book on the new releases rack, *Friday* by Robert A. Heinlein, caught his eye; mainly because it was by one of his favorite authors, but partially because it had a sexy woman on the cover. In fact, the image of the woman even reminded him of Cynthia.

The teaser on the inside flap sealed the deal:

Engineered from the finest genes, and trained to be a secret courier in a future world, Friday operates over a near-future Earth, where chaos reigns. Working at Boss's whimsical behest she travels from far north to deep south, finding quick, expeditious solutions as one calamity after another threatens to explode in her face...

Matt smiled as he carried a copy of the book to the checkout stand. "This should be good," he thought. Everything he liked in a woman, sexy, independent, smart... "This will be a good read to take my mind off Cynthia, while I'm away at sea."

Matt hopped a bus back to the Barracks. Then, he spent the rest of the day reading and napping, and mostly waited for the opportunity to phone Cynthia and make plans for their possible date tonight.

Matt knew that Cynthia would get off work around 5 PM, so he waited until about 5:30, and then he called her.

She answered right away, "Hello Matt, I just got in."

"How was your wonderful day at work?" he asked.

"Oh, it was definitely less than wonderful," she said. "I was run off my feet the entire day. It was non-stop."

"Sorry to hear that," Matt said softly.

Then he changed his tone, "Well, do you know what you need after a long day like that? The answer is... a night out! How would you like to put on your dancing shoes and we'll go out to a club tonight?"

"Oh no, mister," she moaned. "I'm so sorry, Mattie. I'm too tired to go out. I'm so exhausted, and my feet hurt. I can't go dancing. I'm definitely going to stay home tonight."

"Would you like me to come over and keep you company?" Matt asked.

"I wouldn't be good company," she said. "I'm so tired I'm afraid that I'm going to fall asleep. I'm probably going to spend the night in bed."

"Spend the night in bed?" Matt asked. "You know what? That sounds like a great idea. What time would you like me to come over?"

"Oh, you're so funny," she laughed. "No, I really think that I'll have to pass. I am that tired."

Matt knew that there was no way to argue with her on this point. He knew that when she made a decision she could really dig in her heels. In fact, if he kept pressing the issue, he was going to lose badly.

"How about tomorrow?" he asked hopefully. "We can spend some time together. We could go back to the park. The weather is supposed to be phenomenal."

"Oh, I think I already told you, on Sunday I am going to a family picnic in Sooke. Remember, it's my Uncle's birthday?" she explained.

Matt said, "I can go with you."

"It's a family thing, not a boyfriend thing," she clarified.

"I can do family things," Matt countered.

"I don't know, Mattie," she said. "I haven't really told them about you. I don't need all the questions like, when are you going to get married, and when are you going to have babies. I don't need to hear all those particular questions. If you were there with me, it would surely start up."

"Well, maybe we should start talking about some of these topics. Just so you have the answers when your family asks," Matt replied. As the words were leaving his mouth, he knew that he probably shouldn't be saying this.

Cynthia was silent. Apparently, she was dumfounded by his suggestion.

Finally, she replied, "No, let's not do that right now. Now is not a good time for that."

"Okay," Matt said.

"Well, I've got to go now, Matt," she said. "I wish you a good voyage."

"I'll be okay, it's only four weeks. I'll get by, but I'll miss you, mostly," he lamented.

"Okay," she said. "I'll miss you too Mattie, but try to have a good time, will you?"

"I'll try," Matt said. "I'll be in New Westminster next weekend. I'll call you from there."

"Okay, I will look for your call," she said. "It will be nice to hear from you."

"Ah, Cynthia... do you remember, when I asked if you would like to take the ferry over to spend part of the weekend with me in New West? Have you thought any more about that?"

"Matt, I have to work next Saturday," she said.

"I know, but I just wondered if you thought about getting off work, just to come over and see me," he said. "They must owe you a Saturday off, especially since you worked today at the last minute."

"I will think about it," she said.

"Okay, that would be nice. You could come over on Saturday, and we could spend the day together. I would get a hotel room for us for Saturday night."

"I said that I'd think about it," she said abruptly.

"Okay," Matt said sheepishly.

"I'm so tired now. I've got to say goodbye Matt."

"Okay Cynthia, goodbye."

"Goodbye Matt." Then there was a distinctive click as she hung up the phone.

Matt was disappointed. He realized that he would not get to see her again for the next four weeks, unless, of course, she changed her mind about coming to New Westminster for a visit. Still, he knew that the New West thing was a complete long shot. It was all he had at this point in time.

* * *

The rest of the weekend went by slowly. Matt listened to music, read his new book and he slept. The whole time he moped. He was in a sullen mood the entire time.

On Sunday night, just prior to supper, he used a public pay phone in the lobby of the barracks to phone his grandparents in Winnipeg. He knew that they were usually home on Sunday evening, and it was always a good time to call. For over half an hour, he spoke to the only two people in the world that he could truly trust. For the most part, they spoke in Ukrainian, which, for some reason always put Matt in a good mood. Maybe it's because it always reminded him of home.

However, his mirth was short-lived. As he ended his phone call, and placed the receiver back in its cradle, the Duty Petty Officer approached him.

"What is your name and rank?" the Petty Officer asked.

The Petty Officer Second Class was rather menacing looking; tall and fit with an angular face, and his short blonde hair in a brush cut. Matt was in civvies, since it was the weekend, and the Petty Officer's question was a valid one. Matt was obligated to answer.

"I am a Leading Seaman... my name is Petersen."

"Leading Seaman Petersen," The Petty Officer said sternly. "Am I to understand that you were speaking Russian on that telephone?" He pointed directly at the pay phone, which Matt had been using.

Matt stammered, "No PO... Not Russian... Ukrainian."

"What?" said the Petty Officer. "Why were you speaking Ukrainian?"

"I was talking to my grandparents," Matt explained. "They live in Winnipeg. They speak Ukrainian."

"Oh... okay. Just that... it sounded a lot like Russian," the Petty Officer said.

Matt just stared at him. Inside he was angry, especially after having such a enjoyable conversation... and now this?

"Ukrainian is sort of the same language, but it's definitely not Russian," Matt explained.

The Petty Officer pondered the situation for a moment. Then, he made a decision, "You may carry on, Leading Seaman Petersen."

"Yes PO," Matt said as he continued on to the cafeteria for supper.

* * *

The phone incident caused Matt to be perturbed for the remainder of the evening. Grumpily, he packed one final kit bag of essentials. His paperback, some cassette tapes, his shaving kit. Then he decided to head to bed early. He had to be on the *Mackenzie* at 4AM, which meant he had to get up way before dawn. Therefore, he made a conscious effort to sleep off his grumpiness. He needed to be bright eyed and bushy-tailed the next day. It's best that he was well prepared to go to sea with the *Mackenzie*, and to face every challenge that lay ahead.

CHAPTER 4 / BEING IN ALL RESPECTS READY FOR SEA

Monday morning came very early for Matt. He had to be at the *Mackenzie* at 4AM, which meant that his alarm went off at 3AM. It didn't take him long to shower and shave, and his uniform was ready to go, but he had to hurry as his walk to the dockyard would take about 30 minutes. He just pulled on his shirt, pants and tied his boots. He grabbed his kit bag, and he was ready to go. Breakfast and coffee would have to wait until he got onboard the *Mackenzie*.

The stroll from the barracks to the dockyard was quiet as there wasn't a soul awake at this time on a Monday morning. The air was cool, and the sky was clear. Matt could see a few stars twinkling up above as he walked up Admiral's Road. Once he made it to the top of the hill he turned right on Esquimalt Road, which lead directly up to the dockyard gate.

In the east, he could see the horizon brightening as the summer sun was getting set to rise and begin the day. As he walked, he couldn't help thinking about Cynthia and wondering how her family BBQ in Sooke had gone. He realized that he missed her already. This worried him a bit, as he knew that he was going to be away for a while. How would he be at the end of this journey if he was all messed up before it even started? Matt sighed, as he really didn't want to be doing this, leaving for all this time. However, he had no choice, and his only option was to buck up and "take the medicine". Still, every step he took seemed to take him further away from the girl he loved.

The streets were completely deserted at this hour. It was a very quiet walk, until he was about halfway to the dockyard gate, when he heard a lone vehicle coming up the street from behind. Soon, he could see that the vehicle was close, as its headlights were lighting the street next to the sidewalk where he was walking. Matt turned his head to check it out, and he saw that it was a bright yellow Esquimalt Taxi.

"Some poor drunk sailors coming back to their ship, very, very late," Matt said to himself quietly. Just as he said this, Matt was surprised that the taxi was now stopping and pulling up to the curb right next to him.

Matt stopped walking and turned to face the taxi. In the dim light of a streetlight, he could sort of make out Paul Legere's face through the open window of the cab.

Paul called out, "Hey Matt, why are you walking when you can ride in luxury?" Matt noticed that his voice was slightly coarse and gravelly.

"Hey Paul," Matt answered back.

Paul pushed the door of the taxi open, "You might as well ride the rest of the way as we are going to the same place. Come on and get in."

Matt shrugged his shoulders, and then he piled himself into the taxi and closed the door. The taxi continued on its way up Esquimalt Road toward the main gate of the dockyard.

"Good morning Paul," Matt said as he settled into the seat.

"Yes, it is a good morning, isn't it?" Paul replied sheepishly. "It's a little early for what I am used to, but a good morning just the same."

Matt looked at Paul's face. Even in the darkness of the backseat of a taxi, Matt could see that Paul's eyes looked really droopy, and his face looked tired.

"Late night last night?" Matt asked.

"Something like that..." Paul answered, somewhat vaguely. Paul didn't seem very chatty.

At the dockyard gate, a Commissionaire stuck his head into the taxi. Matt greeted him with, "We're going to 'B' Jetty, the *Mackenzie*." Both men showed their ID cards, and the Commissionaire quickly waved the taxi through.

"Some security," Paul complained, as the taxi pulled away from the gate and began to proceed down the street that lead to the jetties where the warships were berthed.

"Oh, come on, grumpy," Matt replied. "He's just doing his job."

Paul sneered, "Doesn't he know there is a war going on?"

"What war?" Matt asked politely.

"The Cold War," Paul sneered. "We're fighting it every day, here." Paul raised his hand and pointed over toward the jetties where several Canadian destroyers could be seen.

Matt didn't reply. He knew that Paul was tired and grumpy, and he was just trying to be cheeky. A response would just prolong the whole event.

The taxi drove right down onto "B" Jetty and stopped right in front of the *Mackenzie*'s gangway. Paul paid the driver as Matt opened the car door and piled out onto the jetty. Paul was right behind him.

Both men boarded the ship, saluting as they crossed the brow and continued down to #4 Mess with their kit bags. As they walked down the flats toward the Mess, Paul continued with his tirade.

"Did you see that? The Quartermaster didn't even challenge us," Paul complained. "He just stood there and nodded in our general direction. He was over 10 yards away. We could have been Russian spies!"

Matt tried to calm his friend, "But we're not spies... we're just here to flash-up the radars and go to sea."

Paul huffed and puffed a bit. He wanted to come up with another piece of sharp criticism...

Matt continued, "All right, take a chill pill. Let's just stow our kit and head up to the Operations Room. We can make a pot of coffee and get started on the flash-up checklist."

"Good idea," replied Paul, more calmly now. "I could really use some coffee."

"Hopefully, it de-grumpifies you," Matt replied with a smirk.

* * *

When Matt and Paul arrived in the Operations Room, they were surprised to see that the Operations Chief, Chief Cartwright, was already there.

This was very unusual to Matt. On the last ship he sailed in, the Operations Chief was never present for flash-up. In fact, he was never around at all, unless there were troubles to sort out. It was becoming more apparent to Matt that this ship was different.

"Good morning men," the Chief greeted them as they entered the space. "I made a fresh pot of coffee to fuel you up as you go down the flash-up checklist."

"Thanks Chief," said Matt. "We are going to need it." Matt looked over at Paul, who was still looking rather grumpy and droopy-eyed.

"Don't worry Chief," Paul assured him as he rubbed his eyes. "We'll have

65

this Ops Room flashed up tickety-boo in no time."

"That's what I thought," the Chief smiled. "It shouldn't be too hard, just be sure to show Petersen how we do things here on the Mack."

"Yes Chief," Paul replied. "I will be sure to show Petersen the ropes." He made a whipping motion with the clipboard that held the flash-up checklist.

Matt went over to the coffee pot to pour two cups of coffee while Paul just stared at the checklist.

"Paul, how do you take your coffee?" Matt asked.

Without taking his eyes off the clipboard, Paul replied, "NATO Standard..."

Matt prepared two cups of coffee, black for himself and one with a large helping of powdered cream and two teaspoons of sugar for Paul. He brought the two steaming cups over to the port-side plotting table where Paul was standing.

"Here you go Paul, NATO Standard," Matt confirmed as he handed the cup to Paul.

Paul took a long sip. Then he grinned and said, "Man-o-man that Operations Chief can make good coffee. This tastes like that gourmet shit."

"Okay, let's get to work!" Paul was suddenly rejuvenated.

"Top of the list, the Gyro," Paul announced. "It was flashed up on Friday, but we'll have to go down below and double-check it and make sure it's reading correctly. Then we'll have to check all the gyro repeaters as well."

Matt agreed, "If the gyro was fucked, we would need to know that right away. We can't sail without a gyrocompass."

Both sailors had another long sip of hot coffee, and then they headed down the ladder to Captain's flats, quietly as they never stomped around near the Captain's cabin. They were never sure when he might be in there. Then they wove their way down three more ladders and three different corridors to enter the space where the gyrocompass was located.

When they entered the space, they could tell that the gyrocompass was operational since it generated a discernable high-pitched whine as it spun at several thousand revolutions per minute. The thought of the gyro spinning so fast was something Matt always remembered from his Radar School training, as the instructor had pointed out, "If the gyro topples it has enough momentum to go right through the bulkhead." However, today everything seemed to be under control.

Paul put his hand on the gyrocompass binnacle, which was mounted on a pedestal at a height of about four feet.

"The Gyro is up and running," Paul said. Matt knew that Paul could actually feel the steady hum of the spinning gyro. From this, Paul had determined that the Gyrocompass seemed stable, "Everything seems good so far. Let's check the heading."

To get the heading, both sailors bent over to peer at the top of the compass binnacle. It said 160 and about a half a degree.

"What's the heading supposed to be?" Matt asked.

Paul replied, "There's a chart on the bulkhead there."

"It says 340° for B Jetty," Matt replied.

"Yeah... but we are pointed south." Paul said. "What's the reciprocal bearing of 340°?"

Matt recalled the method of calculating a reciprocal bearing by either adding two to the first number, or subtracting two from the first number, then doing the opposite to the second number. He subtracted 2 from the 3 in 340° and added 2 to the 4 in 340° to get to the answer of 160°.

"Subtract two, and then add two, so 160°," Matt answered.

Paul replied, "Well this thing is only half a degree off, and that's close enough for government work." He then marked down 160.5° on the flash-up sheet, and made a checkmark.

After the two sailors had confirmed the gyro heading from the master compass, they began a journey throughout the ship to all the gyro repeaters and checked their headings.

Housed throughout the ship were several gyro repeaters. Some were tape repeaters, like the ones in the wheelhouse, Operations Room and on the bridge. The tape repeaters were boxes that had a lighted red window where the bearing was displayed. Others were binnacle style repeats like on the bridge wings. These had a horizontal display with a face like a compass. They had to check them all, to see that they read 160.5° or as close to that reading as possible.

As they went through the ship, they chatted quietly.

Matt asked, "So what is Chief Cartwright like?"

Paul replied, "Oh, he's great. One of the best Chiefs I ever sailed with. He's a bit quirky, though. You know..."

"What do you mean," Matt asked.

"Well, for one thing he likes to talk about the *Bonaventure* and being in the Vietnam War."

Matt knew that *HMCS Bonaventure* had been Canada's last surviving aircraft carrier, and it had been decommissioned over ten years ago.

"I didn't know that the *Bonaventure* served in Vietnam. In fact, I didn't know any Canadian ships at all served in Vietnam," Matt questioned.

Paul laughed, "Yes, none of us knew that. But Chief Cartwright is convinced that he was in that particular war, and on the 'Bonnie' to boot."

Matt chuckled, "There must be a good story there..."

Paul replied, "Yes, there is, and he'll tell you all about it if you ask him."

As they went to each gyro repeater, Matt would read off the heading and Paul would write it down in the corresponding box on the flash-up sheet. Then they would continue on to the next repeater.

"On the Mack, have you ever had one of these repeaters be way off?" Matt asked.

"Yes, and we called in the Tech," Paul answered. "That's when the fun really starts. Radar Technicians hate being hauled out of their cart for anything!"

It took about 20 minutes, but the two men finally made it around to all the gyro repeaters in the ship. At the end, all the repeaters were reading no more than half a degree off what the main compass was reading.

"Well, that's the hard part done." Paul sighed. "Let's go back to the Ops Room, drink the rest of our coffees, and then start on the radars and displays."

* * *

The *Mackenzie* had three radar sets. One was a long-range SPS-12 air-warning radar, used for monitoring and tracking air contacts. Secondly, she had a medium-range SPS-10 surface-search radar, used for discovering and tracking anything on the surface of the sea. Lastly, she had a short-range Sperry navigation radar, which was used for blind pilotage and close-in navigation.

The two sailors made their way to Radar 1, a space that was just aft of the Operations Room. They stood in front of the massive SPS-12 radar switch panel.

Paul said, "Okay, let's switch on the main breaker."

Matt instinctively stood back as Paul put his hand on the breaker switch.

Just then, the Operations Chief came into the space. "Petersen, why did you step back when Legere put his hand on the main switch?"

"I usually stand back, just in case he gets a jolt, I won't get jolted as well," Matt explained. "After all, if he gets thousands of volts coursing through him, he's going to need someone to save his life."

The Chief smiled, "Oh, don't worry about any of that. I've been working around radar my entire career, and I can honestly say that Radar hasn't affected me one bit."

Paul laughed, "Where did your hair go, Chief?"

Chief Cartwright rubbed his bald spot, "That's got nothing to do with any radar. It's got more to do with worrying as to what kind of trouble you guys are going to get into when we go into port."

"Don't worry Chief, we'll be good on this trip," Paul said as he put his hand back on the switch.

"I'm just happy that we are only going to Whiskey 601," the Chief said. "There are no pubs or greasy strip clubs way out there. It should be nice and peaceful for me."

"Uh, Chief... aren't we going on a port visit to New Westminster?" Matt interjected.

"Oh, that's right. I forgot all about that one!" the Chief was shaking his head. "Oh, my fuckness, I recall the last time we were there, a lot of things happened. Some guys got into big trouble!"

"Don't worry Chief," Paul said. "Just for your peace of mind, I will personally keep Petersen out of trouble. We'll just go ashore to the library and read books."

"Why don't I believe you Legere?" the Chief said. Even though he was trying to be stern, he still had a big smile on his rather amiable face. "Now, let's get these radars flashed up, okay, boys..."

"We're on it Chief," Paul replied smartly, but with a smile as the Chief left Radar 1 and went back into the Operations Room.

"Oh, my fuckness???" Matt whispered, after the Chief had completely left earshot.

"Yeah, he says that one all the time," Paul replied. "He's got a few other good ones, like that whole 'radar never affected me' line. He says that one all the time."

"I wonder if he knows that he's repeating himself," Matt chuckled. "I wonder if the radar might be affecting his memory."

"Oh, he knows he's doing it," Paul laughed. "My theory is that he just thinks that if he keeps repeating it, it will come true... okay, stand back I'm going to make the main breaker." Paul put his hand on the breaker for the third time, but this time he snapped it up into the ON position. The power supply came to life with a roar as the circuits began to supply thousands of volts to the radar system.

"It's alive!" Paul said with a mad grin.

* * *

It took about half an hour, but working together the two sailors flashed up all three radars and tuned all the radar displays. They had to wait a while for the SPS-12 and SPS-10 radars to warm up, as you never started them cold. The radars were old, almost museum artifacts, and they were delicate. While the warm-up period was occurring, though, they began to flash-up the radar displays in the Operations Room and on the Bridge. Once the SPS-10 Radar was finally up and radiating, Matt sat down at the centre-line SPA-4 display and began to tune the display for a decent surface picture. He was pretty familiar with the SPA-4 equipment, and this only took about two minutes. Meanwhile, Paul finished flashing up the Sperry Navigation Radar. Lastly, they went back into Radar 1 and switched the SPS-12 antenna to rotate, but they didn't turn the power switch to radiate. They both knew that you didn't radiate the SPS-12 radar in harbour, as it was too powerful.

"Okay, what's next?" Matt asked.

"Now that the radars are flashed up, we can go outside and check the antennas," Paul said.

"I was wondering when you were going to suggest that," Matt said with a grin.

"Why didn't you say something then?" Paul retorted.

"I was waiting for you to say it. After all, the Chief told you to 'show me the ropes'. I'm just letting you do your job."

Paul groaned.

The two men went forward into the bridge and emerged into the outdoors through the door that lead onto the starboard bridge wing. They looked up and witnessed the three radar antennas rotating smoothly.

"Listen, do you hear anything?" Paul asked.

They both paused and listened to the antennas for a moment. However, all they heard was a light breeze and a few seagulls squawking in the distance.

"Nope, I hear nothing," Matt broke the silence. "Were you expecting something?"

"Yes," said Paul. "Sometimes the SPS-12 antenna makes a squeaky squeal, which means that someone has to go up there and grease the bearing."

Matt laughed, "A squeaky squeal?"

Paul looked a little stern. "That's exactly what it sounds like," he said. "If you could hear it, you would agree with me."

"Okay," Matt said. "I believe you. By the way, when is the *Mackenzie* scheduled for her DELEX refit?" Matt knew that when the *Mackenzie* received her Destroyer Life Extension refit she would get all new radars.

"Not for a couple of years... I think," Paul laughed. "Besides, she's not going to get a refit in time for us to sail today. We've got to go to sea with what we have!"

At the height of the bridge wing, they had a decent view of the dockyard. The morning sun was much higher now, and the dockyard was beginning to come to life. Matt looked over at the *Yukon*, which was berthed nearby. As she was sailing today with the *Mackenzie*, her radars were rotating, as well.

"Hey," Paul asked. "Remember that time when we shot radiation through the HQ?"

"I still have nightmares about that. I thought we were going to be charged," Matt replied.

"Nah, they couldn't charge us for that. We were just following the instructions," Paul pointed out. "A good lawyer would have gotten us off."

Matt laughed, "Too bad the navy doesn't have any good lawyers."

Matt thought about that event. He and Paul were on their TQ3 Radar Plotter course in Halifax. Their class was down on a harbour training ship and learning how to flash-up the SPS-12 radar. They followed the sequence, and in the step that said "turn the switch to radiate", they did. After a few minutes, they followed written procedure again and switched the radar off. They found out later that the radiation from the radar had caused all the computer systems in the Headquarters building, which was located right next to the ship, to crash.

Matt said, "Hey, remember when we saw all those people leaving the Headquarters Building early that day?"

"They got the afternoon off. They should be thankful," Paul snickered.

* * *

After a short break on the bridge wing, the two men went back into the Ops Room to complete the flash-up. They switched on the plotting tables and then put a fresh piece of onion skin paper on each table. Then, they switched on the intercoms and performed a test.

They were now done. Both men initialed the flash-up checklist and then Paul placed it on the desk next to the Chief.

The Chief had a good long look at it.

"This looks good gentlemen," Chief Cartwright assured them as he signed the bottom of the sheet. "It's nearly 0630. Why don't you go down to the Galley and get some breakfast."

"Thanks Chief, that's where we are headed," Paul answered.

The Chief nodded and then turned to continue and read the morning messages. However, he suddenly remembered something, "Leading Seaman Petersen, you're fresh out of Fleet School. Maybe you can help with the Fleetex when we are out at Whiskey 601."

Matt looked surprised. The Chief barely knew him, and he was already trusting him.

"How are you at Fleetex?" The Chief asked.

Matt had done plenty of Fleetex's in the past. In fact, he always enjoyed the competition. Basically, the Fleetex consisted of a series of Operations tasks or trivia questions each Operations Room around the task force had to complete, for points. It might sound boring, but it always made a slow watch go a little faster.

"Yes Chief, I guess I'm pretty good. I'll do my best. I'm ready to help out," Matt said. He always tried to be respectful.

"Excellent, that's what I like to hear!" The Chief exclaimed. "Now you two go get some grub in your bellies," he said as he pointed at the exit to the Ops Room.

On the way down the ladders to the main flats, Paul began to tease Matt, "Yes Chief... I'll do my best Chief... Have you seen my merit badges Chief?"

Matt laughed. "I guess he just doesn't like you Paul... what did you do, date his grandmother?"

* * *

Matt visited the heads on the way to the Galley. Being as hungry and hung-over as he had been all morning, Paul couldn't wait and went ahead to get his breakfast. When Matt finally arrived, the galley still wasn't too busy. He could see that Paul had already received his breakfast and was seated in the cafeteria.

Matt grabbed a plastic tray and stepped up to the steam line to order eggs. He was a little dismayed to see that the same cook he had encountered on Friday was working the early shift. The cook was his usual pleasant self, and could only manage a grunt when Matt politely asked him for scrambled eggs. As he waited for his eggs, Matt stood and watched him work.

About halfway through the procedure the cook muttered something unintelligible, to which Matt replied, "Not too dry." Matt knew that it always helped to know the procedure when ordering breakfast at an armed forces galley.

With a large metal spatula, the cook chopped at the eggs one last time, and then scooped them onto a clean plate. Then he brought the plate forward towards the steam line and stood by two trays, one filled with bacon and another filled with sausages. The cook looked up at Matt and sort of grunted again.

Matt said, "Bacon."

The cook took a pair of large metal tongs and grabbed onto three slices of very crisp bacon. He placed them on Matt's plate, and then he handed the plate over to Matt.

"Thanks muchly," said Matt.

The cook said nothing in return. Blank-faced, he just shuffled back over to the rear of the galley, obviously headed back to do some concurrent task.

Matt walked into the cafeteria and sat down at the table, right across from Paul.

"That cook is so chatty," Matt said with a grimace.

"Who him?" Paul said. "He's brain-dead. The guy never says anything. We are just lucky that he can cook eggs." Paul pointed at the eggs on Matt's plate.

Matt asked, "How was your weekend?"

"Pretty good. I scored," Paul said. "How about you?"

"What do you mean you scored? Were you playing hockey?" Matt asked, knowing full well what Paul had meant. He just wanted to tease him a bit.

Paul looked at Matt with a serious face, "You know what I'm referring to, Matthew. Those fancy boys in their expensive skates and short-pants can celebrate their pucks flying into a net, but my game involves something a little more sophisticated, and dare I say more manly."

"So you scored, off the ice then," Matt continued his teasing. "You met a girl, and you deked out her goalie, and then..."

Paul interrupted, "That's right... I slipped one through the five-hole."

Matt laughed. "So, who is this girl? Something serious?"

"No, just a certain piece of trim I've been chasing at the Old Forge the past three weekends," Paul grinned.

"That place is some meat market," Matt said.

"Yes, that's exactly what I like about it..." Paul said as he shoveled scrambled eggs into his mouth. After he had taken a few bites, he reached for the ketchup bottle that was perched in a condiment rack situated at the end of the table.

"Need some navy gravy on these bad boys," Paul said as he opened the ketchup bottle and poured a liberal amount of the thick red sauce onto his eggs.

"So what did you do this weekend? Say goodbye to your sweetheart?" Paul asked, as he scooped a forkful of ketchup and eggs into his mouth.

Matt said, "Friday night, we had a good dinner out. But, Saturday and Sunday, we didn't do anything. I wanted to see her again before I left, but she was busy."

"Too busy to see you before you were going away for four weeks?" Paul asked.

Matt shrugged, "Yep, it's like that. She worked on Saturday afternoon, and then on Saturday night she told me she was too tired to go out. On Sunday, she had a family thing going on."

Paul rolled his eyes.

Matt continued on, "Anyway... I'm hoping she can come and see me in New West next weekend."

"Now you're thinking." Paul grinned. "That's a great idea. Get some seedy motel room..."

Matt frowned. "She won't go for that..."

"Better question... Do you think she'll want to hop the ferry all the way across to Vancouver, and then take a taxi down to New West, just to see you?" Paul asked.

"Yeah, maybe," Matt replied. "I'm hoping she's up for it... but still I don't know." Matt was mulling it over in his head. "I think I'll call her when we get alongside on Friday and see what she says. She has told me that she is supposed to work on Saturday, but I'm still hoping she misses me by then, and cancels her work to come and see me."

Paul smiled at Matt. "I can tell that you've got it bad, my friend. You really like this girl, don't you?"

"No comment," said Matt.

"Why don't you just convince her that she needs to come and see you, you know, like a Jedi mind trick?" Paul suggested as he waved his hand gently towards Matt in an Obi Wan Kenobi-like manner.

"Ya right!" Matt scoffed. "You can't use anything you've seen in any movie on Cynthia. It doesn't work that way with this girl. She is very stubborn. She makes the decisions, and there really is no changing her mind..."

"Plus, she hates any movie references. Just hates them..." Matt added.

Paul frowned, "That's no fun." Paul was starting to wonder about Cynthia, but he felt it was best that he kept his silence. Matt probably didn't want to know how he felt about his girlfriend.

Matt looked down at his plate as he explained, "It's something I'm very familiar with, and I'm still trying to figure out how to get my way, despite this... I'm just not very good at it, yet."

Matt looked up and tried to laugh. Instead, he choked on his scrambled eggs.

"Shitty cook," he exclaimed. "These eggs are too dry!"

Paul pushed the ketchup bottle towards Matt, "Here, try this."

* * *

After breakfast, Matt went back to #4 Mess and grabbed his toothbrush and toothpaste. Then he went forward to the washplace to brush his teeth. This only took a few minutes. Afterward, Matt returned to the Mess and finished stowing all his gear, essentially getting ready for sea. The mess was very busy, and Matt had to squeeze around his shipmates that were basically trying to do the same thing. However, he worked quickly and soon left the mess.

Matt went up to the Operations Room to see if there were any last minute tasks that needed to be done. When he arrived, he saw Paul Legere standing at the port plotting table.

"Hey Paul," Matt said. "Is there anything else we need to do before we sail?"

Paul looked at Matt. "What are you doing, looking for work? That's strange... but I forgot what a goody-two-shoes you could be."

Matt snapped, "Screw you then, buddy."

Paul retorted, "I'm just joking. Sorry... Hey, it looks like my watch is taking it out so your watch will be on top-part ship when we sail."

Matt said, "Yeah, I know that. That's okay. I'm just trying to stay out of trouble until we go." This was only partially true, as Matt knew that if he kept working, he could take his mind off Cynthia.

Paul looked at Matt's sullen face, and he immediately sensed that Matt felt uneasy. "Hey, wait a second Matt I want to tell you something. You know how I was so grumpy this morning. Well, after I heard your story about your girlfriend over the weekend, I don't feel so bad. I am sorry for being gruff this morning."

Matt said, "That's okay, Paul." Matt looked down at the deck. "I shouldn't have told you any of that. Don't worry, Paul, I'm going to be okay about it."

Paul replied, "You know Matt... I think that maybe you could use some time off from Cynthia. Instead of worrying about your relationship, try to put it out of your mind and have a good time instead. Just wait until next weekend. You and I will have a good time ashore in New West."

Matt grinned a bit. "Since when does the 'eminently single' Paul Legere give relationship advice?"

"Since I thought you needed some," Paul responded.

Just then, the ships broadcast system crackled to life with an announcement, "HANDS TO STATIONS FOR LEAVING HARBOUR. DRESS W5 WITH BERETS."

Matt put his beret on, "Okay Paul, thanks for your help. I guess I will see you later."

Before he left, Matt reached out and patted the sheet of onion skin paper on the plotting table, "Try not to fuck up too bad, eh."

Paul smiled as Matt exited the Ops Room and headed for his "leaving harbor" station at top-part ship.

* * *

When it came time for the ship to leave the harbour, the entire evolution required plenty of sailors to work on the upper decks to release the lines. For the radar plotters, they were usually assigned to work at a place on the deck named "top-part". This area was defined as amidships on the upper deck, and was conveniently directly below the Operations Room. As well as being a location for the ship's berthing hawsers, top-part ship was the area where the seaboats were housed on davits located on both the port and starboard sides.

When Matt arrived at top-part ship, he saw that there were already a few other radar plotters working there, beginning to ready the lines for departure. He also saw Able Seaman Morrison there, standing off to one side wearing a sound-powered communications headset.

"Hey, Petersen," Morrison said.

"Hey, Morrison," Matt replied. "You're 'Comms'?" Matt asked.

"Roger," Morrison replied with a smirk.

As the men readied the lines, they kept watch on the action still occurring on the jetty next to the ship. At this point in time, there were several Boatswains from the Deck Department getting the brow ready for landing.

In charge of the Boatswains was the Chief Boatswains Mate, Petty Officer First Class Clarke. Clarke was a gnarly fossil of a sailor.

"Is that the Buffer?" Matt pointed over towards the jetty where Clarke was furiously passing orders to the Boatswains.

Morrison looked over, "Yes, that's Petty Officer 'Nobby' Clarke," Morrison said. "My advice to you, Leading Seaman, is to stay away from him. He's a crank."

Matt looked carefully at Petty Officer Clarke. He was a small man, rather short and skinny, but his arms looked like a bull's legs, muscular and taut, and with hands that seemed to be permanently curled into fists. On each hand, was a tattoo of a swallow in flight. Matt knew what those particular tattoos meant. Swallows on the hands usually meant, "these fists fly".

"Why does everybody named Clarke have the nickname of Nobby?" Matt asked as he scratched his head. Matt knew full well that the reason behind the fact that every sailor in the navy named Clarke or White had the nickname of "Nobby" was a full-on mystery. Nobody really knew why. Still, he liked to ask the question.

"I don't know why. But this one has easily earned that nickname..." Morrison said as the sailors all witnessed Petty Officer Clarke currently bellowing at some poor sailors near the brow.

"Yeah, I see what you mean. He looks like he really whips those Boatswains," Matt said as Petty Officer Clarke began to admonish two Leading Seaman Boatswains, each one twice his size. "He's really giving it to those two right now," Matt pointed down toward the brow. He really didn't have to point as everybody on the starboard side of the ship could easily hear Clarke yelling.

"Tweedledee and Tweedledumbass," Clarke yelled. His face was red, and veins were bulging on his neck. "I told you to have a heaving line ready here for this evolution, but you both fucked up again, didn't you?"

Matt asked Morrison, "What did he call those two Leading Seamen? Tweedledee and Tweedledumbass?"

Morrison answered, "Those are their nicknames. Their real names are Tweed and Dumas, but they sort of look alike and they are always together, paired up..."

"Hey, you!" was suddenly heard coming up from the jetty. Matt looked down and saw that Petty Officer Clarke was just below him, and he was glowering at Matt.

Matt answered, "Who me?"

"Yes, you! YOU... new guy!" Clarke yelled. "Throw me that heaving line!" Clarke was pointing at the guardrail near Matt. Matt looked down and saw a coiled heaving line tied to the guardrail.

"Yes PO!" Matt said as he quickly jumped towards the heaving line and began to fumble with the clove hitch that had the heaving line firmly attached to the guardrail.

"Come on sailor! I ain't got all day," Clarke bellowed.

Finally, Matt had fumbled sufficiently with the knot and had it untied. Then, he leaned over the guardrail and threw it, underhand, towards Petty Officer Clarke. He didn't want his toss to fall short and land in the gap between the ship and the jetty, so he used plenty of force in his throw. Matt was also sure to aim and throw the heaving line directly at the Buffer.

Clarke stood still as the heaving line flew toward him. It seemed like slow motion to Matt, however all he could do was stare as the coiled line hit Petty Officer Clarke square in the chest. Then it simply fell to the jetty in a pile. Meanwhile, Clarke never flinched or moved a muscle. He just stood still, staring at Matt.

Matt didn't know what to say. He remained silent.

Finally, the Buffer broke the silence, "Nice throw, Leading Seaman," he said as he picked up the heaving line from his feet. "You're a new guy, right? What is your name?"

Matt responded, "Petersen, PO."

Clarke turned and began to walk back toward the brow of the ship. As he walked, he spoke out loudly, "Petersen, eh... I'll remember that."

The sailors around Matt were silent for a minute. Finally, Leading Seaman James said something, "Petersen, what the fuck did you do?"

"You saw what I did. I threw him the heaving line," Matt replied, matter-of-factly.

"Ya, I get that, but you hit him..."

"He should have moved," Matt retorted. Matt wasn't too worried about this. He was only here for a few weeks. He could easily avoid the Buffer in that short a time.

Just then, Matt heard the Coxswain on the brow yelling down to the Buffer on the Jetty.

"Knobby, don't land the brow yet. The Captain's not aboard. He should be here in a minute or two."

To this, Petty Officer Clarke scowled, and then he raised his hand to give a thumbs up to the Coxswain. Afterwards, he brought his hand back down to his side, and it resumed the shape of a balled fist. The Coxswain turned and marched aft. Obviously, he had more missions to complete before the ship sailed.

Matt looked up at the main mast and saw that the black and white Captain's ashore pennant was still flying. "Wow," he said. "The Captain sure is taking his time getting aboard on a day when we're sailing."

"He always does this," James responded, rather dispassionately.

* * *

About five minutes later, as they stood on top-part ship, waiting for their next order, Morrison made a slight nod of his head in the direction up toward the head of the jetty. The men saw a dark green Jaguar slowly making its way towards the brow of the ship.

"That looks like the Old Man's car," said James.

"I hope his wife is with him!" said Morrison, with unusual excitement for such an event.

Sure enough, Morrison's wish was granted. Once the car finally crawled to a stop, the passenger door opened and out came the long tanned legs of the Captain's wife. This event alone was enough to make all the sailors on the starboard side of the ship stop in their tracks.

As if in slow motion, the long tanned legs were followed by an equally tanned body that was wearing a stylish pink top, smallish white shorts and tasteful, low heels. To top it off, her high blond hair, liberal makeup and a smile as wide as her face made her look as delicious as anything the eighty sets of eyes, give or take, that were now gawking straight at her had ever seen.

"Not baaaaaaaad," said Leading Seaman James, in a low sly voice. He really wanted to express himself more purposefully, but he still felt the need to be low key about it.

Meanwhile, Morrison couldn't stop staring. Matt noticed that his mouth seemed to be locked open, and his tongue was barely being contained by the microphone of the communications headset that was still positioned in front of his lips.

Nobody was paying attention to the Captain, who had just slipped out of the driver's side door and had opened the trunk to fetch his luggage. The men only noticed him when he and his wife met at the rear of the sports car, where they shared a long kiss and a hug. After an obvious display of affection, and a quick goodbye, she hurriedly hopped into the driver's side seat and hastily reversed the Jaguar back up the jetty from where it came. Then she gunned the engine and roared off toward the dockyard gate.

Matt smiled, as he was always amazed how it only took one hot woman to bring an entire ship to a halt. It was like they had never seen a woman before.

"Holy shit," James said. "The Old Man sure has a hot wife!"

Of course, "Old Man" was the standard nickname for any captain of a ship, but this Captain wasn't really an old man, as he was in his early 40s. However, he looked even younger. Clearly, fit as a fiddle, his body was lean, and his face was chiseled.

Morrison was now ogling at the Captain as he approached the brow. "Ugh, I wonder if he plans it that way. Making sure his hot wife is seen by the entire crew. It gives him an angle I guess."

"Or maybe he's just proud of her..." Matt added. "She's pretty hot."

Just then, the Quartermaster blew the boatswain's call, eight seconds of a steady high note. It was the "Still" and it brought all men on deck, essentially the entire starboard side, to the position of attention as the Captain came aboard his ship. Above, on the mast, Matt could hear the halyard squeal as the Captain's ashore pennant was smartly hauled down in double-quick time.

Looking toward the brow, the men could see the Officer of the Day saluting the Captain as he came aboard. Once the salute ended, the men continued on their business as if nothing had ever happened.

"Are you saying he does that on purpose?" Morrison asked.

"Of course," said James. "If he had an ugly boot of a wife he'd probably take a cab to the dockyard."

"You betcha," said Morrison. "Poor bastard... when you got something like that at home, and you have to go to sea with a bunch of sweaty hairy bags. Meanwhile, she's probably blowin' the pool boy."

"I wish I was a pool boy," James growled.

"Do you even know how to be a pool boy?" Matt laughed. "You do realize that you have to be able to clean and maintain the pool?"

"I could learn," James replied. "I already have all the right pool boy moves," he said, as he swiveled his hips and made thrusting motions with his pelvis.

Morrison was howling with laughter. He was about to reply to the last bit of banter, then he suddenly changed his demeanor and looked very serious as he pressed the sound powered headset to his ear, listening intently.

Quickly, Morrison repeated the order he had heard in the headset, "Top-part, single up, roger."

"Single up boys!" Morrison announced.

Single up means that the berthing hawsers, which were usually doubled, were undone so that there was only a single set of lines holding the ship onto the jetty. This was the last preparation before the ship would actually let go all lines and pull away from the jetty completely.

As they worked hard, hauling the hawser onboard, Matt thought about his buddy Tommy Thompson, from when he sailed in the *Kootenay*. He would always take off his wedding ring when the order "single up" was given. Tommy would chuckle, and everybody knew that it meant that he was accepting the order single up as an invitation to be unfaithful to his wife while the ship was away from home port. Too bad he was such a toad and no women other than his wife would have him. Everybody knew it, but it never stopped the boys from laughing at his gimmick.

Matt was feeling pretty good right now. He had forgotten all about Cynthia as all this joking around had seemed to make the thought of his pending, four-week stretch of loneliness slip away.

At 0759 sharp, the order was given to let go the after lines and heave in on the forward lines. This caused the rear of the ship to spring out a bit, just enough to give clearance for the ship to back out of her berth. Then, at exactly 0800, the order to "let go all lines" was given. There was something about being so precise that made the navy men think that they were in control of all aspects of their voyage. Unfortunately, the ocean always had a big part in the equation. Nobody forgot the dangers of the sea. Most would just put it out of their minds, and go about their business with a chipper grin. Some would feel the effects of the sea, and there was no smiling when you were green. Nevertheless, for now, they were in control and there was no denying it.

With a dull roar of her engines, the light-grey warship backed away from the jetty. The ship's horn sounded one long blast, in a warning to anyone in earshot that she was going in reverse. Even going backwards, the *Mackenzie* cut through the water rather sleekly. As she moved slowly into the harbour, a few people on the jetty waved. Most of the sailors onboard were too busy to wave back as they were beginning to stow the huge hawsers that were once instrumental in securing the great grey beast alongside.

Once the ship was away from the constraints of its berth the Captain ordered the helm to starboard and both engines to slow ahead. The ship shuddered a bit as the twin propellers fought for traction, but soon the *Mackenzie*'s backward momentum was slowed, then stopped, and then she began to move forward slowly... and away they went. To a layperson, the entire event probably looked very simple. In reality, though, it was a grand ballet that required choreography and split-second timing.

After a short delay, the *Yukon* also slipped her berth and proceeded to sea. She followed the *Mackenzie* out of the harbour.

As they passed the entrance to the harbour, which was demarked by the particularly picturesque Fisgard Lighthouse, the men on deck stood in a row facing the Admiral's house, which was located on one of the highest hills in the dockyard. Matt always imagined that the Admiral was up there, inspecting the fleet. You never saw him, but Matt could visualize the Admiral standing in his drawing room with his binoculars, peering at the ships as they went by. You never knew if he was looking, so most sailors stood tall, and with their heads held high, regardless of whether they were being watched or not. Once they were past the harbour entrance, they continued their work and began to stow their lines and hawsers, and continued to get the ship ready for sea.

It had been such a busy morning for Matt, he hadn't thought of Cynthia once. But, now that the ship had left Esquimalt Harbour, Matt looked east and caught sight of the downtown Victoria skyline. He was instantly reminded of Cynthia, as she was currently somewhere in that city.

Matt whispered to himself, "*Cynthia, I miss you already.*"

Morrison was close enough to overhear Matt whispering. "Who are you talking to, Petersen? Are you saying a prayer?"

"Something like that," Matt said, still looking east for a bit. Then, he turned toward Morrison and asked. "By the way, when do you and I go on watch?"

"We are on the 'first dog' watch," Morrison confirmed.

Matt already knew that he wouldn't go on watch until the "first dog", which began at 1600. He just wanted to talk about something else all of a sudden.

"All right let's make a trip of it," Matt replied. This was something that one of his former shipmates would always say, and he still liked the sound of it. It helped to set his frame of mind, and focus on work. Something he really needed to do at this point in time. Matt thought about Cynthia one more time, and then he decided to put her out of his mind until he called her from New Westminster. However, he had to wait five days until that happened, and he wasn't sure if he could actually put her out of his mind for that long. He would certainly try.

The Royal Canadian Navy Mackenzie-class destroyer escort, *HMCS Mackenzie* (DDE 261), passing along San Diego, California. (Public Domain - PH2 M. Correa, USN - U.S. Defense Imagery photo VIRIN: DN-SC-04-15477)

CHAPTER 5 / WHISKEY 601

Now that they were away from the confines of Esquimalt Harbour, the *Mackenzie* and the *Yukon* wasted no time getting out to sea. After each ship had cleared the harbour approaches, there was a distinct rumble and a puff of exhaust as they cranked up their engines to their normal cruising speed of 21 knots. At this speed, they carved through the waves with great ease. They made short work of the transit, racing out towards the open ocean like darts.

Mackenzie led the parade, with the *Yukon* following at a distance of about 500 yards. The two warships sailing together was an ominous sight. Their turns were sharp, deliberate and in synchronicity. To a layperson, it gave the impression of naval potency, as if the Canadian fleet was urgently deploying to some important mission. Though, the reality was closer to impotency. Truth being told, neither one of these ships could withstand even a minute of naval combat against a similar ship from their main rival, the Soviet Navy. Just the same, that never stopped the Canadian Navy from sailing their ships with pride.

It would only take about four hours to be free and clear of the Strait of Juan de Fuca. Soon, *Mackenzie* and *Yukon* would be sailing due west into the wide Pacific.

* * *

In the 1980s, the marketing slogan for the American Navy was "It's not a job. It's an adventure". At the time, American television was hugely popular in Canada and slogans like this often leeched into the Canadian Navy vernacular.

However, if life in the American Navy were anything like life in the Canadian Navy, it was a huge over-exaggeration. The mundane life that awaited Matt at Whiskey 601 was a dreary routine that consisted of standing watches, participating in endless drills and doing cleaning stations. All interspersed with regular meals and fragmented sleeping. Though humdrum, the routine wasn't so difficult. You just had to get use to it.

Matt stood watches in a one in three rotation. That meant four hours on watch, and eight hours off, except for the two "Dog" watches before and after 6PM local time that were only two-hour shifts. During the 8AM to 4PM period, if they were off watch, they still worked. In the morning, they all did Cleaning Stations, then the rest of the working day they performed departmental work, which really meant that they did odd jobs that were assigned by the Operations Chief or one of the Master Seamen… planned maintenance, inventory, cleaning, painting... whatever needed to be done.

* * *

On the first morning out, Matt and Morrison were assigned a cleaning station together. It was the dreaded Coxswain's Office Flats. Matt wondered what he had done to deserve this assignment on the first day, as it was notoriously the worst cleaning station of the lot. But, he just shrugged it off. The cleaning stations usually rotated. If he had a bad one today, he hoped that he would get an easier one tomorrow.

Matt and Morrison went forward to the cleaning gear locker to fetch some gear. They selected a broom, bannister brush, dustpan, a bottle of "Fantastic" spray cleaner, a pile of rags and some green "3M" brand scrub pads. They also got two buckets.

Matt pulled a white, five gallon, plastic pail of detergent out of the locker. He read the label aloud, "Teepol 310 Ships Detergent." Then he ad-libbed, "God's gift to clean decks."

Morrison didn't even respond. Clean decks did not seem to be as interesting to him.

Matt poured about half an ounce of the detergent into a wash bucket, and then he topped up the rest of the bucket with warm fresh water. Thick suds appeared in the bucket. This would be the bucket they would use to scrub the deck. Then, they took the second bucket and filled it with clean, fresh water. This would be the bucket they would use to rinse the rags that would be dirtied with scrub water. After they had collected all the gear they needed, they carried it all back to the Coxswain's Office flats.

The first thing they did was to take a rag and the spray bottle of cleaner and go from one end of their cleaning station to the other, inspecting the bulkheads looking for smudges and fingerprints. The Fantastic cleaner was powerful and could remove almost any type of smudge with one squirt. Matt often wondered what types of chemicals the Fantastic people were putting in that bottle.

The second thing they did was to take the banister brush and clean all the loose dust and dirt out from the edges, corners and crannies of the deck. They even had to get on their hands and knees, just to be sure to get behind the hatch coamings. Once the detail work was done, the broom was used to get the big junk. When it was all in a pile in the center of the deck, they scooped it up with a dustpan.

Lastly, they got the buckets and the rags ready for scrubbing the deck. Scrubbing the deck really wasn't very elegant, but there was a process you followed. If you followed the process, it usually went well. It was too bad the process dictated that you had to be on your hands and knees the entire time. One person would take the bucket of soapy water and spread it onto the deck with a rag. Then he would take the 3M scrub pad and scour the tiles until they were clean and scuff free. The other person would follow the "scrubber" and wipe up the dirty scrub water with clean rags. Periodically, the clean rags would be rinsed in the clean water bucket. Every so often, when the water became too dirty, the "wiper" would dump his bucket and replace the dirty water with clean water.

The rags were made of "deck cloth" a coarse-weave muslin material. It was cut from large rolls in the forepeak. After extended use, the rags started to look ratty and stained. That didn't matter. As long as they could be used to spread, and wipe, the soapy water.

The green 3M scrub pads worked great when they were new, but their effectiveness decreased as they aged. It was always best to choose a newer looking scrubber as all the black marks had to be removed.

The decks were durable as they were covered in tile. It was the same 12-inch tile that you'd see in a household kitchen or cafeteria, but it was industrial grade, and it could really handle the traffic. The tile was a light colour with brown accents. It hid scuffs well, but it became grey with dirt and grime just the same.

Ships never carried mops and Matt always wondered why. He was always told that it was because mops spread germs, but he never thought that this was the truth. He thought it was because the senior people loved to see the sailors down on their hands and knees scrubbing like slaves. But, slavery or not, Matt knew that when they scrubbed the decks they sure got clean.

The two sailors began the procedure with Morrison scrubbing and Matt wiping. They worked well together, and they quickly completed about twenty feet of deck. However, any simple procedure could be made much more difficult by the rolling of the ship...

Suddenly, the ship rolled violently to port. The two men immediately stopped their work and hung on to the bulkhead with their buckets and equipment. They were like two peanuts rolling inside a tin can, and completely at the mercy of the Officer of the Watch, who was currently directing the ship to perform a ninety-degree turn to port. The men below decks couldn't actually see what was occurring, there simply were no windows. Still, they could all tell that the ship was turning drastically.

"Oh crap, we're already at Whiskey!" Morrison gasped as he began to stare directly down at the deck tiles, a trick he had learned to help keep his inner ear on an even keel.

"I doubt it," Matt said. "We're still in the straits. They're probably beginning a serial of Officer of the Watch Maneuvers with the *Yukon*. You know, changing stations, doing circles around each other. Stuff like that."

"Do you think they could ever consider keeping this bastard steady while we peons work making their precious ship spot-free?" Morrison asked as he hung onto the bucket of scrub water. His legs were now splayed out wide to stop himself from skidding across the slanted deck. At the angle he was now at, Matt could see Morrison had a seasick patch on his skin, just behind his left ear.

"The Officer of the Watch is probably showing off," Matt replied. He too was holding on for dear life. The bucket of rinse water was now his best friend as he hugged it with his left arm and clutched onto a nearby hatch coaming with his right.

The deck was easily at a 30-degree angle. Matt was about to ask Morrison about the seasick patch, however, he made a quick decision to remain quiet about it. He knew that when you talked to a seasick person about their affliction, it usually made things worse. He remained silent as both men hung on and calmly waited as the ship finally levelled off. However, instead of remaining level, it now swung back the other way, again at about 30 degrees.

Matt could see Morrison did not appreciate the extra strong rolling. He decided to help by changing the subject.

"This takes a lot of talent," Matt chuckled as he buttressed his body against the roll that was now taking place in the opposite direction. "Do you think I can put this on my résumé?"

"Maybe, not sure. What would be the job?" Morrison replied

"How about a role in Batman?" Matt said.

"I don't get it," Morrison looked confused. He was still hanging on for dear life. The only difference was his entire body was now being forced to the port side of the ship.

"You know," Matt explained. "Batman? You know how the floors were always tilted."

"Oh, I get it now," Morrison nodded. "Sure, you could work in Batman. How do you feel about wearing tights?"

Now, the ship was rolling again, back to starboard, but not as hard this time. Both men stayed relatively motionless. They weren't stupid. They knew that they should wait until things had completely settled down before they attempted to continue their work.

"Ahhhh tights... that was always comical, wasn't it?" Matt laughed. "When you grew up with three channels, and one of them was French, you watched whatever was on. Batman was one of the things that was on."

"Yes, I remember watching all those old Batmans as a kid, usually after school," Morrison said. "Did you see the one where Batman went to a club, and he danced the Batusi while Robin watched on the Batmobile TV screen?"

"Yes, that was a good one," Matt chuckled. "Didn't Batman's date slip him a mickey and knock him out?"

"Typical chick," Morrison shook his head. "You meet a nice girl and she winds up fucking you over."

Matt laughed. "I hear you," he said.

Finally, both men sensed that the ship had settled down enough that they were able to continue their work. Just then, they heard hard footsteps in the flats behind them. Morrison called out, "Wet deck!" in about as commanding a voice that an Able Seaman could venture.

A voice answered back, "I'm coming through. You men will have to wipe my tracks." It was the Executive Officer's voice, Lieutenant-Commander Drapeau.

Matt remained still, but he peered upwards just in time to see the XO marching across their freshly cleaned deck. Both men didn't say a word.

Once the XO had crossed their area, leaving dirty tracks as he walked, he remarked, "It doesn't look like you were doing a great job anyway. You needed to do it again."

By the time that haughty remark had fallen on their ears, the XO had already departed. He had scurried forward toward #2 Mess and the forepeak. Both men still didn't say anything. After a moment, they repositioned their buckets and quickly re-wiped the deck where the XO had crossed. Soon his footprints were rubbed away, and they continued their mission to scrub the remaining area.

* * *

They finished their work quickly, but they still had about twenty-five minutes left in the allotted time for cleaning stations. They just put away their buckets, sat in the corner and chatted while the deck dried.

"So are you enjoying your time in the *Mackenzie*," Morrison asked. "Isn't this a paradise?"

"Yeah," Matt replied calmly. "But, cleaning stations is cleaning stations, no matter what ship you're on. It's the same crap. If I ever start to love cleaning stations just shoot me."

"I promise," Morrison said.

"That's one of the reasons I want to be promoted to Master Seaman," Matt hypothesized. "Once I am a Master Seaman, no more cleaning stations."

"Oh, watch out with that dream," Morrison interjected. "There are plenty of Master Seamen that still have to do cleaning stations."

"Yeah, maybe," Matt said. "But they don't have to do it as often as a Leading Seamen. You don't see Master Seaman Burke out here scrubbing this deck. He assigned the cleaning stations and now he's likely up in the Ops Room doing something far more 'important'." Matt used air quotes with his fingers when he said "important".

Morrison laughed. "Please explain. What 'important' things does a Master Seaman have to do?"

"Oh, I don't know," Matt said. He thought about it for a moment and then he replied. "Maybe he has to do something like go over tomorrow's cleaning station roster?"

"That's it?" Morrison said.

"Well, no. Of course not," Matt answered. "Afterward, you have to take a crap, read two skin mags and then smoke a cigarette." Matt laughed at his own joke. "You know... it's a rough life."

"Soon it will be yours," Morrison snickered.

"Yes, soon it will be mine. All mine." Matt said. "I guess that I'll have to take up smoking."

Though he was laughing it up about the matter, the irony that he didn't know what a Master Seaman actually did wasn't lost on Matt. He supposed that he should start to figure out such things, especially with his promotion just around the corner.

Both men remained pensive now, sitting on the deck side by side, with their backs against the bulkhead. They were well steadied when the ship suddenly rolled again, even more violently than before. First it went to the port and then back to the starboard. The scrub buckets were stowed away, but they still had a spray bottle of cleaner and some rags nearby. Matt merely put his foot against the cleaning gear, pressing it into a nearby hatch coaming, so it didn't skid away down the flats. Morrison had his eyes closed now, like he was napping, but Matt knew that he wasn't asleep. He was just relaxing his mind as the ship rolled so fiercely.

Matt put his head back against the bulkhead and closed his eyes. His thoughts immediately went toward Cynthia. He wondered what she was doing right now. He guessed that she was possibly getting ready for work. Maybe, taking a shower and doing her hair, putting on her makeup and getting dressed. It was a bad choice for him because thinking of her made him even more lonely for her than he was before.

Matt thought that it would be wonderful if he could be with her right now. He wondered if she missed him, and he began to weigh the evidence. She seemed so aloof at times, especially when he seemed to be less distant. Their mood for each other never seemed to be in harmony. When she wanted his attention, he was often not ready to give it, and when he wanted her attention she was often not forthcoming. She loved to tease him instead.

"What are you thinking about?" Morrison asked as the ship's rolling began to settle down again.

"My girlfriend. That's all," Matt replied with his eyes still closed.

"Oh, okay," Morrison said. "Is she pretty nice?"

"She can be," Matt answered.

That was it. Nothing more was said about the matter.

Both men remained silent for the next few minutes. They mainly rested quietly, waiting to hear the announcement to "secure". Finally, they heard the main broadcast crackle to life.

"SECURE CLEANING STATIONS. HANDS CARRY ON WITH DEPARTMENTAL WORK."

That was it. Cleaning stations had officially ended. However, the day was far from over, as they now had to carry on with departmental work. Just as the announcement directed.

* * *

The remainder of the morning went quickly. After a short "Stand Easy", which is how the navy refers to coffee breaks, Master Seaman Burke directed Morrison and Matt to report to "Radar 2" and begin to shred confidential material. When the two men entered the Radar 2 space, they saw three garbage bags of assorted papers and messages that needed to be destroyed in the paper shredder. Working together, it took them about an hour to do the job. Once they were done, they now had four green garbage bags of shredded paper. They would eventually throw the bags over the side of the ship. However, that would have to wait until they were out of the straits and into open water.

Soon enough, though, it was time for lunch. Both men went down to line up at the main cafeteria. There were already about twenty men in line when they arrived. Once the noise of the extended "Hands to Dinner" pipe had died down, they noticed that the lunch line began to move. Slowly, they inched their way towards the front of the line and the promise of naval-style culinary taste treasures.

As the line crept forward, Matt noticed the menu written on a chalkboard near the galley entrance.

"They have steak!" he said.

Morrison also looked at the board, "Be careful, it says 'Yukon' Steak."

"Yukon Steak... what's that?" Matt asked.

"Our cooks always make up fancy names for crappy meals. Actually, I think that Yukon Steak is sled dog," Morrison quipped.

One of the other sailors in line overheard the conversation, and he joined the banter, "Yeah, Yukon Steak. It's malamute meat. Malamute meat... say that five times really fast."

A second sailor tried, "Malamute meat, malamute meat, malameat mute, malameat..." Then he gave up. Laughter ensued.

After a bit more banter, Matt finally arrived at the front of the line.

"I'll have the Yukon Steak," Matt said quickly.

The cook handed him a plate that had a hamburger patty covered with greenish-brown gravy.

"That's the Yukon Steak?" Matt asked.

"That's right," the cook said.

Matt sneered at the plate.

"Do you have a problem with my cooking?" the cook asked.

Matt raised his head and looked the cook in the eye. This was a different cook from before. This one had greasy skin and plenty of zits. In addition, he didn't have a nametag. He just had the name "Chuck" written in magic marker on his white cook's uniform where a nametag would normally be. Matt began to wonder if his first name was "Up".

"No, it's okay," Matt decided to diffuse the situation. "Could I have some veggies with that?"

The cook raised a spoonful of peas and carrots and slopped them onto Matt's plate.

Matt knew that nothing could ever be gained by pissing off a ship's cook. "Thank you very much for the meal," Matt said.

"That's better," muttered the cook. As Matt moved along toward the Main Cafeteria he heard the cook mumble, "Fuckin' ingrates."

* * *

Matt sat down at the table and begin to eat his meal. The Yukon Steak wasn't so bad after all. He wondered why they didn't just call it what it was, a hamburger patty with greasy gravy.

At almost the same time that lunch had begun to be served, the *Mackenzie* had finally left the shelter of the Strait of Juan de Fuca and began to enter the open ocean. Now, her progress through the ocean began to adopt a steady, rhythmic roll. They weren't even in the completely open waters of Whiskey 601, but the rough seas were already beginning to take a toll on the ship's occupants.

Matt noticed that the seas got rougher as lunch went on. Morrison was the first casualty as he ate his meal fast and then quickly scurried back down to #4 Mess. In fact, the entire cafeteria, which had been crowded with lunchtime customers, cleared out pretty fast. When Matt finished and went to the mess, he saw Morrison lying on the settee in the lounge area. He had his eyes closed, and he was clearly feeling the effects of the sea.

Matt was good in rough seas. He had only been seasick a couple of times in his career. However, he knew that there were plenty of sailors that could never really handle heavy seas. It didn't take long for some of the people to start to look green. This was standard, and it usually took about 24 hours for some sailors to be accustomed to the motion of the ship.

You sometimes saw sailors walking around with garbage bags tied to their belts and they would occasionally be puking into them. Matt hoped that Morrison wasn't like this, as he had to work with him. Matt also hoped that Morrison wasn't the "smart ass" type that he had witnessed in the past that used one of the clear garbage bags, so everybody could actually see the vomit in the bag. If that happened Matt would be sick as well, he could almost guarantee it.

Matt sat down on the settee opposite Morrison. "Are you going to be okay?" he asked.

Morrison kept his eyes closed. "Yeah, I'll be just fine. I've got the patch." Morrison pointed to the round patch located behind his left ear.

Of course, Matt had noticed the patch earlier, but he hadn't said anything. Matt knew how the patch worked. It would release a drug called scopolamine, which helped to reduce the sensitivity of the nerve fibers in the inner ear. Apparently, it worked pretty well, but it also makes the person dopey.

"Does that thing work for you?" Matt asked.

"Yes, it always works fine. Usually, after a day or so, I take it off, and then I feel fine." Morrison assured him. "I just need to get over the hump."

"Does it make you dopey?" Matt asked.

"No, it is not bad." Morrison said. "I used to take Gravol, but that made me sleepy," he added.

Matt sensed a pattern. "I know how you feel. When I drink too much coffee, I am grumpy. When I inhale black pepper I am sneezy."

"Shut up with the Seven Dwarves talk, will ya?" Morrison whined. "Just leave me alone for a while."

"Okay, no problem," Matt agreed. "I'm going to read my book. I'll check on you after lunch hour is over."

Matt got up and went over to his bunk. He kicked off his boots and climbed up into his rack. Lying on top of his bunk, he read his Heinlein paperback. Still, he kept one eye on Morrison lying on the settee, partially anticipating that the young sailor might start to go off like a fountain.

Soon after, Paul Legere came down to the mess. He looked very tired, and he quickly took off his boots and climbed onto his rack, which was a middle bunk near where Matt's rack was located.

Matt spoke up, "Hey, Paul. Did you see the casualty on the settee?"

"He's always like that when we first go out," Paul muttered without even opening his eyes. "It lasts a day or so, and then he is fine."

"Okay," Matt said. "Are we at Whiskey yet?"

"Not quite, we are only about 10 miles away. We are rendezvousing with *Saskatchewan* and *Qu'appelle* when we get there... then the fun will begin."

"Fun?" Matt asked.

"Yeah, I saw the OPSCHED. It is non-stop exercises for the next four days."

"Wonderful," Matt said. "Just fucking wonderful."

"It's not just a job it's an adventure," Paul replied quietly. "Now, give me some peace, please. I need to catch up on my ZZZZZ's."

Matt return to reading his book. He still had about half an hour to kill before lunch was over.

* * *

Matt's turn on watch in the Operations Room didn't begin until 1600 hours. After lunch was over at 1315, he still had another full afternoon of Departmental work to kill before he stood his first watch. However, he need not worry that he would be bored, because, just as Paul had warned, there were plenty of drills and exercises planned.

First, there was a Fire Exercise, where Matt found himself donning his flash gear, and then laying out hoses in the flats for a fire team to put out a mock fire in the forward heads. Immediately following, there was a man overboard exercise where the ship had to stop, launch the ship's seaboat, and retrieve a stuffed dummy named Oscar from the ocean.

Finally, at 1430 the ship's broadcast piped, "Stand Easy."

Matt and Paul immediately went aft, down the main flats, and to the canteen for a snack.

As they waited in line, Paul whispered to Matt, "Check out the Canteen Manager."

Matt took a long look at the Canteen Manager, Master Seaman Snow. He was a pudgy, balding middle-aged man. The few remaining wisps of his hair were combed delicately over his shiny scalp.

"What about him?" Matt said. "What's the problem?"

"Oh, just that he is the biggest shyster on this ship, let alone, in the navy," Paul explained.

Matt kept watching Snow as he served his customers, selling packs of duty-free cigarettes for a dollar and candy bars for 75 cents. Matt noticed that Snow was always super friendly to everybody he served, and his customers seemed to love him, calling him "Frosty" or sometimes "Snowman". Matt even heard one sailor call him "Frosty the Snowman". It all seemed perfectly normal to Matt.

"Just take my advice, watch him," Paul warned as they neared the front of the line.

Finally, Matt was next in line. Master Seaman Snow looked at Matt's face, then he studied his nametag for a split second.

"You're the new guy, Petersen, right? Nice to meet you," Snow said with a wide grin. "I'm the Snowman, but most people call me Frosty."

Frosty stuck his hand out towards Matt. Matt took his hand and shook it briefly.

"Nice to meet you... Frosty," Matt said casually, as he surveyed the goodies that were behind the canteen counter. "I'll take a salt 'n vinegar chips and a Coke."

Frosty turned and grabbed a can of soda pop and the chips. He placed them down and slid them across the counter toward Matt. In turn, Matt placed a $5 bill down on the counter.

Matt was surprised to see that Frosty pushed the bill back in his direction. "Sorry, Petersen. Your money is no good here. New guys get their first visit to the Snowman for free."

Matt was surprised by the gesture of hospitality. "Thanks Frosty. Much appreciated," he said with a smile.

After Paul had paid for his snacks, and as they walked away from the canteen, Paul remarked, "He's like a drug dealer. He gives you the first one for free... to get you hooked. Then he doubles the price."

Matt laughed, "Yeah, right. He seems like a nice guy. I like him."

Matt and Paul decided to head up into the open air of the quarterdeck and eat their snacks. There were plenty of sailors out in that area, as the stern of the ship could be a calm place when in heavy seas. The first thing that Matt noticed was that they were almost completely out in the open ocean. There was just a glimpse of land remaining to the east, and miles and miles of emptiness to the west.

Matt was familiar with this place. He knew that they were now at Whiskey... which probably explained the incessant ship rolling!

On the quarterdeck, near where Matt and Paul were standing, there were a couple of guys that looked sort of green. But mostly, the sailors were all standing there with their feet apart for balance, some eating chips, candy bars or drinking pop. Others were smoking. Everything seemed routine, calm and relaxed.

Over in the distance Matt could see three of *Mackenzie's* sisters. They seemed to be sailing in formation with the other ships in the squadron, the *Yukon*, which had accompanied the *Mackenzie* to sea, and the *Qu'Appelle* and *Saskatchewan*, which had joined them here at Whiskey. The four ships were now heading due east in a line abreast formation, meaning that they were all moving together, parallel to each other. Matt estimated that they were moving at about 12 knots, which was a relatively slow speed. Going so slow, and with the long Pacific rollers hitting them on their starboard bow, the ship was rolling steadily.

Matt looked out over the endless ocean of rolling waves, "Whiskey hasn't changed much since the last time I was out here."

"They tried redecorating once," Paul said with a can of soda pop in his hand as he motioned out over the ocean. "They moved that big roller from there and put it over there, but it just rolled back to where it came from."

Matt yawned. The sea didn't usually make him sick, but it always made him somewhat tired.

A few minutes later they heard a voice on the ship's broadcast system announce "Out Pipes". It was time to go back to work, but it seemed that nobody moved. Everybody just kept enjoying the outdoor scenery, including Matt and Paul.

Suddenly, Paul spoke up, "Oh oh. There's the Coxswain. We better move our asses."

Matt looked over and saw the Coxswain coming up through the hatch from the main flats. Then he noticed that the sailors began to scatter.

"We better get moving," Paul said as he quickly finished his can of Coke. Afterward, he squeezed the can and bent it in half a few times, fracturing the aluminum. Then, he flattened the husk of a can into a shingle and with a side-armed throw, whipped the can over the side of the ship.

The two men walked over toward the hatch, and waited in line to go down below. The Coxswain was standing next to the hatch.

"Hello Coxswain," Paul said. "Nice day, isn't it, Chief?"

Chief Czerwinski looked Paul up and down, and then he replied calmly, "Yes it is, Leading Seaman Legere. It's a beautiful day to be a sailor."

Matt smiled at this. The Chief seemed to be agreeable, which was pleasant to Matt.

The Chief noticed Matt's smile. "Leading Seaman Petersen, I see that you're enjoying your trip in the *Mackenzie*?"

"Yes Chief. No problems so far," Matt said as he quickly made his way through the hatch, down the ladder and back to work.

* * *

Being a Radar Plotter, Matt was at home in an Operations Room. When he arrived for his 1600 watch, he knew that he would spend the next few hours either working the plotting table or monitoring the radar display. There may be other odd jobs, such as updating the information on the multitude of stateboards, but his time would be mostly taken up between the plotting table and the radar display.

When the ship was at sea in a peacetime state, the Operations Room was solely responsible to the Bridge for the surface picture, which meant they needed to monitor and report everything that moved on the ocean out to a range of 30 nautical miles.

The routine was simple. The sailor on the radar display monitored all the radar echoes of the contacts and kept a relative plot of each contact using a grease pencil on the plotting head attachment of the radar display. It was only a relative track, though, because the ship was always moving, and this added to the apparent motion of the contacts on radar. However, every few minutes he would report the range and bearing of all the contacts to the man on the plotting table. The contacts would be plotted on the plotting table, in pencil, and the true movement of the contacts would become apparent.

The plotting table was an interesting piece of outdated equipment. In the *Mackenzie,* and in the other older Canadian ships, there were two plotting tables: One on the port side of the Operations Room and the other on the starboard. In normal peacetime operations, the port table was the only one that was used; unless of course the ship was exercising wartime conditions, something the Canadian Navy was very good at. They did it often.

The plotting table was such a specialized piece of equipment. It had a glass top where the radar plotters would spread a large piece of "onion skin" plotting paper. Inside the table was a lamp and a projector that shot an image of a "spider's web'" upwards to the surface of the paper. Your own ship was always in the center of the spider's web, and because the projector was motorized, it always moved with the actual motion of the ship. It got its rate and direction through feeds from the ship's log (speedometer) and the gyrocompass. It managed to scale everything down using a 1960s powered computer, the brain of the entire table.

When Matt first learned of this technology, he thought that it was the coolest thing ever. He always loved physics and motion, and this was right up his alley. Better yet, no one really understood it, outside the world of the Operations Room. It was a secret science.

In fact, in the 1980s, a plotting table was a piece of kit that only Canadian ships relied upon. More modern ships of the time may have had a plotting table, but only as a backup. They relied upon computer systems and displays to provide the surface picture to the command. The Radar Plotters in the Canadian Navy knew that they would soon receive similar computer systems for their ships. In the meanwhile, they continued to do it the old-fashioned way.

To Matt, using the plotting table was an art. To do it well, a radar plotter had to practice, and in fact become in love of the skill itself. There was plenty of pride involved in being skilled at working a plotting table.

First of all, you normally stood on the north side of the table. It should be noted, though, that all the information had to be read from the south side of the table. This meant that the plotter had to write upside down, and do so legibly in block printing. Writing upside down was a skill that was taught in the Fleet School when young sailors first arrived for training. They would receive worksheets where they would transcribe the entire alphabet and the numbers from 0-9 upside down. It was just like kindergarten all over again.

As well, size always mattered. Time marks were always made in one-eight inch high block printing. Courses and speeds were written as one-quarter of an inch, and identifying information and symbols were always one-third of an inch. In Fleet School, you would lose marks if you screwed up the sizes. Neatness and accuracy were essential. However, speed was just as important.

Matt was paired up on watch with Able Seaman Morrison. To Matt, Morrison seemed like a good kid. He was smart and fast, and he seemed to work well with Matt.

"Let's get a round, Morrison," Matt said softly.

"Roger...*Yukon*, friendly two-two, three five zero at two point one miles *(pause) Saskatchewan*, friendly two-seven, three four two at one point six miles *(pause) Qu'Appelle*, friendly three-five, two nine three at one point one miles *(pause)* Skunk one-five, zero two five at ten point four miles, drawing right *(pause)* Skunk one-four, three five five at fifteen point two miles, past CPA and opening."

As Morrison called out each contact, Matt plotted their positions and times on the plotting table. When Morrison paused, he was simply repositioning the cursor to the next contact on the radar display. It was when the pause occurred that Matt would plot the contact, and then add the current time below the freshly plotted position. Just as Matt had finished plotting each position, Morrison was beginning to call out the next contact. Essentially, a rhythm was developed between the radar operator and the plotter.

Aside from the *Mackenzie*, Matt had now plotted the three other Canadian ships, *Yukon*, *Saskatchewan*, *Qu'Appelle* and two unknown contacts to the north, Skunks 11 and 12. The unknowns were referred to using the code word "Skunk", which meant that they were unknown surface contacts. In reality, they were most likely commercial shipping passing through the area.

The ship was rolling ever so slightly. It wasn't so bad, but Matt was keeping an eye on Morrison just the same. As Morrison worked the radar display, he sat on a stool, but had his legs wrapped around the pedestal of the display, so he didn't move. He was pretty much locked-on to that radar display. Morrison looked a little green, but he was concentrating on the radar. Matt knew that he would be okay as long as the motion of the ship didn't increase drastically.

As for himself, he was practically laying on the plotting table as he worked. His feet were on the deck, but his body was draped across the table itself. He had to keep his pencils and dividers off to the side of the plot, lying between two erasers, so they didn't roll off the table and across the deck. As well, Matt had to place the brass rolling-ruler on an eraser, so it didn't roll off the table. When it came to the ship rolling, everything was fair game, and if it weren't secured in some fashion, it would go flying. It was a complicated business. However, Matt had plenty of experience and he knew all the tricks.

As time went by, the center of the plotting table kept on moving at the same rate of speed and direction as the travel of the ship. In three minutes, Matt updated the *Mackenzie*'s position, and he asked Morrison to report another round. As Morrison called out the new ranges and bearings of each contact, Matt plotted the new positions. Finally, the surface picture became more evident to Matt. Instead of relative motion, the plotting table exhibited the true motion of each contact within the designated thirty-mile range.

Now it was the plotter's job to work out the course, speed and closest point of approach of each contact. Matt worked quickly and silently. The course was easy to estimate. You just used the parallel ruler to see what the general direction of each contact was, and then you rolled the ruler to the center of the compass rose and read off the direction of the ruler. Estimating the speed of the contact took a little more talent. The trick was to take the dividers and measure how far the contact had gone in six minutes of time, and then multiply that number by ten. For example, if the contact had gone 1.4 miles in six minutes, then you would assume that he would go 14 miles in sixty minutes, and his speed was therefore 14 knots. It was a trick using ratios called the "six-minute rule", and it was taught to every young radar plotter when they first joined Radar School.

The plotter also had a slide rule, which he could use. It was called an STD ruler, which was short for speed-time-distance ruler. Though, most of the time a good radar plotter didn't need it. They would just use ratios and calculate the speed of contacts in their head. It wasn't too hard once you practiced it, and Matt was good at it.

Finally, Matt had everything he needed to give a "Surface SITREP" to the bridge.

Matt pressed the button on the microphone that was hanging down on a coiled cord from the intercom that was situated over the plotting table.

"Bridge, Ops," Matt said. "Stand by for Surface SITREP."

After about thirty seconds, a voice from the bridge answered, "Ops Bridge, go ahead with surface SITREP."

Matt took a deep breath and began his report. It was rather lengthy, and he paused after reporting each contact so the Bridge staff could give him instructions. If they responded with "report", it meant that Matt was to continue to report this contact to the bridge every six minutes. If they responded with "Cease Reporting" it meant that Matt was to stop reporting the contact, unless it drastically changed its course and speed.

After the SITREP was complete, Matt and Morrison had only one unknown contact remaining to report, Skunk 15, which was currently 10 miles to the northeast.

This is how it went. Every three minutes they plotted the contacts, and every six minutes they reported to the bridge an update of what was happening. Matt could already tell it would be a routine watch... and it was.

The senior hand of Matt's watch was Master Seaman Burke, however, when things were this routine the Senior Hand of the Watch didn't really have much to do. When the watch had begun, Burke had checked in with Matt, "You're good on the plotting table, Leading Seaman Petersen?" he had asked.

"Yes not a problem. I've done it a thousand times before," was Matt's reply.

That was the end of the supervision. Burke was also aware that this was a routine watch, and he didn't want to over-complicate things. Matt appreciated this fact.

* * *

The watch ended at 1745 when Leading Seaman Paul Legere and a young Able Seaman named Ouellette arrived to relieve the watch. Matt gave Paul a very business-like turnover.

"We've got three friendlies on the plot, plus two Skunks. Skunk 16 is cease report and Skunk 17 is report. We are call sign whiskey two delta as of 45 minutes ago. I updated the stateboard," he said.

"Thanks Matt. So, did you have any trouble remembering how all this is done after your cushy job in Fleet School?" Paul teased.

"Did you catch up on your sleep, skin hound?" Matt teased back.

"I don't need sleep," Paul retorted. "I get all my energy from eating pussy. That's all I need."

Matt just laughed, as he didn't have a response. Matt stood back and watched while Paul took the headset and did a radio check with the squadron. Then he received a round from Morrison and did a Surface SITREP with the bridge. For a guy who was operating on a few hours of sleep, he made it look easy.

Matt waited for Morrison, as Ouellette was doing a muster of the Ops Room safe, to confirm that all the classified books and materials were accounted for. It took about five minutes, and then Ouellette took his place on the radar display. Afterward, Matt and Morrison immediately went below for supper. They would be back up in the Operations Room for the middle watch, which began at 2345, but the routine never seemed to end. After their supper, they still had to do a short cleaning stations, in preparation for evening rounds.

* * *

Once the workday was done, the final pipe heard on the Ship's broadcast system was "SECURE. HANDS TO CLEAN INTO NIGHT CLOTHING." It was a routine announcement that was made every evening on Canadian Navy ships. What it meant was that the crew was to wash themselves, change into clean clothing and then relax. Generally, "clean clothing" meant that the sailors were allowed to hang up their uniform shirts and don a white tee shirt.

Matt went into his locker and found one of the clean white tee shirts he had brought along. He took off his work shirt and pulled the tee over his head. Now he felt more relaxed. He sat down in the lounge area of #4 Mess, where the guys were playing cards. Matt wasn't playing, so he just watched and waited for an invitation to join in on the next hand.

Leading Seaman James looked over at Matt's tee shirt. "Nice shirt. *Margaree*, right?" he said.

"You bet. I've had this shirt for a few years. I love it," Matt replied.

"I am going to give you some advice," James said. "If the Executive Officer sees that shirt, he's going to shit on it."

"What do you mean?" Matt asked. "It's a white tee shirt."

"It's not a *Mackenzie* tee shirt," said James stone-faced.

"Is that a rule here?" Matt asked.

"Oh, fuck yeah," James said. "Drapeau is crazy about that stuff. If he sees that *Margaree* badge, he'll have you strip it off on the spot."

* * *

When rounds came through the mess at 1900, Matt noticed that the XO was attending. He remained quiet, sitting on the settee with his side to the inspecting team. He didn't think that the XO would be able to see the badge on his tee shirt. He thought that he would be okay, but he was wrong.

"You!" Lieutenant-Commander Drapeau was pointing directly at Matt. "Why are you wearing another ship's badge on MY ship?"

Matt was trying to think of an answer, but he couldn't come up with anything.

"I didn't think you had an answer," Drapeau snarled, ejecting two fat drops of spit onto the lounge table as he did so. "I suggest to you that the canteen is open until 2000. You should take advantage of that fact, and my good nature, to acquire the proper kit."

Matt just stared straight ahead.

"Did you hear me?" Drapeau said.

"Yes, sir," Matt replied, finally opening his mouth in response.

Drapeau and the rounds team then scurried out of the mess, leaving the men alone. The first thing that happened, is everybody except Matt began to laugh.

"Oh, Petersen. You're royally fucked," James chuckled. "Drapeau fuckin' hates your guts now."

"Oh, fuck you guys," Matt said angrily.

"Hey, don't say we didn't warn you," James said, as he looked warily at the XO's spittle that still remained on the table. "Who's going to wipe this up?" he asked. There were no immediate takers.

* * *

Matt didn't waste any time heading to the canteen to buy a tee shirt. There was no line-up, just Frosty the Canteen Manager standing there behind the counter. He was reading a dog-eared copy of *Penthouse Forum*. Frosty took one look at Matt in his *Margaree* tee shirt, and he immediately seemed to know what was up.

"Let me guess. You need a *Mackenzie* tee shirt?" Frosty snorted. "Did the XO get you?"

"Yes. How did you know?" Matt asked.

"He gives me a ton of good business down here. You'd almost think I'd be giving him a kickback," Frosty said. "Let me see, you're a large, right?"

"That's right," Matt said as he reached into his pocket for his wallet. "How much?"

"They're $18. But, since I like you, I'll cut you a special deal," Frosty said.

"Special deal?" Matt asked.

"I call it the 'XO Special'. Two for $30," Frosty winked.

Matt reached into his wallet and pulled out a twenty and a ten. "Here you go. I'll take two," Matt said.

Frosty took the money and placed the two tee shirts on the counter. Matt immediately took off his *Margaree* tee shirt and pulled one of the *Mackenzie* shirts over his head. It fit well.

"Now doesn't that feel better," Frosty said with a smile.

"Actually it sort of feels the same," Matt said. "But, at least I won't be catching the eye of the XO anymore. I've had two run-ins with him so far. He's just met me, and apparently he already doesn't like me."

"Don't feel bad," said Frosty, as he put the money in the cash box. "He doesn't like anyone."

Matt went back to #4 Mess sporting his brand new *Mackenzie* tee shirt. When he got there, he saw that Paul Legere and Able Seaman Ouellette had now joined the gang playing cards in the mess. He also noticed that the XO's spit was still on the table, but now someone had arranged a square of masking tape around it, and had scrawled "HAZMAT" on the tape in pencil.

Paul looked up. He took one look at Matt in his new tee shirt, and he knew exactly what had occurred.

"The XO got you, didn't he?" Paul snickered.

"What, you too?" Matt said as he sat down on the settee next to Paul. "This is like the biggest inside joke. Everybody seems to be in on it except me."

"Don't take it so hard. This is the XO's thing. He likes to make crazy rules and then have everybody follow them to the letter," Paul explained.

"Uh huh," Matt nodded. "How does this make him different from any other XO that I've sailed under?"

"Where it's possibly different," Paul explained, "Is that this XO is a fuckin' crazy asshole."

Able Seaman Ouellette piped up, "Not only is he an asshole, he knows he is an asshole, and he is okay with it."

Morrison added, "Some people just act like assholes, and they do it without knowing. This guy tries to be the best asshole that he can be."

"Yeah, if there was a contest for assholes, he would enter it, train his heart out and then compete for the gold medal," Paul added.

"Like an asshole Olympics?" Ouellette asked.

"Yeah, just like that. Except, they wouldn't have the five Olympic rings, they would have five assholes..."

Ouellette quickly interjected, "Yeah... but they wouldn't be different colours. They'd all be the same colour... brown."

This was followed by rollicking laughter from all.

Afterward, the banter continued for some time as the men kept playing cards. Matt sat back and watched, and became more comfortable. This type of camaraderie was fun, and certainly one of the reasons that he loved the navy. It was too bad that Cynthia never saw this side of his life.

* * *

For the next few days at Whiskey, Matt laid low. He was determined to stay off Drapeau's radar. He simply stood his watches, ate his meals, slept, read his book and listened to music. That's all he did. Otherwise, the ship's routine was very hectic. During the day, the crew was busy doing exercises: fire exercises, man overboard exercises, nuclear-biological-chemical warfare exercises, bomb threat exercises. They did them all. Matt even helped the Operations Chief with the Fleetex, which turned out very well as the *Mackenzie* received high marks. In the evenings, when he wasn't standing watches in the Operations Room, he usually laid low in the mess and played cards.

By the end of the week, Matt was happy to know that he had no more run-ins with the Executive Officer, and, in fact, he had no run-ins with anybody. Things were finally going his way. He was also happy that they would soon be heading to New Westminster for the weekend. It would give him a chance to call Cynthia on the phone and hear her sweet voice. He was making plans on what to say to her, and how to convince her to come out to New Westminster and visit him. He wanted to see her so badly.

Soon, he'd say goodbye to Whiskey 601. Of course, they would be back, but Matt could only see what was directly in front of him. A port visit, and a possible reunion with the most important woman in his life. All he hoped for, was to lay eyes on his sweetheart.

* * *

On the last night at Whiskey, just as Matt's watch was ending, the intercom buzzed. It was an unusual call from the Electronic Warfare Control Room. Matt knew that the Electronic Warfare Operators in the EWCR listened for electronic emissions from other ships, usually radar and radio signals. Sometimes they called the Operations Room asking what contacts may be visible on the ship's radar, in an attempt to coordinate the signals they detect with actual contacts.

Matt pressed the channel selector and answered the call.

"OPS."

"OPS this is EWCR. What do you have to the north," the voice asked.

Matt replied, "One Skunk, Bearing 015 degrees at 18 miles. He has a large echo, and his course is east. Probably a merchant ship inbound to Vancouver or Seattle."

"EWCR, Roger... What do you have to the northwest at 310 degrees?"

Matt looked at the plot, "We have no contacts on the plot to the west or northwest. Wait..."

Matt called over to Morrison to check his radar display to the west. Morrison quickly checked for new contacts and then he nodded his head, "No".

"EWCR this is OPS. We can confirm we have nothing on radar to the west or northwest of our position and nothing on a bearing of 310."

"EWCR Roger, Out."

"What the fuck was that all about?" Master Seaman Burke asked.

"I guess the Electronic Warfare guys are snooping a signal to the west," Matt explained. "I told them that we've got nothing on radar out there."

"What could they be fuckin' looking for." Burke wondered aloud as he skulked away in the direction of the EWCR.

A few minutes later, Burke returned.

"They're picking up a strange radio signal out there to the west. It's something we've never fucking heard before... in a peculiar bandwidth and low frequency. I put on the headset, and I got to hear it. It's real fucking weird. It's faint, but it sounds like a helicopter blade under water. The EW fuckers are stumped."

"Is it an American carrier group?" Morrison asked. "They've probably got some communications gear we've never heard of."

"Nope, don't fuckin' think so." Burke said. "We've got all the specs and characteristics of all fucking NATO equipment and it doesn't fit any of those parameters."

"Then it could only be one of two things," Matt said.

"What's that?" Burke asked.

"It's either the Soviets or an alien mother ship is coming down to visit us," Matt said stone-faced.

Burke grinned, "Shut the fuck up about that alien crap." He stopped and thought about it. Then, his face turned more serious. "It could be the Russians, but it would have to be something new, something we've never fucking heard before."

"What would the Russians be doing way over here on this side of the

Pacific?" Morrison asked.

"Fuckin' spying on us," Burke said. "Plus, they're evil and they want us all fuckin' dead. Maybe they came over here to blow up fuckin' Ronald Reagan. I don't fucking know. They're insane."

"Well, we're still not sure it's Russian," said Matt.

Burke replied, "Yes, you're right. We don't know fucking squat. Just the same, the EW guys have drafted a flash message to HQ about it. We'll let those fuckers on the fucking hill sort it out."

* * *

At the end of his watch, Matt went into the back of the EWCR and asked if he could listen to the mystery signal. The Electronic Warfare Operator gave him a headset. Matt had to press the earpiece up to his ear and listen carefully, but he heard the signal. It was faint but clear. At first, it sounded like a low rumble, and then he noticed that it was rhythmic. It was like someone strumming an upright bass with a hacksaw, over and over again.

"Wow that sounds so odd," Matt said. "How would you describe that sound?"

"To me it sounds like a far off freight train, with a broken axle," the EW Operator replied.

Matt continued to listen for a few more seconds, then, suddenly it stopped.

"It just went silent," Matt said with a surprised tone. "It's gone!"

"Oh, it does that," said the EW Operator. "It'll start up again in a few minutes."

"What do you think it is?" Matt asked.

"We don't know. But, I'll bet good money that it's the Commies."

CHAPTER 6 / THE AZIYA

Off to the northwest, just a few hundred miles away, the dull grey hull of a Soviet auxiliary was stampeding over the Pacific rollers. She was known as the *Aziya*; the newest hull of a brand new class of Russian spy ship.

Lesser known as Hull #2 of Project 1826, the 4,900 ton *Aziya*, which is Russian for "Asia", was actually one of the first custom-designed electronic surveillance ships built for any navy worldwide. Previous ships used for this type of mission were usually converted fishing trawlers. However, the Soviets had decided that they needed a platform that was purpose-built for spying, so they came up with the Project 1826 ships. For this reason alone, the *Aziya* was very special.

Aziya was currently one of two of this new class of intelligence gathering ships that were currently in the Soviet fleet. She operated in the Pacific and her sister ship, the *Pribaltica*, was currently operating in the Atlantic. The Russians were so enamoured with this class of ships they were currently building two more that were scheduled to enter service in a few years.

The ships were designed to intercept communications via an extensive array of sensors. The collected data could be transmitted back to Russia via satellite uplinks housed in two large spherical radomes. In fact, the dual domes gave the ships a distinctive look that was very hard to miss.

Though heavy in electronics, the *Aziya* was lightly armed. She carried an AK-630 Close in Weapons System (CWIS) and a set of Strela anti-air missiles. Both of these weapon systems were designed for defense. Thus, the *Aziya's* sophisticated suite of sensors remained her best offensive weapon.

* * *

Since being launched two years ago, the *Aziya* had constantly been at sea. She had left Vladivostok 22 months ago, refueling every two months from a fleet replenishment vessel, which also resupplied her with fresh food, water, dry goods and mail. Of course, with a schedule like that, the milk was never fresh and neither was the mail.

The crew suffered because of this aggressive sailing program. However, this minor inconvenience did not concern her Captain or any one of the ship's officers. They were determined to fulfill any and all of the very distinct missions they were assigned. They knew they couldn't carry out the wishes of their superiors if they were visiting foreign ports. It wasn't a pleasure cruise, and the men had to accept it, and accept it they did.

Most of the crew were professionals. In fact, they were professional spies. Many were specialists in electronic warfare, radar and sonar operators, and electronic technicians that kept her suite of specialized equipment running. Plus, there was a complete cadre of scientists that were onboard to test some of the experimental equipment that had been placed in the *Aziya*. There were also KGB operatives. Members of the Soviet secret police, they were onboard mainly to spy on the crew itself, vigilant against any subversive behaviour.

A small portion of the crew were deckhands, cooks and engineers, all tasked with the very important mission of the day to day operation of the ship. Still, despite the necessity for talented crew members, the real stars of the Soviet Union were the technical staff. They seemed to receive all the glory, while regular crew members, like the deckhands, didn't get much recognition at all.

The *Aziya* had already become well known to NATO navies, as she would regularly show up whenever NATO ships got together for a war game. She especially liked to get close to American Carrier groups, mainly because the command and control nature of these ships meant that there was plenty of communications to intercept. However, ships like the *Aziya* were hardly ever interested in the Canadian Navy. The Canadians were small potatoes. Their ships were weak and did not present a threat to the motherland.

This changed, slightly, three weeks ago when the *Aziya* received special orders.

The *Aziya* was to make a course for the west coast of North America, very near Canadian territorial waters, and seek out a location where she could spy on the first operational voyage of *USS Michigan*. The *Michigan* was brand new and notable as the second Ohio Class nuclear submarine to be launched. It was currently based at the US Navy base near Bangor, Washington, in Puget Sound near Seattle.

The Ohio class submarines were a new threat to the USSR. Each Ohio Class submarine could carry enough nuclear missiles to obliterate every major city in Russia. To add to the threat, this class of submarines was built to be extremely quiet and could possibly sneak in very close to the Russian coast. To the Soviets, this was a dreadful threat. A threat they were prepared to defend against at all costs.

The first thing they needed to do was to determine methods whereby they could possibly detect this new class of dangerous submarines. This is where the *Aziya* came in. The Soviets needed to get a spy ship close to where an Ohio Class was known to be operating, and then see if they could "hear" it. To the Soviets, this mission's importance was paramount.

Mind you, the *Aziya* would have sailed right up Puget Sound and anchored herself right off Seattle if she could, but, of course, those were American waters and she could not trespass. In fact, she couldn't even enter the Strait of Juan de Fuca, as those waters were shared by both US and Canada. So, the Soviets were content to place the *Aziya* in international waters, just off of the coast and very near to the entrance to the Strait of Juan de Fuca.

After all, the strait was a perfect chokepoint. When the *Michigan* departed for her first deployment, she would have to pass through the Strait of Juan de Fuca on her way out to sea, and the *Aziya* planned to be waiting there and listening.

That was the plan.

In the past few weeks, Soviet spy satellites had noticed certain activities in Bangor. They were positive that the *Michigan* was about to set sail for the open ocean, and the *Aziya* was ordered to move quickly into position.

Friday morning, at dawn, the *Mackenzie* was getting ready to leave Whiskey 601 for a weekend port visit at New Westminster, near Vancouver. Meanwhile, the *Aziya* was only 24 hours due west, and she was moving towards North America on an easterly heading. Clearly in a rush, the *Aziya's* top speed was 20 knots, and she was currently dashing at 18 knots.

Unlike the *Mackenzie*, the *Aziya* wasn't hurrying to a port visit. She had important work to do at Whiskey 601, and she was very anxious to make her way there.

The Soviet Projekt 1826-class intelligence collection ship *Aziya* (SSV-493) underway in the Pacific Ocean. Circa 1983 (Public Domain - U.S. Navy photo from the USS Wadsworth FFG-9)

CHAPTER 7 / DIAL A SAILOR

In the pre-dawn hours, prior to their scheduled port visit, the *Mackenzie* sailed lazily in a three mile wide square near the eastern edge of Whiskey 601. This tactic was sometimes referred to as "doing a racetrack", as the ship seemed to sail round and round as if on a circuit. Then, just after sunrise, and precisely at 6 AM, the ship suddenly turned east and increased speed to 21 knots. Now, the *Mackenzie* was once more like a dart, cutting through the ocean on a direct path to a port visit in New Westminster.

Matt was still in his rack, but he awoke when he felt the ship shudder and then change pace. He could hear the water rushing past the hull at a greater speed, and he could even hear an increased roar from the engine room. From his experience in this class of ship, he knew that these sounds were telltale signs that they were now heading inbound to their port visit in New West.

New Westminster is actually on the Fraser River, and is a suburb on the south side of Vancouver, Canada. To get there from Whiskey 601 it took a transit of the Strait of Juan de Fuca, then a quick jaunt up the Haro Strait, and then through Boundary Passage into the Strait of Georgia. This was a journey that the *Mackenzie* had made many, many times in the past, and it was almost as if the ship knew the way.

As it was still early, Matt simply stayed in his bunk. He couldn't take his mind off the fact that he would soon be able to call Cynthia. He had only been away for a week, but it seemed like a month. He really needed to hear her voice.

He still hoped that he could talk her into blowing off her work and grabbing a ferry over to the mainland to see him. After all, she *owed* him for last weekend's fiasco. Plus, he really missed her. Surely, she missed him, as well.

As Matt lay quietly in his bunk, he heard Morrison getting up out of his cart. There was still about half an hour before wakey-wakey, but if he got up early he could use the washplace, and shower and shave, before it became too busy. Matt made the decision to get up, as well.

The ship was currently rolling steadily. It usually didn't roll about so much when the ship was moving faster, but it still would take a few rolls as the ship came over the larger waves. Matt had to hang onto his locker door a few times, as the ship rolled fairly hard, but he managed to get his shaving kit and towel. Then he clambered up the ladder and went forward to the washplace.

When he arrived at the washplace he saw Morrison in a towel and flip-flops, standing in front of the mirror, shaving. Morrison had his legs spread wide to balance himself as the ship rolled.

"Good morning," Morrison said. "I guess we are heading in." Apparently, Morrison had also felt the ship's change of movements.

"I think so," Matt agreed. "Have you ever been to New West before?"

"No," said Morrison. "But it's just Vancouver, right?"

"Yeah, that's right," Matt confirmed. "It's on the south side of everything, but it's still Vancouver. Though it's smaller, and it has a few nice clubs right off the waterfront."

Morrison asked, "Is that what you're going to do when we get to New West? Go to a club?"

Matt replied, "Maybe..."

Just then, the ship rolled heavily, which caused Matt to hang on to the sink with both hands.

Matt continued, "...there is one thing for sure. I'm going to get my ass off this bobbing cork of a ship and stand on solid ground. I need to enjoy not being at fuckin' Whiskey 601 for at least one weekend."

Morrison responded, "Well, getting off the ship is a given but what are you going to do after that?"

"I don't know exactly, the first thing I will probably do is go ashore for a beer or two."

Matt had lied. The actual first thing he planned to do when they arrived at New West was to call Cynthia. In fact, there was nothing else on his mind at this moment. Nevertheless, Morrison did not need to know how much he missed his girlfriend. That wasn't something you talked about with shipmates.

Suddenly, the door of the washplace opened, and Paul Legere came in.

"Morning!" Morrison greeted him cheerfully.

Paul just grunted. Matt didn't bother giving any cheerful acknowledgement. Matt knew that if he was grunting like that, there was probably no point. He just nodded at Paul instead.

Morrison continued his chatty discourse, "Hey Paul, Matt said he is going for beers when we get to New West. What are you planning?"

Paul's eyes lit up at this suggestion. "Beers? Just beers? I don't think so! Matt and I are going to do something much more interesting than that."

Matt stopped shaving, "Tell me Paulie... What's this interesting activity you speak of?"

Paul responded, "Three words... Dial-a-Sailor."

"Oh, no! We're not going to do that!" Matt laughed.

Morrison asked, "Please remind me. What's Dial-a-Sailor? Is that the thing some guys did when we last went to Vancouver?"

Paul explained with gusto, "That's right, they had it in Vancouver. It's when girls write their phone numbers on cards, and the cards are delivered to the ship. Then, you check out the cards and choose the one you like. You call the number on the card, and the girl takes you out for the night. Then, at the end of the night, you get laid." He was grinning from ear to ear while he said the last part.

Morrison was interested. "These are just regular girls that want to meet a sailor?"

Paul winked, "Yes, that's exactly what it is."

"And these regular girls are all beautiful honeys?" Morrison needed to know.

"Not all... some are... but they're all... very... how should I put this... very horny. That's the common denominator, and that's why Petey and I are going to do it."

Matt laughed. "Have you ever done this before?"

Paul responded, "Yes, the last time we were in Vancouver. I picked out a card and phoned a girl. She came right to the ship to pick me up. She was very sweet. She took me home, and she cooked me supper. Afterward, we retired to the bedroom for a night of sweet loving."

Morrison piped in, "Was that the girl that you said looked like Miss Piggy from the Muppets? Don't tell me that she was your dial-a-sailor date?"

Paul had a stern look for Morrison, "At least I got something that night. What did you do that night? Spend the night with the Palm Sisters?"

Morrison sneered at Paul, "At least I know where my palms have been."

"Yeah, on your dick!" Paul retorted.

Matt smiled. "I always say, it's not the face you fuck; it's the fuck you face."

"Very poetic. I like the way you think," Paul continued, "anyway... I think I want to try it again... you know better luck this time... I'm hoping."

* * *

It took a total of nine hours to make the journey inbound to the Fraser River delta. Once a pilot was embarked, it took another hour for the dangerous transit up the actual river to the jetty on the New Westminster waterfront. A tugboat was on hand to nudge the ship onto its berth. This was almost always necessary when berthing on the Fraser, as the river normally flowed at a high rate of knots. The current could play havoc when handling the ship at slow speed.

Once the ship was secured alongside, and the "Secure" pipe was made over the intercom system, Matt didn't waste any time to go ashore to find a payphone on the jetty. He really wanted to hear Cynthia's voice.

There was a bank of pay phones conveniently located right near the brow of the ship, and nobody else was there yet, so Matt was able to choose any phone he wanted.

"This is real nice," he thought to himself. "No waiting."

He dialed her number, and then he had to input his credit card number for the charges. He listened on the phone, but it rang and rang. No answer.

"Rats!" he said as he hung up the receiver.

"Maybe I dialed wrong," he thought. So, he then repeated the whole procedure and tried again. Unfortunately, he received the exact same result.

She wasn't home.

Matt stood for a moment and scratched his head, trying to figure out what he should do. Should he wait out here and try again in a few minutes? Should he try again later this evening? He decided to go back onboard the *Mackenzie* and shower and change into clean civvie clothes and then figure it out.

He was feeling rather morose as he crossed the brow to return to the ship. In fact, the Quartermaster had noticed his failed attempts at a phone call and said, "Try again later, buddy."

"I will," Matt replied.

* * *

Once he got back onboard the ship Matt was put off. He didn't really feel like going anywhere at this point in time, except maybe to wait an hour and then go back to the jetty to attempt to call Cynthia once again.

He got into the lineup for the showers, which was long at this point in time. Many sailors were looking forward to a weekend of freedom in New Westminster, and the lineup was pure evidence of that fact. They were talking about clubs they would go to, strip bars they planned to frequent, and girls they wanted to meet. One of the sailors, a signalman Matt thought, was singing "Der Kommisar" loudly, and badly, while he showered.

"Don't turn around, oooh ohhhhh. The Kommissar's in town, oooh ohhhhh." the voice sang very loudly; loud enough to be heard over the sound of the shower.

Several of the sailors laughed aloud when they heard the tortured vocalization echoing out of the shower stall.

From another shower stall, they heard, *"She's a Super Freak, Super Freak!"* in a voice that was clearly trying to emulate Rick James, but doing so very poorly.

Matt began to feel a little better. Everybody seemed to be in good spirits now that they were secure and alongside in port, and right now, he did, as well.

The first voice piped up again from the showers, this time singing the Rolling Stones. It was done in a very strained falsetto, *"Is there nothing I can say… Nothing I can do... to change your mind. I'm so in love with you..."* This time, everybody laughed aloud. However, if Mick Jagger could have heard it, he wouldn't have been amused.

Finally, Matt saw that a washbasin was available. He moved forward to shave and brush his teeth while he waited for a shower stall to open.

Inspired by the vocalizations, Matt looked at the mirror and hummed a bit of "Tempted" and began to shave. Morrison, who had just arrived at the washplace, heard him.

"What is that?" Morrison asked.

It's "Tempted" by The Squeeze. I was listening to it on my Walkman, when I got off watch last night. I guess it's in my head now.

Matt recited the lyrics aloud, *"I bought a toothbrush, some toothpaste a flannel for my face. Pajamas, a hairbrush, new shoes and a case. I said to my reflection let's get out of this place..."*

Suddenly, an anonymous voice from a shower stall loudly repeated the last line, "*Yahhh, let's get out of this place!*" Everybody cheered the sentiment.

Finally, it was Matt's turn to shower. It only took him about three minutes to complete the ablution, and then he quickly combed his hair and trundled back down to #4 Mess. He put on his clean civvies and went back ashore to try to call Cynthia again. Surely, he thought, she would be home by now.

Again, Matt went inside the phone booth and dialed the number. Again, there was no answer, and he had let it ring about 20 times. She simply wasn't home. Matt couldn't help thinking that she might be dodging him. But, just as soon as he had that thought he pushed it back out of his mind. It was a ridiculous notion.

Feeling a little disgruntled, Matt didn't know what to do next. He just stood there looking up and down the Jetty. He noticed that there seemed to be a growing crowd of people standing around looking at the bright grey warship that was now a fixture on the waterfront. There seemed to be plenty of interest in the *Mackenzie* from the local population.

Then, Matt also noticed two white limousines driving slowly up the jetty, toward the brow of the *Mackenzie*.

"This looks interesting..." Matt said aloud.

Matt continued to watch as the limos drove up to the *Mackenzie* and pulled up right in front of the gangway. The driver of the first limo got out and came around to the passenger side. Then, he smartly opened the door. Matt was only about 20 feet away when he saw a red high heel shoe, and then a long white leg, slowly slide out of the open car door.

That one leg was soon followed by another leg, which was followed by the remainder of the whole woman. She was blonde, tall and buxom, wearing a ton of makeup and was outfitted in a tight red dress that started at her hips and only went up to her bust line. In fact, she had to pull the dress down once she got out of the limo, as the dress was riding up dangerously, threatening to reveal too much.

Matt stood there with his mouth open. The whole thing happened in what seemed like slow motion.

Then there was more! The tall blonde was followed by a brunette, which was followed by another blonde and then another brunette. Matt stood in awe.

Then, the other limo pulled forward, and the same thing happened all over again. There was another blonde and another brunette and then a redhead. Then, there was an Asian woman, and then a black woman and another black woman, this time with blonde hair. They were all dressed very provocatively, and they all had curves in the right places. Matt noted that there must have been 15 women standing on the jetty.

This was getting interesting. Matt couldn't help but wonder what was going to happen next.

Just then, Matt witnessed Master Seaman Snow scampering down the gangway to greet the women. Frosty was huffing and puffing, and he was all sweaty from rushing to the brow. Being somewhat disheveled, he had to push the wisps of his hair back onto the top of his head with his fingers.

"Welcome ladies," Frosty said enthusiastically. "Welcome, welcome to the *Mackenzie*. Come on up the gangway. I've got some handsome sailors waiting here to sign all you lovely ladies onboard the ship."

Frosty pointed up at the gangway, where Matt now saw a lineup of sailors waiting by the Quartermaster's station. Each sailor is allowed to sign three guests onboard into the Main Cave. Apparently, Frosty the Snowman had pre-arranged about a half a dozen sailors to be ready on the brow to sign all the women onboard as guests.

Frosty clambered back up the gangway and stood at the top as the girls began to climb the gangway in single file. As each girl arrived at the top of the gangway, Frosty looked her up and down and then greeted her with a smarmy leer.

"Welcome to the *Mackenzie*, my dear," Frosty would say to each girl. He was practically drooling.

Meanwhile, the Quartermaster saluted each woman individually, which was the custom. All civilian women receive a salute when boarding all HMC ships. Matt just wondered how long it would take before the Quartermaster realized that he had just saluted over a dozen hookers.

Matt stood and watched as all the women disappeared down the hatch that lead to Burma Road and to the Main Cave. After the last girl had gone below, Matt noticed that Paul had popped up onto the deck. Paul quickly scurried down the gangway toward Matt. He took the last five steps with a jump. In his hand, he had a blue card.

"Did you see all the hookers?" Paul said.

"I couldn't miss it. They arrived in those two white limos." Matt pointed at the white limousines that were now inching their way back up the jetty from the direction they came.

"Never mind that, Petey! We don't need hookers. Check out the dial-a-sailor, I scored!" He handed Matt the blue index card.

Matt read the card, "Two fun loving gals want to meet two fun loving sailors. Phone us for a home-cooked meal and fun!" There was a phone number at the bottom.

"This is it!" Paul exclaimed. "I can feel it in my bone."

Matt laughed, "Isn't 'fun loving gals' just another word for fat chicks?"

"Who cares? Look, home cooked meal! Plus, they said 'Fun'. That can only mean sex. Let's do it!" Paul grabbed the card and sprinted to the phone booth. He fished in his pocket for loose change. Then, he placed a call to the number on the card.

Matt stood back and watched. He wasn't sure about this. He thought that Cynthia would be ticked if she knew about it. However, Paul needed a wingman and a sailor never let down a buddy.

Matt thought to himself, "I'll just go and be a good boy. Nothing has to happen."

Paul hung up the phone. "They're coming to pick us up at 5:30. They'll be driving a blue Volkswagen Rabbit." He was excited.

"Did they sound cute?" Matt asked jokingly. He figured he might as well play along with the game.

"I asked the one I spoke to on the phone what she looked like, and she said she looked like one of *Charlie's Angels*," Paul said proudly.

"As long as she didn't mean Bosley," Matt quipped.

"I certainly hope not," Paul replied.

* * *

Matt and Paul had about half an hour to kill before their dates arrived, so they went back onboard the *Mackenzie* for a beer or two. When they arrived in the Main Cave, they saw that some of Frosty's ladies were in attendance. The fun and games had already begun.

Matt sat down at a table in the corner while Paul went over to the beer machine and bought two cans of *Extra Old Stock*. He came back to the table and handed one to Matt. "Here you go Matt, your favorite, High Test".

They both cracked the beers and took a sip, and then they clanked the cans together. "Here's to a good night in New West," Matt exclaimed.

In the main cave, there were a few sailors still in uniform. These were the guys that were on duty watch, and they were the bunch that would be staying onboard and looking after the ship tonight. In contrast, there were other sailors that were in civvies, and they obviously had leave as they were mostly drinking. Some were drinking hard, with multiple glasses of liquor in front of them. Some were already looking like they were getting cozy with Frosty's ladies.

Matt and Paul sat back and watched the proceedings. In fact, things started to get wild. Somebody put a porn movie in the VCR that was attached to a large television in the mess. Soon the strains of porn movie music was emanating from the entertainment system. Several of the guys started watching it pretty closely. However, the guys that were remaining on watch just kept eating their supper and going about their business, as if there wasn't a graphic sex video playing a few feet away from their meal. It was a strange scene.

As the party continued, some of the sailors started to pair off with the ladies. At first, they were just flirting and making small talk. However, some had progressed to slow dancing and kissing in the middle of the Main Cave.

Matt pointed towards one of the couples that were dancing and asked Paul, "Who is that tall dude fondling that blonde hooker?"

Paul looked over and saw a tall blond sailor dancing with an equally tall blond prostitute. Both of his hands were busy exploring every recess of her body.

"That's Rick Rottencrotch," Paul replied. "He's usually on a hooker in every port we go to. That's why we call him 'Rottencrotch'. He's had syphilis so many times he has his own chair reserved outside the Doc's office."

Using one of the stanchions as a brass pole, a dark haired prostitute began to perform a strip tease in the middle of the cafeteria. She knew all the moves. Paul and Matt looked on with fascination. A few hours ago, this place was a boring cafeteria filled with greasy men, and now it was a bordello. Matt was fascinated by the transition.

Just then, one of the Master Seamen came into the Main Cave. He was in uniform and Matt thought he must have been the "Duty Tech". The Master Seaman took one look at the porn on the television, and he immediately switched it off.

"We don't play those kind of movies when we have ladies in the mess," he scolded the entire crowd.

Now completely topless, the dark haired pole-dancer took offense. "Hey, I was watching that!" She shouted back at the Master Seaman.

The poor Master Seaman didn't know what to say. He was speechless. He quickly switched the television back on, and he hastily slinked out the door of the cafeteria.

"Nice," said Paul. "She's a keeper."

"I guess she likes her porn," commented Matt.

Things were starting to get even more interesting, when, suddenly, Paul announced that it was time to go.

"Come on Petey, drink up. We don't need prostitutes. We've got Dial-A-Sailor. It's almost 5:30. Our destiny awaits!"

Matt tossed back the remainder of his beer. "It's a shame to leave. This is just getting interesting."

"Maybe, but why pay for it when you can get it for free?" Paul replied.

"Don't count me in on that part of the deal," Matt said. "I've got a girlfriend. I'm only really interested in the home cooked meal part of the invitation."

"Yes, but you'll still be my wingman, won't you?" Paul asked.

"Yes," Matt smiled. "I'll be your wingman."

They slid out of their seats and quietly exited the cafeteria. "Wow," said Paul. "That's some wild party in there. It might be fun, but it's probably a good idea to get out before it gets busted."

* * *

Matt and Paul left the *Mackenzie*. The first thing they noticed was how the jetty was packed with sightseers. It was early on a summer Friday evening in bustling suburb of New Westminster, and many of the locals had come down to stroll the waterfront and see the great grey warship in their backyard. People were asking the Quartermaster if there would be tours of the ship available to the public. He was confirming that there would be tours of the ship offered, both Saturday and Sunday from 1-4PM.

As they walked down the jetty, Matt looked over at the bank of pay phones. The phones were busier now, with sailors getting in touch with friends and loved ones back home. Still, Matt noticed that there was at least one phone open. For a fleeting moment, he considered calling Cynthia one more time, but then he decided against it. He couldn't stomach the thought of facing a third disappointment right now. He thought that he might try to call her a little later in the evening, when there was a greater chance that she would be home.

The guys navigated through all the Friday evening foot traffic and made their way to the entrance to the jetty parking lot. It was there that they spotted a little blue 2-door Volkswagen Rabbit parked at the curb.

"There they are," said Paul. "Let's go take a look and see what we've got ourselves into." They walked over to the car and saw the cute face of a young girl hanging her head out the driver side window. Her long blonde hair was draped over her left shoulder and hanging down on the outside of the car.

Paul approached the car and said, "Are you Mandy and Alison?"

"Mandy?" Matt whispered to himself. Matt always thought that *Mandy* was a silly name, while *Amanda* was perfectly beautiful all by itself.

The girl answered, "Are you Tom and Matt?"

Paul said gleefully, "That's us!"

Mandy smiled broadly. Her smile was so huge that she seemed to have extra teeth. "Well, get in then," she giggled, as she jumped out of the car and pushed the front seat forward. She then motioned for the guys to squeeze into the back seat.

Paul looked at Matt and tried to imitate the excited, happy look that was on Mandy's face, "Let's get in then!"

Matt smiled back, and then he slid into the back seat of the Rabbit. Paul followed him. Miraculously, both Matt and Paul managed to squeeze into the back seat, and the adventure began.

Good thing it was a short drive to Mandy's house. Her Volkswagen smelled badly of diesel, and the way she drove was making Matt more seasick than he ever felt at Whiskey 601. To make matters worse, Mandy was blasting A Flock of Seagulls on the cassette deck and still trying to yell things at the guys in the back seat. They couldn't really hear her.

"Nice car," said Paul. He was trying to compliment her wreck of a vehicle, but she clearly couldn't hear his praise over the rhythmic electronic beats of "Space Age Love Song". Her head was swaying, rhythmically right to left, then back again, to the flow of the music.

Matt looked over at Alison. He couldn't see much of her, other than her dark shoulder length hair that covered the back of her head. He could see the side of her face, and she certainly looked cute enough, but she wasn't bopping to the music like Mandy. In fact, she hadn't said a single word so far. Meanwhile, Mandy was chatting up a storm in the driver's seat. It was obvious that Alison was much less outgoing than her counterpart.

Matt leaned back and whispered into Paul's ear, "Why did you use a fake name, 'Tom'?"

Paul winked at Matt, "Shhhhhh". He held his finger up to his mouth for one second. Matt smiled. This was a typical "Paul" move.

"What's for supper, ladies?" Paul said loudly, loud enough so the girls could finally hear him over the music.

"Perogies and pork chops, Tom!" Mandy yelled back.

* * *

Mandy and Alison lived in a basement suite of a three-story apartment, located at what seemed about twenty blocks from the New Westminster harbourfront. Matt wasn't sure exactly where they were, but he did notice a taxi stand on a main road about two blocks away. He was sure that this would be their escape route when this Dial-A-Sailor date ended. After all, a smart sailor always knew how he was going to get out of any situation.

However, Paul didn't seem like he wanted to escape from anything. As Mandy showed him around the small apartment, Paul gushed at every nuance of the place.

"Oh, that's a nice couch. It looks so comfy," Paul was heard to say.

Matt just grinned, as it was obvious to him which angle Paul was working.

Matt noticed that their apartment smelled of cooked onions. His experience with perogies told him that they were likely being served with grilled onions, something he wholly approved of, as Matt loved onions. The irony that Cynthia wasn't there to scold him for eating onions was not lost on Matt.

Soon, dinner was served. Mandy announced that she had made the pork chops, and Alison had made the perogies. She also explained that the pork chops were prepared in cream of mushroom soup. "They are my specialty!" she added. "I got the recipe off the can!"

Matt had to saw through his pork chop to get a piece to taste. They were anything but tender, and they were far too salty. On the other hand, the perogies were very good. They were served with onions and sour cream and Matt thought they were almost as good as the perogies his grandmother would make.

"These pork chops are so gooood," Paul exclaimed as he chewed a piece of the leathery chop. He was obviously trying to impress Mandy, whom he had clearly taken a liking to.

Mandy blushed, "I'm so glad you like them... Tom... It was easy to make.

Besides, it feels good to prepare a home-cooked meal for some navy guys."

Paul gushed, "Well, it's just wonderful to have a home cooked meal after suffering through navy grits."

"I'll have some more perogies... and onions," Matt said as he reached into the middle of the table. Alison smiled at him. Again, it was obvious that she was the shy one, and certainly much less outgoing than her friend Mandy. Matt noticed that she did have a beautiful smile. Her short dark hair hung over her eyes when she moved. She was always brushing it back with her hand. She was a true beauty, though she was plainer than Mandy.

* * *

It was only about five minutes after supper ended when Mandy and Paul started to get frisky with each other. It progressed rapidly. First, they were wrestling, then they were kissing, and soon after, they disappeared into Mandy's bedroom.

Alison looked at Matt. She shrugged her shoulders and said, "I guess they're gone for the night."

Matt shrugged his shoulders as well, "Yeah, I guess so."

They both looked at each other quietly. They seemed nervous, with some obvious tension caused by what was going on in the adjacent room. After a while, the silence became awkward, and Matt felt he should probably say something.

"So, where did you learn how to make such good perogies?"

Alison smiled, "Oh, my mom taught me how to make them. We made them in my family since I was a little girl, and I pretty much grew up around perogies. Did you like them?"

"I loved them," Matt said. "They were great, and thanks for feeding us... you see... we can't get good food like that where we are from."

"You mean, on the ship?" she asked.

"Yes, for sure," Matt said.

"Wait, if you like the perogies, you should taste my Mom's holubtsi!" Alison was relieved to talk about something other than what is going on in the bedroom.

"I love holubtsi," Matt said. He was also glad to get into a conversation about Ukrainian food. Not just because he loved the food so much, but more because he was getting uncomfortable being around this girl with nothing to say.

"Did you grow up in a Ukrainian household?" Matt asked.

"Oh. Of course." Alison was only happy to respond. "Both my parents are Ukrainian as well as my grandparents on both sides of my family."

"You're pure Ukrainian then... what is your last name?" Matt asked.

"Chomiak," Alison said.

"Where did you grow up," Matt said.

Alison replied, "Not here. I grew up on a farm, in Alberta, near Vegreville."

"Oh, Vegreville... the town with the huge 'Pysanka'," Matt said.

Alison looked surprised, "How do you know about the Pysanka?"

"I've been there, a few years ago with my Ukrainian grandparents. I was younger then, but I definitely recall seeing a giant Easter egg. They had just built it then, I think."

"Yeah, you really can't miss it... it's the biggest in the world," Alison laughed. "So, your grandparents are Ukrainian then? What about you, what is your last name?"

Matt explained, "My last name is Petersen. My father was Icelandic, but my mother was Ukrainian... So I am half Ukrainian."

Matt didn't bother explaining the details of his parent's death. It would just put a damper on the conversation.

Just then, they heard some muffled moans coming from inside the bedroom. Matt looked over at Alison, and she was blushing red. Then suddenly, she glanced over toward the stereo system.

"Do you like music?" she asked.

"Who doesn't like music," Matt responded. "I think some music might drown out the noises from the bedroom."

"That's exactly what I was thinking," Alison said, as she slid onto the floor and positioned herself in front of a milk crate full of record albums near the stereo system.

"Tell you what, let's find out how much you know your music," Alison said. "We'll play a game. You cover your eyes, while I pull an album out of this crate and put it on the turntable. Then, you just listen. You have to guess the artist and the album... and the song... if you can, of course."

"Okay," Matt said as he covered his eyes with his hands. "I'll do my best."

He could hear her fumbling a bit with the album dust jacket and then the sound of her opening the turntable cover. Matt wasn't sure what kind of music she would play, but he hoped that it might be something in which he was familiar.

After a few seconds, he heard the pop of the stylus being placed on the vinyl record.

"Okay, you can look now," Alison announced.

Matt opened his eyes, and he saw Alison facing him, sitting on the floor in front of the stereo. Matt couldn't see the album cover because she had it in her hands, which were behind her back.

Matt heard a few hisses and pops as the stylus travelled up to the beginning of the first track, and then he heard a familiar synthesized hum, followed by a distinctive, rhythmic staccato. Matt knew that it was "Sirius", the first track on the album *Eye in the Sky*. Still, he waited and didn't answer right away. He didn't want to spoil the moment of the music. He just closed his eyes and listened attentively.

After a few more seconds, he answered, "It's *Eye in the Sky* by The Alan Parsons Project. I believe that the first track is named 'Sirius'."

Alison smiled and nodded as she pulled the album out from behind her back, "That's right," she said softly. "Maybe that one was too easy?"

"No, that was a good one," Matt said kindly. "I'm just a big fan. I love this album, and especially the next song 'Eye in the Sky'."

"Yeah, me too," she said softly.

They both listened quietly and enjoyed the music. When the first song began to wane, Matt looked straight at Alison. He noticed that she was looking directly back at him. Was it strange that they were both anticipating what was about to happen?

"This is the good part," she whispered. Then, in unison, they both bobbed their heads slightly with the throbbing bass guitar as "Sirius" segued into "Eye in the Sky".

Alison giggled, "I've never done that in unison with anyone else before."

"That's a shame really. You're a natural," Matt laughed.

They listened quietly to "Eye in the Sky" for a few minutes more before they returned to their conversation. Matt was beginning to notice how easy it was to talk to Alison.

"Does anyone know what Alan Parson's project actually entails?" Matt was trying to be funny.

Alison laughed, "I'm not sure. I always thought it was some sort of secret space station, like on 'Moonraker'."

"I can't believe you just referenced a James Bond movie! That's so unlike many girls I know." Matt was thinking about Cynthia when he said this, but he wasn't about to mention this particular detail to Alison.

"So, shoot me," she said. "I like my movie references."

After the "A" side on *Eye in the Sky* had finished, Alison proposed that they continue their game and Matt should try to guess a new album. So, Matt closed his eyes again as Alison put a new piece of vinyl on the turntable.

Matt kept his eyes closed this time. As the first track began, Matt heard a familiar instrumental introduction followed by the lyrics, *"Won't you take me back to school; I need to learn the golden rule…"*

Matt knew the answer very quickly, "It's 'The Voice' by the Moody Blues. The album is *Long Distance Voyager.*"

"Oh! You're just too good at this," Alison said.

Matt smiled. "This is another of my favorite albums. I can't believe you have it."

"Either you're some sort of music genius, or we have the same taste in music," Alison declared.

"What do you think this song is about?" Matt asked.

Alison thought about it a bit. Matt noticed that she was twirling her dark brown hair with her finger. "I think it's about that little voice inside of us that tells us right from wrong, we sometimes ignore it, but eventually we must listen to it."

"Yes, that's it exactly, isn't it? It is about the intuition in all of us. Usually our inner feelings are right."

Alison smiled at him. Then they sat quietly and listened to the music.

They did the same thing with several more albums. Alison put the vinyl on the stereo while Matt closed his eyes and listened. He guessed them all, *Abacab* by Genesis, *Dark Side of the Moon* by Pink Floyd, *In Through the Out Door* by Led Zeppelin and *Look Sharp!* by Joe Jackson. As they listened to music they continued their friendly chat.

After about two hours, the bedroom door opened and Paul emerged clad only in his underwear. He was somewhat red faced, seeming ashamed in what he had been doing. He didn't make eye contact as he quickly slipped into the bathroom without saying a word. A minute later, Mandy also emerged from the bedroom, wearing a pink housecoat. She said a quick "hello", then she hastily went into the fridge and pulled out two bottles of beer. Simultaneously, Paul emerged from the bathroom, and they both went back into the bedroom, giggling all the way.

Matt looked at Alison. He was about to laugh aloud, but he quickly noticed that she was blushing. She seemed to be embarrassed by the whole affair.

Matt felt that he had to say something. "Did you see that? Did you see that?" he asked repeatedly.

Alison looked at him dumb-founded.

Matt pointed at the fridge. "Did you see what was in the fridge? You didn't tell me you had cold beer!" Matt said with a straight face.

Finally, Alison laughed aloud.

"Yes, there might be a few more in there. Do you want one before they get thirsty all over again and drink them all?"

Alison was smiling now. Apparently, Matt's gag had relaxed her again. She went to the fridge and retrieved two bottles of beer. She opened them in the kitchen and then came back to the sofa where Matt was sitting. She handed him a beer and then held out her own beer towards his.

"Cheers," she said.

"Cheers," Matt replied as he clinked his bottle against hers.

Then, Alison plopped herself down on the same sofa where Matt was seated. But, not on Matt's end of the sofa, she went to the other end. Then she turned to face Matt, putting her feet up on the sofa and wrapping her arms around her knees.

Matt watched as Alison took a sip of her beer. She looked comfortable enough. Matt was a little nervous when she sat down on the sofa with him, but her body language seemed to be neutral, so he didn't actually think she was hitting on him. Still, he was looking for any signs.

However, Matt's wonderment about her intentions were quickly settled when Alison asked him the next question.

"Matt, what's your girlfriend like?"

Matt was taken aback by this question. "How did you know I had a girlfriend?" he asked.

"Oh, I guess you don't know," she began to explain. "When 'Tom' called, he said that he would bring a friend. But, he said that his friend had a girlfriend, and he would just be along as a wingman."

"Okay, I get it," Matt said. "You knew all along, then?"

"Actually, knowing that made me feel much better about this, as I am not the type to jump onto the first guy that comes along," Alison added. "I'm not like Amanda. I really like to get to know somebody first, and since she said that you had a girlfriend I figured you wouldn't want to hit on me."

"Well, I'm glad you brought this up," Matt said. "I was nervous that there might be some pressure for me to hit on you, especially after those two started to hump like rabbits in there." Matt pointed at the bedroom door.

"Good then," she said. "We can just keep talking."

"I'm okay with that," Matt said enthusiastically.

"So, then, let me get back to the original question. What's your girlfriend like?" Alison repeated the question.

Other than his grandparents, Matt had never had to describe Cynthia to anyone before, and he quickly discovered that it was something he couldn't easily do.

"Well... she's very nice. She's a professional. She lives in Victoria. She has red hair, freckles and a cute button nose. She always dresses stylishly. She is very sweet... when she wants to be. I think that's all I can tell you."

"She sounds nice," Alison said.

Alison could see that asking Matt about his girlfriend had made him nervous. She decided that she wouldn't push that button anymore, so she offered to change the subject.

"How about if I change the subject," she said. "Earlier, I told you where I grew up, but you never told me where you grew up..."

"I grew up in Winnipeg," Matt said. "Wait... you changed the subject pretty fast there."

"I had the sense that you didn't want to talk about your girlfriend, especially to some girl you just met," Alison said with a grin.

"Oh, yeah," Matt said. "You're right about that, but what I was getting at, is that you changed the subject before I could ask you a similar question... about your boyfriend!" Matt pointed an accusatory finger at her.

"So... Winnipeg, eh? Cold there, eh," Alison giggled as she faked an evasiveness.

"Aha! Who's nervous now?" Matt laughed,

"Okay, I'll fess up. I have no boyfriend. I did have a steady boyfriend when I was back in Alberta, but that didn't last. Since I've been here in Vancouver I've dated a few guys, but that's all. I'm very selective. Most guys don't get a second date with me. They don't make the cut."

Matt nodded as he took a sip of beer. It was hard for him to believe that Alison was single. She had so many qualities that men desired in a woman.

"That's so hard to believe," Matt said. "I've just met you, but I can already tell that you're wonderful."

"Oh, you're just saying that," Alison blushed. "Keep saying it. Don't stop, keep going..."

Then she laughed aloud. Matt noticed that her laugh was deeper and fuller than most girls he knew. Matt always loved a laugh that seemed to have substance.

"You say that most guys don't make the cut. So, tell me, what is the criteria?" Matt asked.

"I don't know," she said, as she looked deep in thought. "Just someone I can get along with on an equal basis. You know... someone who appreciates me as much as I appreciate them. And, definitely, someone that I can talk to. I mean, really have an intelligent conversation with. You know?"

Matt nodded his head, "Yes, I get it," he said. Meanwhile, Matt was thinking that he had none of these things with Cynthia. But, he was always trying to get there. Still, he wondered what it would take to have this exact kind of relationship with Cynthia? He would have to work on it.

"Is there any more of that beer left?" Matt asked. He really needed to change the subject, again.

"Well certainly, my thirsty friend," Alison said as she went to the fridge and retrieved two more beers.

* * *

Matt and Alison talked until 1:30AM. It was one of those talks where time had flown by, as Matt looked at his watch, and he realized that he had been there with Alison for over 7 hours, talking with her.

Matt didn't want to overstay his welcome, so he decided to say his goodbye to Alison, but not before checking with "Tom" to see if he was okay, and telling him that he was heading back to the ship. Paul gave him his blessing to leave. Matt was certainly surprised that Paul wasn't ready to flee yet, as guys like him seemed to do. Maybe he really liked Mandy?

Getting back to the ship was easy. Matt walked around the corner and spotted a taxi waiting at the cab stand he had spied on the way in. Matt jumped in a cab and $12 later he was back on the jetty next to the *Mackenzie*.

It was around 2AM when Matt got back to the ship. As he walked down the main flats towards #4 Mess, he saw what looked like one of the prostitutes passed out in the flats, forward, just outside the door to #3 Mess.

"Isn't she just outside the Chief's and Petty Officer's Lounge?" Matt whispered to himself, as he stood and studied the scene. "Oh god, I forgot how insane this place was when I left."

He wasn't sure what to do. If the girl was passed out drunk, that was one thing. However, she was lying in the flats all alone. What if she was hurt? He needed to go forward and see if she was okay.

It was a curious thing. As he got closer, he noticed that she seemed to be wearing some sort of furry outfit and a hat with ears. When he got real close, he realized she was dressed in a sheep costume. Her makeup was a mess, with her mascara running down her face. She was definitely passed out, as he could see that she was breathing, but she was unconscious. Matt was impressed that this is something he had never seen before, and probably would never see again.

To Matt's surprise, she suddenly opened her eyes and looked up at him.

"Hey sailor, are you next?" she slurred.

"What?" Matt said, stunned. He could smell her breath, and he knew right away that she was clearly pissed.

"Okay, just let me sleep a little more. I'll be ready soon," she said as she closed her eyes again.

"Wait, are you okay? Do you need help?" Matt asked. He felt that it was his duty to find out if help was needed.

She awoke again, but she was more cross this time, "Sure honey. Just give me a minute. I'm just resting my eyes here a bit... getting my second wind."

Then, the #3 Mess door opened. Out stepped a second prostitute, dressed in a frilly dress, bonnet and carrying a shepherd's crook. She pushed Matt out of the way and bent down on one knee next to the first girl.

"Hey, Andrea. Are you ready?" she said as she shook the sleeping woman's shoulder.

This is when Matt realized that the first girl, "Andrea", was dressed as a sheep, and the second girl was supposed to be Bo Peep. He was astonished.

Matt stood back and watched as Andrea started to get up. "Sure, I'm okay. I'm just getting my second wind," she said slowly. As the two went back inside #3 Mess, through the open door, Matt was sure that he saw the Buffer passed out in his underwear on a couch. Matt tried to get a better look inside. However, the door was abruptly closed before he could confirm what he had seen.

"Crazy times," Matt whispered. Then he hurried back down the flats to #4 Mess. He knew that it was always best to stay away from this kind of situation. It could easily get much crazier than this, and he didn't want to be around when that happened.

* * *

Saturday went by in a blur. Matt woke up relatively early at 8AM with the intention of calling Cynthia in Victoria. If he spoke to her this morning, there was still a chance she might come over on the ferry to see him. Again, though, he was disappointed when there was no answer, even after about 20 rings. Matt surmised that Cynthia must have already gone to work. Where else could she be?

Now in a gloomy frame of mind, Matt wandered ashore. He ducked into a souvenir shop near the waterfront. He quickly spotted a postcard that said "Beautiful New Westminster, British Columbia". It had a picture of a flower garden next to the Fraser River. In the background, on the river, it also showed a tugboat towing a log boom. His grandmother loved postcards and his grandfather loved anything to do with the lumber industry, being a lumberjack in his youth. Matt thought for sure that they would like this one the best.

Matt bought the postcard and a stamp. Then, he borrowed a pen from the shopkeeper and wrote down his Grandparent's Winnipeg address on the back of the postcard.

Matt stopped and pondered for a moment, and then he wrote a greeting on the back:

Dear Grandma and Grandpa, I'm here in New Westminster. It's beautiful here, sunny and warm. Grandma, there are flowers everywhere, you'd love it. Grandpa, you should see the log booms! Everything is wonderful. I miss you a lot. I will come home to see you soon. Love Matthew.

As he returned the pen to the shopkeeper, Matt thought about his dear grandparents. They were such a positive influence on him, and they lead such simple lives. Most important to them was family and friends, and of course good food. They loved to tell stories of the old country, and always spoke in their native tongue at home. Matt loved this about them; they held onto their culture so tightly. It was so valuable to them.

As Matt left the shop, he placed the stamp he had bought on the top corner of the postcard. He put the postcard into a mailbox, which was conveniently located on the corner next to the shop. Then he carried on, walking further down the street to see what else New Westminster had to offer.

Matt had lunch at a café in the middle of town. It was nice to get some food that wasn't navy grub. Afterward, he wandered back to the ship. He thought about trying to call Cynthia from the phone on the jetty, but he knew that she worked on Saturdays, and she wouldn't be home. He would have to call her later after, suppertime.

It was quiet onboard the *Mackenzie*; most of the other sailors were gone ashore. So, he went to the mess and climbed up into his cart to read his Robert Heinlein book, *Friday*. Then the afternoon just slipped by.

Paul came back to the ship just before suppertime.

"Wow!" Matt said. "Did she tie you up, or did you willingly spend the day with Mandy?"

"Very funny," Paul said. "We were up pretty much all night, then she made me breakfast. After breakfast, we went back to bed and slept this time. I just woke up."

"Amazing," Matt said. He was clearly shocked that Paul would spend the day with a girl after being with her all night long.

"Oh, by the way," Paul added. "Alison the roommate says hello. I think she likes you."

"How do you know that?" Matt asked.

"It's all in the way she said it."

Matt thought about it. Alison was very sweet, but he probably shouldn't have anything to do with another girl while he was with Cynthia. Sure, he and Cynthia's relationship wasn't perfect, but he had plans to make it better. He really loved her, and he wasn't about to throw in the towel.

Paul announced, "Well, I'm going to take a very long shower, and then we should have some supper and a few beers. What do you say to that, Petey?"

"Sure thing," Matt replied. "I could use a cold one, but before I get some beer in me I really need to phone Cynthia. You know, just to say hello to the old ball and chain."

"Yeah, good idea," Paul said. "Do that before the beers. Don't let her know that you're actually enjoying yourself over here."

Matt smiled at Paul. He didn't want Paul to know how much he missed Cynthia. He would be teased, and Matt didn't want that right now.

* * *

Now that it was 5:30 PM, Matt figured Cynthia should be home from work and it should be a good time to get her on the phone. So, he scurried back to the bank of telephones on the jetty to place the call. Again, the phone rang and rang. He let it ring over thirty times.

"Enough of that," Matt said aloud, as he forcefully hung up the phone. "I wonder where she could be?"

Matt skulked back onto the ship, head and shoulders down this time. Clearly, he was disappointed. He went straight to the Main Cave and met up with Paul.

"So, did you talk to your sweetie?" Paul asked.

"No, she wasn't home," Matt said. "I wonder if she is okay."

"She's probably late getting off work," Paul said. "You can call her again later. Let's have some supper now."

Matt and Paul went up to the steam line to fetch their supper. The meal was roast beef, mashed potatoes and salad. They both sat down together at their usual table.

"This looks good," Matt said. "But something is missing?"

"I do not know what you could be talking about," Paul answered knowingly.

"Beer!" Matt replied. "Could I get you an ice cold beverage, my good friend?" Matt said politely.

"Yes, please," Paul replied.

Matt went over to the beer machine and fished in his pocket for some change. He bought two ice-cold cans of Labatt's Blue and returned to the table.

"They were out of High Test," Matt reported.

"Beer is beer," said Paul. "It's cold, and that's all that counts."

As they ate their meals, and drank their cold beers, Paul noticed that the cafeteria was much quieter today. "There is a lot less ambiance in here today," Paul said. "Without all the hookers and porn it's just not as much fun." He was always trying to crack a joke.

"Oh, speaking of hookers, I haven't told you what I saw last night when I came back to the ship," Matt said.

"Tell it."

"Get this. In the flats, near the Chief and Petty Officer's Mess, one hooker in a sheep suit and another hooker dressed as Bo Peep," Matt explained.

Paul said, "That's hilarious! I've heard the rumour that they had those costumes up in #3 Mess, but I have never talked to anyone that has actually seen them. Awesome!"

"It was sort of awesome, I guess. But, those girls were really pissed... and it was actually kind of sad."

"Okay whatever," said Paul. "I just think it's great that those old farts in the Chiefs and PO's Mess still know how to have fun."

They continued to eat supper and drink beer. Even five minutes later, Paul was still giggling over the #3 Mess story. A few minutes later, they had finished their meals. Matt took their plates to the scullery while Paul got up and bought two more cold beers from the machine. Then they sat back down at their table together.

"These are going down good," Matt said. He was feeling a little better about missing Cynthia now that he had been drinking.

A few minutes later, Leading Seaman Blair White, one of the *Mackenzie*'s Boatswains, came over to their table. He sat down just across from Matt.

"Hey Blair," Matt said. Matt knew Blair from the barracks, as he was one of the other residents there. Also, Blair was the first friendly face that Matt had seen when he originally arrived on the *Mackenzie*.

"Hey Matt," Blair said. "I have a question for you. Are you still seeing that hot redhead Cynthia?"

Matt was instantly irked. He glared at Blair sternly, "Why? Why do you ask?"

"Oh, I'm not interested in her, if that's what you think," Blair explained hastily.

"Then why would you be asking about her?" Matt was still ticked at the line of questioning.

"Remember, I'm not interested," Blair explained again. "It's just that, I saw her in the Ivy last Saturday, and I didn't see you there with her. That's all.

Were you out of town… or on duty… or something?"

Matt's mind raced back to the moment Cynthia had told him that she was tired that night, and didn't want to go out with him. In his mind, he was freaking out, but on the outside he wasn't about to let on.

"Are you sure it was last Saturday?" Matt asked calmly.

"Yes, last Saturday. The Saturday before we sailed," Blair confirmed.

"That was the night we agreed to go out on our own," Matt lied. "We just don't feel we have to be together every night. You know. We have a mature open relationship. She has her friends, and I have my friends."

Paul heard this, but he remained silent. He knew very well that Matt had said Cynthia blew him off saying she was tired last Saturday. None of this sounded good to Paul.

"When you say open relationship, do you mean that she can hang with other guys?" Blair asked.

Matt was getting annoyed all over again. "What are you fucking talking about Blair?"

"I don't want to tell you this, but I have to tell you. When I saw her at the Ivy, the Gooch was hitting on her pretty hard," Blair explained.

"Mike Gooch?" Matt asked.

"Is there any other Gooch?" said Blair.

Matt was stunned. Apparently, it had only taken that dirt bag Gooch forty-eight hours to horn in on his girl! And, Cynthia was falling for it? He felt sick.

Up until this point, Paul had looked on silently, though, he knew Matt was completely slayed by this news. "Thanks man," he waved at Blair to leave. "I think Matt has heard enough."

Blair White got up from the table, "I just thought you ought to know..."

Paul cut him off, "No problem, thanks Blair. We appreciate it." Paul nodded at Blair. Blair nodded back in agreement.

As Blair White walked away, Paul looked at Matt. Matt's face was pale. He was clearly stunned.

"Matt, don't shit about this," Paul said quietly. "When you get back, you and Cynthia just need to talk it out. That is all."

"Really?" asked Matt.

"Yeah, I'm sure nothing happened," said Paul. "Cynthia's a smart girl, right? She's not going to mess around with a lunkhead like Gooch, right?"

Even as he was saying this, Paul was thinking that he was almost positive that Cynthia was messing around on Matt. He had seen this happen before to plenty of other guys. It was typical. However, he didn't think that his friend Matt needed to know his fears at this point. Nothing could be gained for Matt to worry about something that was beyond his control, right?

CHAPTER 8 / ALISON

Matt lay on his rack, in #4 Mess. In a sullen mood, he was silently listening to music on his Sony Walkman and simultaneously trying to make some sense of the multitude of emotions running through his mind.

"…but I heard you let that little friend of mine take off your party dress…"

Matt scowled. Even his music had turned on him, as Elvis Costello had to pick this exact moment to lament about a girlfriend who had sex with his rival. That was enough! He quickly ejected the tape and forcefully threw it into his bedside box with his other cassettes. Then, he reached in and randomly retrieved a different tape. This time it was The Kinks.

"There's no sad music on this one," Matt muttered to himself. Then he lay back in his bunk, listening to music and staring off into space. He was obviously very morose. He just couldn't understand how Cynthia had lied to him about being tired and then meeting up with the Gooch. He just couldn't get the thought of the whole sordid mess out of his mind.

* * *

Later, Paul came down to #4 Mess and tried to talk Matt into heading ashore.

"You want to go out tonight? It's Saturday night in swinging New West. Me and a few guys are heading out to a bar in a few minutes. It should be fun," Paul said.

"Do I look like I want to go out tonight?" Matt said sarcastically.

"No, but I know that going out and having some fun will do you good."

"I just don't want to go out tonight," Matt reaffirmed. "I'll just stay here. You guys have a good time."

"Look, I can tell you're moping about Cynthia. It's obvious to me, but my advice to you is to put it away. It's probably going to be okay. She's most likely not doing anything. It will be worse if you just sit around here and stew about it."

"What if I want to feel bad?" Matt said stubbornly.

"Nobody really wants to feel bad," Paul said.

"Look, here it is," Matt said sternly. "I'm just going to stay here. I'm on duty watch tomorrow. I'll go to bed early and get a good night's sleep. I'll be fine. I'll see you in the morning."

"All right," said Paul. "Suit yourself. Have a good night."

After Paul had left the mess, Matt was completely alone. He got out of his rack and went over to the bank of light switches by the mess entrance. He switched off all the overhead lighting, and then he went back to his rack. Now he could lay in the dark, alone, and listen to music.

Matt probably could have talked more about his problems with Paul. Likely, it would have done him some good. But, sailors never talked of love for their wives or girlfriends. They certainly will talk about love for their children, or their mother, but never for their significant other.

At about 9 PM, Matt put on his shoes and left the ship. He went onto the jetty and back to the bank of payphones. Those phones were beginning to seem like they were his best friends. He tried to call Cynthia one last time. This time he let it ring about forty times. Once again, there was no answer. Even more frustrated this time, he slammed the phone down abruptly, and then he trudged back onboard the *Mackenzie* and returned directly to his rack.

* * *

Sunday morning came quickly. Matt arose at 0630, showered, had breakfast, and then prepared his uniform for his duty watch. His first muster was at 0745, when they received their assignments and prepared for colours. Matt's assignment was on the brow starting at 0800.

The morning watch on the brow was quiet. It was Sunday. There was nobody awake on the ship, and there was nobody on the jetty.

Matt stood watch as the Quartermaster, which meant that he had to watch the brow of the ship and challenge anyone that came onboard. He was on watch with a Boatswain's Mate, who was an Able Seaman that mostly sat inside a booth and watched the ship's switchboard. The Able Seaman would also answer the odd phone call and make information pipes using the Ship's broadcast system. But, there really wasn't much of any of that happening on a Sunday morning, so they mostly enjoyed the peace and quiet.

Matt was in the final hour of his four hour watch when he saw, in the distance, a young girl walking across the parking lot toward the jetty. He continued to watch her as she purposefully strode right up the jetty to the brow of the *Mackenzie*. When she got very near the ship, Matt recognized her. It was Alison.

"Hey, Alison!" Matt called out to her. "Wow, what are you doing here?"

Alison looked up at the ship from the jetty, and then she placed her hand on her forehead to shield her eyes from the sun. "I brought you some cookies." Alison said with a huge smile. She was holding a medium-sized cookie tin in her other hand.

Matt thought she looked adorable, standing down on the jetty in the sunshine. He couldn't help but smile himself. "You have cookies?" Matt said with a grin. "Come onboard then."

Alison climbed the stairs, and then crossed the brow. Matt stood at attention and gave her a salute.

"Wow, I'm glad I came here," she gushed. "I get saluted by a real live sailor? I never expected such a wonderful welcome."

"Well, you did bring cookies," Matt explained. "Maybe I was saluting the cookies."

Alison took a long look at Matt. "It's always nice to see a man in uniform," she smiled.

Matt felt like he might be blushing.

"Your girlfriend is a lucky girl," she said.

Now, Matt knew that he was definitely blushing.

She handed Matt the metal cookie tin. "Here you go Matt. A treat for your long voyage ahead," she said. "I wanted to thank you for the wonderful time we had on Friday, and this is the best thing I could think of."

Matt cracked open the tin and took a peek inside. He smelled the cookies, "Oh, they smell great. Are they oatmeal?" he asked as he poked one of the cookies with his finger. It felt soft.

"Oatmeal chocolate chip," she said.

"Oatmeal chocolate chip is one of my favorites," Matt said. "Thank you. This is just what I need for the weeks ahead at sea."

"Just as I suspected," Alison said. "You can always give someone cookies when they are going on a long trip."

Matt couldn't help but notice how thoughtful Alison seemed to be. This was something he had always hoped to see in Cynthia. But, he quickly put the thought out of his mind.

"Thanks for coming by, and thanks for the cookies," Matt said. "It's good to see you."

"Yeah, it's good to see you too..." she replied.

Matt felt he owed her something for the cookies. But, what?

"How would you like a tour of the ship?" he asked. As he was saying it, he recalled how most girls didn't like warships, or navy things. He had probably made a mistake by offering.

"Actually, I was going to ask you if the ship was offering tours. But, if you were to give me a tour, that would be more than awesome," she said with a smile.

"Okay," Matt said. "When I am relieved off watch in about 15 minutes, I will give you the special grand tour."

* * *

After Matt's relief came to the brow, and Matt was finally free, Matt toured Alison through the entire ship from stem to stern. Mind you, he didn't take her down Burma Road, or into the Main Cafeteria, as he knew that there were plenty of sailors down there at this time of day. He didn't want any of those greasy, hairy bags gawking at Alison. She was too nice for that.

When they went forward, on the forecastle, Matt referred to the deck as the "Foc's'le".

"What did you call this place?" she asked.

"I called it 'Foc's'le'. Sorry if I confused you with that term, it is short for forecastle. But we all just say 'Foc's'le'," Matt explained. "I guess I just didn't think when I said that word just now, I'm so used to it."

"No, that's okay," Alison said. "I find this all very interesting. Don't hold back, show me everything."

Matt said, "Okay, let's look at the forward gun next."

Then, they toured around the forward gun. "Wow," she said. "It's so huge, how do you fire it?"

Matt opened the door of the gun and showed her where the operator sat.

Then he took her through the door in the superstructure to show her where the magazine was located.

Matt pointed down to a hatch on the deck. "They just throw the rounds up that hatch. A guy stands here and catches them, and then he passes them to another guy that loads them in the clip."

Alison looked at all of this with fascination. "You must have to be coordinated to do that," she said.

"It takes practice," Matt said. "When they do their drills, they sometimes put a brand new Ordinary Seaman on that job, just to see how discombobulated they can get him."

Alison laughed. "Ordinary Seaman?" she asked.

"That's what we call a brand new recruit," Matt explained.

"So he's just so plain that he is considered 'Ordinary'?" she asked with a grin.

"That's right," Matt replied, also with a grin.

As they went aft, Matt avoided taking Alison down the hatch to Burma Road.

"What's down there?" Alison asked as she pointed at the hatch.

"That's Burma Road where you have the Main Cafeteria and the Mess Decks, which are the sleeping quarters and such. I won't take you down there, as it's probably full of 'Hairy Bags' right now."

"What did you say?" Alison asked. She seemed to be slightly shocked.

"I'm sorry, I should have said 'sailors' or 'men'," Matt explained. "Hairy Bags is a term we sometimes use to refer to a bunch of sailors. We use it so much I often forget that ordinary people would think it was dirty."

"I was just shocked," she laughed. "You guys have a funny way of putting things."

"We love to joke around," Matt said.

* * *

After the tour, they sat on the quarterdeck, further aft on a set of bollards. The bollards were like two café stools, side by side, and served as a place where they could sit and chat.

"So, I hear you're having trouble with your girlfriend," Alison said.

"How the heck did you hear that?" Matt asked. He was completely shocked that Alison would know anything about his problems with Cynthia.

"Oh, Paul told me," she said.

"Paul?" Matt asked, curiously. As far as he knew, the girls still knew of Paul as "Tom".

"Yeah, Paul," Alison said with a grin. "Actually, yesterday he told Amanda that his name was Paul, and not 'Tom'."

Matt laughed. "I see that he finally had to come clean on that one. I guess he must like Amanda."

Alison nodded, "I think so. They seem to be getting along famously."

"Wait," Matt said. "When did you see Paul?"

"Last night at the bar," Alison explained. "We were there, and Paul was there, and a few more guys from your ship, but you weren't there. It's too bad. We had a lot of fun."

"Oh. I wasn't feeling good last night," Matt said sheepishly. All of a sudden he sort of wished he hadn't moped around last night and that he had gone out. He could have spent time with Alison.

"That's sort of what Paul told me," she said. "Plus, he told me to come here today, and catch you while you were on duty."

"I can't believe he told you that," Matt groaned. "...and going back to the initial question, I can't believe he told you about the whole Cynthia thing."

"He didn't say much. He just told us that you had heard that your girlfriend might have been out with another guy, and that's why you didn't feel like going out last night," she said softly.

"Oh, he told you all that," Matt said.

She nodded.

"Well, he's got a big mouth then," Matt said. "Anyway, it's true that she was out and that she was seen with another guy, but I haven't spoken to her yet. I don't really know what was going on."

"Do you trust her?" Alison asked.

"Of course I trust her," Matt said firmly.

"If you trust her, then, there shouldn't be a problem," Alison said. "That's my advice to you."

Matt understood what Alison was saying, and he knew that she was right. However, he still felt that there were definite issues between himself and Cynthia. Logically, then, didn't that mean that he didn't trust Cynthia? He guessed that it did, but he didn't want to consider it at the moment.

Matt and Alison sat and talked for about two hours. Matt missed his lunch hour, but he didn't even notice. Finally, at 3PM she had to go. Matt had enjoyed her company.

"Don't eat all those cookies at once," she said. "But don't save them forever," she added.

"Don't worry," Matt assured her. "With the cooks on this tub, these cookies are a god-send."

Matt watched Alison as she crossed back over the brow and walked back down the jetty towards the parking lot. As she was about halfway back up the jetty, she turned to look back at the ship. Matt waved at her. She smiled and waved back, and then she continued on her way.

Matt wondered if he was ever going to see Alison again. After all, he got along with her so well. It would be a shame never to get the chance to talk to her again.

Mind you, she lived in New Westminster, and he was in Esquimalt. It wasn't too far away, and he would be able to call her sometime. Then, he realized that he didn't even have her number.

But, of course, Paul had it. He could get the number from Paul!

Perhaps she didn't want him to call her? After all, she knew that he had a girlfriend. He wasn't completely sure until he opened the cookie tin to get a cookie. At the bottom of the tin, he noticed a slip of paper. He pulled it out and unfolded it.

> *Matt, I thoroughly enjoyed our talk last Friday. Here is my phone number, just in case you wish to talk some more. Call me anytime. I'd love it.*
>
> *Alison*
>
> *PS. Have a cookie!*

Below the writing, he saw a smiling happy face and her phone number.

Matt whispered, "How thoughtful. Wow."

CHAPTER 9 / COLD SHOULDERING

Over the course of the weekend, Matt had tried to phone Cynthia several times. Each time, he had been getting more frustrated, and even more distraught. Now, it was Sunday evening, and he really had just one more chance to call her before they sailed the next morning. Surely, she would be home now.

Still in his duty watch uniform, Matt slipped off the ship to return to the bank of pay phones on the jetty. The phones were busy now, as many of the *Mackenzie*'s sailors were taking this opportunity to phone home before the ship sailed. Matt found an open phone and attempted to place the call.

The phone rang three times, and then, to Matt's utter surprise, Cynthia answered.

"Hello."

"I can't believe you're home," Matt said excitedly. "I've been trying to call you all weekend."

"I'm sorry, I've been busy. You know. Working and stuff," Cynthia explained.

"Yeah... I know. You're always so busy... it doesn't matter... I'm so, so glad I finally have the chance to talk to you. We're going to be at sea for the next three weeks, and I needed to hear your voice just once before we left." Matt wasn't kidding.

"Uh huh... So you'll be at sea for three weeks you say? Where are you going?" Cynthia replied.

"I can't exactly say where we are going. I can tell you though, that we aren't going anywhere important. We'll just be at sea... in the middle of nowhere."

"Oh, that's too bad," Cynthia said. "It sounds kind of boring. I wouldn't want to be you." She giggled a bit.

"Yeah, it will be boring," Matt laughed. "But you can rest assured that our country is safe when I'm defending the coast." He was trying to be witty, to lighten the mood, as he knew that he did have an important question to ask.

"Uh huh," Cynthia replied. She didn't appear to be amused.

Matt noticed that Cynthia didn't seem too talkative tonight. Usually she wanted to chat about work, but not tonight. Maybe she was tired?

"Ahhh Cynthia..." the phone line had gone silent. "Are you still there?"

"Yes, Matt."

"Ummm, I have a question to ask you."

"Okay, ask me," she said.

"Do you remember last weekend, on Saturday night, you said you were too tired to go out. Did you go out?"

"What are you talking about?" she asked.

"I just need to know if you wound up going out that night," Matt repeated the question.

She paused for a long while, and then she gave Matt the answer that seemed to be inevitable. "Yes. As a matter of fact, yes I did, and I apologize for not telling you about it. How did you know?"

"One of the guys I know here on the ship said he saw you out at Ivy's last Saturday night. As I recall, you told me that you were too tired to go out..."

Cynthia snapped back, "I knew this would happen! Oh, my lord, you navy boys are sure a bunch of gossip hounds aren't you?"

Matt was surprised by her drastic change of tone.

Cynthia continued to rant, "My girlfriend had called me and asked me to go out. I thought since I had just seen you the night before, I could go out somewhere on my own. I didn't want to bother you with the details because I didn't want the third degree like I'm getting now. I went out with her because she is my good friend and we never go out anymore... and she asked me at the last minute. As for you and I, sure we see each other a lot but we have our individual lives and friends."

Matt was silent. He was surprised by her rant. He had never heard her speak like this before.

The phone line remained silent for a few moments.

"Are you still there?" she said. "Hellooo? What do you have to say? Do you agree with me, or what?" She was demanding an answer.

Matt stammered as he spoke, "Well... I guess that I sort of agree... I'm not sure. You know that I wanted to see you lots before I went to sea for four weeks. I hardly saw you, and now I miss you like crazy."

"It's not my problem that you're gone away, now, is it?" she retorted.

"Yeah," Matt said. "I know that it was short notice, and all, but I have no control over that."

"Maybe you should find a different job, then."

"Okay, let's not get into that right now. I can't just rush off and give the navy two weeks' notice. It doesn't work that way," Matt explained.

"I know," Cynthia said. She had softened her tone a little bit now. But, there was still another important point that Matt felt the need to discuss.

"Cynthia, there is something else I need you to explain to me," Matt asked. "My friend that saw you at Ivy's also said that you were with the Gooch."

"Who is the Gooch?" She paused for a moment. "Do you mean Michael?" she asked.

"So you DO know Mike Gooch then?" Matt was a little more confident now.

"Yes, I know Michael. I have seen him before, in the bar. He is a friend of mine."

Matt continued, "Was he hitting on you Saturday night?"

Cynthia sighed, "Lots of guys hit on me. It doesn't mean anything."

Matt shot back, "Then he was hitting on you Saturday night?"

Cynthia was defensive. "Matt what are you getting at? What are you trying to say? Just say it already..."

Matt thought about it, and then he said calmly, "I think that I might as well get to the point. I think you're mad at me for leaving you this summer... that's what I think. And I think you're trying to punish me by going out with other guys."

Cynthia sighed, "You know what? You're right. I wish you weren't away this summer, and I wish we could be together. Since we can't be together, my life goes on. I want to have a good summer. I work hard, and I deserve to have fun. I can't have fun if I'm constantly thinking that you're away, and I can't just sit here like an old maid while you're sailing the seven seas. I'll hang out with whomever I want, and if they are other guys, then so be it. You'll just have to get used to it."

Matt didn't have anything to say in reply. Cynthia obviously didn't share the heartache he felt when they were apart. She seemed content to go out and be with other friends. Meanwhile, he ached for her every hour of the day. His feelings were bruised. His heart was breaking.

Matt lamented that this was something that he couldn't possibly repair right now. He felt that they could talk it through, and figure it all out. But he was miles away, and he wouldn't be back for three more weeks. He couldn't talk to her, face to face. He felt helpless.

"Cynthia, I'm sorry you feel this way," Matt said. "There is nothing I can say, or do, especially over the phone... Look, I'll be back in three weeks. I will see you then. Promise me that we will talk about this then?"

In a soft tone Cynthia said, "Goodbye Matt." Then she hung up the phone rather suddenly.

Matt was left holding the silent phone to his face. He realized that he didn't get an answer, and he didn't even have the chance to say goodbye. Finally, after a long minute, he hung up the phone himself.

He couldn't believe how badly that went. He started to think about what he was going to say when he was able to see her again in three weeks, but something in the back of his head told him that he might never get the chance. It was in the way she had said goodbye. Even if there really was a glimmer of hope to reconcile with Cynthia, Matt sensed that it was about to fade while he was hopelessly mired out at Whiskey 601.

* * *

The next morning was a blur to Matt. As the ship was scheduled to sail at 0800, the morning had started early for the crew of the *Mackenzie*.

As the great grey warship slipped her berth, there were only a few locals there to bid her farewell. It certainly wasn't as exciting as when they arrived. Of course, the leaving was always anti-climactic when compared to the arriving.

A small tugboat was on hand to pull the warship off her jetty and into the stream of the Fraser River. The tugboat slightly rotated the *Mackenzie* and pointed her in the correct direction, downstream toward the Pacific. Then, the tug cast off her lines and let the *Mackenzie* begin her outbound transit of the river under her own power. A pilot had been brought onboard to guide the ship down the narrow and treacherous Fraser and back out into the relative safety of the Strait of Georgia.

During the entire transit, the *Mackenzie*'s blind pilotage team had been "closed up" in the Operations Room, and Matt was very busy on the plotting table. Thankfully, all the action took his mind off his previous night's phone call with Cynthia.

Once the *Mackenzie* was clear of the Fraser River, the pilot was sent away by boat, and then the warship immediately cranked it up to 21 knots and sped away down the Strait of Georgia. Within a couple of hours, after navigating Boundary Passage and the Haro Strait, she changed course to the west and headed into the Strait of Juan de Fuca. Soon she would be out of the strait and back into the broad expanse of the Pacific Ocean.

Matt was just about to finish his forenoon watch in the Operations Room when the *Mackenzie* whizzed past the Victoria waterfront. They were miles offshore, but Matt still recognized the familiar radar echo of Ogden's Point and the Victoria Harbour entrance. He recalled his conversation with Cynthia the night before, and he began to wonder what Cynthia might be doing right now somewhere in that city. If only he could see her, just once, and talk to her. All he could do was sigh as the *Mackenzie* sped past, leaving Victoria behind and making a beeline for the Pacific.

Soon afterward, his relief, Leading Seaman James, showed up to take over the plotting table. He was right on time, as usual.

Always the cheerful one, James greeted Matt, "What's happening, Petey!"

Matt sighed, "It's not just a job it's an adventure, Jamesy."

James blurted out his response, with a smile, "I'm just trying to be all I can be..."

Matt smiled. He always thought it was hilarious when Canucks used these hackneyed US recruiting slogans. At least, James had managed to cheer him up a bit.

"Okay James, here is the situation report..."

As part of the watch turnover, Matt gave James a SITREP prior to him being relieved on watch. It went quickly as things were relatively routine at the moment. There were only three contacts on the plot, all merchant ship traffic inbound in the Strait of Juan de Fuca.

Just as Matt was completing his watch turnover, the ship's broadcast system came alive with the Executive Officer's voice:

"Do you hear there, this is the XO speaking. I feel it is very important to inform you of

our very special mission while we are at Whiskey 601. Over the weekend, while the ship was alongside in New West, Admiralty was formulating plans for us to intercept a brand new Balzam Class Soviet spy ship which we expect to find operating out at Whiskey 601. Now, we've seen these types of ships before close to our coasts, however, this time the situation is different. First, this is one of their best brand new ships. This is not one of the dirty trawlers we have seen in the past. Second, the Russians are here to spy on certain submarine operations of our American allies. The Americans are getting ready to sail their new Ohio Class platform, the Michigan, out of Bangor, Washington, and the Soviets are hoping to find it and track it. I shouldn't have to tell you that we certainly don't want them to do that. So, our mission for the next three weeks, or until we are relieved, is to make life a living hell for those Soviet spies! More information will be passed on to you in the coming days. That is all."

Matt knew that this type of announcement wasn't out of the ordinary. In fact, it was a regular occurrence on any warship for the Executive Officer to use the ship's broadcast system to make ship-wide announcements, usually about the ship's upcoming routine. However, it wasn't too often that the message was about operations with the Russian fleet.

Leading Seaman James looked at Matt. "Well that'll make things interesting for us at Whiskey. Don't you think?"

Matt grinned, "I guess!" Matt was surprised to hear that the *Mackenzie* was actually deploying on an important mission.

Matt quickly went over to the Operations Room safe and pulled out the latest edition of *Jane's Fighting Ships*. He placed the large book on the starboard plotting table, and he began to look up the entry for *Balzam* Class. When he got there, he noticed that there was already a bookmark on the page.

"I guess there has already been some interest in this class of vessel," Matt said as he read the entry.

He noted that there were two *Balzams* built, and only one served in the Pacific. It was named the *Aziya*. He looked at the photo of the *Aziya* that was in Jane's. It looked impressive; dark and ominous, long and bulky with two large domes forward.

"Interesting," Matt whispered. "I wonder what those domes are used for?"

Matt was always fascinated by the Soviet Navy, and this development was exciting for him. He read the entire entry in *Jane's Fighting Ships*, and then he read it again.

* * *

As soon as the *Mackenzie* returned to Whiskey 601, she had orders to begin shadowing the *Aziya*. The *Aziya* wasn't difficult to locate, as she was the only ship in the area. She was about the same size as the *Mackenzie*, but she was bulky and lacked any sort of stealth. On the radar, she produced a well-defined echo.

Soon, in the Operations Room they were tracking the *Aziya* as "Hostile 13". Now that her position course and speed were known, it only took a few minutes for the Operations Room to calculate an intercept course. Once this was done, the *Mackenzie* immediately changed course. On her new course, it was calculated that she would meet the *Aziya* in just over two hours.

* * *

Later that evening, the Executive Officer, Lieutenant-Commander Drapeau, entered the Operations Room. He made a beeline for the Operations Officer, Lieutenant Heywood.

"Lieutenant Heywood, tomorrow morning starting at 0800, I order you to double the watch in the Ops Room. I want both plots closed up, medium range and short range. We are going to begin 'shouldering operations' in the morning. We are going to war, and we need this place functioning as if we were at war."

"Shouldering? Are you sure?" Heywood questioned. "Is this coming from the Captain?"

"No, it's coming from me," Drapeau said. "Don't you worry. I will speak to the Captain about it. I just need you to be ready here in Ops."

"Isn't shouldering illegal?"

"Illegal? Mr. Heywood, would you please explain how you think I'd order something illegal."

Lieutenant Heywood rephrased his comment. "What I mean is, isn't there a treaty that disallows shouldering?"

"Yes, of course, but I believe that it's still a grey area. Don't forget, this is a Cold War. These Russian bastards in their brand new spy ship have come all the way over here to sneak up on our country. It is OUR home and native land. We owe them a little welcome, don't we?"

The Operation Officer relented, begrudgingly. "Sir, I will speak to the Operations Chief. On your order, we will double the watch in the morning."

* * *

Being back on watch in the Operations Room, Matt and Able Seaman Morrison had overheard the entire conversation. After the Executive Officer and the Operations Officer had left, Morrison asked the question, "What's shouldering?"

"I've read about this in one of the tactics manuals," Matt responded. "Shouldering is a Cold War tactic. It is when ships get close to each other at high speeds, and one tries to force the other to turn. Like if we get close to the Russian ship, and get just ahead of it, and then we turn into its path. It has to turn or hit us."

Morrison said, "That sounds dangerous."

"It's playing chicken," Matt explained. "Each ship just tries to keep their bow ahead of the other ship's bow and try to cut them off. If they turn into you, it's their fault. I've read during the Vietnam War Russian ships would even try to get in front of American aircraft carriers. You know, to try to force them to change course."

"What did Heywood say about the practice being outlawed?" Morrison asked.

"I'm not sure, but I think there was some sort of treaty laid down in the 70's that banned shouldering. I think that's what the Operations Officer was talking about."

"All I know is that it looks like we are going to 'one in two' tomorrow," Morrison said. He was disappointed, as he knew they were currently standing a "one in three" watch rotation, meaning they stood one in every three watches. However, if they went to a one in two rotation, the Radar Plotters would be required to stand every second watch.

"Yeah, you betcha. One on, seen off," Matt laughed.

"What does that mean, one on seen off?" Morrison asked.

"What? One on seen off? It means that you stand every second watch and that you're 'seen off' as a result," Matt explained.

Matt knew that he didn't have to explain "seen off" to Morrison. Every sailor knew that seen off meant that you were screwed over.

* * *

When Matt got off watch, he and Morrison headed back down to #4 Mess. They wasted no time telling the other Radar Plotters what they had heard, or more importantly that they were doubling their watch in the morning. This really got the ball rolling, as Master Seaman Burke muttered something about "fuckin' rumours" and then immediately stormed off to speak to the Operations Chief. It only took about twenty minutes, but Chief Cartwright himself came down to #4 Mess to settle the rumours.

"Okay lads, don't go spreading rumours. You're not going to one in two," the Chief assured everyone.

Matt responded, "But Chief, we heard the Executive Officer give the order, and he said we would be shouldering the Russian..."

The Chief cut him off, "Unfortunate for the XO and his grandiose 'shouldering' plans he doesn't actually call the shots. The Captain calls the shots, and he has said there would be no high-seas high-jinx with his ship. Those were his exact words. So, as I said, you guys can all stand down. Business as usual, do you understand?"

"Yes Chief," several of the sailors chimed in, in unison. Consensus wasn't hard to achieve in this situation.

Morrison said, "Stand down? You don't have to tell me twice Chief!"

"That's exactly what I figured, Morrison," the Chief responded. "Hey, what are you guys watching on TV? Is that some sort of workout program?" The Chief was pointing at the mess television, which was playing *20 Minute Workout*, yet again.

"That's *20 Minute Workout* Chief," Morrison answered. "One of the Signalmen has made an eight hour VHS tape of it. They play it continuously on Channel 5. We like to watch it. It relaxes us."

"I don't know how that can be relaxing for a young guy like you," the Chief noted as the TV program showed a closeup of a leotard-covered rump.

As the Chief was leaving the mess Matt took the opportunity to tease him a little, "Chief, what type of programs do the Chiefs and POs watch in the Chief's Mess?"

"Nature programs, mostly," the Chief responded. "Nature programs." Then he left the mess.

* * *

All through the evening, and into the night, the *Mackenzie* shadowed the Russian ship. It mostly remained on the starboard side of the *Aziya* keeping a distance that averaged at about 500 yards. In nautical terms, this was relatively close, but it was a safe distance being a quarter of a mile.

At 0345 hours, Matt returned to the Operations Room for the morning watch. When he arrived, he found that Able Seaman Morrison was already there, closed up on the radar display.

"I came a little early. I couldn't sleep. So punish me, send me to sea and make me a lowly Able Seaman," Morrison apologized.

Matt laughed. He thought that Morrison was a good egg.

Matt got his turnover from Leading Seaman James, and then he took over the plotting table.

"Centreline, report Hostile One Three," he asked Morrison to give him a fresh position on the *Aziya*.

Morrison responded, "Hostile One Three, three two zero, 500 yards."

Matt updated the position of the *Aziya* on the plot. Then he made a fresh calculation of her course and speed, and made a report to the bridge.

Matt pressed the intercom switch. "Bridge, Ops. Hostile one three. Three two zero at 500 yards. Course two nine five at 14 knots."

"Bridge roger. Report hostile one three."

Matt thought to himself. This was setting up to be an easy watch as there were no other vessels on the plot at the moment. Right now, all they had to do was update the position of the *Aziya* every three minutes and give an update to the bridge every six minutes, unless of course, the *Aziya* changed course and speed. Then he was to report that immediately.

"Why is the Russian ship identified by a hostile designation?" Morrison asked. "Isn't that just prejudicing the situation? We don't actually know that she is hostile to us. I mean she hasn't done anything hostile like point weapons at us?"

Matt waited for Morrison to finish his rambling before he answered. "Well, she is not friendly, she's definitely not an unknown and she is far from neutral. The only category left is hostile. Don't worry about semantics, that's the way we do things here... Russian ships are always referred to as hostile."

Morrison responded, "Okay, I just thought it was a good point to make."

Matt thought to himself that it was a valid point. After all, they weren't actually at war with the Soviet Union, so why was there a "hostile" when there were no "hostilities"?

"A Cold War is still a war," Matt said.

That pretty much ended the conversation.

* * *

By the next morning, the *Mackenzie* had been shadowing the *Aziya* all night, though she had been keeping her distance. At precisely 0800, the Captain arrived on the bridge and sat down in his special chair that was situated on the port side of the bridge.

"Okay, we don't want to run into this son-of-a-bitch but let's get a little closer, say 200 yards. Officer of the Watch, close the distance between us and the Russian. I want to take a good look at these boys."

The Officer of the Watch ordered "Starboard 10" and a speed change to 21 knots in order to close the distance between the Canadian and the Russian ships.

The bridge crew watched as the *Aziya* steadily got larger and larger until the *Mackenzie* took up station only 200 yards off her port quarter. From this distance, the Canadians could make out much greater detail of the Russian ship. The *Aziya* was bulky and high. Her main deck traversed all the way from the bow to the stern, but she had a main superstructure that was relatively large, likely to house the various operations activities that were going on inside. Furthermore, unusual for a ship her size, she had three major masts. One was forward; it was bristling with radar antennas of all shapes and sizes. The other two masts, one amidships and another aft, were outfitted with her suite of electronic warfare measures. Aside from the masts, her most predominant features were two large domes. They looked like large grey tennis balls, and they were situated both forward and aft of the radar mast.

"Look at all the antennas," the Captain said. "I wonder what they are hiding beneath those grey domes?"

It wasn't just the Captain that was agog by the sight of this new Russian ship. The entire bridge staff was ogling the Russian, plus there were many more sailors gawking from various positions on the upper decks of the *Mackenzie*.

"Let's move up abeam of her," the Captain said as he brought his binoculars up to his eyes. He was scanning the Russian ship for activity.

"That's odd. I don't see any activity. She's quite buttoned up," the Captain remarked as the *Mackenzie* moved up to a position on the beam of the *Aziya*.

The *Aziya* appeared deserted as she moved through the water at a steady 14 knots. From this distance, you could hear the groan of her engines and the roar of her bow through the ocean waves, but her empty decks made her seem like a ghost ship.

Just then, the starboard lookout pointed out that there was some activity aft.

The Captain scanned the after part of the *Aziya* with his binoculars, "Yes, I see it, near the quarterdeck. There is a crew working on a piece of deck equipment very near the stern... maybe planned maintenance or maybe repairs... that might be their towed array sonar?"

"How can you tell if it's the towed array?" the Officer of the Watch asked.

"It's very near that large object that seems to be shaped like a reel. It's covered up, so it's hard to tell, but I'm thinking that it's the reel that holds the towed array tube."

The Captain thought he might be onto something. He ordered, "Pipe the Combat Officer to the Bridge."

The pipe was made. A minute later, the Combat Officer arrived on the bridge. "Lieutenant Whitehall, excellent," he pointed over toward the Russian ship. "Take a look aft and tell me what you see."

Lieutenant Whitehall picked up a pair of binoculars and scanned the stern of the Russian ship. "They're working on some fitted equipment, Sir," he said.

"I can see that, "the Captain replied. "What I am wondering… is that their towed array sonar winch?"

Lieutenant Whitehall, who also doubled as the Intelligence Officer aboard the *Mackenzie*, was the closest thing they had to an expert. In fact, he and the Executive Officer had attended a special briefing back in Esquimalt on the weekend, while the crew was languishing in New Westminster.

"Sir, from our intelligence reports, that is exactly what we believe that piece of equipment to be. From the briefing though, it was still only a guess, and the briefing officers couldn't even say with one-hundred percent certainty that this ship even had a towed array system."

"Really?" said the Captain. "Well if she didn't have a towed array sonar system then she wouldn't be here trying to track the *Michigan* would she? She likely needs something like a towed array to hear an Ohio Class submarine. They are very quiet, aren't they?"

"Well, that's just it sir. The Ohio Class is very quiet. Still, the *Aziya* has come to this place at this moment in time. The Soviets clearly feel that they can find the *Michigan*. As well, she is exhibiting the tactics of a towed array search. These reasons indicate that she indeed does have a towed array system."

"Yes, that's true… and it looks like they're having trouble with it. Let's open up the distance to 500 yards but let's still keep an eye on them."

* * *

Unlike the *Aziya*, where the decks were mostly empty of sailors, the

Mackenzie's decks were busy. Being naturally curious, many of *Mackenzie*'s crew were out on the deck checking out the Soviet ship, many even peering through binoculars to get the best view. With this many sailors on deck, the banter is usually lively.

"What are these Russian bastards doing way over here in Canadian waters?"

"You know, we are out past 12 miles. These are actually international waters."

"I thought Canada had a 200 mile limit?"

"Yep, but that's just for fishing. These guys aren't fishing... I don't think."

"There is no fishing rig on that monster. Look at those huge domes, what do you think is inside those?"

"Secret radars, I think. They put the domes on them to hide them from the Americans."

"I think they are for space communications. You know, to talk to Russian satellites."

"Oh, really?"

"Yeah, and that's high-powered shit. Do you think that they are beaming our nuts with radiation right now, especially now that we are this close?"

"Those fuckers! You know if I had my hunting rifle I could take out one of those commies from here."

"Just like hunting gophers back in Saska-bush, eh?"

"We could take out all these commie motherfuckers. Then we could go straight home and get laid."

"Do you think that there might be some greasy Russian bastard over there with a rifle pointed at your head right now? I wouldn't doubt it."

"I'd like to see him try it. We'd launch our full arsenal in retribution."

"What full arsenal?"

"The Americans of course. They'd push the button. They'd launch everything in one second."

"Are you sure?"

"Yes, they're just looking for a reason to go off. Aren't they?"

"So they blow up the world. How will that work for us?"

"We'll just stay at sea until the radiation goes away. A year or two."

"That sounds boring. What'll we do for fun?"

"We'll sail down to Tijuana. You can have all kinds of fun there."

* * *

In the Operations Room, Matt was plotting tracks on the *Mackenzie* and the *Aziya*, and nothing else. There was one merchant ship in range of the radar, but he was out at a distance of 30 miles. Too far away to worry about at this point in time.

"Where is this American sub everybody keeps talking about?" Morrison asked.

"Who knows," Matt replied. "It's stealthy and it's underwater. We'll never hear it or see it."

"Couldn't we pick it up on sonar?"

"No way, we don't have a decent passive sonar on this tub." Matt explained. "We would have to switch on our active sonar and ping the shit out of the ocean. We don't want to do that."

"Of course not," Morrison agreed. "Then we would give away the sub's position."

"That's right," Matt confirmed. "There is nothing we can do, but keep on shadowing the Russian. Watch him, maybe get in his way... you know."

"...basically, we would be a gnat on a buffaloes' arse," Morrison added.

"That's right."

"Do we even know which day the American sub is supposed to set sail?" Morrison asked.

Matt replied, "We don't know. But, I'll tell you what. The day that they tell us to stop being a pest is the day after it has occurred."

* * *

Now it was twilight. In the darkening night, the ocean was a single dark mass that rolled perpetually. Daylight had gone. Any wisps of fading sunlight had now completely disappeared. The landscape now consisted of dark ocean wave tops that were lit somewhat by a mostly full moon.

On the upper deck of the *Mackenzie* the two Leading Seaman, Matt Petersen and Paul Legere, looked out over the darkening ocean. It was a common occurrence on a Canadian ship, especially when the weather was nice, to stand out on the deck and get some fresh air. Nobody likes being cooped up indoors for too long.

The ship was rolling very steadily, so they stood with their backs to the after superstructure, as a shelter from the breeze. Also, leaning against something solid helped to steady themselves against the rolling sea.

Matt complained, "These damn seas are always rolling out here at Whiskey. When does this stop?"

"Probably never... hell never freezes over, does it?" Paul lamented.

The two sailors stared across the wave tops at the *Aziya*, silhouetted in the growing moonlight about 600 yards off their beam. The *Mackenzie* seemed to be on a parallel track but positioned ever so slightly astern, though she was keeping pace with the *Aziya* at about 14 knots.

"What do you thing they're doing over there right now?" Paul asked.

Matt was pretty sure he knew, "Same thing they've been doing all day. She's conducting towed array sonar operations. She is trying to discover a track for an American sub. That's why she's on a steady track. Her towed array sonar tail is probably deployed. We're here to make so much noise that she won't be able to hear her target."

Paul nodded in agreement. "That's all the Canadian Navy is good for these days... providing background noise for the Americans."

Matt heard Paul's remark, but he kept on talking about the sonar. It was far more fascinating to him. "The only thing is that her sonar is likely deployed deep, so as to listen beneath a thermal layer in the ocean."

"So, if the American sub is also beneath that layer?"

"That's right," Matt affirmed. "She won't hear us at all, she'll hear the sub."

"It's very complicated," Paul said.

"Still, we can always do our best to make her life miserable."

Paul sighed. "Look at all the antennas. She's a radar and comms behemoth! I thought this was all there was to these ships, but you're saying she has sonar too?"

"Actually this ship is brand new, and she was built with everything but the kitchen sink," Matt explained. "Radar, electronic warfare suite, both passive and active sonar. See those big domes, we are not even one-hundred percent sure what kind of system they are covering."

The two huge domes were silhouetted in the moonlight. They were the most striking feature on the *Aziya*.

"Wow. So dark and forbidding," Paul said. "I wonder what kind of commie bastards crew a ship like that."

"I'm sure she's full of sonar and radar operators as well as dozens of electronic warfare specialists. All trained to spy for mother Russia. Plus there must be a section of KGB that is onboard to keep everybody in line and make sure nobody defects... I'm guessing," Matt said.

"Why do we do this?" Paul asked.

"What do you mean," Matt replied.

"What I mean is that they've got enough nuclear missiles to blow up the world a thousand times, and so do we. Yet, nobody really wants to blow everything up. Still, we keep facing off like we just might do it."

Matt sighed, "Isn't that the truth." After a moment he added, "It seems that war is something mankind desires. It's inevitable."

"That's deep", Paul said. "You're thinking way too much..." he teased Matt a bit, but then he relented to the conversation. "I recall reading George Orwell's 1984 in high school. He said that wars will come and go, but they were always desirable as they helped preserve the special mental atmosphere that a hierarchical society needs. In other words, we always wanted to be fighting a war or preparing for a war."

"I remember 1984. Didn't he also say something like 'War is not meant to be won. It is meant to be continuous'. Basically, he meant to imply that governments needed wars to stay in power."

"I believe so," Paul agreed.

"1984. Huh... isn't that next year?" Matt asked, though the answer was evident.

"Yes, it is. Watch out for Big Brother," Paul said. "He's watching you right now." He pointed over towards the *Aziya*.

"Yeah, they're probably listening to this whole conversation. I hope they aren't as bored as I am," Matt sighed.

Paul said, "Yeah, probably..."

Matt was now staring off towards the horizon. He was looking east, back towards Vancouver Island. He remained silent for a long pause.

Paul noticed that Matt was suddenly unengaged in their conversation, "Are you thinking about the Cynthia thing?" he asked.

"Yes. Sorry," Matt apologized. "I can't help but think that she is off somewhere with the Gooch. It's pissing me off to no end that I'm out here, and I can't do anything about it."

"You gotta be sure that she is messing around before you go off," Paul recommended. "My advice to you is to put it all out of your mind until we get back to Esquimalt."

"Yeah maybe," Matt said.

"It's for the best. Stewing about it is just going to mess you up even more," Paul said.

"I just don't get how she can be so nonchalant about misleading me. She knew that I wanted to see her as much as I could before I went to sea," Matt lamented. "Then, to find out she stepped out anyway, and even met up with the Gooch. I can't believe it."

"But you still don't know that anything actually happened with the Gooch," Paul replied.

"Yeah," Matt said. "That's right."

"So, maybe nothing happened."

"It was the way she was so evasive about it. I am sure that something happened," Matt sighed.

"Your only course of action is to figure it all out when you get home. You can't do anything out here, except worry yourself stupid about it," Paul said.

"Yeah," Matt said quietly. "You're right about that."

Of course, he knew that Paul was right. He knew very well that he shouldn't think about the situation, but he couldn't help himself. He may have agreed with Paul's advice, but his mind was tugging in a different direction.

* * *

On the *Aziya,* they could have listened in on the conversation if they had wanted to. They had the equipment to do so. However, they weren't really interested in listening in on two Canadian Sailors. They were far more concerned about listening for a brand new American submarine. The *Michigan* represented an immediate threat to their homeland; a war machine so powerful it could single-handedly annihilate everything and everyone they loved.

The Canadians were suspicious that the *Aziya* was conducting sonar operations, and, in fact, she was doing just that. She was equipped with an experimental towed array sonar, and the hope was that this new and advanced towed array would be sensitive enough to detect the *Michigan.*

A towed array sonar is a passive system, meaning that it doesn't transmit a ping, it merely listens. The sensor consists of a tube, hundreds of meters long, that is filled with very sensitive microphones that are referred to as "hydrophones". The tube is trailed behind the ship, providing a very long and sensitive listening device that is able to detect contacts at extreme ranges. Also, because of the length of the sensor, bearings to contacts can be triangulated and the actual positions of the detected vessels can be calculated.

The value of having a towed array sonar is that you are able to clear the detecting ship's "baffles", which is a blind spot that normally affects a hull-mounted passive sonar. As well, the towed array is always able to detect a contact at a much longer range, hundreds of miles in some cases. The downside is that the ship needs to remain on a steady course and at a relatively slow speed. If rapid maneuvering is required, the tube needs to be reeled in quickly.

The *Aziya's* crew was getting good use of this brand new system. The tube was currently deployed deep, well below a thermal layer that currently lay at a depth of 80 meters. Though it meant that she had to plod along at a relatively low speed and on a steady course, they hoped that they would be able to hear the near silent whisper of the *Michigan* as it slipped out of the Strait of Juan de Fuca.

Currently the sea swell was hitting her broadside, which meant that the *Aziya* rolled steadily. The rolling was a nuisance, but she kept on a steady course regardless of the sea, and also despite the pesky Canadian destroyer that was always on her beam.

Since the towed array system on the *Aziya* was rigged at the last minute, it did have some problems. The remote control system had been faulty in the past, and had been repaired. However, it only operated properly for a few days before it was accidentally damaged by a crewmember. It required another repair, but now it needed a part that would have to be obtained in their next resupply. Meanwhile, the actual sonar system still worked well. They just couldn't deploy or retrieve it remotely.

This was not a huge deficiency. Once it was deployed, they usually didn't need to retrieve it, except in the case of an emergency. The Officer of the Deck simply ordered a sailor be required to stand by on the upper deck next to the winch system, just in case they needed to raise or lower the tube quickly. Essentially, the faulty remote control system was replaced by a lone deckhand.

CHAPTER 10 / SEAMAN BONDARENKO

Seaman Bondarenko was the lone man on deck. It really wasn't fair that he had to stand this unfamiliar watch alone at night. However, since the remote control circuits for the towed array sonar winch were "fried" two weeks ago, this had been one of his many duties. Perhaps the engineer that sprayed the seawater into the winch control panel could stand this horrible watch. After all, he was the one that had destroyed the panel in the first place.

It made sense that someone had to stand by the switches, ready to raise and lower the system just in case there was a required change in the equipment. However, he had been here for over two hours! Nobody had relieved him, and he had received no orders. It was almost as if they had forgotten him. It certainly was strange, and it wasn't the place he wanted to be, but his orders were clear. He was to stand by the winch and listen to the intercom for further instructions. Nevertheless, there was nothing to be heard from the intercom but static.

It was a cool night out on the deck, even though it was summer. There wasn't much wind, but the seas were still fairly high. The ship wasn't going very fast, so the *Aziya* rolled dramatically every time one of the high Pacific rollers came by. Bondarenko tightly clutched onto a nearby railing. He had been there so long he thought his hands might be actually locked onto the cold steel pipe.

Vitaliy Bondarenko was a young man only 20 years of age. He grew up on a state-run farm near Popeliany just outside the Ukrainian city of Lviv. When he turned 18, like all good citizens, he reported to Lviv to be conscripted into the Soviet Navy. It was to be a mandatory term of three years' service. His hope was to do his three years and return to Popeliany where he would be reunited with his sweetheart Natalya.

Now, it had been 26 months since leaving home and Vitaliy was terribly homesick. It wasn't so bad when he was in the Seaman's school at Vladivostok, but things quickly got worse. Since he had been posted to the cursed ship *Aziya*, it was like being in prison. They hadn't been in port for the past 18 months, and no mail for the past six!

In his present situation, he couldn't help but to ponder his fate.

"What am I doing here?" he thought. "Thousands of miles away from home, and now I'm hanging onto this railing for dear life!"

He could always take his mind off his predicament simply by thinking of his girlfriend back in the Ukraine. Thinking of Natalya soothed him. He began to contemplate what it would be like to return to Natalya and see her again. She would meet him at the train station. They would hug and then they would kiss. He could even imagine that he could smell the sweetness of her beautiful red hair.

Vitaliy closed his eyes and sighed deeply. He continued to think of Natalya as the steady roll of the ship lulled him.

* * *

In the *Mackenzie*, the "Big Eyes" binoculars were an impressive optical instrument. As the name implied, they were, in fact, really large binoculars. Of course, the *Mackenzie* had dozens of pairs of binoculars. However, this pair were so large they had to be mounted on a special pedestal just aft of the bridge.

Although they were especially powerful in daylight use, they did not have a night vision attachment. Even though, on a night when there was plenty of ambient light, even moonlight, they could be very useful. Tonight was one of those nights, and there just happened to be a set of eyes on the *Mackenzie* that was watching Seaman Bondarenko.

The *Mackenzie's* Signalman of the Watch was rather bored. There wasn't too much action for a Signalman when your ship was sailing alone. When you were out at sea with the squadron, there was always activity such as flashing light communications and semaphore, which you would have to decode for the Officer of the Watch. But, the *Mackenzie* was out here all alone. There wasn't much to do.

It was quiet. However, he did know that when there was this much moonlight, there were still things you could look at, even in the middle of the night. Right now, they were sailing close to an interesting subject, a huge

Russian spy ship that was currently conducting an intelligence gathering mission. Of course, when you had access to Big Eyes binoculars you could actually spy back.

The night air was cool, but he was still comfortable. His biggest environmental issue was with how the *Mackenzie* rolled something awful on this current course. He needed a way to steady himself, and the Big Eyes pedestal doubled as a solid base in which to hold.

Therefore, the Signalman of the Watch spent his time with his arms clutched onto the binocular pedestal and his eyes on the eyepieces. As the ship rolled, he swayed from left to right. It was almost as if he and the pedestal were slow dancing.

He mostly kept his eyes on the *Aziya*. In fact, it was about 30 minutes ago that he had first noticed a single individual standing out on the deck of the Russian ship. He had been watching him steadily since. When the Russian ship rolled to the starboard, the individual's face became illuminated by the moonlight. He saw a round white face, but that's all he could see at this range.

He wondered, why is that sole person standing there? Is he having a smoke, or is he taking a break? Maybe he is just trying to get some fresh air, or he is a seasick sailor that feels better out on the deck.

"What are we both doing out here," the Signalman whispered to himself. "We should be at home in our warm beds."

* * *

The *Aziya* had been rolling very steadily. However, it was at this time that an unusually large wave lifted her awkwardly. Suddenly, the *Aziya* rolled abnormally, causing Vitaliy to be thrown forward abruptly. The surprise of this violent roll and the numbness of his hands were just enough to make him lose his grip on the railing. Without a handhold to steady him, he clumsily waltzed forward toward the side of the ship, all the while trying desperately to control his momentum. Now completely off balance, the steep angle of the deck sent him crashing into the outer guardrail at the side of the ship. Vitaliy tumbled over the guardrail and fell face first into the grey foaming sea. He hit the water with a dull splash. The wind, and the roar of the ship through the water, swallowed up any sound that was created by his hitting the water.

"Holy shit," the Signalman on the *Mackenzie* said, aloud.

He was sure that he had just seen the Russian sailor flip over the side of the ship. Now, he kept on scanning with the Big Eyes, and he did not see the man on deck anymore. Even more frantic now, he scanned the deck again just to confirm that he hadn't been imagining what he had seen. It took a second for what he had seen to resonate in his own mind.

"He's gone over the side," he said aloud.

* * *

The first sensation Vitaliy had was the coldness of the water. It immediately shocked him, and he began to hyperventilate. As he was panting uncontrollably, he attempted to stay afloat by treading water frantically. He flailed his arms and legs desperately, but he found that he was barely able to keep his head above water. Twice, he slipped below the surface, and twice he managed to rise up and gulp a breath of air. Each time, despite his frenetic struggle to stay afloat, he again sank below the water. Unfortunately, he was fighting a losing battle, as his boots were filling with water and his quilted jacket was becoming waterlogged. He struggled as hard as he could, but as his buoyancy became negative, he began to sink. All he could manage to do was to hold his last gulp of air as he was mercilessly dragged down, beneath the ocean waves.

Vitaliy held his last breath as he sank. He had ceased his frantic fight to stay afloat, and he now felt more at peace as he slipped deeper beneath the waves. Completely submerged, his body was not active, but his mind was racing. He thought about how he so wished he was at home, and not in the dreadful navy. He wanted to be with Natalya again. His dear sweetheart Natalya, the one who had kindly knitted a gift of red wool socks for him to take on his journeys. He recalled their last day together; she was in a brown sweater that matched his brown hair; he was in a red sweater that matched her red hair. He could also picture her last letter to him. It was covered in lipstick kisses. He remembered how she had filled the margins of the letter with hearts and the words "Natalya plus Vitaliy", over and over again. He imagined what it would be like to kiss her again. He could almost smell her.

Then, he thought that he could smell his mother's homemade bread. He couldn't help but think how wonderful it would be to be back on the farm and to see his dear mother again. He pictured her, but she was crying. She was sobbing uncontrollably after being told the news that her beloved son had drowned somewhere in the Pacific Ocean.

Then he recalled Natalya again. He remembered her at the train station, with him, as he was about to depart. He recalled how she made him promise to return to Popeliany as soon as his three years in the navy had ended. Vitaliy felt an overpowering sadness, now that he wouldn't be able to keep that promise.

Suddenly, Vitaliy snapped out of his underwater daze. It had been over two years since he had received drown-proofing training in Vladivostok, but he began to recall what he had been trained to do. Methodically, he reached down with both hands and located the life-vest pouch at his waist. How could he have forgotten that he was wearing this basic item of a seaman's kit? He opened the pouch and pulled the life vest up and over his head, and then with one quick motion he reached back down and pulled the inflation tab. Finally, he felt the satisfaction of the vest filling with gas. His ascent back to the surface was rapid. He popped out of the water like a cork, and gasped a deep breath.

He continued to breathe deeply as his eyes began to clear. He looked around in wonderment. He was alive! However, his elation quickly turned to horror as he saw the dark silhouette of the *Aziya* clearly sailing away from his position. It was a sailor's dread; he was overboard and his own ship was leaving him behind!

Vitaliy yelled as loud as he could. He waved his arms in panic. Nobody saw him, and nobody heard him.

He was now alone. A mere dot among the high rolling waves of the Pacific Ocean.

* * *

Back on the *Mackenzie*, training had taken over. The Signalman had immediately begun to raise the alarm by shouting, "Man Overboard, Man Overboard, Man Overboard" at the top of his lungs. This caused the Starboard Lookout, up on the right side of the Bridge, immediately to hit the Man Overboard alarm button. The alarm began to ring loudly and frantically, alerting everybody in the vicinity of the bridge there was a man overboard situation.

A few seconds later, the Quartermaster rang the Action Alarm and began to make an announcement throughout the ship, "MAN OVERBOARD, MAN OVERBOARD, RED WATCH TO RESCUE STATIONS". It only took seconds, but the entire ship had now sprang into action.

Meanwhile, the Signalman was pointing at what he thought was the position of man in the water astern of the *Aziya*.

The Officer of the Watch ordered, "Report the man in the water, range and bearing!"

The Signalman replied, "He's astern of the Russian Ship. I spotted him on

Big Eyes. I can't see him now. I am continuing to scan the water for him."

The Officer of the Watch yelled back, "Confirm that the man overboard is from the Russian Ship?"

"That's affirmative sir!"

* * *

Leading Seaman Matt Petersen was on watch in the Operations Room when he heard the ringing of the Man Overboard Alarm. He too was well trained in how to react to this situation.

When the Man Overboard Alarm rang, it was standard operating procedure to switch the plotting table to a lower scale, half mile to the inch, and then to place a special symbol on the plot. The symbol was two black concentric circles, one-third of an inch high, and it was to be placed 500 yards astern of the ship.

Matt instinctively switched the scale of the table. Then he picked up the dividers and measured 500 yards, which was one-quarter of a mile. On the plotting table, this distance was one-half of an inch. Matt did the math in an instant, and in his head, as he had been trained to do. He plotted the symbol as quickly and neatly as possible, and marked the symbol with the current time.

Just then, the bridge intercom crackled, "OPS BRIDGE, MAN IN WATER IS FROM HOSTILE ONE THREE."

Matt immediately responded, "OPS ROGER, MAN IN WATER IS FROM HOSTILE ONE THREE."

Able Seaman Morrison was on the radar. Once he heard this exchange, he immediately reported the position of the *Aziya*, "HOSTILE ONE THREE, BEARING 314, RANGE 900 YARDS."

Matt quickly updated the position of the *Aziya* on the plot, and then he placed a second Man Overboard symbol the standard distance of 500 yards astern of the *Aziya*. He put a line through the first symbol he had made, thus nullifying it. Then, he quickly gauged the range and bearing to the new symbol.

"BRIDGE OPS, MAN IN WATER BEARING 325, RANGE 850 YARDS." Matt made his initial report to the Bridge.

"BRIDGE ROGER, REPORT MAN IN WATER EVERY MINUTE", the Bridge responded.

Matt would follow the order with precision. Every minute, he would use the intercom to report the current range and bearing to the Man Overboard symbol. He would continue to do so until the Bridge told him to "cease reporting".

* * *

On the bridge, all eyes were on a patch of ocean that was now hundreds of yards astern of the *Aziya*. "If you spot him again, point at him and don't take your eyes off him!" the Officer of the Watch ordered.

Meanwhile, the *Aziya* had continued on her course. She was clearly unconcerned of the action occurring to her stern. Even as the *Mackenzie* made a hard turn to starboard, and proceeded on a course to intercept its wake, the Russian ship continued on its way. The *Aziya's* officers knew their towed array sonar tube was deployed deep, and there was no way for the *Mackenzie* to cause any real disturbance to their operation.

Over the bridge intercom Matt's voice was heard, "MAN IN THE WATER BEARING 035 RANGE 500 yards."

The Officer of the watch ordered to the Wheelhouse, "STARBOARD 10 STEER 035!" The Wheelhouse acknowledged the order, and the ship's bow came a little further to the right as the ship settled on a course of 035.

The Signalman of the Watch remained on the Big Eyes, methodically scanning the ocean waves ahead of the *Mackenzie*. Despite his effort, he did not see anything.

* * *

Vitaliy Bondarenko was still bobbing up and down, a victim of every high swell that passed through his position. With the inflated life vest, he floated like a cork on the very top of a vigorous ocean.

He felt he was totally alone. Without hope, he imagined exactly how it was going to end... he was going die slowly of hypothermia. He was already cold. His teeth were chattering and he could feel his lips tingling. There was no way he was ever going to get out of this mess. Sure, he could begin to swim for it, but he didn't know which way to swim. He knew that he would have to head east, but he had no way to determine which way was east, and he didn't know how far it was to land. It could be hundreds of miles.

From his training, he also recalled that he would get hypothermia quickly in the cold ocean and that he lost most of his body heat through his crotch, armpits and the top of his head. In Vladivostok, he was instructed that he should cross his legs tightly and keep his arms close by his side. Also, he was to place a special cap on his head that was enclosed in a pouch on his life vest. It was made from white reflective material and was designed to insulate his scalp. Vitaliy dutifully opened the pouch, and then unrolled the reflective cap.

He placed it on his head, and then he fastened the velcro chinstrap. Finally, he crossed his legs and his arms and tried to preserve as much body heat as he could.

Vitaliy just rested his body as the big Pacific rollers threw him up and down like a cork. He tried to take his mind off his dilemma, but he knew from his training, despite his precautions the cold water would make him hypothermic within minutes. He would perish soon afterward.

Vitaliy knew that it would take a true miracle to save him. He didn't want to think about it. As he grew even colder, he kept his mind on his home; his home back in the Ukraine.

* * *

Meanwhile, the *Mackenzie* had turned and was now on a course that was surprisingly near where it had to go to pass right by Vitaliy Bondarenko. They still did not have visual contact with him, but they had an idea where he was, based on the Operations Room plot. But, that's all they had. They would have to continue to search and hope that they got lucky enough to find the man.

The bridge team were the primary eyes in the search. Both the Port and Starboard Lookouts had their binoculars trained forward and were scanning the waves for anything unusual. In fact, any non-essential persons were also on the bridge scanning the ocean. They saw nothing.

"BRIDGE OPS. MAN IN THE WATER BEARING 036 AT 300 YARDS", the Operations Room made another report over the intercom.

The Officer of the Watch quickly replied, "BRIDGE ROGER." As he did this, he noticed that the Captain had entered the Bridge.

Without hesitation, the Captain came directly to the Officer of the Watch and ordered, "SITREP?"

The Officer of the Watch, experienced at giving situation reports to the boss, quickly summed up the proceedings, "We've got a man in the water from the *Aziya*. He was spotted going over the side on the Big Eyes by the Signalman of the Watch. The alarm was raised immediately. The Operations Room has the man on the plot at 036 degrees 300 yards."

"Roger," the Captain said. "How long?"

"The man has been in the water for seven minutes. The current sea temperature is 45 degrees Fahrenheit. The manual says severe hypothermia is estimated in 20 minutes."

"We better find him soon," the Captain said. "He's only got just over ten minutes left."

The Captain adjusted his *Mackenzie* ball cap and then announced aloud to the entire bridge team, "A Russian in the water? Let's pick him up shall we! We can show him some Canadian hospitality!"

The bridge team all paid credence to the Captain's remark. In fact, they were already busy trying to fulfill his wishes.

* * *

The Signalman of the Watch was still using the Big Eyes binoculars, scanning the ocean waves ahead of the ship. Finally, he thought he saw an object about 10 degrees off the starboard bow. It was a little white dot, reflecting light off the moonlight. It was only visible intermittently as it rose and fell at the mercy of the giant waves, but it was definitely there. The signalman thought it might be flotsam, maybe a piece of floating styrofoam, but he had to report it.

"OFFICER OF THE WATCH, SIGNALMAN OF THE WATCH. RED ONE ZERO, WHITE OBJECT IN WATER, MEDIUM RANGE."

Now, many eyes scanned ahead at 10 degrees off the Starboard bow looking for the white object. First, the Starboard Lookout said he saw it, and then the Officer of the Watch himself said he spotted it. Finally, when they were a little closer, the Signalman of the Watch on the powerful Big Eyes actually confirmed that he could see the man's face, and he was now positive that it actually was a man in the water. Apparently, the white object that he had initially spotted now looked to be a reflective cap that the man in the water was wearing on his head.

The Officer of the Watch ordered the engines to slow, and finally to stop. As the ship shuddered to a stop, he then ordered, "LAUNCH THE SEABOAT."

* * *

Down on the boat deck, the boat crew was already in the seaboat, a 27-foot fiberglass whaler suspended over the side of the ship on two davits. It hadn't taken long for the boat crew and the deckhands that would do the lowering to get to their rescue station, three minutes on the average from their bunks to the boat deck. The response was usually very quick, as they were well practiced due to the multitude of drills they performed. But, this was the real deal, and not an exercise. There was an edge to everybody's conduct. There were no mistakes. They were ready to go.

When the order "Launch the Seaboat" was given, the deckhands on the two capstans began to lower the two sets of boat falls in unison. Launching the seaboat can be tricky in rough seas, yet the Canadian Navy had ample expertise. There was plenty of tension on the blocks and tackles, as the ship continued to rise and fall, and sway to the port and starboard with the ocean swell, however, the gear was built for these types of conditions. As well, each man in the boat had a vertical steadying line that he hung onto tightly in order to have a safe descent with the seaboat. It was the type of procedure that needed to be done carefully.

As the seaboat was almost low enough to be touching the water, the Boat Coxswain squeezed the fuel bulb on the outboard motor fuel tank, engaged the choke and then pulled on the starter cord of the outboard motor. Everyone on the boat deck heard the motor sputter to life. Seconds later the boat hit the water, and the motor was revved by the boat Coxswain.

The order was given to remove the lifting gear, and the seaboat was now free of the ship. In fact, in rough seas, this was something that needed to be done quickly as it could be dangerous for the seaboat to be thrown up against the ship, even with forward and aft steadying lines. The sooner the seaboat was free, the better.

The Boat Coxswain looked up to see if anyone on the boat deck was indicating a bearing to the man in the water, which was something that was done when the boat deck could see the man, but they couldn't see anything in the dark. The Boat Coxswain would have to rely on directions from the bridge, via radio, to pinpoint the location of the man in the water.

* * *

The Bridge had eyes on the Russian. They could see his white cap bobbing up and down in the ocean swell. He would disappear when he was in the trough of the swell, and he would reappear when he rose to the top.

"Does it appear that he is moving?" the Officer of the Watch asked the Starboard Lookout.

"No, Sir," he replied. "It's just his head visible and I can't see any movement."

The Officer of the Watch could also see the seaboat heading out in his general direction with two searchlights scanning the water as they went forward, but they were not even close to the man in the water. However, after a few directions were given via radio, the seaboat started to move directly towards the Russian.

* * *

Vitaliy Bondarenko was already groggy and numb from the cold water, and he was shivering uncontrollably. He was trying desperately to battle a chill that now seemed to have invaded his entire body.

In his mind, though, he thought that he could hear the sound of an outboard motor. At first, he imagined the sound as part of a wonderful dream of being rescued. Then, he also thought that he saw searchlights scanning nearby on the surface of the ocean. He tried to wake himself up and convince himself that this was not a dream, but he found that he was just too numb.

Vitaliy's mind began to ponder, "Maybe my replacement on the *Aziya* arrived early and noticed me gone… and now they have turned around and are looking for me. I need to wave my arms and speak up, so they notice me." He tried, but his arms did not move. He could not speak, as he realized that he was already too cold for speech. He shivered uncontrollably instead.

He looked upward and saw a light shining directly into his eyes. Now, he seemed to appreciate he was very far-gone, and the light must be something he was imagining. He put his head back and closed his eyes, merely trying to accept that he was close to the end, and the light he saw was heaven sent.

The outboard motor sound got closer and closer. It ebbed and flowed with the rise and fall of the big Pacific rollers, but it got closer, and closer, and closer. It now sounded like it was maneuvering. Vitaliy opened his eyes once again to see the hull of a large grey boat rise over the top of the swell, and settle in the water right next to him.

All of a sudden, there was such a commotion. The sailors in the boat were yelling orders to each other. Then, the hull of the boat was right next to him, and two different hands seemed to stretch down toward him. Vitaliy stared at the hands in disbelief as they reached out at him. One grabbed a hold of his collar, and the other had a hold of his life vest. They both heaved up on him as a third hand reached for the small of his back and grabbed his belt. All three hands pulled together, and they managed to yank him into the boat.

Delirious, Vitaliy lay in the bottom of the boat. He was unsure of where he was, and he still wasn't sure he hadn't died and gone to heaven. He looked up and saw a young face looking down at him. It was a young face just like his; it was a friendly face, but it seemed to be a stranger's face just the same.

This was the last thing Vitaliy remembered before he passed out completely.

CHAPTER 11 / CALLING ALL UKRAINIANS

In the *Mackenzie*, Sick Bay was generally well equipped. It wasn't as worthy as a hospital emergency room, but it could certainly deal with cases of hypothermia.

Seaman Vitaliy Bondarenko was still mostly unconscious when they brought him in, but his lips were blue and his face was pale. That was all the evidence the medics needed to spring into action. First, they stripped off his wet clothing and quickly gave him a bed bath with warm water. Then they dried him completely and covered him with an electric blanket that provided even warmth. They also placed warm water bottles on his sides and under the small of his back. They wanted to warm him slowly.

As most hypothermia victims become moderately dehydrated, the medics also began to administer intravenous fluids of dextrose and saline that were warmed to just above body temperature.

They were taking good care of their visitor.

This is about the time that the Executive Officer arrived on the scene. Medically, things had been relatively straightforward up until this time. However, Lieutenant-Commander Drapeau was the type of leader that loved to add complication to even the simplest situation.

"Is the Russian going to live?" Drapeau asked.

"Probably, it is a moderate case of hypothermia, however, he is already showing signs that he is recovering," the Chief Medic said. "We'll warm him up and see how he does."

Drapeau was pleased with this answer. "Good," he said. "There is far more paperwork for a dead body than for a live one."

Petty Officer First Class McKay, the Chief Medic, didn't respond. He pretended that the XO didn't say what he had just said. He was a much lower rank than the Executive Officer, but his title as Chief Medic gave him greater power. As well, he was usually referred to as "Doc", despite the fact he wasn't officially a medical doctor. Anyone that was called "Doc" seemed to have inordinate authority.

"Okay Doc... Just tell me this. When will he be able to talk?" Drapeau asked.

"We need to get his core temperature up to normal, and he's going to need rest," McKay replied. "Likely, he will be able to speak to us in the morning."

"Okay, do your best Doc," Drapeau agreed. "Make sure you have him handcuffed to the bed so when he wakes up he doesn't try to wander around. We don't want him to leave this space and sneak around. He will likely try to conduct espionage operations."

Petty Officer McKay looked at the patient's face. It was a young face... so innocent. How could this boy conduct espionage, especially in this medical state?

"Sir, I believe that it's in the Geneva Convention that patients should not be restrained."

McKay had found a way to disagree with the XO's wishes. In fact, he really didn't like the Executive Officer, and he was happy to find a way to countermand his order.

The XO sighed, "Oh, cripes!" he said. "There is a fucking rule for everything, isn't there?"

He scratched his hairless scalp for a minute and came up with an alternate plan.

"If we can't restrain him, we'll guard him." He dramatically pointed at the Sick Bay door. "Be aware that I am going to have two armed Boatswains posted at that door twenty four hours a day while this commie is onboard my ship."

Drapeau nodded his head with a perceived aura of triumph, "Our physical security is paramount! Let's always keep that in mind."

"Yes, Sir. I'll inform the medics," McKay agreed with the XO. In his mind, he didn't see that the threat was so imperative. However, he recognized that the XO had a job to do and his actions were reasonable.

Drapeau had a long look at the Russian before he departed. Sure, he looked young and innocent, especially in this fragile state, but he was still a Russian.

He sneered at the patient, one last time, and then departed the Sick Bay. He would get a few hours' sleep and then return in the morning, when he hoped to have the opportunity to interrogate the prisoner.

* * *

For the remainder of the middle watch, the activity in the Operations Room was relatively quiet. This didn't upset Matt too much. His adrenaline had peaked during the man-overboard incident, and it was nice to relax after all the excitement. It was a strange feeling for Matt, as they exercised man-overboard all the time, and he knew the standard operating procedure. But, this was the first time he had been involved in a real incident, and it was a Russian to boot! He never imagined this could have happened when he first found out he was attached posted to the *Mackenzie*.

Close to when the middle watch was about to end, Chief Cartwright made an unexpected visit to the Operations Room. Matt thought it seemed odd for the Chief to be checking out Ops in the middle of the night. Matt stared across the plotting table at the Chief, wondering what could be happening now...

Chief Cartwright soon announced the reason for his visit, "Leading Seaman Petersen and Able Seaman Morrison, before you complete your watch, I wanted to pass on a message to both of you straight from the Captain."

Matt was nervous, "Yes, Chief?" Morrison looked over from the radar display, and he was visibly surprised and nervous over this development.

"The Captain wanted me to tell you 'good job' in Operations tonight. You men did your job well. He said you plotted the man in the water perfectly." The Chief grinned broadly, knowing full well that he had initially scared the young sailors.

Matt was relieved, especially since he could only ever imagine bad news coming from the Captain.

"Chief, we just followed standard operating procedure." Matt downplayed the whole affair.

The Chief responded, "Yes you did, and you did it well. That's the whole point. When people do their jobs properly, it's okay to tell them. So, good job."

"Thanks Chief," Morrison said. "Can you tell me, though, how is the guy that was rescued?"

"He has hypothermia, but I understand that he is doing okay. He's in Sick Bay, and he's resting now."

"Okay, thank you, Chief," Morrison replied.

* * *

At 0400, after they were relieved from their watch and had completed the watch turnover, Matt and Morrison walked back down to #4 Mess feeling pretty good about themselves.

"What do you think they're going to do with him," Morrison asked as they walked together.

"I don't know. Probably return him to his ship," Matt surmised.

"Do you think technically he's a prisoner?"

"I guess he is... maybe... but we're not really at war are we?" Matt said.

"Not really," Morrison said. "It just seems like we are always at war, that's all."

Matt nodded, as he went down the last ladder leading to the main flats. "Just get used to it, Morrison. The Cold War could go on forever. As long as we are in this navy we are forever destined to be part of it."

"Uh huh," Morrison grunted as he grabbed both of the handrails and lifted his feet. Then, he slid down the ladder. Once he was down on the deck he said, "Did you hear what the Chief said? I'm a hero!"

"Yes, you are," Matt laughed. "You should include that in your next letter to your Mom."

Morrison smiled, "Don't think I won't."

As the two arrived at the hatch leading down to #4 Mess, Matt looked forward, up the flats toward the entrance to Sick Bay. He could see two Boatswains standing guard outside the Sick Bay door. Even from this distance, Matt could see that they were sporting holsters and armed with Browning 9mm pistols.

Matt nudged Morrison in the ribs, "Check it out. They've got two armed deck apes guarding the Sick Bay."

"Oh, wow. Do you think the Russian is a dangerous spy?" Morrison asked. "We should go over there and ask them."

"Count me out. I don't want anything to do with that! I'm staying out of

180

the spy business," Matt said as he started heading down the ladder to the Mess. The only thing that Matt cared about right now was his warm bunk.

A little later, as Matt was finally in his rack, and drifting off to sleep, he couldn't help thinking that a few spaces over and up one deck, there was an actual Russian. The whole thing seemed so very unusual. As he went to sleep, for the first time in days, he wasn't thinking about his problems with Cynthia.

* * *

Matt slept uninterrupted until 0700, when wakey-wakey blared out of the speaker on the forward bulkhead. He decided to get out of his rack, and go forward for a quick shower and shave. He made his way down from his cart to the deck, being careful not to step on his lower bunkmates as he climbed down, as they were still curled up nicely in their carts.

Matt was at his locker, getting his shaving kit and towel, when a peculiar pipe was made through the ship's broadcast system:

"LEADING SEAMAN PETERSEN, SICK BAY, LEADING SEAMAN PETERSEN."

"What the hell?" Matt whispered aloud. He couldn't imagine why he was needed in Sick Bay.

Somebody's voice in the far corner of the mess teased him, "Petey probably needs a shot of penicillin after doin' a load of hookers in New West." This was followed by anonymous laughter from another corner of the mess.

"Very funny guys," Matt replied as he put down his towel and shaving kit and reached for his uniform instead. He quickly put on his shirt, pants, socks and boots. He combed his hair with his fingers and grabbed his beret, just in case he needed it. It only took him a minute and then he was quickly up the ladder to the main flats.

Matt walked forward to the Sick Bay. The first thing he saw standing guard in the main flats, right outside the Sick Bay door, were two Boatswains. Looking like bookends, it was Tweedledee and Tweedledumbass. Matt grinned. He just loved those nicknames, though he wouldn't dare call them that to their faces.

Leading Seaman Dumas put his hand up and stopped Matt, "Wait for the XO, Petersen. He'll be right back."

"Is the XO the one that piped me here?" Matt asked.

"We can't tell you anything," Tweed said. "You'll have to wait for the XO to answer any questions."

"That's odd," Matt said as he stood aside, waiting for the Executive Officer. Matt was nervous about this development, however, as he stood there waiting he remembered that the Chief had mentioned that the Russian was in Sick Bay. Still, he couldn't figure out why this concerned him at this time of the morning.

Soon, Matt could hear the XO's voice in the flats, further aft. He was yelling at someone about coffee. "Probably some poor cook or a steward getting a tongue-lashing," Matt thought. "Poor bastard."

Lieutenant-Commander Drapeau finally walked forward, and arrived at the Sick Bay. "Petersen, excellent. I understand that you speak Ukrainian?"

Matt stammered, "Yes Sir. My grandparents taught me Ukrainian... I lived with them since my parents were killed in a car accident when I was six years..."

"I don't need to hear your life story..." Drapeau cut him off. "I just need to know that you can help me to interrogate the prisoner?"

"What?" Matt said. He couldn't believe that Drapeau had said the word "interrogate".

"Apparently he was muttering in his sleep last night," Drapeau explained. "The Coxswain thinks that it may be Ukrainian."

Matt nodded.

"No one has been able to talk to this guy," Drapeau added. "So I need you to see if you can get him to talk."

"Isn't he a Soviet?" Matt asked.

"Some Soviets are Ukrainians," the XO replied with a snarky tone.

"Okay, sir. I will try," Matt said. He wondered how the XO knew that he spoke Ukrainian. He remembered that he had mentioned it to the Operations Chief. Other than that, he recalled that he had checked the box for "other languages" and written "Ukrainian" on the enrolment form when he joined the navy, but that was years ago. This was very odd to Matt, as he couldn't imagine how Drapeau could have access to his enrolment file way out here at Whiskey 601.

Drapeau opened the Sick Bay door and motioned for Matt to follow him inside.

The first thing Matt saw was the Russian sitting upright in a chair. He was wearing a hospital gown but was also covered with a blanket. On a table in front of the Russian were a bowl of tomato soup and a spoon. The space was uncomfortably hot and humid, like the air conditioning was switched off. One of the medical assistants was sitting at a small desk in the corner.

Matt looked at the Russian. He wasn't at all what he expected. He was young, pale and skinny. His demeanor was weak, and he was obviously avoiding eye contact by staring down at the deck. This certainly did not look like the tough Russian he had been expecting.

"Petersen, why don't you sit down in that chair," the XO said as he pointed to a grey folding chair that was placed across from the patient. "See if you can communicate with him."

Matt sat down in the chair. Meanwhile, Drapeau stood off to one side. Matt looked at the man, though there was no eye contact. The Russian did not look up at all.

Drapeau blurted out, "Talk to him! Talk!"

Matt said, "Hello."

Now, Drapeau seemed to be disgusted, "No, Petersen. Say it in Ukrainian."

Matt knew that his Ukrainian was rusty, but he had no trouble saying, "Vitayu", which was a simple way of saying "Hello".

Vitaliy looked upwards at Matt. He saw Matt's face, and immediately noticed that it was similar to his in many ways. It was a young face, and, in fact, the face even seemed friendly.

What was going on, he thought? Should I answer to this person? Was this a safe person to talk to? Would I be in trouble if I talked? Should I say something, or should I stay clammed up? Vitaliy just didn't know whom to trust.

Vitaliy said nothing. Instead, he shifted his gaze back down toward the deck.

The XO sighed, "What the Fuck is this?"

Matt shrugged his shoulders.

"You can't get him to talk? I don't believe it." The XO moaned. "Is everybody on this ship useless?"

Matt said, "He's definitely not talking to me, Sir." Matt thought about it for a moment, "Maybe he doesn't speak Ukrainian."

"This is crap," said the XO. "Who was the one that said he spoke Ukrainian?" He directed his question to no one in particular.

It was the Duty Medic that answered first, "It was the Doc, Sir."

"What," Drapeau said.

"Yes, the Doc," the Medic confirmed. "He wrote down what the prisoner said right here." The Medic produced a notebook, which contained a few scribbles.

Drapeau took the notebook and scanned the text. "This is complete gibberish," he said. "Petersen is this Ukrainian?" He passed the notebook over to Matt.

Matt looked at the words on the notebook. The XO was right. It looked like gibberish, but mostly because the Doc's handwriting was horrible. It seemed more like chicken scratching than anything else.

"Petersen, is there anything there?" Drapeau demanded.

"There is one word I think I can make out," Matt said. "It's a woman's name, I think."

"What is it?" the XO asked.

"Natalya," Matt said.

Vitaliy quickly looked up. "Natalya?" he said.

Matt replied, "Natalya." He was looking at Vitaliy and now he was making eye contact with him.

Matt continued in Ukrainian, "Who is Natalya?"

Vitaliy responded in Ukrainian, "My sweetheart."

"Your girlfriend?" Matt asked.

"Yes," Vitaliy responded.

"Is she back home?"

"Yes, back in the Ukraine," Vitaliy confirmed.

Drapeau was very pleased that there was now some communication happening. Though, he couldn't understand what the two young men were talking about, he could tell that they were definitely communicating.

"What exactly are you talking about?" Drapeau asked.

Matt looked up at the XO and said in English, "His girlfriend, Natalya. She is back in the Ukraine."

Vitaliy heard the word "Natalya" in what Matt was telling the XO. With a concerned look on his young face, he looked up at the XO, as well.

Drapeau noticed that the prisoner was now making eye contact with him. This pleased him. "Good job Petersen. You got him talking. Now, we need to get him talking about something other than his girlfriend."

"What should I ask him, Sir?" Matt asked.

Drapeau thought about it for a moment, and then he said, "Ask him his name and rank... Wait... I'll make a list. Give me that clipboard!"

He reached for a clipboard that was on the Medic's desk. The Medic grabbed the clipboard and passed it to Drapeau. The clipboard had a pad of blank, white lined-paper as well as a pencil on a string attached. The XO began to scribble madly. After a minute or so, he handed the clipboard to Matt.

"Here," Drapeau said. "Ask him all of this."

Matt scanned the list. It had some basic info like name, rank, ship and trade. Then, it also had some more sensitive questions about the *Aziya*, like number of officers and crew, top speed, range, mission details, weapons onboard, fitted sensors, last port, next port, Commanding Officer's name, etc...

Matt broke into a cold sweat. He suddenly realized that he was supposed to interrogate this person. They never trained him for this at Radar School!

"You want me to ask him all of this?" Matt confirmed.

"Look Petersen," Drapeau sighed. "I wouldn't think I need to tell you how important this is, but it seems that I need to tell you anyway. If we could gather details about this brand-new vessel's capabilities, it would be of paramount importance to NATO. If we could collect the very first intelligence on it, we would be famous."

"Famous?" thought Matt. He was starting to think that the XO was a little too full of himself for his own good.

"Do you understand?" asked the XO.

"Yes Sir," Matt said. "I understand that this is very important."

"Good," said Drapeau. "Now, do it!"

Matt looked at the Russian, who was now looking him directly in the eye. He began the interrogation by asking some of the simple questions.

"Could you tell me your name," Matt asked in Ukrainian.

Vitaliy looked at Matt with a definite distrust. He just stared at him, sternly, but he did not answer.

Matt realized that the prisoner did not want to say anything about himself. Therefore, Matt changed the question, "If you tell me your name, then we will be able to report to the Soviet Navy exactly who has been rescued."

Vitaliy pondered for a second, and then felt it might be safe to answer some simple questions. "My name is Vitaliy Bondarenko."

Matt began to write down Vitaliy's name on the clipboard, but then he paused.

"Please excuse me Vitaliy, but could you spell your name. I wish to be very accurate."

Vitaliy spelled his name out completely as Matt checked his notes. Meanwhile, Drapeau hovered nearby. He was excited by the fact that the information was beginning to flow.

"Next thing," Matt said. "What is your rank and service number?"

Vitaliy replied, "Seamen Third Class. 1174545768."

"Okay," Matt said as he continued to write down the information.

"Now," Matt said. "I want to ask you a few questions about your ship."

Vitaliy quickly averted his gaze. Again, he was staring down at the deck. Matt asked a few of the questions that the XO had written on the clipboard, but Vitaliy did not respond. Not even with a single grunt.

"Oh fuck," Drapeau cursed. "He's going to play that game now, is he?"

Matt didn't know what to do. "Maybe I need to get him talking more first," Matt suggested aloud, in English. "Maybe I need to chat him up a bit, you know, to gain his trust?"

"Yes. Why don't you do that, Petersen," Drapeau said. "I'll step out for a few minutes and leave you alone. You see what you can do, okay?"

"Yes Sir," Matt said awkwardly. He now wondered what he had just agreed to.

The Executive Officer left and closed the door behind him. Now it was just Matt, Vitaliy and the Medic remaining in the Sick Bay. Without Drapeau, the overall mood did seem to be calmer.

Vitaliy looked up from the deck. "Where am I?" Vitaliy asked, quietly.

Matt immediately wondered if he should tell Vitaliy anything. He thought about it. He really didn't have the authority to pass any information to Vitaliy.

"You're safe," Matt replied, in Ukrainian.

"Safe? Where?" Vitaliy asked again.

"Safe on our ship," Matt answered vaguely.

Vitaliy sighed and rubbed his forehead with his left hand. He seemed so confused.

Vitaliy made direct eye contact with Matt. "Okay, since when do Americans speak Ukrainian?" Vitaliy asked.

Matt grinned slightly, "That's because we're not Americans. We are Canadians."

Vitaliy seemed astonished. He studied Matt's face closely, and what he had thought was an American face, he now saw as a Canadian face. He didn't know what to think. In all of his training, he had been told to distrust the Americans, but there was never any mention of the Canadians. He wasn't sure what to make of this.

"Is there a Russian ship nearby?" Vitaliy asked sheepishly.

"Do you mean your ship, the *Aziya*?" Matt responded.

Vitaliy replied enthusiastically, "Yes, the *Aziya*! Is it nearby?"

Again, Matt wasn't sure if he should be that direct with this information. Still, he was happy that the prisoner was now talking, but he noticed that the questions now seemed to be directed at him, rather than the other way around.

"I believe that your ship may be nearby," Matt said. "Though, I cannot be completely sure where the *Aziya* is at this exact moment. I can tell you for sure that she was nearby last night when we rescued you."

"Oh, you rescued me?" Vitaliy asked.

"Not me exactly, but people from our crew did pull you from the water," Matt answered.

Vitaliy rubbed his eyes. He was still exhausted, and the questions and the information were wearing on him. Matt noticed this, and decided to soften the questions.

"Vitaliy, do you remember being rescued?" Matt asked.

"Not really," Vitaliy said. "I recall falling into the water, and remember being in the water for a long time... and being so cold. That's all I remember."

"So, you don't remember when they pulled you out of the water?" Matt asked.

"Maybe I do," Vitaliy combed his memory. "I seem to remember a dream where I was praying, and then I heard voices yelling out to me to stop praying and to reach up to the sky. I remember hearing a motor, and then I looked up to see faces looking down upon me. They pulled me out of the water. But that all seems like a dream to me."

"I guess that it wasn't a dream. It was all real," Matt said.

Petty Officer McKay entered the Sick Bay. Just as he arrived, Vitaliy vigorously rubbed his eyes. He was clearly exhausted, and the Doc was quick to notice this.

"No more questions for now," the Doc said. "Let's get you back in bed." He motioned for Vitaliy to go back to the nearby bed. Vitaliy looked up and immediately understood the Doc's instruction. Quickly, the Medic came to Vitaliy's side and helped him up out of his chair and back into the bed. Then he packed warm water bottles around Vitaliy and tucked him in with two blankets.

"No more questions, Petersen," the Doc said. "His body temperature is still not quite up to normal. He won't be able to talk anymore this morning. You can report to the XO. He is in the flats outside the Sick Bay."

"Okay PO," Matt said. "Thanks."

Before he left, Matt came to Vitaliy's bedside. "Goodbye Vitaliy, sleep well."

Vitaliy opened his eyes again and looked at Matt. He said, "Goodbye... wait... what is your name?"

Matt wasn't immediately sure if he should answer the question, however, when Matt looked at Vitaliy's young innocent face, he felt that he could answer such a simple question, "It's Matthew, but you may call me Matt."

"Okay, Matt. Goodnight," Vitaliy said.

Matt turned to leave when he heard one more question from Vitaliy.

"Matthew, when can I go home?"

"I don't know the answer to that," Matt replied.

* * *

Matt left the Sick Bay. The XO was waiting in the main flats, right outside the door. Matt had barely closed the Sick Bay door when Drapeau lunged towards him.

"What did you find out?" he asked abruptly.

"Not much, Sir," Matt said. "I have his name, rank and service number, as you know. But, not much else."

"So, you didn't find out anything else?" Drapeau asked.

"No, but he was beginning to talk to me when the Doc put him to bed," Matt explained. He hoped that the XO would at least appreciate a partial effort.

"This is going too slow," Drapeau lamented. "We really need to suck as much information out of him before he leaves the ship."

"Is he going home soon?" Matt asked. "That's one of the things he asked me."

"No, not until we get the information we need," Drapeau said. "I'll do everything in my power to keep him here as long as I can."

"Okay," Matt said.

"But, don't you dare tell him that, Leading Seaman Petersen," Drapeau said in a threatening manner. "You keep your mouth shut."

"Yes, Sir," Matt said.

"Petersen, you best be ready to come back here at a moment's notice. When he wakes up, I want you inside that Sick Bay interrogating him. You got that?"

"Yes, Sir," Matt said. "Sir, I am scheduled to go back on watch in the Operations Room at 1145. I'm on the afternoon watch."

"Don't worry about that. I'll look after that. You just be ready to go back in there and get the information I want."

"Yes, Sir."

Matt looked at his watch. It was now 0845 and too late for breakfast, but he was hungry. So, he scampered down to his locker in #4 Mess and got some of Alison's oatmeal chocolate chip cookies from a secret stash in his locker. They were so good.

As he ate the cookies, he pondered what had just occurred. This development was unexpected! Matt began to think about the young Ukrainian. The poor guy was lost, and now he was here, but at the whim of the Executive Officer. He really felt bad for him. Surely, the XO couldn't actually delay his return to the Russian ship. Then, Matt thought about how he was going to accomplish the herculean task of siphoning information from the Ukrainian. How would he ever manage to do that?

* * *

At about 1300, when Matt was on watch, the Executive Officer and the Operations Officer both entered the Operations Room. Their demeanor was purposeful, which gave Matt the hint that this had something to do with his new duties as an "interrogation specialist".

"Master Seaman Burke. The XO is stealing Petersen, to help him speak to the prisoner in Sick Bay."

Burke nodded as he took over the plotting table duties. "We'll be okay," he said. "I seem to remember how to drive one of these things."

The XO and Matt walked down to Sick Bay together. As they walked, he gave Matt explicit instructions.

"The Russian is awake again, and the Chief Medic has informed me that we can ask him more questions."

"Yes, Sir," Matt said.

"This time I want you to ask him every question on that clipboard. Don't let up. You got it?"

"I will do my best sir," Matt started to break out into a brand new cold sweat. "I just have one question, Sir?"

"What is it?" the XO replied abruptly.

"When do you think the Ukrainian will go back to his ship?" Matt wanted to know this for two reasons. He wanted to know when things were going to return to normal for him, and he wanted to be able to tell Vitaliy something in case he asked again.

"Don't worry about that," Drapeau said. "You just worry about getting the information I want. That is all you need to concern yourself with."

As Drapeau opened the door to the Sick Bay, Matt could feel a bead of sweat running down the small of his back. Once they were both inside, Matt saw that it was exactly as it was before. Vitaliy Bondarenko, dressed in a hospital gown and covered by a thin yellow blanket, was sitting in an armchair.

There was one other person in the room who Matt recognized. The Duty Medic, a Leading Seaman Medical Assistant named Daryl Webb was sitting at a desk in the corner. Matt recalled that he went by the nickname "Spider".

There was a grey folding chair situated just across from Vitaliy. Drapeau motioned for Matt to sit in the chair, and Matt dutifully sat down. Drapeau took up a position behind, and to Matt's right.

"Good afternoon," Matt said in Ukrainian. "How are you feeling this afternoon? Are you improving?"

Vitaliy looked directly at Matt's face. He did not make eye contact with Drapeau, whatsoever.

"It's too bad for me that I have been rescued and brought back to good health only to become a prisoner here on this ship." Vitaliy raised his right hand for Matt to see that he now had a handcuff attached to his wrist and to the arm of the chair.

Matt, with an astonished expression, turned to look at Drapeau.

"It's only for everyone's safety," Drapeau said. "He is now well enough to cause problems. We don't want any problems."

Matt looked back at Vitaliy and spoke in Ukrainian. "I am so sorry for this, Vitaliy," he said as he pointed at the handcuffs. "It is merely a security policy. That is all."

Vitaliy shook his head in dismay. "I am very uncertain about all of this Matthew," he said. "I thought that I was the luckiest man in the world. I thought I was dead, and then it was a miracle as I was rescued. Now, I realize that my rescuers are not friendly. I'm locked up, and I'm a prisoner."

"You're not a prisoner," Matt said. "The Executive Officer only wants to be safe." Matt tried to explain. He only hoped that this worked, as he still needed to ask Vitaliy the list of questions. How was he going to achieve this?

"Okay," Vitaliy said.

"Vitaliy, you might remember earlier that I had asked you a few questions about yourself."

Vitaliy nodded, "Yes, I remember."

"Thank you for answering those questions," Matt said. "But now, I still have some questions about your ship."

Vitaliy's face suddenly turned from a slight defiance to complete terror. "...and if I don't answer your questions I'll be beaten and fed to the swine."

Matt had to correct him immediately. "No, you've got it wrong. We won't hurt you."

"I'm not sure I can trust you," Vitaliy said.

"Where did you get this idea that you'd be fed to pigs?" Matt asked calmly.

"In Seamanship School," Vitaliy said. "They told us to never get captured. You will be interrogated, tortured and fed to the pigs."

"We won't feed you to the pigs. We don't have any pigs here." Matt said.

"What if I don't answer your questions?" Vitaliy asked. "What will you do then?"

"Vitaliy, remember you are on a Canadian ship. In Canada, we don't do such things." Matt felt like he had just made a promise for the entire nation. But, who would know? Nobody else in this space spoke Ukrainian. It was completely between him and Vitaliy.

Vitaliy's concerns seemed to be eased. "Matthew, you're the only person I trust right now, and this is only because you speak my language."

"All right then," Matt said. "I appreciate that."

"You seem like you're a man of your word. I will trust you Matthew."

"Good then. You can trust me," Matt said. "Now my problem is this. That man behind me wants me to ask you some questions about your ship. He won't stop until the questions are asked. Vitaliy, I really need your cooperation."

"I'm not sure I should," Vitaliy said.

"Well let's just try, shall we?" Matt said. "Let's start with this question. What is your job on the *Aziya*? What is your navy occupation?"

Vitaliy thought about it for a second. He couldn't see how admitting your job on a ship could really cause a breach of security.

"I am a Seaman, Third Class," he said.

"I already know that," Matt said. "Do you have a specialty?"

"No," Vitaliy said. "I am merely a seaman."

"So you don't work with weapons or systems and such," Matt asked.

"Only if they need cleaning or painting," Vitaliy said.

"Okay," Matt said. He wrote down Boatswain on the XO's clipboard. All of a sudden Matt realized that this was going to be easy, as Vitaliy probably didn't know very much of the technical and mission details of the *Aziya*.

"Okay. Next question," Matt said. "What is your last port?"

"That's easy," said Vitaliy. "Vladivostok."

"When were you there?" Matt asked.

"Two years ago," Vitaliy said glibly.

"Are you serious?" Matt asked.

"Yes, we have stayed at sea every day for two years. We are replenished every few months. That's it."

Matt wrote this down on the clipboard. The XO read the information, and he shook his head.

"Damn fuckers," Drapeau said. "They stay at sea forever. Are they robots?"

Vitaliy heard the XO's remark. "What did he say?" Vitaliy asked as he peered at Drapeau nervously.

"It was nothing," Matt assured him. "He's just as surprised as I am that you have been at sea so long."

Vitaliy nodded. "Yes, it's been too long."

Matt looked at the clipboard and saw that the next question fit the conversation. "Vitaliy, when is your next port visit?" he asked.

"I don't know," Vitaliy said.

"Are you not told such things?" Matt asked. "Is it not posted somewhere on your ship?"

"No."

"Then how do you know when you will see your family again?" Matt asked.

"We don't know. We just accept that we need to be at sea to protect Russia. That's all we need to know."

"Okay," Matt said. "I get it." Then, Matt wrote, "undetermined time at sea" on the clipboard.

* * *

As time went by, Matt was surprised that the questioning went very smoothly. It was simple really; Vitaliy didn't know much. Most of the questions on Drapeau's list were met with answers of "I don't know", "I am not sure" or "I think". There certainly weren't any major discoveries.

Later, after they had left the Sick Bay, Matt handed the clipboard back to Drapeau.

"This is all I found out, Sir," Matt said.

The XO scanned the list of questions and answers. "This is UNSAT," he said gruffly. "He is obviously lying."

"I don't think so, Sir," Matt said.

"What makes you an expert?" Drapeau asked.

"Sir, he sounds sincere," Matt explained. "Plus, he is a Boatswain."

"What does that have to do with anything?" Drapeau asked.

"Sir, just go and ask an average Boatswain on this ship any of these questions about the *Mackenzie*," Matt said. "Do you think that they'll know the answer?"

"Maybe you're right," Drapeau said as he began to rub his sweaty scalp. Matt noted that he always seemed to do this when he seemed to be scheming.

"Here is what I want you to do," the XO instructed. "You go back in there, and you be his friend. Talk to him. Figure out if he is telling the truth. I will stay away. It'll just be you and him. You got that?"

"Yes, Sir," Matt said. "I will do my best."

Matt was being an obedient subordinate, but inside he was wondering when his special detail as an interrogator was going to end. After all, hadn't he done enough already?

"Okay, you go back in there and chat him up," Drapeau said. "I'll send down one of the stewards with some tea and cookies." Drapeau opened the Sick Bay door and motioned for Matt to go back inside.

Matt re-entered the Sick Bay. Vitaliy looked up and nodded, as if to welcome him in.

"Hello Matthew, I see you are back," Vitaliy greeted Matt. "Wait... tell me, what is your last name?"

"Petersen," Matt said.

"Then, hello Matthew Petersen," Vitaliy said. "Wait... you're making a joke, right? Petersen is not a Ukrainian name. How is it that you speak my language?"

"I am a Petersen, but my grandparents are Ukrainian. They're Ukrainian Canadians," Matt said with a smile.

"So, they taught you Ukrainian? How interesting," Vitaliy said. "Your Ukrainian is good. They taught you well."

"It's relatively simple," Matt explained. "I grew up living with my grandparents, and Ukrainian is all we used when at home."

"Really?" Vitaliy said.

"Yes. It's a beautiful language, and my grandparents will never give it up. Even though people speak English all around them, they are determined to hang onto this link to their culture."

Vitaliy nodded in fascination. This was something he had never heard of before. Yes, he knew that there were plenty of Ukrainians living in Canada, but he was surprised to hear that they were keeping their language and culture.

Just then, the door opened and one of the Wardroom stewards entered with a tray. He placed two cups of tea and a plate of sugar cookies down on the side table next to Vitaliy, and then he left. The two men just looked at the goodies, and then Matt picked up the plate and offered a cookie to Vitaliy. Vitaliy took the cookie and nibbled the corner. It must have tasted okay, because he then took a regular sized bite of the cookie.

Now that the cookies and tea were served, Matt continued their chat. "Where is your hometown?" he asked.

Vitaliy was still thinking cautiously about giving up information. However, since Matt had already told him so much about his life he naturally felt that it would be okay to reciprocate.

"I am from a town near Lviv, Ukraine," Vitaliy said. "It is called Popeliany."

"Is it a small town?" Matt asked.

"Yes, very small. It's really just a hamlet. Where are you from Matthew?"

"I am from Winnipeg? Have you heard of it?"

"I know where it is," Vitaliy said. "It is in the middle of Canada. Right?"

"How did you know that?" Matt asked.

"I've heard of Winnipeg," Vitaliy said proudly. "It has many Ukrainian immigrants, doesn't it?"

"Yes, of course. I take it for granted everybody in Canada knows that. I just wasn't aware that you knew it."

Vitaliy went on to explain, "Everybody in the Ukraine knows that Canada has the largest population of Ukrainians outside the Ukraine, and of course, Russia. In the Ukraine, I know plenty of people that have relatives who live in Canada. Of course, they never hear from them much, and they can't keep in touch with them. It's because of the Iron Curtain. They can't call and they can't visit. They can write, but the letters hardly ever arrive. Still, they always know they are there. They're always remembered."

"That's fascinating," Matt said. "I never thought of things that way. I keep forgetting how much you folks don't know about what's going on outside the Soviet Union."

"Does Natalya live in Popeliany?" Matt asked.

"Yes, she is there," Vitaliy said. There was a definite hint of sadness in his tone.

"What does she do there?"

"She works on a dairy farm. She is a cook."

"Is she a good cook?" Matt asked.

"Oh yes, she is very good. Before I was in the navy, I worked on the same farm, as a farmhand. I have eaten her meals many times. Maybe that's why I like her so much," He rubbed his stomach and grinned.

"Natalya is a remarkable woman," Vitaliy continued. "I plan to marry her the minute I get home."

Matt was impressed by Vitaliy's resolution to marry his sweetheart. However, he found himself feeling slightly cynical about this. What if she were with another man already?

"Does she write to you," Matt asked.

"Yes, she writes to me almost every day," Vitaliy said.

"Really?" Matt said. Every day sounded like an embellishment to him.

"Well maybe not every day," Vitaliy said. "She misses a few days, here and there."

"Oh, of course," Matt said. "You must have plenty to read then?"

"Yes, I do, when the mail arrives. Unfortunately, we do not get much mail. It comes once every few months. When it arrives there is always a whole bundle of mail for me."

"Really?" Matt asked again. He was impressed by Natalya's supposed dedication to Vitaliy.

"Yes, really," Vitaliy said. "I sort it by postmark and spend a few days reading it. I want to read it in order, as she tells me everything that is happening on the farm. She also tells me how my mother is doing."

"Oh, your mother lives on the farm as well?"

"Yes, she is there as well," Vitaliy said.

"And your father?" Matt asked.

"He is gone," Vitaliy said. "He was killed while serving in the army."

"Oh, I'm sorry to hear that," Matt said.

"My mother was glad when I went into the navy. She didn't want me to be in the army," Vitaliy said.

"How long has it been since you've seen your family?" Matt asked.

"It's been over two years since I have joined the cursed navy," Vitaliy explained. "I didn't want to leave, but I had to. After all, it is our duty to serve in the military." He pointed at Matt and then at himself, as if to imply that Matt also had the responsibility to serve in the military.

"So, you were conscripted?" Matt asked.

"If you mean that I was forced to join the navy, then yes," Vitaliy confirmed.

"I volunteered for the navy," Matt said.

"But, you would have been forced to go... if you hadn't volunteered...

right?" Vitaliy looked confused.

"No, there is no conscription in Canada. We all volunteer."

"You know," Vitaliy explained. "We are told that all countries force their people into the military."

"Maybe that's what they need to tell you to make you feel like it is okay," Matt said.

Vitaliy shook his head. It was as if he was a child, and he had been told that Santa Claus doesn't exist.

"How much longer do you have to serve?" Matt asked.

"I have to serve three years," Vitaliy said. "I have less than a year left, and then I can return home to the Ukraine."

Matt nodded.

"Before I left the Ukraine, Natalya knitted a nice pair of wool socks for me. She used bright red wool. She told me that they were for me to wear to keep my feet warm when I was so far away at sea."

"They're red?" Matt asked.

"Yes, absolutely. She knows that red is my favorite colour, but I'm sure that she made them red so I would always be reminded of her red hair."

Matt's thoughts swirled. As he listened to Vitaliy's story, he was instantly reminded of Cynthia, who also had red hair. How he missed her dearly, but then, she would never knit him a pair of socks. Never in a million years. He was both jealous and moved by Vitaliy's story.

"I was wearing the red socks when I fell overboard," Vitaliy said as he looked down at his feet. All he saw were a pair of flimsy, pale yellow hospital slippers. "Now, I see that the socks are missing."

Vitaliy paused to take a drink of tea. Matt waited for him to continue.

"The one thing I've been wondering, for the past hour, is where are those red socks of mine? Do you think they fell off my feet when I was in the water? Maybe they are with my uniform. Does anyone know the location of my uniform?"

"Hmmm, I'm sure that your uniform couldn't be too far away," Matt pondered. Then he spoke in English to Spider Webb, the Duty Medic. "Do you know where his uniform is?"

Spider looked up and answered quickly, "We bagged it, and sent it to the laundry."

Matt nodded, "Thanks." Then he spoke to Vitaliy, "Your uniform is in the laundry. I will see if I can retrieve it for you."

Vitaliy smiled, "That is what I need. But, you can forget the rest of the uniform, if you want. I just need the red wool socks."

Matt replied, "Red wool socks?"

"Yes, bright red," Vitaliy said.

"Okay..." Matt said. "I suppose that I can try to locate them."

"Remember, I don't care about the uniform at all," Vitaliy said. "I just need the red wool socks."

"Red wool socks," Matt repeated again.

Vitaliy looked right into Matt's eyes.

"Matthew, those socks are one of the only things that ties me to my Natalya."

"You still have her letters," Matt pointed out.

"Yes, she does write to me. But, the mail schedule is so poor." Vitaliy explained.

Matt nodded.

"Matthew, when she gave me those socks, we were at the train station in Popeliany. I was about to leave when she promised me that she would wait for me to return. She said that she would wait for three years. I told her that I would want to marry her when I returned. But, she began to worry that when I would return I would have changed too much. She became very afraid that I wouldn't love her anymore, especially after I had seen the world."

Matt nodded thoughtfully, "Okay, I understand. What did you tell her?"

"I promised that I would return and that I would still love her. No matter what."

"And that worked?" Matt asked curiously.

"Yes it did, but then she gave me the red socks and told me that I should wear them as a reminder of her. Also, when I returned, and she saw me again, she would look to see if I was wearing the red socks. If she saw me wearing the socks, she would know..."

"So, the red socks would be the signal that tells her that you still love her?" Matt asked.

"Yes," Vitaliy said. He thought for a moment and then continued, "I am sure that I can explain to her that I lost the socks and she will just be happy to see me."

"You could do that," Matt said. "She will be so thrilled to see you she might just forget about the socks."

"But Matthew, those socks have become my spiritual connection to her over the past two years. Without them, my connection to her will be lost. I might stop thinking about her. I might even lose my love for her," Vitaliy said.

Then Vitaliy suddenly declared, "Matthew, I need them back."

This was something that Matt had never seen before. Vitaliy, this poor man, was completely lost without a pair of red wool socks. How could it be that the mere symbolism contained in an item of clothing was the only thing that mattered to a man? Matt rubbed his head and looked at the deck as he pondered the scope of this dilemma.

"Could you try to find my socks Matthew? It would mean so much to me." Vitaliy was now pleading.

Matt knew exactly what to say in this case. Matt said two words to Vitaliy, "YA obitsyayu."

Vitaliy nodded, "Thank you, Matthew."

Suddenly, Matt recalled the time, once, long ago, when he heard his very own grandmother say those very same two words to him. It was when he was a child, and was right after his own parents had suddenly passed away:

> *"Grandma, will you be my new mommy?"*
>
> *"YA obitsyayu."*
>
> *"Forever?"*
>
> *"YA obitsyayu."*
>
> *"You promise?"*
>
> *"I promise."*

Those two important words, coupled with his Grandmothers' comforting smile, were forever lodged into Matt's consciousness. Matt's promise to Vitaliy was as genuine as his memory.

Matt looked at Vitaliy. He was getting tired again, closing his eyes and rubbing his forehead. He was due for more sleep. Matt decided to leave. After all, he had work to do.

He had "promised" Vitaliy that he would locate his red wool socks, and he had even given the promise by using two of the most important Ukrainian words in his memory, "YA obitsyayu." Matt needed to get started locating the uniform.

Sometimes, items of kit tended to grow legs in the navy. He had to work fast.

CHAPTER 12 / RED SOCKS GAME

"He wants his red wool socks back," Matt said to Paul.

"What's the big deal with a pair of socks?"

"His girlfriend in the Ukraine knitted them for him," Matt explained. "Then, when he left home for the navy, he made a solemn promise to her that he would someday return and that he would be wearing those same red socks."

"That sounds touching." Paul was rolling his eyes as he said it.

"You don't get it?" Matt asked.

"No, I don't get it. So, he comes home with a different pair of socks. What's the big deal?"

"It's the symbolism of the thing," Matt explained. "To him, losing the socks is the same as losing his girlfriend."

Paul rolled his eyes again. He was starting to get the feeling that Matt was transferring his own girlfriend troubles onto this poor Ukrainian fellow.

"I'm sorry that you aren't moved by this, Paul," Matt said. "Besides missing his girlfriend, this guy has been at sea for two years and he is really homesick. Now that he is onboard the Mack, he thinks that he is never going to make it back home. He's convinced we are going to torture him and feed his corpse to pigs."

"Pigs?" Paul said. "The only pigs we have on here are working in the Engine Room. This guy's really messed up."

"Yes, he is," Matt agreed. "Do you know what? If the tables were turned, the same thing would happen to any of us."

"Explain," Paul said.

"I mean if you or I fell overboard and found ourselves on a Russian ship," Matt clarified. "We would be pretty screwed up, just like him."

Paul thought about it a bit. "Yes, I would probably spill my guts in a second," he said. "Hey, did he know any secrets?"

"No, he doesn't know squat," Matt said. "He's just a boatswain. He's pretty much like one of us. Meanwhile, the XO is treating him as if he is the Russian James Bond, and he knows all the codes for the missiles. This guy doesn't even have the combination to the padlock on the paint locker."

Paul laughed, "So your saying he's a frickin' dummy?"

"No, not at all. He seems smart enough. He's just a regular guy, that's all."

"Well screw him then. He's a Russian after all. He's the enemy. He'd fuck us all over in a second if we gave him a chance."

"I doubt it," Matt said. "Yes, he is the enemy... but then again he's not really... an enemy. He just doesn't seem like a bad guy." Matt weighed the factors, but he was swaying back and forth.

"Well, bottom line is that you can't be his friend. He's the enemy after all. There is no way someone like you... someone with a security clearance can make friends with a Russian. You'd end up in big trouble," Paul explained.

"Yah, I know... I can't be his friend," Matt said. "But I don't have to be mean to him. I can help him, just as I would help any other human being."

"Not in this case," Paul said.

"Wait a minute. If he is the enemy, then he is a 'prisoner' on our ship," Matt said.

"I suppose so."

"Then as a prisoner, he has rights... and one of those rights is to be treated fairly. Right?" Matt was still trying to make a case.

"Maybe," Paul said. "Just take my advice though, and be very careful. Okay?"

"Okay."

* * *

Matt thought about when he was a young sailor in Fleet School. The Chief Instructor had lectured them on watching out for friendly Russians that wanted to steal NATO secrets.

He specifically recalled one story the Chief had told, "Watch out for a beautiful woman, maybe in a foreign port. She may or may not have a Russian accent. She likely wants to buy you drinks, and she wants to take you home. This is a Russian spy!"

The guys in his class would always joke that if this ever happened they would let her have everything but the secrets. They clearly thought it was a joke. Matt also thought it was a ridiculous scenario. But, now he had been face to face with a Soviet sailor. Is this similar to what the Chief had been talking about? Is this just a big game? Maybe Vitaliy was just using him, trying to get inside his head? Could it be that the missing his home and his girlfriend story was a ploy? He needed to consider it.

Matt gave it some thought. Vitaliy has never asked anything about the ship or about Matt's job. How would Vitaliy know he was in an Operations trade anyway? He shows no curiosity for anything like that. Look at the circumstances. It's obvious he simply fell overboard, and we rescued him.

Right then, Matt decided that Vitaliy was obviously not a spy, and that this couldn't be a game. This was real, and Vitaliy's only desire was to go home.

Still, he thought he needed to be cautious. He knew that he couldn't show any friendship towards Vitaliy, otherwise he might be branded as a communist sympathizer. He didn't want that to happen. In fact, he could imagine all kinds of terrible consequences that might occur, such as his getting kicked out of the military, charged as a spy and sent to military prison. Nothing good would come of it. The consequences were all horrible. Whatever he did to help Vitaliy, he couldn't show any favoritism. He had to remain at a distance.

So, how would he find those red socks?

* * *

Matt trooped aft to the laundry room. When he arrived, he opened the door and peered inside. He saw an Ordinary Seaman with a nametag that said "Cross". He was folding laundry, so Matt assumed that this was the person that might know the answers.

Matt called out over the noise of the washers and dryers, "Hey there, Ordinary Seaman Cross."

Cross looked up. He didn't recognize Matt, but he saw Leading Seaman Rank badges. He dutifully came over to speak to Matt.

"Yes, Leading Seaman," Cross said.

"Have you seen the Russian uniform?" Matt asked.

Suddenly, Cross turned away. He appeared to be nervous.

Matt asked again, "Have you seen it?"

Cross turned back toward Matt and stammered, "It was here for a while, but now I don't know where it is."

"What do you mean, you don't know?" Matt demanded.

"I just don't know," Cross said. "You know, things go missing here."

"Is that your best excuse?" Matt asked.

Cross waved his hand across the laundry space. "Look at this place. Look at all this crap. There is so much stuff here... I can't keep track of everything."

"Surely, you would know about something as special as a Russian uniform?" Matt asserted.

Cross stuck to his story, "I don't know anything about it."

Although, Cross was adamant that he was wholly innocent, Matt was positive that he knew something.

* * *

The Laundry Room operator wasn't of any assistance, other than to give a strong hint that something dishonest had happened to Vitaliy's uniform. Matt had only been onboard for a few days, but he was already aware that if there was one guy who knew everything that was going on in the *Mackenzie*, it was the Canteen Operator, Master Seaman Frost.

That evening Matt went to the canteen, at 2000, right when he knew it was about to close. He scouted out the location, and waited until nobody else was nearby. He wanted to be able to speak to Frosty privately.

"Hello Master Seaman Frost. How is business this evening?"

"Hey, Petersen. How are you enjoying your time in the *Mackenzie*? How are those tee shirts working out for you?"

"Yes, they are fine," Matt said politely. "Thanks for asking."

"Can I get your usual?" Frosty asked. "A Coke and a bag of salt and vinegar chips, right?"

"No, not tonight Frosty. I had a big supper," Matt said as he patted his stomach. "Actually, tonight I have come for information, and since you're the guy that knows everything that goes on aboard this ship, I figured you'd likely know the answer."

"Flattery will get you everywhere," Frosty said. "Tell me, what's on your mind?"

"I'll just be blunt," Matt said. "Have you seen the Russian's uniform?"

Frosty started to smirk. "Maybe I know something about those particular items of kit and maybe I don't. Right now, I'm not sure if I remember anything. However, if you pay me for, say, twenty packs of smokes, I will see if my memory improves."

Apparently, Frosty wouldn't take cash for info. He didn't want to risk being caught for bribery or any other military offence. But, a shyster always figures out how to get his money.

Matt nodded, and then he opened his wallet and pulled out a $20 bill. He handed it over to Frosty. Frosty held the bill up to the light, seemingly to inspect it. Then he grinned at Matt and put the bill directly into his trouser pocket.

"I can tell you what I know, Petersen. The Russian's uniform went from the Sick Bay straight to the ship's laundry. However, they only had it for a mere 10 minutes before I walked in and bought the whole shooting match from the Ordinary Seamen for fifty bucks. He couldn't believe his lucky stars. It was great. I made that boy $50 richer, and all he had to do was be in the right place at the right time."

"So, he wasn't afraid that the XO would find out he sold private property for profit?" Matt asked.

"I told him to say it was lost," Frosty said glibly. "You're aware that things get lost in the laundry, aren't you? It happens all the time."

"Do you think the XO will buy that story?" Matt asked. "He's not stupid."

Frosty replied, "Who cares? The problem is not mine. Once Cross sold me the uniform, that's all I really cared about. Besides, I made him happy."

"So, he profited from the sale. Good for him, he can buy himself something nice," Matt said. "I assume then that you're in possession of the kit?"

"Well, yes I was in possession of the kit. However it is no longer in my possession." Frosty was being vague.

"Okay," Matt said. "Where is it now?"

"Why do you want to know?" Frosty asked.

"Look Frosty," Matt said. "I paid 20 bucks for information, so just give me what I paid for."

"Okay, okay, just keep your pants on," Frosty said. "I'm just messing with you anyway."

"So, where is it then?" Matt asked again.

"Earlier today, before supper, we had a teensy-weensy little auction back aft in the mortar well. The Russian's dungarees went for $300; his quilted jacket went for $250, his boots were $150."

"Were there red socks?" Matt asked.

"Oh yes, I forgot about those gems," Frosty said. "The red commie socks went for $100. Piggy the Stoker, from #8 Mess, was quite taken by those."

"Really? That much?" Matt said.

"Yes, it was wonderful. Everybody was quite surprised to learn that commies wear red socks. They were the hit of the auction," Frosty exclaimed. "They got double than what I thought they would go for!"

Matt was somewhat shocked by Frosty's self-centred attitude. He really didn't seem to care about anyone or anything other than himself.

"Okay. Thanks for the info, Frosty," Matt said as he started to walk away.

But, before he got even three steps, Matt stopped. He turned and called back to Frosty, "Hey! You didn't give me my 20 bucks worth of cigarettes."

Frosty smiled, "I only said you had to pay me for the smokes, I did not say you'd actually receive any product. Besides, it's past closing time." Then, Frosty abruptly rolled down the canteen window shutter with a bang.

Matt knew this, but he still wanted to toy with Frosty as he was completely disgusted by this man. Still, he was further ahead as he now knew that "Piggy the Stoker" from #8 Mess was in possession of the vaunted socks.

Matt heard Frosty locking the shutter from the inside of the canteen, then he saw Frosty step out through the canteen door.

Frosty called back to Matt, "Hey, Petey. I have a question for you. Why are you so interested in those socks?"

"No reason," Matt said. In fact, Matt was now trying to feign evasiveness, mostly because he wanted to tease Frosty.

Frosty sensed Matt's evasiveness and his wits told him that something was afoot. Without really trying, Matt had turned the tables on Frosty. Now, Frosty was the one who was seeking information.

"Okay Petersen, now you really have to tell me. Why would anyone be so interested in those socks?" Frosty asked again.

Matt saw the opportunity to tease Frosty even further. "Really now, Frosty... I can't tell you that. It's a secret."

Frosty looked at him strangely. He was wondering what the secret could be. If there was a secret on this ship, he was usually one of the guys to know about it.

"If it's a secret, you can tell me," Frosty said with an evil grin. "You can trust me."

"Okay, I will tell you," Matt said. "But, only on one condition."

"Anything," Frosty said. "Just tell me the condition."

"You give me my 20 bucks back."

Frosty reached into his pocket and pulled out Matt's $20 bill. He handed the banknote back to Matt. "Okay, here's your money back. So, tell me now. Why are you so interested in the red socks? Are they worth a lot of money?"

First, Matt pocketed the $20 bill, and then he began to explain, "I want the socks to keep my feet warm, especially this winter when I visit my family in Winnipeg."

"What?" Clearly, Frosty had trouble buying it. His lips were pursed and his eyes were all squinty.

Matt continued the ruse. "I've heard Russian wool is the warmest ever. It's something to do with the contented sheep on the Steppes."

"The Steppes?" Frosty asked. He was now much closer to the belief that Matt Petersen was leading him down the garden path.

Matt did not answer. Instead, he turned and walked away. Frosty couldn't see it, but Matt was grinning from ear to ear.

* * *

Back at #4 Mess, Matt gave the current situation a little thought.

If Piggy had paid $100 for the socks, he's probably not going to let them go for less than $200. Matt checked his wallet. He only had $100. There was no chance of going to the bank when you're away at Whiskey. Ironically, he realized that he could have asked the canteen manager, Frosty, for a loan. But, even if Frosty wasn't too ticked off at him to float him some cash, the interest rates would probably kill Matt. Matt needed to find a different source for the cash.

So, Matt went to his best friend Paul, for a loan.

"I've got $60 I can loan you," Paul said as he pulled out his wallet. "It's yours if you need it. I know that you're good for it." Paul pulled out three $20 bills and handed them to Matt.

"Thanks Paul, you know I'll pay you back." Matt put the money in his wallet.

"Just tell me," Paul asked. "Is this something to do with the Russian?"

"Yes, I'm trying to put together at least $200 to buy the red wool socks back from a stoker named Piggy."

"What?" Paul said. "Are you bonkers, man? You're going to pay $200 for a pair of sweaty socks to give back to a stranger?"

"Well, when you put it that way..." Matt smiled.

Paul couldn't help himself. He smiled back. "I know that smile. You're not going to give up, are you?"

"No, I promised that I'd help him," Matt said. "You should have seen his face."

"He's not a pound puppy," Paul said. "He's a Russian Commie."

"Actually, he's a Ukrainian Commie," Matt corrected. "That's a big difference in my books."

"Okay, okay. A Ukrainian Commie then. Like there is a huge difference."

"That's better," Matt said with a grin.

Morrison was on his bunk, but he overheard the entire conversation. "Hey, Leading Seaman Petersen. I've got $40 I can lend you until payday."

Matt went over to Morrison's rack. "Thanks Morrison. That would be awesome."

Morrison pulled out his wallet and handed Matt two $20 bills, which Matt quickly put into his wallet with the rest of the cash.

"Thanks Morrison, I owe you one."

"Correction. You owe me forty," Morrison smirked.

"That's right," Matt said. "Forty it is."

* * *

The next morning, it was busy in the Main Cave when Matt, Paul and Morrison went for breakfast. Both Paul and Morrison decided to wait in line for bacon and eggs, but Matt was less patient, and he decided just to have toast and cold cereal. All three sat down together at a table in the middle of the cafeteria.

Matt looked over at the television and saw that the show *20 Minute Workout* was on, yet again. Currently three different women in skintight body suits were squatting in three different positions; each position equally presenting their backsides to the camera.

Matt pointed at the TV, "I think you've explained this before, but tell me again. What's up with that? How are we getting that? We are hundreds of miles away from a television transmitter, and I know that the cable TV provider doesn't have a cable that goes this far."

Morrison explained, "Oh, it's not live, it's a VHS recording. We have hours of that show on tape. Everybody loves it."

"I don't love it, I think it's ridiculous," Matt moaned.

"I for one consider it to be educational," Paul replied. "Open your mind Petey, enjoy the wonders of the world." He was staring at the television.

Morrison said, "Oh, this is my favourite one. I love it when they do this one! Check it out!"

"I like how healthy they all look," Paul said. "All those 20 minute workouts are really working out for them."

"Which is your favorite," Morrison asked.

"I like the blonde," Paul said.

"I like the brunette. The one that is the leader," Morrison said. "She seems smart."

As they ate, two of the men couldn't take their eyes off the television. However, Matt didn't want to look anymore. It only made him think about his girl problems. Plus, he had other more immediate concerns that he needed to concentrate on.

"So which one is Piggy?" Matt asked, as he scanned the cafeteria.

Paul took his eyes off the television long enough to point across the Main Cafeteria to the corner known as the "Stoker's Table".

"Do you see that rather rotund Master Seaman with the dark beard? That's him, Master Seaman Forrester."

Matt glanced over to where Paul was pointing. Piggy was a big man. He looked like he was over six feet tall, and he must have been at least 300 pounds. He was eating a stack of pancakes about four inches high. A second plate accompanied the first plate, and it was full of bacon and sausage.

"He doesn't look very wiry," Matt said. "How does he fit into all the spaces in the engine room?"

"He's a Master Seaman. He doesn't do anything but sit on his fat butt near the controls. The Killicks and Able Seamen do all the grunt work."

They watched as Piggy pushed a sausage into his mouth.

"Oh, look. A pig eating a sausage. Isn't that cannibalism?" Paul quipped.

Matt smiled at Paul's joke. "Really though, how did he get his nickname."

"Well, I think it's mostly because he happens to have a tattoo of a pig on his knee, but I have heard that it's more likely because he likes to be a disgusting pig," Paul explained.

"A disgusting stoker?" Matt said. "Nothing unusual, they're a dime a dozen."

"Not this one," Paul said. "This one is special. Word has it, he grossed out the most disgusting man in the world."

"That's crazy! What could you be talking about?" Matt exclaimed.

Paul began to tell a story.

"It was in San Diego, last year. Piggy and a bunch of the stokers were out on the town when they came across a bar that had the advertisement 'Tonight only! The Most Disgusting Man in the World' written on the marquee sign above the entrance. It was written in big letters, apparently, and you have to understand that these boys never back down from a challenge..."

"Uh huh..." Matt said. "The Most Disgusting Man in the World? What was that, some sort of joke? Was it a comedy club?"

"No, it was a regular club," Paul explained. "They just had this performer that would do really gross stuff as entertainment."

"So he was a gross-out artist?" Morrison asked.

"That's right," Paul confirmed.

"Sounds delightful," Matt said.

"As the story goes, the boys entered the bar, and then Piggy challenged the bar's headliner to a spur-of-the-moment gross-out contest. Legend has it, once the contest was over the 'Most Disgusting Man in the World' was puking his guts out."

"Wow!" said Morrison.

"That's not all. After Piggy had won the contest, they forced the bar owner to take down the marquee."

"Really?" asked Matt.

"Yes, they threatened to bust up the entire place unless the bar owner told the truth on the sign. So, they forced him to get a ladder and take down the sign right then."

"What? I don't believe it," Morrison exclaimed. Morrison then asked the very question so many others that have heard this same story had asked, "What did he possibly do to disgust the most disgusting man in the world?"

Paul grinned, "That's just it. Nobody will say. Apparently, it is so disgusting you will wretch just to hear it!"

"Good story," Matt said. "It's perfect folklore for a pig... it's a good nickname then." Matt somewhat believed the story, though he thought that it may have been fictionalized a bit. He did know that if there was one thing that was common throughout the navy, it was how sailors would demonstrate how badass they were by trying to gross out their shipmates. Piggy was clearly just trying to uphold his reputed nickname.

They all sat quietly, looking over at Piggy as he shoveled pancakes and bacon into his mouth. Every one of them was still having visions of what the mysterious disgusting act might have been.

Finally, Morrison broke the silence, "What's that saying I keep hearing about a tattoo of a pig on a knee."

"It's pretty simple," Paul said, "It goes 'pig on the knee, good luck for me'. Or, sometimes it said as, 'pig on the knee, safety at sea'."

"Yeah, I have heard that one, "Morrison said. "Now, what's the one about a pig and a cock?"

"That's another way to do it," Paul said. "You get a tattoo of a pig on the left knee and a tattoo of a rooster on the right. Then, it signifies 'Pig on the knee, good luck for me. A cock on the right, never lose a fight'."

"Do you guys really believe this stuff?" asked Morrison.

"It's really not a belief. It's a naval tradition," Matt corrected. "If you're asking if I believe in the sanctity of naval tradition, then yeah, I believe in it."

"The only tattoo I have is a bright red maple leaf on my bicep. That's all I need to show people who I am," Paul said. "I'm a true Canadian," he grinned.

"I wonder what kind of tattoos they get in the Soviet Navy," Morrison asked. "I wonder if the Russkie has any tattoos. I should ask the medic. He's seen him... you know... without his shirt. Maybe he has a hammer and sickle?"

Paul shook his head, "Don't ask the 'pecker-checker'. He's only good for handing out throat lozenges," Paul quipped. "Just ask Petey here for the answer. You know he has spent time with the commie. What's he got Matt? A hammer and sickle on his tit?" Paul teased.

Matt didn't respond to the teasing. He decided to counter by treating Morrison's question in a serious manner.

"You know Morrison, the only tattoo I noticed was a pink flower on his forearm."

"Huh?" Morrison said. "I wonder what that means."

"I'm not sure," Matt said. "But, it's no hammer and sickle."

* * *

After breakfast, Matt quickly ducked into the heads to do his business. After he finished washing his hands, he exited the washplace and ran smack-dab into the Buffer, Petty Officer Clarke.

"Leading Seaman Petersen," Clarke growled. "I'm glad to see you're enjoying yourself here in the *Mackenzie*." His tone was dripping with sarcasm.

Matt noticed that Clarke seemed to be irritated about something. He was surprised by the Petty Officer's abrasive bearing, "Yes PO," he said nervously. "I am enjoying myself."

"Tell me Petersen," Clarke said as he stared at Matt intensely. "How is it that you can speak Russian?"

"No PO," Matt explained. "I can speak Ukrainian. I can't speak Russian."

"That's not what my Boatswains are telling me," he said. "They say that you're fluent in Russian."

"Ukrainian sounds a lot like Russian."

"Maybe," the Buffer said. He relaxed his stare for a moment, and then he regained an even more intense glare as he continued his cross-examination. "Tell me then, smart guy. How is it that you speak Ukrainian?"

"I am Ukrainian," Matt said sheepishly, as he shrunk under Clarke's interrogation.

"No you're not. That's bullshit," he said. "Your name is 'Petersen'. That's not Ukrainian."

Being cornered by Clarke was wearing on Matt. How could he explain his life story to this snarling Petty Officer?

"I don't trust you Petersen," Clarke continued. "There is something about you I don't like, especially since I saw you lurking around outside #3 Mess when we were in New West. You didn't think that I saw you sneaking a peek inside the Chief and PO's Lounge, did you?"

"What are you talking about? I wouldn't..." Matt was sputtering, as he wasn't sure as to what Clarke was referring. Then, he suddenly recalled that night in New Westminster when he tried to help the prostitute outside of #3

Mess.

"You should know that it's none of your business what goes on inside #3 Mess," Clarke snarled.

"I'm sorry PO. I was just checking on the girl..." Matt attempted to explain.

Clarke cut him off, "I bet you were."

Matt looked down and noticed that Clarke's fists were balled up tightly and his forearms were taught. He seemed to be ready for a fight. Matt had never been punched by a senior rank before, but he was suddenly afraid that it was about to occur. Mind you, they were in a common area, and there might be a witness...

Matt looked around to see if anyone else was nearby. To his luck and surprise, he saw the Operations Chief strolling jauntily up the flats in their direction.

"Hello Petersen. Hello Buffer," Chief Cartwright said merrily, as he approached the two men.

The Buffer looked up at the Operations Chief. "Hello 'Ops'. The young Leading Seaman and I are just discussing how it is that he speaks the language of the prisoner." His tone was accusatory.

Chief Cartwright furrowed his brow. He could instantly tell what was happening. "Now Knobby, cool your jets," he scolded. "This young fellow is just trying to help us out by translating."

"I don't trust him," Clarke said firmly.

"Well, I do," Cartwright said calmly. Then, he raised his voice to the Buffer, "That should be good enough for you now, shouldn't it?"

Clarke stayed silent. He simply furrowed his brow as a response.

"Petersen, you may carry on," Cartwright ordered.

Matt didn't waste any time getting away. As he retreated, he looked back up the flats to see that Chief Cartwright and Petty Officer Clarke were continuing the conversation.

CHAPTER 13 / PIGGY IS THE NAME, STOOK IS THE GAME

Matt blinked as he slowly descended the ladder into the darkness of #8 Mess. He couldn't see a thing.

It was unusual for a mess to be so dark at this time of the day. However, as Matt should have known, this was one of those mess decks that were always dark. Due to the fact that the off-watch stokers were notoriously in their racks during the day, the overhead lights usually stayed dark. The other departments had sailors that did work during the daylight hours, but not the Engineering Department. Matt always wondered why they got away with such things. It might have something to do with the ongoing joke about how the "Stoker's Union" was such a powerful force.

When he reached the bottom of the ladder, he had to let his eyes adjust for a few seconds. Matt noticed the mess smelled of sweat, diesel and grease; the same as every Stoker's mess in the navy. In fact, the diesel smell was in their pores. It was an occupational hazard of working in the engineering spaces.

The darkness extended to all corners of the mess. However, he quickly noticed a lounge area that was well lit over to his right. Heavy blackout curtains surrounded it, but a few slivers of light were still managing to slip out.

Matt spotted an opening, grabbed the edge of the blackout curtain, and slightly drew it aside. He sheepishly poked his head through the space. As soon as he did, seven sets of eyes focused directly at him. Sitting around a small table in the lounge area were seven sailors. Some were sitting on the bench seats and even more were sitting on chairs that were drawn close to the table in a tight circle, as if they were playing cards. As well as their faces, Matt quickly scanned their nametags, just to see if there was a name he recognized. Parker, Simpson, Kerchenko, LaBouef, Lachance and an Ordinary Seaman with just a piece of masking tape sporting the name "SLUT" as a nametag. Matt recognized some of the men as stokers, but in his mind, he had already assumed that they were all stokers.

Finally, at the far right of the table, Matt saw the king of the stokers, Piggy.

Piggy stared straight at Matt, as if to challenge his presence in the mess. "Can I help you Leading Seaman?" He spoke forcefully, and he seemed to be growling with his eyes.

Matt looked at Piggy. It appeared as if he had just gotten off watch. His work shirt had large patches of sweat stains around both armpits and on his belly. His face was glistening and oily, and his beard seemed that it was matted with a layer of sweat. It took a second for Matt to take in the sight.

Finally, Matt answered, "I'm here to see you, Master Seaman Forrester."

Piggy stroked his sweaty beard as he looked Matt up and down. "Who are you? Are you the new ping bos'n replacing Sully?"

Matt cringed. To Matt a "Ping Bos'n" was slang for a Sonarman, and of course, he wasn't a Sonarman, he was a Radar Plotter... and to add to the error, radars don't actually ping.

Still, Matt knew that he wasn't here to educate this bunch of Stokers. He had to get to the point. "Yes, I am Sully's replacement," Matt replied. "Can we speak in private?"

Piggy scowled at the suggestion. It didn't occur to Matt, but someone like Piggy made it a point to never grant a request to someone with a lower rank.

"No, we will not speak in private," Piggy scolded. "If you have something to say, you say it in front of all these fine gentlemen." He waved his upturned hand around the table. Matt looked at the faces of the men, and he saw that there were a few smirking grins thrown in Matt's general direction.

Uncomfortable as he was by the situation, Matt still managed to make his request, "I'm looking for a certain piece of the Russian's uniform. I understand you may be in possession of it?"

Piggy's reply was curt, "Be more specific."

"A bright red pair of wool socks?"

Piggy laughed, "You're seeking the Russian's dirty laundry? What are you, the Russian laundry service?"

"So, you have them then?"

"Yes, I do, and they are rightfully mine. They are spoils of war."

Matt stammered, "Well... not really..."

Piggy ignored Matt's plea, and continued his rant, "I am the proud owner of an authentic pair of Russian issue red commie bastard socks. Who knew that the commie Russians actually wore bright red socks, but now I have the proof."

Piggy was grinning as he expounded his plans, "They are a personal memento of when we captured that pinko commie. Do you know what? I'm going to have them mounted and framed... that's what! Then, I'm going to nail the frame to the bulkhead. When I leave the navy, or the navy kicks me out, I'm going to take those socks and show them to my grandkids and tell them the story of when we bested the Russians by capturing one of their own."

Piggy was clearly boasting, trying to get Matt excited. Matt even thought that he might be trying to raise the intrinsic value of the socks. However, he wondered whether Piggy could really be that crafty?

Matt decided to downplay, "You can't be serious, they're just a pair of worn out wool socks."

Piggy's face didn't change. He continued to look stoic.

Matt sighed. "Would you be willing to sell them?" Matt asked.

"Fuck off. Not on your life!" Piggy scoffed. He looked away from Matt as if he had received a horrendous insult.

But, as he looked away, a plan was forming. Pigs were crafty animals, and this Piggy was no different, especially now that Matt had mentioned money was involved.

Piggy turned back to Matt and asked, "How much ya got?"

It turns out that there may just be a price. Piggy just couldn't resist a deal.

Matt reached into his pocket and pulled out a wad of bills. "This is what I have, $200. Is it a deal?"

Piggy looked at the wad of cash. His eyes glistened. He loved this situation, and he wanted to make the most of it. "Not enough bud. It will cost you $300," Piggy replied as he twisted the beard hairs near the corner of his mouth.

"This is all I have." Matt wasn't lying.

"Well that's the price, $300. No less." Piggy was standing his ground, for the moment. He held all the power in this deal, and he knew it.

However, Matt did not have any more money with which to deal. Disappointed, he turned to leave, going back out, through the opening in the blackout curtain.

Piggy was slightly stunned by this, realizing that the wad of cash he coveted was now leaving the mess. Surely, he could find some way to get his greasy hands on that cash...

As Matt was politely closing the curtain behind him, Piggy spoke up, "Hey, Petersen, I've got an idea! Here's how you can get those red wool socks. How about we play cards for them?"

Matt turned around. He could now see that there was an opening, a way to get the socks back. "Cards? I don't know... what is the game?"

Piggy was boastful, "In 8 Mess, 'Stook' is always the game."

The stokers all laughed. Matt looked around and witnessed their faces. He knew that these guys were up to something, but he figured he'd have to play along. It seemed like the only path that might lead to his getting the socks.

Piggy waved at one of the stokers, Leading Seaman Parker, who was sitting at the opposite side of the table as Piggy.

"Nosey Parker why don't you slide over and give our new friend Petey a place to sit," said Piggy. Matt noticed that Piggy was much more congenial all of a sudden.

Matt sat down. As he placed his wad of cash on the table he was trying his best to look confident. "I've never played stook before. Is it like blackjack?"

Some of the Stokers looked at each other and smirked. Matt took notice of this, and he began to feel more uneasy. Piggy sensed Matt's apprehension and he attempted to soothe Matt's insecurity. After all, this wouldn't work out in his favour if Matt chickened out.

"It's pretty much the same as Blackjack. It's not too hard. Anyone can play it. Even my grandmother plays it."

Matt nodded.

Piggy continued, "You try to get as close to twenty-one as you can. Whoever is the closest, wins the hand." He made it sound simple.

Matt was even more disconcerted though, as he noticed Piggy unconsciously cutting the deck of cards continuously with one hand, as he was giving the explanation.

"Who's the dealer?" Matt asked. Matt had begun to realize that he didn't want Piggy to deal.

"We'll cut the cards to see who deals. That's the fair way to do it," Piggy replied.

Piggy shuffled the deck quickly and vigorously. Matt watched him intensely, but Piggy was very fast. Finally, Piggy finished shuffling, and then he squared the deck and placed it at the centre of the table.

Piggy looked at Matt and said, "Okay Petersen, cut the deck. Low card deals."

Matt wanted to deal. He reached over and cut off about twenty cards from the deck, and then he turned the cards over. The top card was the six of clubs. Matt was slightly relieved. At least he now had the odds in his favour.

Piggy saw the six, and he sneered. He cracked his knuckles once, and then he carefully reached out to cut the remainder of the deck. His large hand covered the deck, almost completely, but Matt could still see that his cut was very near the bottom of the pile.

Piggy turned the cards over to reveal that the top card in his hand was the two of diamonds.

"I guess I'm dealing then," Piggy announced.

Matt frowned.

"Well, we better ante up," Piggy said as he pointed toward the Ordinary Seaman with the masking tape nametag. "Mess Slut, go get those red socks from my locker."

The Ordinary Seaman dutifully scurried off into whichever corner of the dark mess that Piggy's locker was situated. Somewhere off in the dark, Matt could hear a locker door being opened, and then being shut.

The young sailor returned with a beautifully bright red pair of wool socks. He quietly placed them down on the table in front of Piggy.

Piggy put his hand on the socks and pushed them towards the centre of the table. "Here is my bid. For the purposes of our wager, I will call it 200 bucks."

Matt looked down at his wad of cash. He picked it up and placed it on top of the socks. "Okay," he said. "I'm covering your bet."

Piggy smiled.

Piggy shuffled the cards quickly. Again, Matt tried to watch closely. He was trying to pay attention to Piggy's shuffling, but Piggy was so quick it almost seemed futile.

Suddenly, Piggy stopped shuffling, and he began to deal the cards. He placed one card face down in front of Matt. Then he placed one card in front of himself, also face down.

Piggy then dealt Matt his second card face up. It was the Jack of Clubs. Matt smiled. He was getting some confidence now.

However, Matt's smile faded when he saw Piggy deal an Ace of Hearts as his face up card.

Matt was now worried. However, before he went into sheer panic, he decided to peek at his downturned card. Matt pried the corner of the card up, just enough so he could see it, and nobody else. It was the King of Spades.

Matt made sure that he did not smile. In fact, he just sat stone-faced.

Piggy looked at Matt's face, scanning for a clue as to what kind of card he had. He saw nothing, though it didn't really matter. Piggy didn't plan on losing.

"Do you need another card?" Piggy asked.

"No, I'll stay," Matt replied.

Piggy said, "I bet you have twenty, don't you?"

Matt didn't reply. He just sat silent, waiting for Piggy to show his hand.

As Matt waited, he happened to notice that Piggy and all the stokers around the table seemed to look confident, even though they all thought that he had twenty. This was especially surprising to Matt, as he doesn't recall that Piggy had even peeked at his hole card. Then, suddenly, the suspense was broken, as Piggy reached down and quickly turned over his hidden card. It was the Ace of Spades.

"I win," declared Piggy. "Thanks for visiting 8 Mess." He grabbed the wad of cash and the red socks off the table.

The whole table burst out in laughter. In fact, everybody was laughing, except, of course, Matt.

Matt sputtered, "Wait a minute... that's not right. You had two aces. That's either two or twelve. It doesn't beat twenty!"

"Not in Stook!" Piggy laughed. "In Stook, two aces are a Stook! Stook beats everything!"

Matt's jaw hung open. Clearly, he had been swindled. He didn't know what to say.

Piggy continued, "Petersen, maybe learn the rules, practice a bit, and then come back for another round. Your money is always welcome here."

"Come on back now ye hear!" Parker hooted. The rest of the stokers were howling with laughter.

Matt knew when he was done. He stood up and began the long trudge back to #4 Mess, broke and without the socks that his new friend Vitaliy so dearly desired.

Piggy saw the look on Matt's face. It was obvious that he had bested him; however, Piggy was still curious about one thing. Why was Petersen so willing to lose all his money just for a pair of red wool socks? Piggy wondered if those socks might have more value than he had originally thought.

"Hey Petersen, before you leave, tell me something. What's so special about those commie socks?" Piggy asked.

Matt stopped in his tracks. Suddenly, he began to think that this thing wasn't over. Maybe there was another opening? He turned and approached the table.

"I'll tell you what the plan was, Master Seaman Forrester," Matt explained. "When I heard that he wore red socks, I realized that red was a Canadian colour. Essentially, it was our colour. So, I was going to have Canadian maple leafs stitched onto the socks, and then return them to the guy, just so the Russians know who is the boss."

Matt couldn't believe that he made up that whole story on the spot. He knew that it was lame, but it was all he could think of. He just hoped that Piggy was dumb enough to buy it.

Of course, Piggy didn't buy it. "That's the lamest thing I've ever heard," Piggy groaned. "Embroider his socks?! Give me a fucking break!"

Matt sighed. He had fears that the story was bad, even as the words were leaving his lips. His imagination had failed him at the worst time.

"I'd say, let's tattoo the bastard instead," Piggy bellowed. "Now that's a great idea!"

The stokers around the table loved that suggestion. They all howled in chorus.

"We could put property of Canada on his ass," Parker chimed in.

Again, the mess roared with laughter.

Matt was becoming a little ticked off now. His plan to retrieve the socks now looked more impossible than ever. He needed to figure out how to get this back on track, right now.

"Look, Master Seaman Forrester, I've got to come clean." Matt began to explain. "Those aren't actually Russian issue socks; they are just regular civvie socks that were hand-knitted for him by his girlfriend."

Matt pointed at the socks that were sitting on the table. All the sailors looked at the socks. Piggy actually picked up the socks and gave them a close look. When he did he could see that the woolen weave of the sock looked rough; a little uneven; handmade maybe?

Matt continued his explanation, "His girlfriend knitted him those socks for his long voyage when he was conscripted into the Russian Navy... and he's not actually a Russian, he's a Ukrainian."

Piggy's eyes lit up. "Like from the actual Ukraine?" he asked.

Matt explained, "Yes, from the *actual* Ukraine. He is a farmer that was forced to go into the Russian Navy. He had to leave his home and his family for three years and go to Russia. Now, he is halfway around the world and has fallen off his own ship. He almost died... think about it. However, he was rescued by us... the Canadians! I think we should show him how the good countries in the world treat people. We should show him how it is to be a Canadian."

Matt was much more satisfied by this story. He just hoped that it would work.

"Yeah, right," Parker said. "He could still be a commie spy."

Matt replied, "He's not a commie he's a farmer. On his ship, he's basically a deckhand. I'm pretty sure he doesn't want to harm us, he just wants to go home."

"You're saying this guy is a Ukrainian? You're shitting me, right? I thought he was from a Russian ship?" Piggy was somewhat doubtful.

"Ukraine is part of the USSR," Matt said.

Piggy softened, "Really? Part of the USSR?"

"Yes, these Ukrainians are ordered to leave their homes and serve for Russia. He had no choice," Matt said, trying to use a more convincing tone.

"Poor bastards..." said Piggy, as he stroked his beard and pondered this new information. Then, he held the socks up, again looking at them very closely, turning them over in his hand. Piggy thought about his own Ukrainian grandmother that would knit him socks and mitts for Christmas. Her socks looked a lot like this. After taking the time to think about it, he was sure that these red socks were hand-made.

"Nosey, I told you that these looked hand-made. You said they were probably knitted by prisoners in a Siberian Gulag." Piggy laughed as he put the socks back down on the table.

Parker didn't say anything. He just shrunk down into his seat.

"Petersen," Piggy asked. "I still have a few questions. How do you know all this about the Russian?"

"Ukrainian," Matt corrected.

"Sorry, how do you know all this about the Ukrainian?" Piggy repeated his question.

"I've been speaking to him. Apparently, I am the only person on this ship that speaks Ukrainian. The XO has been using me as a translator," Matt explained.

"So you spoke to him, and you're sure that he is a Ukrainian?" Piggy asked.

"Absolutely," Matt said.

Matt noticed that Piggy's demeanor had been slowly changing from being confrontational to a more understanding tone.

"My mother is Ukrainian," Piggy said. "Well, she's not actually from the Ukraine like your friend in Sick Bay, but her parents were... but you know what I mean, right Petersen?"

Matt nodded.

Piggy then pointed across the table, "Kerchenko you're Ukrainian, right?"

Kerchenko replied, "My parents are 'Ukes'. Me, I'm a Canuck!" He said proudly as he pointed to a red maple leaf tattoo on his forearm.

"Doesn't matter," Piggy pointed out. "We've heard you play your Nestor Pistor tapes. We've all seen you inhale dozens of cabbage rolls in one sitting. There is no doubt that you've got Ukrainian blood pulsing through your veins."

Everybody laughed, including Matt. Piggy was grinning now.

"Since those socks aren't actually Russian issue, like I thought they were, I say we give them back to the Ukrainian," Piggy decreed. "He wasn't hurting anyone when he fell overboard. He is a sailor just like us, and we should treat him as we would want one of our own to be treated."

Matt couldn't believe what he was hearing. It looked like this little venture was actually going to be successful!

"But I still want to put the maple leafs on them," Piggy decided. "You know, as a souvenir of Canada."

Matt nodded in agreement. His crazy idea was actually starting to sound like a good idea.

Piggy continued, "Just call it a token of goodwill. Consider it my part in keeping relations between the east and west sort of sane, so the two sides don't wind up blowing up the world ten times over."

Piggy had spoken, and the stokers all nodded in agreement. After all, they would never disagree with their leader.

"Nosey Parker, do you know that bunting tosser that sews like a Mexican whore? What's his name?" Piggy asked. He was scheming now.

Parker had to think for a second, "You mean Jonesy?"

"Yes, Jones! That's it. Let's get him to stitch the maple leafs," Piggy declared. "Then, Petersen, can you get the socks back to the Russian... I mean Ukrainian?"

Matt answered enthusiastically, "Yes! That is something I can do. But, get him to do it fast. The Ukrainian will be sent back to his own ship real soon. I'm certain of it."

CHAPTER 14 / A DEBACLE

"He's not such a bad guy," Matt said to Paul.

"Really? You're talking about that big fat stoker? He doesn't seem like such a great guy to me," Paul countered.

"Listen to this," Matt said. "You think he is just a mean asshole, right? Well, I convinced him to return the red socks to the Ukrainian."

"How did you do that? What did you do, promise him a tray of bacon?" Paul said drolly.

"No, all I had to do was appeal to his good sense. It turns out that he's actually a pretty smart guy and he's going to return the socks because it's the right thing to do. We've got a deal."

"So, you didn't have to spend the $200 then, right?" Paul asked.

"No... he's got the $200," Matt couldn't help but to pause and consider the irony of it all. However, he decided to shrug it off.

"Doesn't matter... the good news is that we're getting the socks back."

Paul sighed. "I can't believe that you did all this for a pair of socks."

Matt had already considered what Paul was aiming at. "They aren't just socks. They are the only thing that ties him back to his home, his family and his girlfriend."

Paul looked Matt in the eye. It was time to confront him, "You're doing this because of the Cynthia thing, aren't you?"

Matt thought about it for a second. "No," he decided. "I'm doing this because it's the right thing to do for another human being."

Matt still had a notion that Paul was right. He knew that the Cynthia mess was constantly in the back of his mind. Even though Paul might have been correct, Matt still wasn't ready to admit it.

"Bottom line," Matt explained. "He deserves to be treated like a human being, and his personal property not just stolen and auctioned off to the highest bidder."

"Okay, I get that," Paul agreed. "You're a real humanitarian, Matt Petersen."

Just then, Matt heard the announcement on the ship's broadcast system:

"LEADING SEAMAN PETERSEN, SICK BAY, LEADING SEAMAN PETERSEN."

"Duty calls," Matt said. He quickly went up the ladder, and then up the flats toward Sick Bay. As he approached the Sick Bay, he saw that as well as the two Boatswain guards, both the XO and the Coxswain were also standing outside the door.

Drapeau looked particularly angry.

"Petersen," he scolded. "Move it. I need you right now."

"Yes, Sir," Matt said as he stood before the XO. Matt had a real look of concern on his face, as something was up, and he wasn't sure what antic Drapeau was about to pull.

"Petersen, the prisoner is likely going to be returned to his ship very soon. Regrettably, I left it up to you to get the answers to these questions," he said as he pointed at the clipboard.

Matt nodded.

"Unfortunately, you have failed. So far we have nothing." Drapeau said. His brow was furrowed, and his unblinking eyes were drilling holes directly into Matt's face. "We are going to go back in there right now, and I am going to ask the questions. You're going to translate. You got that?"

"Yes, Sir," Matt said.

"I wouldn't need you," he added. "Except you're the only idiot around here that can speak the language. So I HAVE to use you."

"Yes, Sir," Matt repeated.

"Think about it Petersen. If we can get the Russian to tell us anything, even if we can get him to tell us about their passive sonar system, we will be of huge service to the navy. More importantly, I can finally get my Command. As for you, if we succeed, I will be sure that you get a commendation."

Matt couldn't help but think that the XO had gone completely off the deep end.

Drapeau moved forward and opened the door of Sick Bay. Then he motioned for Matt to head inside. When Matt went inside, he saw Vitaliy and the Duty Medic, Leading Seaman "Spider" Webb. Vitaliy was seated in his armchair and Spider was on the far side, seated at the Duty Medic's desk.

As Matt turned to face Drapeau, he suddenly noticed how the XO had remained outside the Sick Bay. Through the open door, he saw how the Coxswain and the Executive Officer were now having what appeared to be a rather animated conversation. It seemed that Drapeau was mad about something and Chief Czerwinski was responding in his usual calm and professional demeanour.

"Typical shit," Matt muttered under his breath.

Since the XO was delayed, Matt simply waited inside. He was trying to be obedient, as Drapeau didn't seem like he could handle any sort of disobedience right now. Matt was getting nervous.

Vitaliy was there, in the easy chair as usual. He looked up at Matt and greeted him, "Hello Matthew. Is there any news about when I am going home?"

Matt stood for a minute, waiting to see if the XO was going to enter the space. When he did not enter, Matt turned to Vitaliy and said, "I am sorry Vitaliy I have no good news for you yet." Then, Matt remembered that the XO had hinted that Vitaliy would be returning soon. "I am sure though that it will happen soon."

"I'm just so worried. It's taking too long; I'm worried that something bad is happening."

"What could happen?" Matt asked.

"They could ship me off to prison," Vitaliy said.

"Why would they do that?" Matt asked.

"For being stupid and negligent..." Vitaliy said, as Drapeau entered the space. He was in a snit, as he completely red-faced, and huffing and puffing like a freight train. Matt stepped out of the way and stood right next to Vitaliy.

"Are you okay, Sir," Webb asked.

"Yes, I'm okay," he roared back to Leading Seaman Webb. "You nitwit. Why would you think I am not okay?"

Webb did not respond. Visibly disturbed by the XO's verbal assault, he just quietly remained at his desk.

"Okay Petersen, you sit down across from the prisoner, now," Drapeau ordered. He wasn't huffing and puffing as much now. He seemed to want to get down to business.

Matt sat down in the chair. Now he was face to face with Vitaliy.

"Petersen, I will ask the questions. You will do a direct translation for the prisoner. You got that?" Drapeau ordered.

"Yes, Sir," Matt said to the XO. Then he turned to Vitaliy and said in Ukrainian, "Vitaliy, the Executive Officer is going to ask you some questions, okay?"

Vitaliy had been looking concerned. However, Matt's kind explanation seemed to put him at ease, but only for a few seconds as Drapeau exploded again.

"WHAT THE FUCK ARE YOU TELLING HIM?" Drapeau screamed. Spit flew out of his mouth onto Matt's face.

Both Matt and Vitaliy winced at this outburst. Matt wiped his face with his bare hand. Spider Webb remained at his desk, looking down at a notebook and avoiding all eye contact with anyone.

Matt looked up at the XO, who was now hovering right next to him. "I just told him that you will be asking him a few questions," Matt tried to explain. "That's all I told him."

"DID I TELL YOU TO SAY THAT STUPID?" Drapeau shouted.

"No, Sir. You didn't," Matt apologized. "I am sorry, Sir."

"Petersen, you fucked up again," Drapeau moaned. Then he muttered, "If only I had someone that spoke Ukrainian that was also intelligent, we wouldn't be in this mess."

Matt didn't know what to say. He was dumbfounded by the XO's shouting, and the accusation that he wasn't intelligent bothered him. He wanted to tell Drapeau off, but he knew that things would only get much worse if he was to respond. He knew that it would be best to remain silent until this blew over. He just hoped that it would be over soon.

"I will repeat myself just so you understand," Drapeau instructed, a little more calmly now. "I will talk to the prisoner. You will only translate exactly what I have to say. Do you understand Petersen?"

"Yes, Sir," Matt said. "I understand."

Drapeau turned and studied the clipboard. He was pondering which question to lead with, in his interrogation. Vitaliy had been sitting in the armchair, observing this entire event. He didn't know exactly what they had been discussing, but he could see that it was heated. This made him very nervous; more nervous than he had ever been before in his life. He imagined all sorts of nasty unknown outcomes he was sure he was about to undergo. Would he be questioned and tortured, just as they had warned him about in his training? Would something much worse happen? He seemed like he was alone and trapped, with no recourse or escape...

Suddenly, Vitaliy couldn't control himself, and he began to shake. It was a classic panic attack. At first, he tried to calm himself by breathing deeply, but his breathing quickly progressed to hyperventilation.

Matt had been watching Vitaliy closely, but now he was seeing something that he had never witnessed before. Normally calm, Vitaliy was now a mess! He was shaking and breathing heavily. Matt wanted to keep his mouth shut, as per the XO's strict orders, but this was something else. Something had to be done.

"MEDIC!" shouted Matt.

Spider turned to look, and then he quickly jumped up out of his chair and came to Vitaliy's side. Matt backed off to give Spider some room to work.

Drapeau couldn't stand it.

"Oh FUCK," he said. "This is obviously a delaying tactic. He's just faking it so I won't question him."

Matt and Spider couldn't believe what they were hearing. They were sure that Vitaliy's panic attack was real, and they were jumping into action. However, the Executive Officer, the second in command of their own ship, was ignoring the emergency. They didn't know what to think.

Spider knew exactly what to do. He returned to his desk and pressed a button on the nearby intercom. Then he quickly spoke into the intercom, "Pipe the Chief Medic to the Sick Bay." Three seconds later the ship's broadcast system came to life and the announcement was heard, "CHIEF MEDIC REQUIRED SICK BAY. CHIEF MEDIC."

"Oh, great!" Drapeau snorted. "Do we really need a second opinion from that quack? He is clearly faking."

Leading Seaman Webb didn't respond to Drapeau's question. He certainly wasn't about to argue with the Executive Officer, so he simply ignored him. However, he had called for the Doc and he knew that Petty Officer McKay would be able to straighten things out.

But, Drapeau wasn't done! "Petersen, ask him this question, immediately. What types of Sonar do you have on your ship? Do you have a towed-array system?"

Matt looked across at Vitaliy. He was breathing so very deeply, and he looked as if he was going to pass out any second. Vitaliy looked over to Matt. His eyes were plainly pleading for help.

Matt pointed at Vitaliy, "Sir, look at him! He can't answer any questions right now!"

"I'm looking at him, Petersen. I can see him, and I can see that HE'S FAKING!" Drapeau screamed.

"No, Sir," Matt said. "This is a medical emergency. We need to wait for the Doc to get here."

"I'LL SAY WHEN THERE IS A MEDICAL EMERGENCY AND THIS IS NOT A FUCKING MEDICAL EMERGENCY," Drapeau howled.

Matt was very angry and frustrated. He had reached his breaking point. "NO, SIR. YOU'RE WRONG!" Matt yelled back.

Suddenly, Matt heard a booming voice coming from the Sick Bay door, which had now been opened.

"WATCH YOUR BACKS! Chief Medic coming through!" Incredibly, it was Chief Czerwinski's voice, and he was holding the door open for the Ship's Doc, who was answering the request for his presence. Relieved, Matt moved aside as McKay rushed by, and immediately went to Vitaliy's aide.

The Executive Officer was suddenly silent.

"Clear the Sick Bay," the Chief Medic said calmly.

The Coxswain held the door open as Matt, and then the XO left the space. Matt saw that the two Boatswain guards were both standing right outside the door and both had their mouths open about a mile. They hadn't witnessed the debacle directly, but they had heard the entire affair through the door.

"XO, Sir," the Coxswain said, rather plainly. "The Captain has requested your presence in his cabin."

"What?" Drapeau said. "Oh cripes, what does HE want now?" Drapeau then scurried off, down the flats and up the ladder, in the direction of the Captain's cabin.

"Fuck, I'm glad he's gone," Matt sighed.

"What did you say, Petersen?" Chief Czerwinski asked. He was being stern, as usual, but this time he had a slight grin on his face.

"Nothing, Chief," Matt said guiltily. "I'm just glad that the Doc showed up to help the Russian."

"Yes, it's a good thing the Doc got there," the Coxswain said. "The Russian looked like he was in real distress. The Doc should be able to sort things out."

"I hope so," Matt said. "He didn't look good. I hope he is okay."

Matt waited outside the Sick Bay for a few minutes. He was hoping that he would be able to get an update as to Vitaliy's condition from the Doc. But, he was also fearful that the XO would return and start up again. Finally, the Coxswain came over and spoke to Matt.

"Petersen, you may carry on," he said. "We'll let you know if we need any more translation. I'm sure we will, just not now."

"Thanks Chief," Matt said. Then he went back down to #4 Mess. It was quiet down in the mess, so he plonked himself onto the settee with his paperback and began to read. He needed to calm himself and take his mind off everything. After about twenty minutes, he noticed that someone was coming down the ladder. It was Spider Webb, the same Leading Seaman who was in the Sick Bay when the XO had gone bonkers. He sat down on the chair across from Matt.

"Petersen, I saw how you stood up for the Russian," he said.

"Yeah, that wasn't very smart of me," Matt said. "Drapeau is a bastard and now he is probably going to lay a charge on me, or something."

"I doubt it," Spider said.

"What do you mean," Matt asked. "He's probably drafting up a disobeying a lawful command charge right now, and I'm sure that he's naming you as a witness."

"No, I don't think so Petersen," Spider said. "Drapeau has been relieved of duty."

Matt blurted out, "What? Why?"

"Stress. I just saw the paperwork. The Doc was asked to prepare it. He and the Coxswain were even there when the Captain signed it."

"You're joking!" Matt said.

"No, it's completely true, I've seen the signed copy," he said. "Apparently, Drapeau had it out with the Coxswain just before he had come into the Sick

Bay, then he told the Captain off when he was summoned to his cabin. I would say, not a good way to further your career. I didn't read the whole report, but I saw those two parts, for sure."

"Get the fuck out of here," Matt said. He couldn't believe it. How crazy has this been?

"I just wanted you to know that you did the right thing," Spider said.

"What do you mean," Matt asked.

"You stood up for the Russian. It was the right thing to do."

"I guess so. I wasn't sure what I was doing at the moment. I just did it. It was sort of a reflex," Matt said. "How is Vitaliy?"

"You mean the Russian?" asked Spider.

"Yes," Matt said. "His name is Vitaliy. How is he?"

"It was a panic attack. The Doc has calmed him down. He is fine now."

"Did he pass out, from all the hyperventilating?" Matt asked.

"No, the Doc eventually calmed him down. He made him breathe into a paper sack. That worked, but it took a while. But, he still seems to be very nervous about every little thing. He doesn't seem right."

"Oh, crap! I hope he is okay. He's supposed to be sent back to his ship soon."

Earlier, Matt had decided to cloak his friendship with Vitaliy, but now he was obviously showing a real concern for his new friend. He couldn't help it.

"You know that he is just a young kid, and he's not a Russian he's a Ukrainian," Matt explained to Spider.

"Really?" Spider said.

"Yeah," Matt said. "He's not a spy. He's really just a farmhand."

Spider nodded. He understood.

"By the way," Spider said. "He's asking to speak to you. The Doc wants you to come back to Sick Bay."

"Okay," Matt said. He had just discovered how genuinely worried he was about his new friend.

* * *

Matt returned to the Sick Bay. When he arrived, he saw that the two Boatswain guards were now accompanied by the Buffer, Petty Officer Clarke.

"Well, here is the famous sailor, himself. Men, make way for Leading

Seaman Petersen," the Buffer announced.

Matt looked on, puzzled by the Buffer's sudden commending tone. He was very wary of the Buffer, especially since their conversation a day ago. Luckily, Chief Cartwright had come to his aid. Otherwise, Matt wasn't sure how that would have ended.

"Soooo," the Buffer drawled. "You're the man who told the XO to 'Fuck Off'."

"What?" Matt said, astonished.

"Someone had to do it Petersen," Clarke said as he patted Matt on the back with his meaty fist. "You're the man."

Matt shrugged his shoulders. He knew what Clarke was referring to, but he didn't exactly recall that he told Drapeau to "Fuck Off." Maybe he did say it. It had been a crazy moment; maybe he doesn't remember?

"...and Petersen," Clarke continued. "I apologize for that conversation we had yesterday. Cartwright explained your whole story to me. I understand it. I also lost my parents when I was a youngster."

Matt was surprised. "That's okay Buffer," Matt said. "I'm just glad he explained it."

Then the Buffer did something that surprised Matt. He held his open hand out toward Matt, as if to invite a handshake.

Matt looked down at the Buffer's outstretched hand. It was strange to see Clarke's hand offered in this way, as it was normally balled up, into a fist. Matt reached out and took the Buffer's hand, and then they shook hands.

"I apologize," Clarke said. His face had softened somewhat, but he somehow remained as his stoically gruff self.

Matt said, "Thanks PO." Matt couldn't believe it. A handshake and an apology from Clarke were so unexpected! Matt couldn't help but smile.

"Okay then," Clarke said. "You better get inside. They're waiting for you."

Matt nodded, and then he slipped past the guards and entered Sick Bay. When he saw Vitaliy, he was back in his armchair, but now he was sitting back casually and eating a candy bar. Matt recognized the wrapper; it was a Coffee Crisp bar.

"Vitaliy, you are looking much better now," Matt said in Ukrainian. "I'm glad for you."

"I feel better," Vitaliy said as he munched on the candy.

"Where did you get the candy bar?" Matt asked.

Vitaliy smiled and pointed towards the Sick Bay door.

Spider chimed in, in English, "Dumas, one of the Boatswains that is standing guard outside, gave it to him. He did it right after I told him that Vitaliy is just a Ukrainian farm boy and not really a Soviet spy."

"Oh," Matt said. He was pleased.

"Matthew, I'm glad that you are back," said Vitaliy.

"And you," Matt said. "How do you feel, spiritually?"

"I wish I knew what was going to happen to me," Vitaliy said. "I feel like I am trapped here and there is no reprieve."

Matt tried to understand what Vitaliy was enduring. It probably seemed like he had been here forever, especially considering that he was in an unfamiliar place and faced with the unknown. Vitaliy was showing obvious signs of stress. Matt thought that he could possibly help him with friendly conversation.

"I noticed that you have a pink flower tattoo on your forearm," Matt said as he pointed at Vitaliy's right arm.

Vitaliy lifted his arm to display the tattoo. "I had that done in a tattoo parlour in Vladivostok, only a week after I arrived at Seaman's School."

Matt looked closer at the tattoo. "It's nice," he said. "What kind of flower is it?"

"It's a mallow. In the Ukraine, the mallow is a very popular flower to be in flowerbeds around homes. It is symbolic of the Ukrainian native land, and it represents love for one's parents, or their home."

"You know, now that I think about it, my grandmother had similar flowers in her flower bed at home. I didn't really know what they represented, much more than just flowers."

Matt noticed that Vitaliy's eyes were welling up with tears as he had given Matt the explanation. He could see that the tattoo carried a great deal of meaning for Vitaliy.

"Do you have many mallows where you come from in the Ukraine?" Matt asked.

"Oh, yes. Of course! My mother has a huge flowerbed in front of our house full of mallow, and other flowers like petunias and chrysanthemums. They are behind the house as well, in her garden. They are everywhere. She loves them."

Matt noticed that Vitaliy had real tears on his cheeks now.

"When I left home for basic training, I was very sad to be going away. My mother gave me a Bible as a gift for my voyage. Later, when I was on the train to Vladivostok, I opened the Bible and found a single mallow flower pressed between the pages."

Vitaliy was crying now. He looked down toward the deck, and was wiping his tears with his sleeves, trying to cover up his weakness. But, there really wasn't much he could do to hide his despair. Matt looked on, and what he saw was a boy who missed his family. It made Matt realize even more that what Vitaliy really needed was to go home.

"She had put it there to remind me of home," Vitaliy sobbed.

Matt tried to console him, "I'm sure you'll be going home soon. You'll be going back. I'm sure of it."

Vitaliy, tears streaming down his cheeks, looked up at Matt and nodded.

"And won't your family be so surprised to hear of all your adventures!" Matt added.

With his sleeve, Vitaliy wiped away his tears. He looked right into Matt's face, and he said, "I will go home? You promise?"

"Ya obitsyayu," Matt said. "Ya obitsyayu."

CHAPTER 15 / THANK YOU CANADIANS

"I heard that you told the XO to pound sand," Paul said as he brushed his teeth.

"What did you say?" Matt asked.

Paul spit a glob of toothpaste into the sink, and then he repeated himself. "Actually, to be more specific, I heard that you told him to 'Fuck Off'." Paul was grinning broadly. "I have to say, this is a side of you I am not familiar with."

Matt laughed. "I don't recall using those words. Maybe I did, but I'm not sure now. Who did you hear this from?" Matt was wondering who was spreading these rumours.

"I heard it from Burke, who heard it from one of the POs, who heard it from the Buffer. I understand that the Buffer heard it from one of the Boatswains that was standing on the other side of the door when you said it."

"Really?" Matt said. He just realized that a good many people on this ship were now walking around thinking that he told off Drapeau.

"That Sick Bay door is thin," Paul laughed. "Apparently, they all heard what you said."

Matt realized that this could explain why they may have gotten it wrong. After all, how accurately can you hear something through a closed door?

"I still don't think I said it," Matt said as he spread shaving cream across his chin and neck.

"It doesn't matter," explained Paul. "You're now a legend. Everybody thinks you did it and that's all that matters."

"I guess that I'll have to work it then," Matt said as he began to shave.

"Hey, it's 6:30 AM," Paul said. "What are you doing up so early. Weren't you on the middle watch? I would think that you would still be in your cart?"

"I had to get up early," Matt said. "Something important has come up."

"What's that?" asked Paul.

"My Ukrainian friend is being sent back to his ship, first thing this morning," Matt said with a smile.

* * *

Matt approached the Sick Bay. This time, the Boatswain guards, Dumas and Tweed didn't challenge him. Mind you, he had been there so many times they ought to have just moved aside whenever he walked up to the door.

"I'm going to talk to the prisoner," Matt announced with an air of authority.

They both nodded at Matt, indicating that he should enter. Dumas even opened the door for Matt and held it open. Strangely, they both seemed to have wide grins on their faces.

"Thanks Dumas," Matt said.

Matt entered the Sick Bay and closed the door behind him. Vitaliy was just inside, still dressed in a hospital gown. He was sitting in the lounge chair, and he appeared to be attempting to read a 10-year-old copy of MacLean's Magazine. Of course, the magazine was in English; he wasn't making much progress.

Vitaliy looked up and saw Matt. "Ah, Matthew, my good friend. Hello, could you translate this magazine for me."

Matt laughed. "There is no time for reading, besides that's old news. You should be more interested in current events, such as this... Vitaliy, you're going home today."

"What you mean going home?" Vitaliy asked. "I'm going back to the Ukraine?"

"No, sorry, not that home." Matt hoped he hadn't disappointed the young man. "What I meant is... today, you're going back to the *Aziya*."

"Oh..." Vitaliy actually looked nervous.

Matt decided that he might be able to relieve his fears.

"Don't worry, it will all be okay. They're looking forward to you returning," Matt told a white lie. Of course, he didn't actually know that this was true.

"Really?" Vitaliy sounded surprised. "I am thinking that I'm going to be in a lot of trouble for falling overboard and causing all this."

"I don't think so," Matt said. Actually, he wasn't sure about anything. He realized that he just didn't know how things really worked in the Soviet Navy.

Vitaliy still looked very worried. "Matthew, I know how MY navy works, and I am sure I will be punished. They do not miss a chance to punish a lower ranked sailor, never," Vitaliy said as he shook his head from side to side. He was worried.

"Don't worry Vitaliy," Matt said. "The path from here to you being home in the Ukraine leads through the *Aziya*."

"But what if I never get to go home, ever again? What if they punish me, and send me to a work camp? People go there, and they never return!" Vitaliy lamented. "Poor Natalya, I will never return. She will never know what has happened to me."

Matt thought about the circumstances. Poor Vitaliy was in a desperate state. He wasn't sure of what was ahead. At this moment, he felt that he needed to help Vitaliy. He quickly devised a plan. Matt just hoped that this wouldn't be a useless effort, but anything will be helpful at this point.

"What if you write a letter to Natalya?" Matt asked. "You could tell her what has occurred and tell her that you love her."

Matt's idea seemed to bolster Vitaliy.

"I would love to write her a letter, but how would I get it to her?" Vitaliy asked.

Matt already knew the answer, "I would mail it for you," he said calmly. "From Canada," he added.

"You would do that for me?" Vitaliy asked, wide-eyed.

"Yes," Matt assured him.

"And she would get my letter mailed by you from Canada?" Vitaliy was still somewhat skeptical.

"I'm sure of it," Matt said. "My grandparents would send letters to the Ukraine all the time. It is slow, but it usually arrives."

Matt went over to the medic's desk and came back with a pad of paper and a ballpoint pen.

"Here you go Vitaliy. You write it, and I'll make sure that it gets mailed," Matt said as he placed the stationery on the table in front of Vitaliy.

Vitaliy wasted no time. He began writing very swiftly while Matt sat nearby and watched.

Dearest Natalya, I love you dearly though I'm not sure if I will ever see you again for I may never return...

Suddenly, Matt interrupted. "Are you sure you want to go with that?" he asked.

"What do you mean?" Vitaliy said sternly.

"If you tell her that you may never return, she will be heartbroken until you get home. She will assume the worst," Matt explained.

Vitaliy thought about it. "But, what if I never return?" he said. "She needs to know."

"Don't worry. You will return. I am sure of it," Matt assured him. Matt even smiled with his patented crooked smile. It was the most convincing face he could muster.

Vitaliy studied Matt's friendly face. He looked so sincere. That did it! Vitaliy was convinced as well.

"You are right Matthew. I need to be positive. I will go back to the *Aziya*, and then someday, soon, I will return to Vladivostok and then afterward back home to Natalya."

Matt noticed that Vitaliy smiled broadly when he said "Natalya".

"That's the spirit," Matt said. "Now write the letter like that."

Vitaliy took a fresh piece of paper and began to write a new letter.

Dearest Natalya, I love you dearly and miss you every day. I am fine and I will be coming home soon...

As Vitaliy wrote the last phrase, he looked up at Matt. Smiling, he nodded to Matt. Matt smiled back and nodded in agreement.

As Vitaliy continued to write the letter, Matt tried to remain positive, but he was now the one who was worried about Vitaliy. What if the Soviets punished him and sent him off to military prison for being careless? A dozen awful scenarios rushed through his mind. Nevertheless, he remained calm and just showed a smile for Vitaliy. There would be no point in worrying him now.

Meanwhile, Vitaliy was grinning as he wrote. Matt thought that he must have been thinking about his Natalya waiting for him back in the Ukraine.

After about five minutes, Vitaliy was finished.

"Would you like to read it Matthew?" Vitaliy asked.

"No, it's a private letter," Matt declined.

Vitaliy insisted, "I want you to read it, Matthew. I trust you, and I want you to make sure it is good."

Matt nodded in agreement. He took the letter and began to read it silently.

Dearest Natalya, I love you dearly and miss you every day. I am fine, and I will be coming home soon. I have so much to tell you when I get home to Popeliany. I have a fantastic story to tell you about new friends I have made. You see, I fell overboard from my ship, but before anything bad happened to me, a Canadian ship rescued me from the Pacific. They are very nice and have looked after me wonderfully. Soon, I will go back to my ship and soon after, in a few months, I will return to Vladivostok and then home. I can't wait to see you, Mother and everybody else. I really hope that you are not worrying about me, as I said I am okay, and excited to see you again. Once I get home, I want to stay at home and be with you forever. Remember? We talked about getting married and having plenty of red-haired children? I still want to do that, and I only want to do it with you. You are my only love. I have been away so long, and I have seen many wonderful things. But the only thing I really want to see with my eyes is your lovely face. Love always, Vitaliy.

Matt finished reading the letter. "It looks good," he assured Vitaliy. "It looks just fine."

After reading Vitaliy's letter, Matt felt an unusual rush of emotions. His outward appearance did not give away how he felt inside, until he suddenly felt tears welling up in his eyes. He fought to keep the tears inside, but he failed, as one of the tears eventually rolled down his cheek. He brushed it away quickly, hoping Vitaliy hadn't noticed.

"What I need you to do is write the address on the back of the letter," Matt instructed.

As he watched Vitaliy carefully write the address down on the back of the letter, Matt searched his emotions. Soon, it was clear to him that he had reached a decision. It was a point of epiphany, and things were now obvious to him. He could never write a letter like this to Cynthia. She didn't want to talk about children and family, let alone talk about love. It was clear to Matt that Vitaliy and Natalya had a true love. Meanwhile, he and Cynthia surely did not have the same. The more he thought about it, the more he realized that Cynthia never really loved him, and Matt just knew, now, that she never would; especially the way that he wanted her to love him. He realized that it would never happen. He was suddenly tired of wasting his time with her. His attitude had changed completely, and in fact, he had even just surprised himself.

Once Vitaliy finished, he said, "You'll be sure to mail it, Matthew?"

"What..." Matt said. He was still deep in thought.

Vitaliy now noticed that Matt was suddenly disengaged. "Are you okay Matthew?" he asked as Matt stared off into space.

Matt turned his head and looked Vitaliy in the eye. "Vitaliy, my friend. I am more than okay. I am fantastic!" Matt said.

"Excellent," said Vitaliy as he handed Matt the letter. "You'll be sure to mail it then?" Vitaliy asked.

"I promise you," Matt said as he took the letter. Then he purposefully folded it and put it into the left-breast pocket of his work shirt. He buttoned the pocket shut and then patted it with his hand. "I guarantee it," he said stoically, with his right-hand remaining over his left-breast pocket.

Vitaliy smiled. "I feel much better right now, Matthew. Thank you," Vitaliy said.

Matt nodded in agreement. "I'm more than happy to help," he said. He too felt much better about things, right now. Ironically, Vitaliy had helped him. Matt knew it.

"Matthew," Vitaliy asked. "How do you say thank you in English?"

Matt said, "Thank you," clearly, in English.

Vitaliy practiced the phrase a few times. With Matt's coaching, he could say it fairly clearly.

However, Vitaliy wasn't done. He kept asking Matt how to say other phrases in English. Matt obliged him, and with Matt's help, Vitaliy became proficient in a few choice English phrases.

"Matthew, how does this sound?"

Then, Vitaliy paused and said in English, "Thank you Canadians. Thank you for rescuing me from the ocean."

Matt said, "It's perfect."

After a few minutes, the Coxswain entered the Sick Bay.

"Oh, good. Petersen you're here," the Coxswain said. "Could you tell the 'Russian' that he is going on a boat trip in about twenty minutes?"

"Oh that soon Chief? I will tell him," Matt said.

Matt noticed that Leading Seaman Budge was there, as well. Budge placed a pair of white disposable coveralls and a pair of white "pusser" running shoes, the kind that they issue in military clothing stores, on the bed across from Vitaliy.

"Thank you Leading Seaman Budge," the Coxswain said as he pointed at the kit. "Petersen, you make sure he puts on that kit. We can't have him flopping about on the Pacific in a bloody hospital gown."

"Yes Chief. No problem," Matt said as the Chief and Budge left the Sick Bay.

Matt explained what was about to happen to Vitaliy. Vitaliy started to put on the white coveralls. However, Matt had a better idea.

Matt said, "Wait a minute. I'll be right back."

Matt rushed out of the Sick Bay and past the guards in a flash. He quickly went aft to #4 Mess and then he returned to the Sick Bay, in about two minutes, carrying a small pile of clothing.

"Here are a T-shirt and a pair of blue jeans to wear underneath your white coveralls," Matt said as he handed Vitaliy a bundle of clothing. "It's just something for you to wear under those nasty coveralls, since your uniform has gone missing. Those things can be very uncomfortable."

Vitaliy looked at the clothing. "You're giving me your blue jeans? Amazing gift! Denim jeans are so hard to get in the Ukraine."

"I have several pairs. Consider them a gift," Matt said. "Now, you'll have a good pair of jeans to take home with you when you're released from the navy."

"Thank you Matthew," Vitaliy said as he slipped into the blue jeans and fastened them at the waist.

"They even fit," Vitaliy said. "Thank you again. You are a good friend."

"There's also a T-shirt," Matt said. "You should take it as a souvenir."

Vitaliy looked at the white T-shirt. He saw on the right breast of the shirt it said "Mackenzie" and had the badge of the ship.

"What does this mean?" he asked as he pointed to the badge on the white t-shirt.

"That's the name of the ship you are on, *Mackenzie*." Matt explained.

"And what is this emblem?" Vitaliy asked as he pointed towards the *Mackenzie* badge.

"That is the ship's badge." Matt pointed to the emblem on the shirt. "It's the symbol of the ship."

"Mackenzie?" Vitaliy asked. "What does that mean?"

"Mackenzie is the name of a river in northern Canada. This ship is named after the river."

"Mackenzie! A mighty river!" Vitaliy exclaimed. "It's a very nice name and a wonderful souvenir. Thank you very much Matthew."

"Now put on the tee-shirt and then put on the white coveralls over top of everything and zip it up fully," Matt instructed. Vitaliy followed the instructions and the white overalls covered up the civvie clothes nicely. Matt thought that his gift to Vitaliy would be best if it remained relatively secret.

Matt looked at the white running shoes that Budge had brought. He hoped that they would be the right size for Vitaliy.

"Well, those shoes will have to do," Matt said. "But you will need some socks to go with them."

From his pants pocket, Matt produced Vitaliy's cherished red socks.

"Here you go my friend. Here is your treasure," Matt said as he held the socks in his hands for Vitaliy to see.

Vitaliy couldn't believe it. He looked at the socks and then he looked up at Matt and said, "I don't believe it. Natalya's socks! Thank you Matthew. Thank you very much. I will always appreciate this."

"Go ahead, take them. Put them on," Matt said cheerfully.

Vitaliy took the socks, and then he noticed that there was something embroidered on them. He said, "What's this?"

"We had them decorated," Matt explained.

Vitaliy saw what they had done on the socks. Each had a Canadian maple leaf embroidered on the side of the ankle. The maple leafs were done in white thread, and they stood out blatantly on top of the deep red wool.

"We wanted you to remember us Canadians," Matt said.

"Perfect," Vitaliy said. "Thank you Matthew, thank you very much. My sweet Natalya is going to be amazed at what you've done."

Vitaliy sat down and put on the socks, then the running shoes. Then, he stood up.

"That feels good," said Vitaliy. He was grinning from ear to ear. "It's time to go home!"

"It's time to go home," Matt repeated.

Just then, as if on cue, the two Boatswains, Tweed and Dumas entered the Sick Bay. They were very business-like. Leading Seaman Tweed went behind Vitaliy, and motioned for him to put his arms behind his back. Vitaliy obliged, and Tweed began to fasten a set of handcuffs to his wrists.

"Is that really necessary?" Matt protested in English.

"We've got our orders," said Dumas flatly.

Vitaliy shrugged his shoulders and looked over at Matt. He said in Ukrainian. "It's okay Matthew, I'm going home. That's all that matters."

Matt replied to Vitaliy in Ukrainian, "Yes, it's for security. Don't worry."

The two Boatswains marched Vitaliy out of the Sick Bay, one in front and the other behind. The Buffer and then Matt followed along. Meanwhile, slack-jawed sailors had congregated in the flats in an attempt to get a first look at a real live "Russian". What they saw was a cheerful young man, almost a teenager really. He was nodding his head, smiling and saying "Hello" to every person he saw. A few said "Hello" in return, but most just stood there stunned.

When they came to the ladder that lead up to the boat deck there were a few sailors currently using it. Leading Seaman Dumas yelled out "MAKE A HOLE". The sailors on the ladder instinctively cleared out and left the ladder for the entourage going upwards.

Leading Seaman Tweed steadied Vitaliy by placing his palm on his back as they went up the ladder. Vitaliy trundled up the ladder purposefully. This would be the first time he had been outdoors for three days, and he was determined to get there immediately. The entire entourage, once up the ladder, went through one more door, and then they were all standing outside on the boat deck.

It was a bright and sunny day. Vitaliy breathed in the warm air and blinked as his eyes became attuned to the sunlight. Once they adjusted a bit, he looked to the left and managed to spot a long, light-grey fiberglass boat hoisted up on two davits and currently being turned out over the side. Soon, the boat would be lowered to the surface of the ocean.

"Ahhh, there is my beautiful carriage," he said in Ukrainian. Matt was a few feet behind him, but he still heard the comment and he smiled.

The Buffer looked at Matt and snarled, "What are you smiling at Petersen? Did the Russian say something awful about my motor work boat?"

"No PO. He said it was beautiful," Matt explained.

"Darn tootin'. She's a beauty," said the Buffer with a grin.

Vitaliy looked further, out over the ocean. Across the waves, under a bright blue sky, he saw the *Aziya.* Normally a dark silhouette, today she was brightly illuminated by direct sunlight. Even her dark grey domes seemed to shimmer and twinkle as they reflected the sunshine.

Vitaliy smiled broadly. He recalled how desperate he had been only three days ago, lost in the troughs and peaks of a heavy Pacific swell and facing sure death, and now this! It was the culmination of what seemed like a pure miracle. He had been given a second chance! Now, it was time that he began his long journey home.

Home would come soon enough, though. First, he needed to thank his rescuers.

A loose gathering of curious sailors had now formed to one side of the boat deck. Vitaliy moved to a position in the centre-front of the congregation and began to speak out, "Thank you for rescuing me from the ocean. Canadians are very kind. Thank you." He spoke these phrases in English, just as Matt had taught him.

The sailors on the boat deck looked on in wonderment. They had come here to witness the notoriously hated Russian return to his ship, but they were witnessing something unexpected. Some actually broke out into a smile, realizing almost immediately that this man was just a sailor that was overboard and lost at sea, and he was genuinely thankful to be rescued, as anyone would have. However, most still didn't make the connection, and they were very wary of the "Russkie". They never even cracked a smile.

Nevertheless, Vitaliy wasn't finished. There was more.

The Buffer pointed at the handcuffs and then Leading Seaman Tweed moved behind Vitaliy and unfastened the restraints. Once the handcuffs had been removed, Vitaliy, with a broad smile, immediately began to approach the throng of sailors on deck offering his hand for a handshake.

"Thank you, thank you, thank you", Vitaliy said as he moved through the crowd. He seemed like he was on a mission to shake hands with everybody he met. For the most part, the Canadians were surprised by this act of gratitude. Again, some demonstrated genuine appreciation, but there were still a few that backed away, wanting no part of Vitaliy's handshake.

Matt noticed that Piggy was in the crowd. When Vitaliy went up to Piggy to shake his hand, Piggy took Vitaliy's outstretched hand into both of his meaty paws and gave him a double-handshake.

Piggy said, "Goodbye and good luck."

Vitaliy nodded at Piggy and said, "Thank you." Then Vitaliy continued on his mission to meet and thank everyone on deck.

Matt had a smile from ear to ear. He was very proud of Vitaliy. He was using these English phrases exactly as he taught him, and now everybody was getting to meet him much in the way that he had. In actuality, Vitaliy was just a boy, barely a man, and now he had his whole life ahead of him. To Matt, this alone was a reason to celebrate. He smiled broadly.

As Vitaliy continued to say his goodbyes, Piggy approached Matt. "So, he got the socks?" Piggy asked quietly.

"Yes, he's wearing them," Matt whispered proudly.

"Perfect," Piggy said. "Good job Petersen... and good job on telling the XO to 'go fuck himself' and getting away with it. You're the first guy to pull that off."

Matt grinned, as he replied, "No problem." Matt still wasn't sure what he had said to Drapeau, but it must have been good, as it seemed to have taken on a legendary status.

After a bit, the Buffer decided that this was enough fun, and it was high time to get down to business. He stepped in front of Vitaliy, and with his arms outstretched, he attempted to corral the wayward Ukrainian.

"Okay sonny, that's enough goodbyes. You've said your piece. Now, it's time to go." Petty Officer Clarke nodded towards the *Aziya*, which now lay only a few hundred yards off the *Mackenzie*.

Vitaliy smiled at the Buffer, and upon noticing he had his arms extended, Vitaliy threw his arms wide as well and unexpectedly gave Petty Officer Clarke a giant hug in the process.

"Thank you Canadian!" Vitaliy shouted as he hugged the Buffer. Everybody on deck cheered and laughed, even the sailors that were still frowning up to this point. Vitaliy couldn't have picked a better person to hug. The normally stoic Clarke turned beet red; then he actually smiled a little bit, but only a little Grinch-like bit.

Matt looked across the boat deck, and he noticed the XO was also lurking nearby. Matt was surprised that he even saw Drapeau crack a smile.

"Okay sonny, time to go," the Buffer said one more time. Finally, Vitaliy obliged and released him from the hug.

Vitaliy looked over at the *Aziya*. He took a deep breath and said, this time in Ukrainian, "Okay, time to go".

The Buffer motioned towards the cargo net at the side of the ship. Vitaliy took another deep breath and climbed over the side and then down the cargo net into the boat. The sailors in the boat helped him with the final few feet.

Matt looked down over the side of the ship and saw Vitaliy finding a seat in the boat. He was surrounded by Canadian sailors, and he saw Vitaliy now shaking their hands and obviously continuing to say "Thank you" to everyone in the boat. Matt smiled at this.

Vitaliy looked up and saw Matt's smiling face looking down at him. He waved at Matt and said the words, "Thank you Matthew". Matt couldn't hear him, but he understood the words and he waved back at Vitaliy. A few seconds later, the seaboat roared off in the direction of the *Aziya*.

Matt watched as a Russian boat came from the direction of the *Aziya* and headed towards the Canadian boat. The two boats met briefly, halfway between the two ships. Matt noted how quickly the transfer occurred; it only took a few seconds. Matt watched as both boats quickly began to head back to their respective ships. It certainly seemed that Vitaliy's re-introduction to his ship was just as quick as his untimely departure.

That was it. Seaman Third Class Vitaliy Bondarenko had finally returned to his ship. Matt could only hope that eventually he would make it back to his real home in Popeliany and to his sweetheart Natalya, red socks, and all. Then, they would be able to have all those red-haired children they had planned together.

Matt continued to stand on the deck, staring at the Aziya as the nearby sailors prepared to retrieve the motor work boat back onboard the *Mackenzie*. He was pondering the moment, and enjoying the bright sun. He continued to watch the *Aziya* in the distance, waiting to see if he would be able to see the moment that it retrieved its seaboat and moved off again.

"She's kind of pretty in the sunlight," Paul Legere said. He had appeared on the boat deck, and had snuck up behind Matt.

Matt turned to see Paul. "Hey, Paul. Are you referring to the *Aziya*?"

"Yep."

"I never thought you would ever say anything nice about a Russian ship," Matt laughed.

"Well, I'm just glad things are going to get back to normal around here," Paul said. "Maybe that's why she's so pretty."

"When have things ever been normal here?" Matt laughed.

"I guess you're right... but you're okay, right? Things are back to normal for you, right?" Paul asked.

"I'm better than normal," Matt said. "Things are going to be much better from now on."

EPILOGUE / IT'S THE BIGGEST IN THE WORLD

It had been 30 years since Matt had sailed in the *Mackenzie*.

In fact, Matt hadn't even laid eyes on a navy ship for almost five years, and it had been twenty years since he had completely retired from the Canadian Forces. These days, he certainly didn't think much about the *Mackenzie*, a ship he had only sailed in for a few weeks in the summer of 1983. He'd had many other adventures since then, but the memory of that trip and the recollection of the Ukrainian sailor, Vitaliy Bondarenko, still lingered.

Of course, the *Mackenzie* was no more. She had long since been retired as a warship. She had been fully decommissioned in 1993, and then she was purposely sunk off Sidney, British Columbia. This is where she remains today, at the bottom of the ocean. She was serving eternity as an artificial reef at a dive site near Gooch Island.

Ironically, whenever Matt heard the name Gooch Island, he thought of his old rival, "The Gooch". He sometimes wondered what ever happened to him. However, he wasn't too concerned with the Gooch, or even Cynthia for that matter. He had broken it off with her the day he returned to Esquimalt. She didn't seem to take it hard, and that helped him to understand that it was the right thing to do. Besides, he never wished her to be hurt. He always hoped that she was happy, somewhere, but he really couldn't imagine how she could ever be happy. He knew that Cynthia did date the Gooch for a little while after he broke up with her, but he was sure that they had not stayed together. Matt wasn't concerned about the fate of that relationship, mainly because he had found true love himself… a true love with his perfect match, Alison.

He had called Alison the very same day that he broke it off with Cynthia.

She was delighted to hear from him. After that, they got together a few times. One weekend, Matt would take the ferry to New Westminster. The next weekend she would take the ferry back to Victoria. Soon after, she moved to Victoria to attend university. This sealed the deal. Once she was located so close, they officially became a couple. Their bond was real and long lasting. To Matt, it was perfect.

As for Paul Legere, he remained as Matt's good friend for many years. Even now, when Matt lived hundreds of kilometers away from Paul, they still kept in touch. Paul had remained as a lady's man for many years, but finally he did meet his match and was married. He now has six children and lives in Victoria, BC. His life has done a complete one-eighty. If you asked him, though, he'd tell you that he was as happy as a clam.

Despite not having fond memories of many people from that time, Matt often did think about his friend Vitaliy. Even though he had only known Vitaliy for three days, he still often wondered if Vitaliy had been punished for falling overboard, or whether he had eventually made it back home to the Ukraine. Even more importantly, he wondered if Vitaliy was ever reunited with his sweetheart Natalya. After all, Matt had told Vitaliy that he would be fine, and that he would make it home. He had convinced him to think positively and promised everything would work out. However, Matt could only hope that things had actually turned out for the best. He could never be completely sure.

To ease his mind, Matt always told himself that he was sure that Vitaliy had escaped punishment, and that he had gone home to be with his family. If only he knew this was true. Matt always thought that one day he would discover the answers to his questions. He just knew it, somehow he would find out. He wasn't sure how, but he had an intuition.

Today though, memories of the navy really had no place in his mind. Since his time in the military, Matt had gotten married, moved back to Winnipeg, gone back to school, started a job as a school teacher and had fathered two children, a boy and a girl. So many good things had happened in his life. He was very happy and satisfied, but he still often wondered about Vitaliy Bondarenko.

Of course, Matt kept his promise and had mailed Vitaliy's letter. At the time, though, he was very nervous about it. Even though the contents of the letter was innocuous enough, and was clearly a love letter, Matt didn't want anyone from the military to know he had helped Vitaliy. As well, back in the 1980s, anyone in the military that mailed a letter to the Ukraine might be put under investigation. Matt had mailed the letter from a mailbox in downtown Victoria, and he didn't mark his return address on the envelope. While he was in the navy, he didn't want the government tracing any such letter back to him. He just mailed it anonymously and hoped for the best.

He also recalled how, thirty years ago, he had returned to Winnipeg on military leave to visit his grandparents. He had told them all about Vitaliy and the story of Natalya, the red socks and the love letter. His grandparents fell in love with the story. His grandmother had even cried whenever she would re-tell the story to her friends, and she told it often. She had made Matt promise that he would try to find out what had happened to Vitaliy. However, there was no way at the time for Matt to contact anyone behind the Iron Curtain, especially given his connection to the military. Vitaliy's final story seemed to be left to the unknown. It was only after Matt had insisted that he was positive Vitaliy had made out fine, that his grandmother would stop her fretting.

In 1991, the Ukraine broke free of the Soviet Union, and became the independent country we know today. At this time, there was a renewed hope that Matt could possibly locate Vitaliy. However, the task still proved to be next to impossible. From Canada, there was no way to track down a citizen in rural Ukraine.

Since his grandparents had both passed away in 1999, the idea of locating Vitaliy had faded somewhat in Matt's mind, but the notion was still there, albeit tucked away behind his family and job. Every now and then, he would mention Vitaliy to Alison, and she would just sigh and say that she was sure he was happy and living well in the Ukraine.

"Of course, he must be alive and well," Matt thought. Still, there was always a nagging wonderment. The last memory of Vitaliy, the moment of the two seaboats coming together for a few seconds, was something he could never completely put out of his mind.

* * *

If you wait long enough, something will eventually happen...

Everything changed thirty-one years after meeting Vitaliy, in March 2014, when Matt became a user of Facebook.

He had managed to avoid all of the social networking nonsense for years. However, he decided to get started when he realized that he needed to know more about social networking so he could stay in touch with his children, who had now grown and had left his home.

Since getting on Facebook, he had established friendships with a few of his cousins, some co-workers, a handful of school chums and a few guys from his navy days, such as Paul Legere. Matt was surprised how people found him on Facebook. Like when his grade school girl pal had sent a friend invite. "Wow," Matt wondered. "How did she find me?"

However, this was nothing compared to the day when he received an email from Facebook with the subject line, "Vitaliy Bondarenko has sent you a friend request".

At first, Matt stared at the email in disbelief. He thought that this had to be a practical joke. He considered the request for a few minutes and realized that to pull this off would require knowledge that he hadn't shared with anybody. Only his wife would know enough to do this, and she would never do it. She knew better than to tease him about Vitaliy Bondarenko.

Matt logged-in to Facebook and looked at the request more closely. The photo that accompanied Vitaliy Bondarenko's profile showed the face of a man that was the spitting image of the Vitaliy he had known. Mind you, he was much older, fatter and balder, but Matt knew in an instant that it was the real Vitaliy. Matt checked further, and it said that Vitaliy lived in Lviv, Ukraine. Matt recognized Lviv as the city near Popeliany, the village where Vitaliy had mentioned he had grown up. For Matt, this clinched it. Matt went ahead and accepted the friend request. It had been decades, but with a simple click of a mouse button, he and Vitaliy were reunited.

Vitaliy and Matt had a chance to chat online. Sometimes they chatted in Ukrainian, which was difficult at first for Matt because his Ukrainian was very rusty; however, it improved as they went along. Matt had to figure out how to switch his keyboard to Cyrillic, which wasn't too hard to do. He had just never needed to do it before.

Vitaliy described his wife Natalya, and his two children Met'yu and Vitaliy Jr. Matt realized that Vitaliy had named his first boy Matthew, and he was beyond flattered. Matt also shared his family details with Vitaliy, telling him all about his wife Alison, and their two children.

Matt asked Vitaliy how he was treated when he arrived back onboard the *Aziya*. Vitaliy told him that he was extensively debriefed by the KGB officers at first, and the ordeal was somewhat rough. Afterward, though, the crew treated him as a returning hero. He had survived being lost at sea! He was an oddity, and everyone wanted to hear his story.

Once returning to the *Aziya*, he had spent another six months at sea before being discharged, and then returned home to Popeliany. He and Natalya were married as soon as he arrived home. Vitaliy also said that when he returned home, Natalya was holding the letter he had written to her; the love letter that Matt had mailed.

To Matt it was a relief to hear the news. He smiled for days, after finally being in contact with Vitaliy. He was a happy man. However, it was when Vitaliy told him that he and his wife were coming to visit Canada that he really got excited.

* * *

Vitaliy and Natalya arrived in Winnipeg on July 1st. When Matt and Alison met them at the airport, Matt greeted Vitaliy, in English, with "Happy Canada Day".

Vitaliy responded, in English, as well, with a spirited "Thank you Canada." They both laughed aloud.

They shook hands and then they hugged. Vitaliy introduced Matt and Alison to Natalya. She was as beautiful as Matt had imagined her, with a soft round face and bright red hair.

Then, Vitaliy lifted his right pant leg and revealed that he was wearing bright red socks.

Matt was astonished. "Are those the same red socks?" Matt asked.

"Yes they are!" Vitaliy said as he lifted his pant leg a little more, revealing a white maple leaf embroidered on the ankle.

"Those are the same socks!" Matt said excitedly.

"I only wear them for special occasions, and I felt that this was special enough," Vitaliy said.

After the reunion at the airport, Matt and Alison took Vitaliy and Natalya on a quick tour of Winnipeg that ended at their home. Then they started the barbeque grill on the patio, and prepared a wonderful meal for their guests. After the meal, they remained on the patio until the sun began to go down, and the mosquitoes began to come to life.

A while later, after all the navy stories had been told, Matt asked Vitaliy. "You finally made it to Canada. What do you want to see first?"

"That's easy," Vitaliy declared. "We are renting a van and travelling to Alberta. We are determined to see the giant Pysanka in Vegreville."

"Wow. That should be a wonderful trip," Matt said.

"I want you and Alison to come with us," Vitaliy said with a grin.

Matt looked stunned. "You do know that it's over 1000 kilometers from here?" he asked.

Vitaliy suddenly looked saddened. "It looked real close on the map," he said with a dismayed tone.

"Well, it's a big country..." Matt said.

Vitaliy seemed crestfallen. Matt looked at Vitaliy's disappointed face. It took him back to the time in the *Mackenzie* 30 years ago.

"You know Vitaliy. My wife is from Vegreville, and she has relatives out that way. We could probably go on a trip. I'll have to check with the boss." Matt winked at Vitaliy.

Matt turned and called out to Alison, who was chatting with Natalya in the next room. "Alison, would you like to go to Vegreville to see the Pysanka?"

She looked at Matt and smiled. Then, she nodded, "Yes."

"So you will come with us then?" Vitaliy asked.

"I wouldn't miss it," Matt said. "After all, it's the biggest in the world." Matt was grinning from ear to ear.

Vitaliy smiled broadly, "All right Matthew, I knew you wouldn't let me down. You have never let me down!"

Acknowledgments

I would like to thank those that helped me in the writing of this story, specifically Lynn Gibson, Paddy Burt and Bettina Allen who kindly took the time to read my draft manuscript and gently advised me on several important revisions. Also, thank you to Fred Haight, my old navy winger, who took the time to read the first draft and to let me know that I was on the right track.

About the Author

Mark Nelson first joined the Canadian Navy on Canada Day in 1980, at HMCS Chippawa, Winnipeg. He trained first as a Radar Plotter and later as a Naval Combat Information Operator. After 26-years of service, serving in almost every platform the Navy owned, plus different stints in fleet schools on both coasts, he finally landed back in Winnipeg as Coxswain of HMCS Chippawa. Today, he works at Red River College in Winnipeg as the Library Systems and Services Coordinator. He is also a part-time teacher, web site developer and author. *Whiskey 601* is Mark's first novel.

Other titles by Mark Nelson

Jackspeak of the Royal Canadian Navy:
A Glossary of Canadian Naval Terminology (2014)

Winnipeg's Navy: The History of the Naval Reserve
in Winnipeg, 1923-2003 (2003)

For more information about this title

Visit WHISKEY601.COM